SUSAN
LEWIS

Who's Lying Now?

HarperCollins*Publishers*

HarperCollins*Publishers* Ltd
1 London Bridge Street
London SE1 9GF

www.harpercollins.co.uk

HarperCollins*Publishers*
1st Floor, Watermarque Building, Ringsend Road
Dublin 4, Ireland

First published by HarperCollins*Publishers* 2022
1

A catalogue record for this book is available from the British Library

ISBN: 978-0-00-847181-1 (HB)
ISBN: 978-0-00-847182-8 (TPB)

Typeset in Sabon LT Std by Palimpsest Book Production Ltd,
Falkirk, Stirlingshire

Printed and bound in the UK using
100% Renewable Electricity by CPI Group (UK) Ltd

MIX
Paper from
responsible sources
FSC
www.fsc.org   FSC™ C007454

Who's Lying Now?

Susan Lewis is the internationally bestselling author of over forty books across the genres of family drama, thriller, suspense and crime – including the novel *One Minute Later*, which was a Richard and Judy pick. She is also the author of *Just One More Day* and *One Day at a Time*, the moving memoirs of her childhood in Bristol during the 1960s. Following periods of living in Los Angeles and the South of France, she currently lives in Gloucestershire with her husband, James, and her dog, Mimi.

To find out more about Susan Lewis:

www.susanlewis.com
www.facebook.com/SusanLewisBooks
@susanlewisbooks

Also by Susan Lewis

Fiction

A Class Apart
Dance While You Can
Stolen Beginnings
Darkest Longings
Obsession
Vengeance
Summer Madness
Last Resort
Wildfire
Cruel Venus
Strange Allure
The Mill House
A French Affair
Missing
Out of the Shadows
Lost Innocence
The Choice
Forgotten
Stolen
No Turning Back
Losing You
The Truth About You
Never Say Goodbye
Too Close to Home
No Place to Hide
The Secret Keeper
One Minute Later
I Have Something to
Tell You

Books that run in sequence

Chasing Dreams
Taking Chances

No Child of Mine
Don't Let Me Go
You Said Forever

Featuring Detective Andee Lawrence

Behind Closed Doors
The Girl Who Came Back
The Moment She Left
Hiding in Plain Sight
Believe in Me
Home Truths
My Lies, Your Lies
Forgive Me
The Lost Hours

Featuring Laurie Forbes and Elliott Russell

Silent Truths
Wicked Beauty
Intimate Strangers
The Hornbeam Tree

Memoirs

Just One More Day
One Day at a Time

For the Corona Girls
With love

Jill Lewis, Grace Lewis,
Denise Hastie, Lesley Gittings,
Sonia Gourlay, Pat Cockram,
Fanny Blackburne

Wednesday 6 January 2021

Jeannie was pacing back and forth in her study, engaged in a lengthy and complicated call, when she realized she was being watched from the garden. She came to a stop, still listening to her assistant's updates, while allowing her eyes to fix on the landscaper's. She experienced a pleasing frisson of their unusual and deepening connection.

She'd come to know many things about this man since he'd taken on the contract to transform the gardens surrounding her home, things that excited and amused her, intrigued and perplexed her. All that dismayed her about him was the fact that he was married to the wrong woman.

He waved and she raised a hand too before he disappeared from view, no doubt to continue his work. She returned to her phone call, feeling irritated by the fact that he'd probably be long gone before she was finished. She hadn't actually been expecting him today; presumably he was just dropping something off, or collecting up what remained of the Christmas lights.

January the sixth already, and here they were, as a country, back in lockdown.

1

How fortunate she was to have this beautiful coastal home to work from, with all its wonderfully high ceilings, walk-in fireplaces and large bay windows overlooking the bay. It wasn't unlike the manor she'd grown up in, large, dignified, welcoming and quietly settled into its own place in the world.

Her parents' house didn't exist anymore. It had been destroyed by fire, but that was a firmly closed chapter in her life.

She and her husband, Guy, had been the owners of this rambling old pile – Howarth Hall – for over three years now, but she still hadn't delved into the history of the place. Maybe Guy had and was keeping it to himself.

It was Wednesday lunchtime now, and she knew already that he wasn't going to make it back until Friday. His work often kept him away longer than he'd like to be gone but, though she missed him, she rarely pressured him to try to spend more time here. It wouldn't be fair when so many people's lives depended on him.

After finally finishing her call, Jeannie wandered out of the study and along the wide, wood-panelled hallway to the spacious kitchen-diner that occupied the whole of the east-wing ground floor. Three sets of French doors opened out to a covered terrace where low-rise stone steps descended to the magnificent lawn, a landscaping triumph in such steep and rocky terrain.

She was so deep in thought that she didn't spot the note on the centre island as she went to the Aga and set the kettle to boil. Her mind was still full of the information she'd just received. However, as she waited she raised her head and closed her eyes, inhaled deeply and satisfyingly – and found, not unusually, that even when Guy wasn't there, she could catch the scent of him. He might have left only a few minutes ago rather than a few days.

How she missed him.

She wondered what sort of surprise he'd have for her when she came home on Friday. He invariably brought something: chocolates, champagne, a piece of jewellery . . . Her fingers went to the white-gold Chopard pendant he'd given her last summer, an open heart with encrusted diamonds, small, elegant and wickedly expensive. She hadn't taken it off since he'd fastened it at the nape of her neck, his long fingers brushing her skin and sending shivers of pleasure all the way through her.

He was the perfect man for her – complex, fascinating, largely unpredictable, and with a penchant for the kind of mind games that she adored. His latest was perplexing her – a simple phone number that she was certain she'd been meant to find. Since calling it she'd felt uneasy and not quite as sure as she'd like to be of where this might go.

After making herself a cup of tea, she turned around and finally spotted the note. Her heart gave an unsteady beat of surprise. She hadn't heard anyone come in, but her study was far enough away that she wouldn't have.

Unfolding it she read the few words and experienced a bizarre feeling. She wanted to laugh out loud at how welcome the summons was, but there were more serious and troubling thoughts to sober her.

Pouring her tea down the sink, she went to collect up what she would need and, minutes later, she was letting herself quietly out of the door.

Not that anyone was around to hear her – it just seemed the right way to leave.

PART ONE

CHAPTER ONE

CARA

Monday 18 January 2021
Twelve days since Jeannie's disappearance

'Cara, we have a bit of a mystery on our hands here that I'd like you to take a look at.'

Cara Jakes, still officially a trainee investigator, composed her naturally sunny features into an expression of alert and sober interest and sat a little straighter in her chair. There were three of them in the room, unmasked, but seated in a suitably distanced fashion at one end of a huge conference table that they were using for this meeting. It was adjacent to the chief superintendent's office; he was someone she'd never spoken to and he was, thankfully, nowhere to be seen.

Not only eager to find out more of what this was about – who didn't love a mystery? – she was also proud to be included in this attempt to solve it. At twenty-four, with eight GCSEs, three A levels and some chequered work experience behind her, she knew she was seriously lucky to have this job. The competition had been fierce – dozens, maybe hundreds of applicants had come in from all over – but for some fabulous reason she'd been chosen to work alongside Kesterly's CID detectives as a dogsbody, basically, or a backup when they required extra assistance with their cases. From day one she'd been determined to excel in every way possible and this, if she was reading it correctly, could be her big chance, for it seemed Detective Sergeant Natalie Rundle was coming to her first with an issue.

'A woman has disappeared,' DS Rundle continued, her smooth brow puckering in a frown, while her piercing black eyes moved between Cara and the notes in her hand. She was a frightening woman in some ways – fierce, demanding, critical – and quite beautiful in others, with her mixed-race colouring and striking red lipstick.

She hadn't yet been introduced to the third woman in the room, but Cara knew very well who she was. Her name was Andee Lawrence and she'd once been a detective here in Kesterly-on-Sea. She was also a favourite of DCI Gould, a good friend of DS Rundle, and was much beloved by the community at large. She was tall, slender, with a gorgeous tumble of shoulder-length curly hair, stunning aquamarine eyes and the kind of poise that Cara, at five two and a little on the scrawny side, could only dream about.

DS Rundle was speaking again. 'The woman's name is Jeannie Symonds. She's married, no children, high-powered career, and she usually lives in London. Since the summer she's based herself here, at Westleigh Heights, where she has a second home. As you're local you might know the place – Howarth Hall; it's the large house up on the western headland that you can see parts of from Westleigh Bay.'

Cara knew it all right, or at least she'd seen it a thousand times from the beach where she used to go foraging as a kid with her sister and dad. Look up and there was this illusion of an amazing mansion at the top of the cliffs – like a fairy-tale castle almost – with acres of woodland sprawling out behind it and a dreamy sort of descent over the cliffs in front of it. She'd never been there, obvs, but she'd driven past the gates plenty of times on the way to the moor. It seemed totally massive to her, although she understood that one person's massive was another's *just a little place on the coast, darling, you must come to stay with us one of these days.*

'This is Andee Lawrence,' DS Rundle continued. 'She's going to fill you in on what she knows about Jeannie Symonds and why she's decided to bring the matter to us.'

Responding to Andee's open smile, Cara produced one of her own with dimples and said, 'Would it be all right to take notes?'

'Of course,' Andee replied.

'And I'll give you what I have when we're done,' the DS added.

Doing her best to remain calm in the face of so much trust, Cara created a new document on her laptop and made ready to type. First up came basic background info on Jeannie, aged fifty-one, and her husband Guy Symonds, aged forty-five. Apparently he was a neurosurgeon working out of St George's Hospital in London, and she was a senior executive at a major publishing house based in South Kensington. They'd been married for seven years and their main home was in Kew, which was where they'd stayed for the first lockdown. After that Jeannie had moved to Westleigh Heights, while Guy had carried on working in London, joining her at weekends. More often if he could.

'On Friday January the eighth,' Andee said, reading from her own laptop, 'Guy Symonds arrived at Howarth Hall at around five o'clock to find no sign of Jeannie. He searched the house and immediate grounds, tried ringing her, but her phone was either turned off or had run out of battery. He then discovered that her car had gone, so he assumed she'd popped out for something and so didn't think much more about it until another hour had passed and she still wasn't back.'

Cara was typing furiously, picturing it all in her mind as best she could, and not asking any questions yet as she felt sure most of the answers were coming.

'That night, and over the weekend, Guy contacted everyone he could think of who might know where Jeannie was: her colleagues, friends, family; the neighbours both in London as well as those up around Westleigh Heights. By then – three days later – he'd discovered that her handbag and wallet had gone, but her passport was still in her desk at the Hall. Her computer was also still there, along with her work files and calendar of upcoming commitments. Apparently she hasn't made one of them since the morning of January the sixth, when she spoke with her personal assistant, Maurice Bisset, about complications that had arisen in Ireland due to Brexit. That call lasted about forty minutes, according to Bisset, and started at around one p.m. We're pretty certain the call was made from the Hall – we have no phone records as yet, so can't actually confirm that – but she was seen by her landscaper at around that time. He says she was in her study and when she waved out to him he could see she was on the phone.'

Cara suppressed the urge to ask one of the many questions buzzing around in her head and concentrated on listening to the account.

Andee said, 'No one has seen Jeannie since then – at least no one that Guy, or Jeannie's assistant, Maurice Bisset, have been able to find.'

Cara glanced at DS Rundle, and, receiving a nod, she said, 'So she could have left at any time between one o'clock-ish on January sixth and five p.m. on January eighth when her husband got back?'

Andee nodded. 'As things currently stand, that's correct,' she confirmed.

Cara wrinkled her nose. 'It's January eighteenth now,' she pointed out. 'So it's between ten or twelve days since she disappeared.' *What's taken so long to get here*, she wondered, but didn't add.

Andee said, 'Guy contacted the police on January the eleventh – that's between five and seven days after Jeannie disappeared – but he was told there was nothing anyone could do. No accidents had been reported – we've run a virtual nationwide check – and Jeannie is an adult with no physical or mental health problems. In other words, if she wants to absent herself from the family home, that's her business and no one else's.'

Seeing the point, Cara said, 'Has she ever gone off without telling anyone before?'

'Good question,' DS Rundle commented approvingly.

'Indeed,' Andee agreed, 'and actually, yes she has, but apparently she's usually back within a few days.'

'Do you know where she goes?'

'I think it's best if I let Guy tell you about that.' Andee checked the time on her phone. 'He should be here any minute.'

Cara's heart gave a flip of nervous excitement. These weren't the sort of people she normally mixed with; it would be interesting to see what he was like.

'I have a list of people he's already spoken to,' Andee told her, 'locally and elsewhere. I'll email it as soon as we've finished here, along with all the notes I've made.'

'Thank you,' Cara responded. 'Do you mind if I ask whether or not you are a friend of the Symondses?'

Andee smiled, seeming to approve of the question. 'I've never met Jeannie, and the first time I was properly introduced to Guy was when Fliss from the Seafront Café called me to ask if I could help with the search.'

'And when was that?' Cara asked.

'On January the twelfth, the day after the police turned him away. He wasn't ready to let it go, so he asked Fliss if she'd mind putting up a photograph of Jeannie in the café in case anyone had seen her. Fliss did so and then she rang me.'

Neat move, Cara was thinking. She'd want Andee on-side too if any of her loved ones did a 404.

'I met with him that same day,' Andee continued, 'and since then I've been following up on all the calls he's made in an effort to try and find his wife. In every case I've received the same response he did. No one knows where she is and no one has stood out for me so far as being someone who needs further questioning. However, I know Natalie here will tell you that you should satisfy yourself of that and I would urge the same.'

Cara was already working out in her mind how she was going to introduce herself when she made the calls. *Hello, I'm Cara Jakes of Kesterly CID* seemed to do it;

at least it made her sound like a detective, even if she officially wasn't.

Andee was speaking again. 'I've also been pulling together a general picture of what Jeannie is like as a woman, a wife, a boss – and I would say family member, if I'd managed to speak to her brother. He lives in New Zealand – Paul Haines, he's called – and he's divorced with a daughter, Mallory – that's Jeannie's niece, obviously. According to Guy, Jeannie and Paul are not close.'

'For what reason?' Cara asked.

'Nothing that seems immediately relevant,' Andee told her, 'but you'll find everything I know in my notes.'

Happy with that, Cara said, 'No other family?'

Andee shook her head. 'But feel free to double-check with Guy when you talk to him.'

DS Rundle weighed in with another question. 'Did you get the impression she had enemies or business rivals with a grudge, someone from the past who might want to cause her harm?'

Andee shrugged as she said, 'Nothing specific was mentioned during my questioning, but several colleagues referred to her as having a fiery temper, someone you wouldn't want to be on the wrong side of. According to one of her senior editors, her moods can change at lightning speed, and sometimes she can be quite intimidating.'

'Sounds like me,' DS Rundle quipped cheerily.

Cara dutifully laughed, while thinking the DS wasn't wrong there.

'So as yet no concrete reason to think any harm has come to her,' the DS said.

'No,' Andee admitted, 'but the length of time she's been gone is concerning. Obviously, I understand why you're

13

reluctant to launch an official investigation when there's no suggestion of a crime being committed, and she's someone who could easily stage her own disappearance if she wanted to. Nevertheless, just in case, I'd really appreciate some help at this stage.'

'And that's where you come in, Cara,' DS Rundle announced grandly. 'You'll have all our resources at your disposal, which is what Andee needs to further the search, so you'll work closely with her from here on in, without anything being official unless it becomes necessary. And I can't think of anyone better for you to learn from than Andee.'

Thinking exactly the same, Cara felt warmth in her cheeks as Andee smiled in her direction.

DS Rundle was saying, '. . . so you'll start by duplicating much of what Andee's already done – speaking to all the main players, mainly to see if you get the same answers she did. There could be a lot of ground to cover, Andee will guide you, and you know where to find me if anything interesting turns up, such as the woman herself.'

Cara felt terrible for hoping that didn't happen – it hardly made her a good citizen to wish someone kidnapped or dead, which, for all anyone knew, was where this was heading. But it was such a great opportunity for her as a newbie investigator, it would be a disaster if it got solved before she even got started.

'Is there anything else you'd like to ask before we go on?' Andee prompted gently.

There was, so Cara said, 'The landscaper who saw her on the phone on January sixth. I guess you've spoken to him yourself?'

'I have. His name's Neil Roberts and I know he'll be more than happy to talk to you when you call.'

'Is there anyone else who works at the Hall?' Cara asked.

'Yes, they have a regular housekeeper, Magda Kaminska, but she was self-isolating around the time Jeannie disappeared, so she hasn't been able to throw much light on things. You'll find her number, and Neil's, in my notes.' She checked her phone as it pinged and broke into a smile.

'Great! Fliss from the café is here,' she declared. 'I asked her to bring coffee and pastries if she could. I don't know about you, but I say better late than never.'

'Absolutely,' DS Rundle agreed. 'I was about to leave you to it, but I'm not passing up on Fliss's elevenses.'

'Shall I go and get her?' Cara offered, her mouth already watering at the prospect of an almond croissant.

'Someone's bringing her,' Andee replied. 'And Guy should be here by now. I'll just text to make sure he hasn't been held up.'

A few minutes later, they all looked up as the door banged open and Fliss, carrying an enormous tray of flasks, covered dishes and cardboard mugs, eased her way in, helped by a uniformed PC.

Cara beamed; Fliss always had that sort of effect on people, especially when her mask had a great big smile sewn on the front of it. She had thick, glossy blonde hair, high cheekbones and large, slanty blue eyes. Cara's mum always said that if she could be anyone else it would be Fliss, and not just because she was so gorgeous and outgoing and friendly, but because she had the sweetest soul. Cara's crabby old nan used to say, don't be deceived, everyone has a dark side, even that sexpot Fliss and I know what I'm talking about. Well, crabby-nan would know all about dark sides, given it was where she'd spent most of her sorry little life; even her own son, Cara's dad, used to say that about her.

'Sorry I'm late,' Fliss declared, hurrying to the table before her arms gave out. 'It's been hectic this morning, people queuing right along the Promenade, all thanks to the sun showing its face for half an hour.'

Knowing that she could only allow a single customer at a time into her brand-new café – the alterations had happened just prior to the first lockdown and then she'd been unable to open up – Cara wanted to ask how things really were for her, but didn't quite have the nerve. It wasn't as if she actually knew Fliss; she just felt as though she did, which was probably the same for everyone in town.

'It's Cara, isn't it?' Fliss asked. 'How do you take your coffee?' She got ready to pour, while massaging the bottom of her back. Cara almost said, *however you take yours*. Luckily she rescued herself from the idiocy and said, 'White, no sugar, thanks.'

'Help yourself to something wicked,' Fliss encouraged, as she passed the coffee over and indicated the pastries. 'That's right, Natalie, don't hold back. I'm not taking them home with me.'

Andee was pouring her own coffee. 'Did you happen to see Guy outside?' she asked, taking a moment to select a Danish.

'Yes, he was just parking up,' Fliss replied. To Natalie she said, 'I'm so glad you've decided to give Andee some help with this. It's been a terrible couple of weeks for Guy.'

'It's not an official search,' Natalie warned, 'and it won't be unless I'm convinced some harm has come to her. As yet, no one's been able to say that it has. So for now, you

16

have my best investigator on it, who will be reporting to Andee and obviously to me.'

Cara blushed to the roots of her hair to be described so glowingly.

Turning to her, Fliss said, 'Ever since I heard you'd got the job here I've been waiting for you to come into the café so I could give you a cupcake and coffee to say well done. Your mum must be thrilled. You will say hi to her when you get home, won't you?'

'Oh, of course and she says hi too. Or she will when I tell her, you know my mum.'

As Fliss smiled, the door opened again and Cara put down her almond croissant for a moment as a tall, dark-haired bloke came in. From what she could see of him, thanks to the mask, he was more like a movie star than a surgeon. Her mum would be having hot flushes for a week if she ever saw those eyes.

'Guy, I'm glad you made it,' Andee said warmly, keeping her distance, because everyone had to, of course. Fliss did a Namaste and Cara couldn't help noticing the way he kept his eyes on her a moment longer than seemed necessary. He liked her, Cara decided, and from the way Fliss reacted she reckoned the feeling was mutual. Well, who wouldn't like Fliss? And who wouldn't like him too? He seemed so . . . friendly.

'This is Natalie Rundle,' Andee said, directing him to the DS, 'and this is Cara Jakes. I've already told you about her.'

Cara watched him adjust his mask slightly while saying to the DS, 'I'm grateful to you for giving this some time. To be honest, I'm not sure what else to do. I've tried everything and everyone I can think of.'

'Cara will organize a check on the phone and credit card logs,' the DS assured him, 'and there should be a way of tracking the car.'

'Would you like some coffee?' Fliss offered.

'I'd love some, thanks,' he said, and again Cara picked up on the warmth between them. She knew Fliss wasn't married; in fact, come to think of it, she'd never seen her with a bloke. Guy Symonds was definitely not single, though; unless he was but didn't know it yet. That was a grim thought. Realizing her brain was shooting off in too many directions at once, she deliberately shut it down and watched him take the chair the DS was pointing him to – distant, but not so far along the table that he'd have to shout to be heard.

'I should leave you to it,' Fliss said, checking the time. 'I'll come back later for the tray.'

Guy Symonds rose to his feet. 'Thanks for coming,' he said. 'Thanks for everything.'

'We'll find her,' Fliss assured him softly, and leaving them to it, she let herself out of the room.

'Jeannie and I don't know many people around here,' he said as he sat down again, 'so I'm not sure what I'd have done without Fliss, and now Andee.'

'And now Cara,' Rundle added. 'I'm sorry the police weren't able to help when you came to us before, and I regret to say not much has changed on that front. Cara will of course do her best, but I'm afraid it's not possible to commit this Force's resources to a full-scale search when – as far as we're aware – no crime has been committed. Added to that, your wife isn't from this region and this isn't your main home, so she could be anywhere. She's also, I believe, of sound mind and in good health.'

'She is,' he confirmed. 'And I understand everything you're saying – and please know how much I appreciate the help you are prepared to give.' He looked at Cara, a smile visible in his eyes. 'I'm guessing,' he said, 'that you think she was having an affair and has decided to run off with whoever it is.'

Since it had very definitely crossed her mind, Cara was keen to know the answer.

'If she was involved with anyone else,' he said, 'I knew nothing about it, and presuming her friends and colleagues are being truthful, nor did they. Actually, if anyone knows her secrets it would be Maurice, her assistant, but he swears there wasn't anyone, and right now I'm inclined to believe him.'

DS Rundle nodded slowly as she took this in. 'So do you have any theories at all?' she prompted.

'I wish I did. I'm completely at a loss . . .'

'Did you argue before she disappeared? You say you last spoke to her on . . .'

'January the fifth,' Cara provided.

'Was anything said then that might have prompted her to leave? Or even before that?'

He shook his head slowly. 'We had words the weekend before, but it was just a spat that didn't actually amount to anything.'

'What was it about?'

His tone was wry. 'I told her she worked too hard, she accused me of the same. I said we should retire and travel the world. She said I wouldn't do it even if she were prepared to, and she wasn't. It was a pointless argument – actually, I wouldn't even call it that. We were both tired and some-times we snipe at each other, the way married couples do.'

'And what happened after?'

'About that? Nothing. It was just forgotten. I returned to London the following day and the next time I spoke to her was on January the fifth, as Cara says, although not for long. I'd just finished a Gamma knife procedure and I wanted to talk it over with my team so I said I'd call again later.'

Gamma knife. What was that? Cara wondered.

'And did you?' Rundle prompted.

'Yes, but she texted to say she was tied up in a meeting with her American colleagues that was likely to drag on, so she'd call me back the next day.'

'But she didn't?'

'No. And before you ask, yes, I've already checked to find out if the meeting was real and it was. It ended at ten forty-five in the evening, UK time, and there were eight of them on screen.'

Rundle nodded thoughtfully.

'Excuse me,' Guy said as his mobile rang. 'I need to take this.' As he clicked on, he drew a notebook out of an inside pocket and began to jot down whatever he was being told. At the end he said, 'Thanks for this, Ed. Yes, it will be a craniotomy, but I'm in a meeting right now. I'll call him as soon as I'm free.'

As he rang off, he apologized and put his phone and notebook on the table in front of him.

'The world keeps turning,' DS Rundle commented by way of understanding, and turning to Cara said, 'It might be a good idea for you to review everything Andee's sending your way before you and Mr Symonds have a chat. Does that work for you?' she asked Symonds.

'I'm happy to play it any way that works for you,' he assured her.

'OK, is there anything you'd like to ask now, Cara, before we break this up?'

Swallowing, Cara said, 'Yes, just a couple of things, and I expect Andee's already covered them, but first of all, can you tell if any of her clothes are missing?'

Symonds seemed troubled as he said, 'There are a few empty hangers in her dressing room, but I can't honestly say whether they were empty before, as we have separate dressing rooms. As for shoes and boots, maybe some have gone, but again I couldn't tell you for certain. She has a lot to choose from.'

'Suitcases, holdalls?' Cara prompted.

'She has a large navy Mulberry bag that I can't find either at the Hall or in London.'

After noting this down, Cara said, 'Do you know if she has a second phone, one she uses for personal calls, maybe?'

'Not that I've ever been aware of. Again you could try asking Maurice, but I'm sure he'd have mentioned it by now if he knew of one.'

Sensing how closely she was being watched by Andee and the DS, Cara pressed on. 'Have you contacted her doctor at all?'

'Yes, I have,' he replied. 'She hasn't seen him for over a year, so no undisclosed health issues that we know of.'

She glanced down at her notes. 'My last question is about the landscaper,' she said. 'Do you know how close he was to the window that day when he saw her? I mean, could he tell whether she seemed upset or in a hurry, or anything at all that stood out for him?'

Frowning, he said, 'I didn't ask, but I'm sure if he had noticed anything unusual he'd have said so right away.'

'Do you know if he spotted anyone else at the Hall that day? Was there another car, maybe, that he hadn't seen before?'

'Again, he hasn't mentioned anything like that, but I think he was only there for about half an hour.'

'What was he doing there?'

'He was dropping off some materials for a wall we're planning to extend, and I believe he replaced a couple of fleeces that had been torn off by the wind.'

'Fleeces?' Rundle queried.

'It's what he wraps around the large plant pots to help protect the roots from the frost.'

Nodding, she turned to Cara. 'Is that it for now?' she asked.

In spite of having loads more she wanted to ask, Cara said, 'I think so, but it shouldn't take me long to go through Andee's notes. Can we speak again later today?'

'Of course,' he replied, and he might have smiled, but thanks to the mask she couldn't know for sure. 'I have quite a lot of administrative work to catch up on,' he said, 'so I'll go to Howarth Hall. Let me know when you're ready and perhaps we could connect by video-link?'

'That sounds a good idea.' Rundle started getting to her feet. 'Thanks for coming in, Mr Symonds, it helps a lot to meet someone in person before enquiries get under way. And of course, if you hear anything at all, you'll get in touch with us right away.'

'Of course,' he confirmed. He was on his feet too and checking his phone as it rang again. 'I'm sorry,' he said. 'It's another call I have to take. As you said, the world keeps turning.'

'I'll go downstairs with him,' Andee said as he made

for the door. To Cara, she added, 'I've already emailed everything including my number. Call if there's anything and I'll join you later when you speak to Guy on video-link.'

As Andee left, Cara turned to the DS, glad to be alone with her for a moment. 'I was thinking,' she began, 'I don't actually have a proper desk—'

'Don't worry about that,' Rundle interrupted, 'you can set yourself up in the second-floor incident room. It's not being used at the moment. Obviously you'll have to move out if something comes in, but for now it has everything you'll need – phones, computers, whiteboards, video screens. Remember to record every interview, won't you, either on your phone or the computer, so you can share it with me and Andee, if she's not actively involved in it herself. This means you'll have to start each one with a caution, so don't forget that. Just try to make it sound chatty, not too official, because as far as we know no one's done anything wrong.'

CHAPTER TWO

FLISS

Thursday 20 August 2020
Five months before Jeannie's disappearance

It was coming up to lunch time and the Seafront Café's bustling kitchen was steamy and noisy and setting tastebuds zinging as the cooks began removing quiches, lasagnes, hunter's pies and homemade pasties from the hot ovens. These days there was plenty of space for everyone to work, which certainly hadn't been the case back at the beginning of the year – in other words prior to the 'big expansion', as Fliss's son, Zac, termed it.

Or, put another way, pre-pandemic.

Andee Lawrence, in her guise as interior designer, had overseen the entire project, turning the tired old corner caff the Seafront had once been into a cross between an American-style diner – with its long, welcoming countertop, deluxe bar stools, colourful soft-drink optics, and cosy banquettes – and a Parisian café, with huge bifold doors at the front opening onto an awning-shaded terrace facing the sea. It had been a wide pavement pre-pandemic, but the local authority had recently allowed it to be used for outdoor dining.

Fliss had been so giddy with excitement over it all on completion in March that she'd planned an enormous 'grand opening' party with everyone invited. As bad luck would have it, a national lockdown had been announced before she could serve so much as a coffee. The blow of what it was likely to mean for the future had sent her reeling.

All her money had gone on the expansion and lavish makeover of the upstairs apartment, every last penny of it, and none of the banks wanted to help her. She was already mortgaged to the hilt, and besides, she desperately didn't want to borrow any more funds that she might not be able to pay back.

The only good thing that had happened back then was when her wonderful, thoughtful, treasured eighteen-year-old son, Zac, had turned up on the doorstep with his keyboard, bags and books, declaring he was going to spend the lockdown with her, and planned to study for his A levels in the spacious flat above the café.

How blessed she was in that boy – young man now. She simply adored him, and their bond couldn't have been stronger, in spite of his father having had full custody of him since he was four.

Bolstered by Zac's return, and growing concerned for so many in the area who'd started to suffer hardship, some for the very first time, Fliss had forced herself back into action. She was going to get food to those who needed it; after all, she was the owner of the Seafront Café, a cornerstone of the town, a place everyone relied on in so many ways, not only for breakfasts and lunches, afternoon teas and takeaway snacks. Virtually since she'd taken the place over ten years ago, people had seemed to flock to it, not only locals, but tourists, second home-owners and romantic weekenders. And she'd made so many friends that she'd almost been able to forget why she'd needed to escape her previous life to come here in the first place. In fact, in recent times, she'd felt as close to happy as it was possible for someone like her to be, and no one, apart from Andee, knew why she'd resolutely remained single since her divorce, and always would.

'Mum! There's a delivery,' Zac called out, putting his head round the kitchen door and promptly helping himself to a juicy Scotch egg from a tray ready to go through to the café. 'Don't worry, I've got it, but the storeroom's locked.'

Continuing to stir the day's special, asparagus, pea and mushroom risotto, Fliss used her other hand to dig into the pocket of her jeans, pulled out a heavy set of keys and tossed it over. 'Is it olive oil?' she asked.

'I hope so. We need it. More Corona Girls have just turned up, by the way, they're out front taking orders from all the tourists coming over from the beach.'

Fliss sent silent blessings to the WhatsApp group Andee had started to support the café through these difficult times, as she handed the risotto over to another cook and went to check that everything was in place for the afternoon duties. This was when three or four of the Corona Girls would box up the many donations that came in throughout the day, ready for delivery the following morning, while Zac, her right-hand man now that his A levels were over, usually took on the heavy jobs. He also found time to work with his father a few times a week, helping to keep struggling residents' gardens in order. Just a couple of weeks ago, he'd heard that he'd received the necessary grades to go to Edinburgh, his uni of choice.

Fliss couldn't be prouder of him; luckily for him, given the times they were living through, he'd already planned to take a gap year following his A levels – although, not so luckily for him, it wasn't now going to involve travelling the world.

At last five o'clock came round, time to close the café doors for the evening and start to work out the day's takings. She hadn't done badly today, considering the awful weather and reduced number of diners owing to social distancing, but it was a fraction of what she'd have made in normal times. And she didn't even want to think about all the food that was going to waste.

Stuffing her Turbo Smart spin mop into the wringer, she gave the remainder of the floor a final swipe-over, while sending silent thank yous to Leanne and Claudia, the Corona Girls who'd cleaned and disinfected everything before leaving. She truly wouldn't have been able to manage without them, and would never have known how willing and dedicated they'd be until Andee had called them to arms.

Hearing someone trying to open the door, she turned, and as often happened when she saw her son unexpectedly, she felt her heart contract with beautiful and joyful emotions.

Except it wasn't him, she realized, as she went to open up; it was his father who, if truth be told, also made her heart sing. The fact that they were no longer together was entirely her fault; he hadn't wanted the break-up, in truth, he'd done everything he could to talk her out of it. But after what she'd done, she simply hadn't been able to accept that she had any rights left as a mother or a wife.

'Hey you,' she said, unlocking the door to let him in. Not unusually, she turned away quickly, as the powerful attraction she still felt for him sprang to life. It didn't always happen, thank God; they'd been apart for so long it would be a living nightmare for her if it did. However, there was no doubt it still existed, and at times it was as though the chemistry between them was going to take over her body completely and restore her to the fully functioning and deeply sensuous woman she used to be. 'I wasn't expecting you,' she said, going back to the counter.

'I've just dropped Chloe at a ballet class around the corner,' he explained, referring to his nine-year-old daughter, 'so I thought I'd see if there was any chance of a cuppa while I wait for her to finish. By the way, I dropped some roses at the back for your boxes upstairs. They're already in bloom, but should see you for another month or so, then we'll sort out what's best for winter.'

'That's lovely, thanks,' she smiled, watching him kick off his boots before stepping off the mat, and feeling grateful to him, as she always did, for making sure the four, sea-facing balconies of her apartment were colourful and cared for. 'Everything's turned off, I'm afraid,' she said, 'but we should have a kettle somewhere.'

'How about an ice-cream?' he suggested, going to peer into the display case where only half a dozen flavours remained to tempt him. They'd had a run on ice-creams and lollies today, thanks to the good weather. 'Aaah, rum raisin, my favourite,' he declared, thumping his heart to confirm the truth of it.

With twinkling eyes she said, 'OK, but I'm warning you, your son won't be happy with you if you finish it off.'

'Ah, but he'll only know it was me if you tell him.'

With a laugh, she scooped two generous boules into a cornet and passed it over, watching him as his eyes closed in ecstasy at the first taste. When they opened again, they came to hers and stayed. She knew instantly what he was thinking, feeling, that the currents between them were affecting him too, making him want her right now, right here. Her heart was thudding too hard, the longing was sharp and demanding, but she forced herself to look away. How could she still love him so much after all these years, still feel as though he, and every part of him, belonged to her, when he was married to someone else?

'Tell me you made this,' he said, savouring the next creamy mouthful almost as though those few intense seconds hadn't happened. It was the only way they could get through them and remain apart, to talk over them as if they weren't real.

'I made it,' she replied, and helped herself to a small boule of vanilla.

Though they both knew she hadn't, they continued with the illusion as he licked and swooned and finally said, 'Business seems to be good. There was quite a bit of activity when I went past at lunch time.'

'It wasn't bad,' she admitted, 'but we're still only serving at half-capacity and I'm starting to fear we'll be locked down again before we know it. Have you heard that?'

Grimacing he said, 'Some rumblings yes, but if it does happen, maybe it won't be as severe as before.' His eyes narrowed as he regarded her closely, inquisitively. 'These

29

restrictions are hitting you harder than you're admitting to,' he stated, seeming to know she'd deny it, so not making it a question.

Waving a dismissive hand, she said, 'Everyone in hospitality is feeling it, you know that, but I'm sure we'll get through. Well, obviously not everyone,' she quickly added, thinking of the pubs, restaurants and cafés all over town – all over the country – that had already been forced to close their doors and would never open them again. She felt herself panic inside at the mere thought of it. Thank God she wasn't in that position yet, for she couldn't imagine what she'd do, how she'd survive even, without her beloved café. 'Where's Zac?' she asked. 'Isn't he working for you today?'

'He's digging out a pond in Blenley Park, so don't expect him to be smelling too good when he gets back.'

'Thanks for the warning.' Treating him to the last half-scoop of rum raisin, she said, 'I saw Estie earlier. She seemed a bit strung out. Is she OK?' Since his wife was often in a state of agitation over one thing or another, Fliss wasn't particularly worried, and knew he wouldn't be either; she just thought she'd mention it.

Glancing at his phone as it rang he said, 'Speak of the devil,' and clicking on he continued to look at Fliss as he said, jokily, 'Kesterly Landscaping, Neil speaking. How can I help you?'

With a roll of her eyes, Fliss tuned out the call and went to busy herself in the kitchen for a while. The last thing she wanted was to eavesdrop on his conversations with Estelle, mostly out of dread of them turning romantic. She couldn't bear even the thought of them sharing any kind of intimacy. Not that she hadn't witnessed it over the years; spending so much time with them in order to be with Zac had meant having to suffer it way more regularly than her sanity, or heart, could really bear. However, given a choice of seeing Zac or not, she'd decided that the relationship with her son had to come before her sensibilities over his father's second marriage.

'Everything OK?' she asked as she returned to the café to find him off the phone and perched on a bar stool gazing at nothing.

With a playful roll of his wonderful blue eyes he said, 'Apparently Estie got recognized earlier, in the florist's. You know how she loves it when that happens. She was just leaving the shop when the woman behind the counter said, "Thanks, Estelle."'

Fliss said dryly, 'And that counts for being recognized? Maybe she'd paid with a credit card?'

Holding back a laugh, Neil said, 'It's possible, but let's not burst her bubble.'

Feeling mean for attempting it, Fliss said, 'I've told her plenty of times that lots of women who come in here still talk about the book she wrote, and they'd love it if she'd agree to give a talk. When we're back to normal, of course. We couldn't do it now with the way things are.'

Lowering his voice conspiratorially, he said, 'I'm sure she'd come in a heartbeat if you hadn't already invited Jeannie Symonds to advise on how to get published. She's got a bit of a bee in her bonnet about Jeannie, in case you didn't know.'

Fliss tried not to laugh, because of course she knew. Anyone who knew Estie was aware of it, and to her shame Fliss even wondered if she'd invited Jeannie first just to annoy Estelle. It wasn't very admirable, the way she got a kick out of that at times. Anyway, it had come to nothing, thanks to the lockdown, and since they still weren't able to hold any gatherings it wasn't going to be an issue for the foreseeable future. 'So how are the preparations going for Jeannie's summer party?' she asked, starting to pack up the cake display stands.

Perching on a stool he said, 'They're about done, for my part. Garden's ready, gazebos are up, lights are in the trees in case it goes on into the evening, which I'm sure it will. We'll go back tomorrow to help bring in the tables and chairs and set up for the musicians.'

'Sounds as though it's going to be quite a do,' she commented, easily able to imagine how lovely he'd made it look, 'and the forecast is good. Will you be going?'

With a sigh he said, 'I'm invited, but obviously I can't go without Estelle.'

Fliss grimaced. 'Did they expect you to?'

'I'm not sure. We didn't get into it. I just thought it would be better to stay away rather than risk any awkwardness. One of the lads will be on hand in case of emergencies.'

With the cake trays ready to go through to the kitchen for cleaning, she started to tie off the tops of loaded bin bags. 'Does Estie know she's not invited?' she ventured.

'I'm afraid so. Obviously she says she couldn't care less, and wouldn't go even if she had been, but I know she's hurt. As she has been every other time Jeannie has failed to invite her.'

Feeling a little sorry for Estie, always on the outside, Fliss said, 'Guy Symonds was in earlier.'

'Oh, is he back already?' he responded, looking up from his mobile. 'Jeannie'll be pleased, she was starting to worry

32

he wouldn't turn up until the last minute. I might see if he fancies hitting the surf on Sunday, if his hangover's not too bad.'

Surprised, she said, 'I didn't know you two surfed together.'

'We just talk about it, but hey, if he's around . . . It's been an age since I caught some waves, and I know Zac's dying to.'

'If I had time I'd come and watch,' she said wryly, 'three ripped dudes in wetsuits riding the boards. Not one to be missed.'

With a raised eyebrow, he said, 'So Guy does it for you, does he?'

Feeling a tell-tale heat in her cheeks, she pulled a face at him and turned away to busy herself. 'Not just me,' she countered, wondering how he might feel about her finding another man attractive. Obviously he couldn't be ignorant of the fact that she'd never been involved with anyone since they'd parted, although it wasn't something they'd ever discussed. Maybe he told himself that she simply kept it discreet.

'You should hear some of the things the ladies say about him after he's been in,' she continued, determined to keep things light, 'or maybe you shouldn't – they might make you blush.'

With a laugh, he said, 'I'm sure they would, and I'm equally sure they know he's happily married.'

'Which isn't surprising when he's thoughtful enough to stop by here to pick up some of Wilkie's handmade truffles to take home for his wife.'

Looking eagerly around, he said, 'Any left?'

'Afraid not. He had the last ones, but she's delivering

some more tomorrow. She's got quite a cottage industry going up there at the farmhouse.' Fliss was looking at the door now, her expression turning to one of horror as their son appeared.

Following her eyes, Neil started to laugh. 'Well, look at you,' he declared as Zac trod onto the mat and let his sodden self drip all over it.

'Why are you coming in this way?' Fliss cried, rushing to push him out again. 'Oh my God, you stink.'

'I fell in,' Zac laughed. 'I swear someone pushed me, and you're not going to like the truck too much, Dad, but I had to get home somehow. Anyway, I must have left my key behind this morning – and before you say anything, Mum, at least it was me this time. It's usually you who forgets stuff.'

'Because I've always got a lot on my mind,' she retorted defensively. 'Wait there, I'll go and unlock the back door.'

As she sped through to the rear exit, she heard her mobile start to ring and Neil say, cheerfully, 'Hey, Andee. How's tricks?'

Used to him answering her phone if a name came up that he knew, she continued on to open up the back. By the time she returned, Neil had apparently settled into a nice cosy chat with Andee, while Zac had decided to strip off right there in the doorway.

Unable to stop herself laughing at his nearly nude state, she spun him around, shoved him outside, threw his filthy jeans and T-shirt after him, and turned back to Neil just as he was saying, 'I often wish she'd tell me what was really going on with her, but she never will.'

Not knowing whether he was talking about her or Estelle – it had to be Estie, she was always an issue – Fliss tried to grab the phone, but he held it at arm's length to tease her.

She eyed him meaningfully, and reached for it again. Letting it go this time, he took himself off to join Zac in the apartment upstairs.

She continued to stand where she was, forgetting for a moment that Andee was waiting. She was trying to collect her thoughts, but for some reason they seemed to be escaping her.

CHAPTER THREE

CARA

Monday 18 January 2021
Twelve days since Jeannie's disappearance

Cara was by now installed in her very own freezing cold incident room, all wrapped up in hat, gloves and scarf until the heating kicked in. There were six desks all pushed together at the centre of the space, a wall filled up by a partially cleaned whiteboard and another with windows overlooking the alley below. She even had her own coffee maker, or would have once all the mould had been cleaned off; and next to it was a very small fridge that thankfully didn't turn out to be growing the next virus.

Delighted with everything and already bursting with eagerness, she started by firing up all the computer terminals and was soon checking the National Database for both Symondses – Jeannie and Guy.

Nothing.

Unsurprised by that, she went to Andee's email on her laptop and dug out Jeannie's mobile phone number and bank card details in order to submit the relevant requests for information. Same for ANPR – automatic number plate recognition. Could be several days before she heard back from anyone, so best to get the process started right away. She then turned to Google, typed in 'Jeannie Symonds' and up came just shy of four hundred thousand results.

'Could be here a while,' she murmured to herself, but in fact she was on the Athene Publishing website in next to no time, and a few more clicks took her to the only Jeannie Symonds that interested her.

'So this is you,' she murmured, taking in the catlike, wide-set green eyes, delicate bone structure and thin-lipped but attractive smile. Her hair was fair and collar length, and there was no way she looked like a woman in her fifties, not in this shot anyway. It could have been airbrushed, of course, or it could have been taken some time ago; nevertheless she had a much more youthful look about her than Cara had expected. You wouldn't have known Guy was younger than her.

Going onto Facebook, she found Jeannie's page had no security settings, and so was soon surfing through the hundreds of photos Jeannie had posted over the years. The most recent were of Howarth Hall's gardens, including some aerial shots of a seriously glam-looking party on the front lawn overlooking the bay, attended by dozens of people. The weather looked lovely – on checking the date she saw it had taken place last August, when things had kind of opened up for a while, before restrictions had returned in September.

Next were dozens of before-and-after shots of the gardens, loads of heavy machinery digging into the rocky soil, old stone walls being constructed, turf laid, plants and trees going in. It had clearly been an enormous project that had no doubt cost a fortune. Cara guessed that the well-ripped workman with short dark hair and a shadow beard was Neil Roberts, as he looked to be in charge. There were shots of him with Jeannie as he explained something to her, and of the two of them laughing together over something out of frame. Then there was Neil Roberts high-fiving Guy Symonds over what looked like a wishing well; another of the two men up to their ankles in a pebbly stream, and a dozen or more of them with Jeannie, all three of them in muddy boots and old clothes, with champagne glasses in hand and woollen hats pulled down to their eyes.

Scrolling on, Cara found lots more shots of Guy, often in scrubs or gym gear, and then there were pictures of their wedding, which had apparently happened on a Greek island. They were a good-looking couple, no doubt about that, him more than her, it had to be said, but Jeannie had shone on their wedding day, in clouds of ivory chiffon and flowers in her hair. She didn't look half bad in a swimsuit either. Cara wondered who'd taken the really dreamy shots of them lying together on a hammock, or her sitting between his legs and him kissing her hair. Maybe they had a tripod, or some of the wedding guests had still been around.

Moving on, or back in time, she came to Jeannie during her pre-Guy years, mostly depicting her professional life because they were shots of launch parties, or bestseller lists, or movie premieres of books she'd published. Cara recognized some of the authors' names, but most she didn't. There were plenty of shots of holidays with mates, boyfriends, and an older couple Cara presumed were her parents. Intermingled with these, almost as if she were sewing her husband into her past, were some fantastic photos of her and Guy on their travels, and it seemed there was nothing those two hadn't ridden in or on –

speedboats, small planes, luxury yachts, camels, jet skis, hot-air balloons, donkeys, Land Rover safaris, and some sort of space rocket that turned out to be a theme park ride somewhere in New Zealand. They'd definitely packed it all in during the time they'd known one another, that was for sure.

A sudden change came next, as if a lift had dropped a couple of floors, and opened up to show Jeannie as a child with her parents, and a knobbly-kneed boy, presumably her brother. There was a large country house, no doubt where she'd grown up, given how often it appeared. Cara couldn't help being impressed by it all. Jeannie's parents had clearly been loaded.

Cara's heart suddenly lurched as she found herself looking at Jeannie in her thirties, or thereabouts, holding a tiny baby, and seeming so entranced by it that she might not even have known the picture was being taken. There were dozens more of the child, not only in infancy, but also as she grew into a toddler, a schoolgirl, a teenager, and almost always with Jeannie. Some were with Jeannie's parents, but there was no sign of a possible father, although he could have been behind the camera. There was nothing to say who the child was – no name, only dates going back about twenty years.

Guy presumably knew who the child was or the shots wouldn't be public on Facebook. Andee presumably knew too, though Cara hadn't got that far in the notes yet, and if Andee had felt it was relevant she'd surely have brought it up already.

Going back to Jeannie's profile picture, Cara sat studying it for a while, almost as if it might speak to her, although she wasn't familiarizing herself with Jeannie's features as much as remembering what DS Rundle had told her not very long ago.

'Photographs are frozen moments in time; they can as easily tell a false story as they can disguise what's happening outside the frame.'

She'd gone on to say, 'It's important to remember that when it comes to social media, people only upload what they want you to see.'

Returning to Jeannie's most recent posts, Cara began going through them again more slowly this time. The gardens at Howarth Hall, sunsets over the bay, the woods behind the house; the stream that appeared to run through the grounds and trickle into a waterfall down over the cliffs. Then she was once again at last summer's party, with photos and videos of Jeannie looking radiant, as did all the guests, dressed up in their cocktail finery, champagne flowing, live musicians playing, barefoot dancing on the grass, uniformed staff keeping it all going.

Sitting back in her chair, Cara began to unwind her scarf now the room was warming up. Although she hadn't learned anything immediately helpful from this trawl through Facebook, she definitely felt she was getting to know Jeannie a little better. It had also made her feel a bit like a stalker, going into someone's personal life so deeply, but she'd get past that. The point was, as far as she could see, Jeannie was everything her friends and family had said she was: attractive, successful, healthy, happily married and pretty rich. So what on earth would make her leave her apparently wonderful life and loving husband to go . . . Where?

She stared at the smiling woman on the screen again, and this time felt as though Jeannie was staring right back at her. And the longer she looked at those eyes, the more unsettled she started to feel, as if beneath the friendly façade, Jeannie Symonds was warning her to stay away, to mind her own business and stop digging into her life right now.

A cold chill went down her spine.

She blinked, looked at the profile picture again, and this time she saw nothing unusual at all.

CHAPTER FOUR

ESTELLE

Friday 18 September 2020
Four months before Jeannie's disappearance

Estelle cut a small, dainty figure at the large desk in her upstairs writer's room where a floor-to-ceiling A-frame window looked out onto the colourful and rambling garden, over to the orchard and on out to the far slopes of the moor. The bookshelves around her were all neatly arranged, and the many posters of her own book *A Crow Amongst Blackbirds*, plus marketing brochures and publicity shots from the time, were filling up all the available wall space and shelves. It was a small gallery in honour of her single publishing achievement, which had not, by any means, been small. It had just been quite a long time ago, and though she still came into this room every day, and told everyone that she was busy on another book, it wasn't true.

Everything in her life felt wrong, out of kilter, moving along a strange and unnavigable path, and as time went on, she only seemed to become even more distant from herself and who she really was. She knew that she'd lost a sense of it after Jeannie had thrown her out of her office all those years ago, as if she were last week's garbage, someone of no importance at all. The hurt she'd suffered then had felt as bad, maybe worse, than all the other rejections she'd suffered throughout her life.

She might have got over it, managed eventually to rebuild her self-esteem and go on to write again, but then Jeannie had bought the house on Westleigh Heights. It had seemed like a deliberate provocation, a way of rubbing salt into barely healed wounds; it was the kind of monstrous act only someone like Jeannie would commit.

Estelle still wondered if she'd contracted Neil to spite her. He said not, but why had Jeannie chosen him when there were at least two other perfectly good landscapers in the area? And why had he taken the job when he knew better than most how terrible it would be for his wife?

'It's a major job and we need the money,' he'd reminded her when she'd tried to argue him out of it. 'I know you don't want to hear that, but right now things are tight . . .'

'And it's my fault because I'm not earning?'

He'd denied it, but she'd known it was true, and so she hadn't been in a strong enough position to talk him out of it.

She'd never admit that deep in her heart being back in Jeannie's favour was what she wanted more than anything, to laugh and joke with her again the way they used to, and to share the joy of success. She'd felt whole and purposeful and even invincible when Jeannie had believed in her, and she could feel that way again if Jeannie was ready to take back all she'd said.

It had never happened, though, and so here she was, sitting here alone with the world outside in turmoil, people dying, the virus spreading, tighter restrictions being imposed again and warnings of a new lockdown to come, and all she could really think about was herself. Lately she'd come to believe that the only person she ever felt really comfortable with was her daughter, Chloe, although she couldn't be entirely sure Chloe felt the same. She was always so busy with other people and other things, and had spent so much time with Neil over the summer that she was becoming quite the little gardener herself.

She was back at school now, mixing with all her friends again, no doubt the life and soul of it all, although there was still no socializing after the school day ended. Chloe never complained, or seemed down about the way things were. She was like her father in how adaptable and easy-going she was, and sometimes when Estelle watched them together, she found herself wanting to cry for her young self who'd known so little joy at home.

It was impossible to know why her parents had adopted her when they'd always seemed so detached, even unin-terested in her. Apart from feeding and clothing her, sending her to school and taking her on holidays to West Wales or a Scottish island, they'd done so little with her.

Thank God for her friends' parents, she used to think – and still did – or she might not have known what real family life was like at all. As it was, she'd mostly had to watch from the sidelines, hurting, longing and envying to within an inch of her lonely little soul.

She'd just turned twenty-five and was working as a receptionist at a literary agency in London when her parents had got in touch to let her know that they were moving to Canada. If she wanted anything from the house in Somerset, her mother had said, she should come to get it.

What a joyless, desperate visit that had been, the place full of boxes, and empty already of what little warmth it had ever seemed to possess. Her parents had been excited about the move, she could see that; they were more animated than she could ever remember, and so proud of her father's new position as head of a civil engineering firm in Montreal that they hadn't even thought to ask if she might like to go too. (She wouldn't have gone, not in a million years, but it would have been nice to be asked.)

The only bright part of the visit – which actually turned out to be one of the best things that had ever happened to her – was meeting Neil when he'd come to survey the garden for the new owners. She was attracted to him from the off – it was hard not to be when he was so charming and good-looking, but what had really set him apart was that he'd talked to *her*, seemed genuinely interested to know all about her – from where she lived, to how much she enjoyed her work, to the kind of things she did in her spare time. When she told him she was writing a book, he'd seemed so impressed that, for the first time since she'd started it, she'd actually felt she might finish.

And finish it she had, the following year, by which time she and Neil were seeing one another regularly at week-ends and he'd even introduced her to his little son Zac. Everything was going so well – she couldn't imagine life being any better – and then it was as though a whirlwind picked them up and threw them into a world where dreams actually did come true. Her book was published and became a million-copy bestseller, Neil inherited a huge plot of land near Kesterly-on-Sea, and she found out she was pregnant. So they'd married (her parents didn't make it back for the wedding), built a house, and in what seemed like no time at all they were a family.

Obviously she'd known he was a great dad from

watching him with Zac, but when Chloe had come along and she'd seen how much his daughter meant to him too, she'd realized that her precious girl was always going to have someone waiting for her at the school gates with a big smile and open arms and feeling so pleased to see her that they could have been at the end of a rainbow.

She wasn't thinking about Chloe, or rainbows, or her own childhood now, as time ticked on and she still didn't move from her desk. She was – not for the first time – reliving the day in August – the twenty-second to be precise, so not quite a month ago – that had changed everything for her. Simply allowing it to enter her mind sent shivers of hope and happiness coasting through her like gaily coloured ribbons tying up parcels of promise.

She'd been standing beside the kissing gate on the edge of the woods next to Howarth Hall, watching the summer party that Guy and Jeannie were hosting on their front lawn. She'd thought no one would notice her there, that she was far enough away not to be recognized even if someone did spot her, but Guy had seen her and had walked all the way across the field to come and invite her in.

She'd wondered later why she hadn't disappeared back into the woods before he could reach her, why her own sense of self-preservation and dignity hadn't kicked in. For all she knew, he might have been on his way to tell her she was trespassing and it was time to leave, but that wasn't what he'd said at all.

'Hi, Estelle,' he'd smiled, 'fancy seeing you here.'

The gentle irony of his tone had made her smile too. This was the first time she'd seen him since her book launch, five years before, and yet he was greeting her as easily and warmly as if they were in touch most days.

'Why don't you come and join us?' he suggested, and he actually seemed to mean it.

'Oh, no, thanks,' she protested. 'I was just admiring the view from here . . . I didn't realize . . .' How could she claim not to know about the party when Neil had been at the Hall preparing for it every day this past week?

'You'd be very welcome,' he assured her.

She laughed awkwardly. 'That's kind of you, but I don't think Jeannie would agree.'

He smiled and she felt her heart turn over. She remembered how much she'd always liked him, and had understood perfectly why Jeannie was so crazy about him. He wasn't only good looking, sophisticated and very successful, he had a quality about him, a genuine warmth that seemed able to unknot tensions and inhibitions and melt them away. 'It's my house too,' he reminded her dryly, 'and I'd like you to come.'

Although he really did seem to mean it, she'd said, 'No, honestly. In fact I should be going now anyway.'

She didn't move and nor did he.

After a while he said, 'I'm sorry things worked out the way they did with Jeannie. She was going through a very rough time . . .'

'With her parents dying, I know.' She didn't add it was still no excuse for Jeannie to have behaved the way she had, but she got the sense he knew that and maybe even agreed with her.

'Do you often walk in these woods?' he asked, changing the subject as he watched a flurry of noisy gulls swoop down over the bay.

She glanced over her shoulder at the trees sheltering many pathways and hidden nooks, a stream, slumbering animals, wild berries, mosses, mushrooms, and the infamous Devil's Scoop way over on the other side above the cliffs. She'd never admit to how often she came simply to get a glimpse of the house, but mostly in the hope of spotting Jeannie. It was her own form of self-torture, like someone who kept pulling the scab off a wound to make it hurt and bleed all over again. 'Occasionally,' she said, 'but I prefer to walk on the moor.'

He appeared delighted. 'Me too,' he said. 'Jeannie adores the woods, she's coming to know them quite well, in fact, but every now and again I manage to persuade her to join me on Dunkery Hill or in the Doone Valley.'

Suspecting Jeannie was learning about the woods from Neil, and knowing how charming and funny he could be when waxing lyrical on his favourite subject, Estelle pushed down her jealousy and said, 'They're two of my favourite moor walks, but I like Nutcombe Bottom too.'

He tilted his head. 'I don't think I've ever tried that one. Are there a lot of trees?'

She smiled. 'Do you have something against trees?'

He laughed. 'Not at all. I love them, but I like wide open spaces as well. It's probably why I enjoy sailing and surfing. I know your husband's a keen surfer.'

'He is, although he hasn't had as much time to go lately.' Had that sounded like a criticism of how many hours he seemed to spend at Howarth Hall? It wasn't, because he had a lot of clients, and she didn't know for sure how often he was there.

'We were hoping to go tomorrow,' he said, 'but I don't think Jeannie would forgive me if I disappeared when there's bound to be a lot of clearing up still to do.'

Estie didn't answer that; she wasn't even sure what she

thought about Neil becoming so friendly with the Symondses, whether it was good or bad, so they stood quietly for a moment, absorbing the view and heady scents of scorched grass and salt air, listening to the distant sound of voices and laughter drifting over from the party. In the end she said, 'Shouldn't you be getting back?'

He glanced over to the gathering and said, 'Yes, I probably should.'

He still didn't go, and as he looked down at her, Estie's breathing seemed to stop. His eyes were intense and yet tender, full of concern. 'It's been nice talking to you,' he said. 'Please try not to think too badly of Jeannie. I know she can be difficult, but I'm sure things will work out.'

Swallowing she said, 'I hope so.'

He continued to look at her, and for a heady moment she wondered what it would be like to kiss him, to feel his arms around her . . . 'Would you care to show me Nutcombe Bottom?' he asked kindly.

Her heart skipped a beat. 'I'd love to,' she replied.

He took out his phone and, after they'd exchanged numbers, he'd promised to be in touch soon, leaving her at the gate with a brief wave of his hand.

He'd texted three days later and they'd walked through Nutcombe Bottom for over two hours, talking about so many different things while soaking up the sun as it blazed down through the trees. They'd met again a week later to wander through the Doone Valley, which was when she'd first told him how much she'd like to meet her birth mother. He'd listened and seemed to understand in a way she hadn't expected of anyone, least of all a near stranger. Except she'd stopped seeing him that way since their chat at the kissing gate.

It was because he'd encouraged it that she'd finally found the nerve to take the first steps in finding out more about the woman who had let her go when she was only a day old. As yet she'd gone no further than contacting a private investigator to ask for his help, but she'd hear back from him soon, she was certain of it, and then . . . Well, she had no idea what she'd do then, but as Guy had said the last time she'd seen him, 'There's no point trying to make decisions about something that hasn't actually happened yet.'

She wondered if he'd told Jeannie she was hoping to meet her birth mother.

No, of course he hadn't – what kind of an idiot was she, to think he might have?

The kind of idiot who loved her husband, was becoming increasingly besotted with another man, and who was so lonely at times she hardly knew what to do with herself.

She desperately wanted to hear from Guy. He'd said, when they'd first discussed the idea of her contacting her birth mother, that it would probably help to free her from all the complex and contradictory feelings she had towards Jeannie if she were to focus more on herself and how important it was to find out about her roots.

She knew in her heart he was right, but she wanted, needed, to hear him say it again.

CHAPTER FIVE

JEANNIE

Friday 18 September 2020
Four months before Jeannie's disappearance

Jeannie was curled up in the window seat of the magnificent bay window in her private study at Howarth Hall. It was so large and plushly upholstered it could have been a day bed. Her neat fair hair was tucked boyishly behind her ears, and her normally pale complexion was slightly flushed as she stared through her ghostlike reflection out at the view. Some said she had a knack for seeing through things, or people, or the page of a book to another, truer story. Some found her gaze unsettling, usually because she meant them to. It was a silent, effective weapon she used to make a point without having to waste words. Guy called her the cruellest and gentlest of Svengalis.

'All the new talent you discover, and dreams you make come true,' he'd tease, 'it's no wonder everyone wants to be in your world, but woe betide those who don't fit anymore.'

It was true, she had no time for fools and lost little sleep over moving people on, telling them they'd be a better fit with another publisher, or even to reconsider their life goals. Life was too short and the competition too fierce to spend time or energy on anyone who couldn't get past their own ego, or who wasn't productive, positive and efficient.

Fortunately she didn't have any super-inflated egos on her publishing team. At all levels they worked well together, were quick thinkers full of creative ideas, who understood each other's needs and issues as well as their own. Their meetings were electric, inspirational, deeply analytical when called for, and often hilarious too, for there were a number of ready wits amongst them.

How Jeannie missed those meetings, those electrifying, heady days when they'd all been able to sit down together in the same room, unafraid of touching one another, taking biscuits from the same plates, drinking coffee or juice or champagne from a glass someone else might already have used. Video conferences just weren't the same; they didn't allow for the same degree of spontaneity or banter. If anything they seemed to suck up more energy than they created.

It was why she took breaks whenever she could. She needed some respite from the screen, from her desk, from the incessant demands on her time to recharge, calm down even, or to prepare for what was next on the agenda. It had been such a good idea to relocate here to Howarth Hall once they'd all been able to move around again in July. She'd hated not being able to come during the lockdown, had worried about the place standing empty for so long in spite of Magda, the housekeeper, popping in twice a week to make sure everything was OK.

It was the garden that had caused her the most frustration, for she'd missed an entire season of its constantly changing magic. Of course Neil, the landscaper, had regularly sent photos, and even a few videos to walk her around the rhododendrons and azaleas; the rose bushes and cherry trees and wisteria-covered pergola. He'd captured a sunburned mist floating in from the bay, bees pollinating, butterflies skimming the buddleia and black-eyed Susans, and birds splashing about in the stone baths. On a couple of occasions he'd taken her on a trip through the wild-flower meadow behind the house and over to the woods. His running commentary was captivating and inspiring as he talked about the leaves of rowans, maples, limes, hazels and oaks. He described the feel of bark, the scent of lichen and mosses, and the taste of a wild berry, or even a mushroom. He knew what was and wasn't poisonous, where badgers had created a run and weasels had taken over a den. He made her laugh with his imitations of bird calls and wildlife, but most of all he'd made her long to be there with him so she too could inhale the wonderful woody scents and perfumed flowers, spot deer tracks and chaffinch nests, listen out for wood-peckers and murmur along with the distant sough of waves.

She gazed out across the handcrafted green oak terrace beyond her window to the beautiful flat lawn he'd created in time for them to host a party back in August, and felt a flutter of calming contentment. It was a lush, inviting expanse of green surrounded by dry-stone walls and flow-ering beds, and if she half closed her eyes she found it easy to recall that wonderful summer day. How exhila-rating it had been to see some friends and close colleagues after so many months behind closed doors. No one had been able to stay the night – that restriction hadn't been lifted – but it hadn't stopped anyone from coming. There had just been a little less champagne consumed than normal by those who had to drive.

Catching a rainbow drift of spray out in the bay, she watched as the world seemed to turn into a real-life impressionist painting. Her thoughts moved to Guy, as they often did. How fortunate she was to have met him just over seven years ago. They'd known almost as soon as they'd been introduced that they would be going home together that night. The attraction between them had been so powerful and irresistible that they hadn't even tried to pretend it wasn't happening. Instead, from that day on, they'd spent all their available time together, and no one had been surprised when they'd announced, several months later, that they were getting married. Her parents had been thrilled and relieved in equal measure; it had mattered a great deal to them to know she wouldn't be alone when they were gone.

Their sudden and terrible death, a year after the wedding, still haunted her, and she knew it always would. No one, apart from her brother Paul, had ever blamed her for the fire that had swept through the house and claimed both their lives. It was an accident. Tragic, devastating, a cruel twist of fate that could have been visited on anyone, but it had been inflicted on her parents, and Paul would probably have seen her hanged for it, had such a draconian punishment actually been an option. Their relationship had never been good; these days it was beyond repair.

With a quiet sigh, she uncurled her legs and stretched them across the padded seat, whose patterns were crossed with diamond-shaped shadows from the leaded lights in the window. She'd get back to work in a minute. There was a meeting she was supposed to join, and Maurice, her trusted and beloved assistant, would soon start to wonder if she was going to make it.

'Hello, darling.'

Starting, she turned and felt her heart expand as Guy came into the room. Even now, after all this time together, he could still make her feel as though they were only just falling in love. 'Hello you,' she said, holding out a hand for him to take. 'You're back early.'

'I've been in for a while,' he told her, 'you just didn't hear me.'

He was wearing a white shirt and black jeans, with a neutral-coloured sweater draped over his shoulders. His hair was damp, telling her he'd not long since had a shower. 'Am I interrupting?' he asked, popping a chocolate into her mouth and another into his own.

'You called into the café again,' she said, after swallowing the delicious caramel and hazelnut truffle. 'Did you see Fliss?'

'Actually no. I think she was at the back. Someone else served me today.'

'Oh, that was disappointing for you.'

'Mm, yes, I suppose it was.' With a playful twinkle, he nodded towards the window as he added, 'Don't tell me, I've caught you watching Neil at work.'

Turning to the garden, she said, 'Is he here? I haven't seen him. He must be around the other side.'

'His truck's in the drive.'

'Which doesn't necessarily mean it's him. It might be his son, Zac, or one of his workers.' Dismissing it, she said, 'Tell me how you are. You look tired.'

With a sigh he said, 'I am, and frustrated, and glad to be home.'

'Why frustrated?'

'Too much bad news to break today. I could do with an antidote, something to cheer me up.' He arched an inviting eyebrow.

Irresistible.

Did he want to go upstairs for a while, or stay right where they were? The thought of Neil spotting them caused wicked frissons to leap into life like hot, liquid stings. This entire, enormous house with all its staircases, landings, attics, cellars, bedrooms, salons, vast kitchen, stone terraces and outdoor gazebos was at their disposal, but they could choose to remain here, in front of the window.

Her eyes went to Guy's. He knew Neil was possibly around. He wouldn't want to embarrass him; on the other hand, he might want to show off that she was his.

'What's going through your mind?' he asked darkly.

Sliding a foot along his thigh, she said, 'I'm sure you'd like to know.'

'Will I like it?'

'I think so.'

He laughed and glanced at his phone to see who was calling. 'I should take this.' He grimaced, and held on tightly to her foot to stop her from going anywhere as he spoke briefly to the caller about a spine surgery he had scheduled for next week. When he rang off, he took a notebook from his shirt pocket and jotted down the information he'd just been given.

Removing the book from his hands, she let it drop to the floor, wanting it to be known they were to have no more interruptions. He kissed her first on the diamond pendant at her throat, then deeply, tenderly on the mouth, as their hands moved beneath their clothes to the places most eager for attention. She wasn't surprised, or sorry, when he closed the shutters before laying her down; sometimes the idea of something was more enjoyable than the reality.

CHAPTER SIX
CARA AND ANDEE

Monday 18 January 2021
Twelve days since Jeannie's disappearance

Nicely warmed up in her incident room now, Cara felt as though she'd been living an alternative life for the past four hours as she'd familiarized herself with the case so far. She'd become so engrossed in Guy and Jeannie Symonds's world that she hadn't noticed the time passing, had remained entirely focused on reading through the notes that Andee had made on the dozens of interviews she'd carried out with Jeannie's friends, London neighbours and publishing colleagues.

For the past half an hour she'd been concentrating more on Guy Symonds. He was obviously a top bloke in his field, specializing in many types of brain and spine conditions, and with a ton of letters after his name. He worked both privately and for the NHS, and was currently involved in trials for a new drug to do with immunotherapy treatment for something called glioblastoma. He'd studied at Oxford, Nottingham and London, had spent a few years at Johns Hopkins in the States before taking up his position now; he was also an 'honorary clinical lecturer' at

Birmingham University. There was a lot to read about him and his achievements – all the papers he'd written, posts he held, research he was involved in – although much of it had gone straight over Cara's head. Nevertheless, it was impossible not to be impressed by his CV.

Less impressive was the fact that, if it turned out something bad had happened to Jeannie, then Guy – as her husband – could find himself in the role of suspect number one. Weird to think of him that way. In fact Cara couldn't see it at all, especially with him having Andee Lawrence on-side. However she ought to stay mindful of what DS Rundle had said before leaving her here to get on with things, 'Don't rule anything out.'

Taking a deep breath, she decided she was just about ready to start her first interview, although she had to admit she could do without the nerves.

'You'll be fine once you get into it,' Andee assured her when she came online for a quick chat prior to the big event. 'Just put aside all you've read about him. I know it can be daunting, all those qualifications and achievements, but keep in mind that – in spite of it all – he's still just a man. And frankly, he's very easy to get along with, unlike many in his profession who do tend to hold themselves apart.'

Brightening at this levelling down of her new idol, Cara said, 'Did you have time to look through the questions I sent over?'

'I did and they're excellent. You're obviously already on top of things. Don't worry about repeating anything I've already asked; he's expecting it and is more than willing to go through everything again.'

'Good to know,' and asserting herself with a straightening of the back she said, 'I have one for you first. Has he given you the impression at any time that he's holding back about anything?'

Andee gave it some thought. 'I can't say that he has, but we'll see where we are at the end of this.'

'OK. I've emailed over a Statement of Witness for him to sign and send back to me when we're done.'

Andee smiled approvingly. 'Then it sounds as though we're ready to go. I won't say much when he joins us, I'll just listen for now, but I'm ready to step in at any point if you need me to.'

Cara's insides leapt about wildly, but she could do this, was as determined about it as she'd ever been about anything – and also relieved to know Andee was there to take over if necessary.

As soon as Guy Symonds appeared on the screen, she could see just how good looking he was now the mask had gone. Similar to Bradley Cooper she thought. He looked tired, though, and worried. She guessed that going home to an empty house and feeling overwhelmed by his wife's absence had upset him all over again. However, he sounded OK as he identified himself for the recording, and confirmed that he'd received the Statement of Witness.

'OK,' Cara said, checking that the agenda she'd drawn up was clearly displayed to one side of the screen on her laptop – she didn't have to stick to it, but it could be a good prompt if she got lost along the way. 'I think, for the record, Mr Symonds, that we should go through all the efforts you've made over the past twelve days to find your wife.'

'Of course,' he agreed, and the next few minutes were taken up by the details of his search, which Cara had to admit were impressive. From exploring Jeannie's computer, to speaking to her many colleagues, contacting their army of friends and continually calling her mobile just in case she picked up. The phone's locator app had either never been activated, or had been turned off. Regardless, he didn't seem to have missed anything. He'd even got Neil Roberts, the landscaper, to help him search the grounds of Howarth Hall and the woods beyond, and had knocked on neighbours' doors (not that they had many up where they were) to ask if anyone had seen his wife, but apparently no one had.

He'd also been in touch with Jeannie's brother Paul in New Zealand. Apparently she wasn't there – unsurprising given that her passport was still at Howarth Hall and that the two of them were said not to get on. However, it seemed as good a place as any for Cara to ask one of her questions.

'You haven't mentioned anything about Jeannie's parents. Are they still alive?'

Guy grimaced, and looked more strained than ever as he explained how they'd died in a fire around six years ago. 'It was a very difficult time for her,' he said bleakly. 'They were extremely close, and it wasn't helped by the way her brother reacted.'

'How was that?' Cara asked.

'Paul got it into his head that it was her fault. It wasn't, of course, but he's always resented her for being the favourite, while he was very definitely the black sheep. He actually stole money from his own father, but that was a long time ago, before I knew any of them. I only contacted him because I'd run out of anyone else to try.'

'Is there any other family?'

'Yes, she has a niece, Mallory, who she adores. That's Paul's daughter,' he added.

'I think I saw Jeannie with a baby on Facebook – was that her?'

He nodded. 'She's nineteen now, and they're as close as ever, in spite of Mallory being in Auckland. You know Jeannie travels a lot for her work, so she's often down that way, and Mallory was over last year as well.'

Satisfied that the Kiwi connection had been sufficiently covered for now, Cara said, 'Is there anyone else? Cousins, aunts, uncles, godparents?'

Symonds shook his head.

'OK.' A quick consult of her laptop brought her to her next question. 'Are there any stand-out events from recent days, weeks or months that could be seen as relevant to Jeannie leaving?' She'd decided to term it that way, mainly because the car was gone and there was nothing so far to say she hadn't been driving it.

He took a deep breath and let it go slowly. 'Believe me, I've been racking my brains, trying to come up with something, anything that might give me some sort of lead, but there's nothing that stands out.'

'So no unusual behaviour on her part?'

He gave a dry sort of laugh. 'To be honest, there are a lot of things about my wife that could be described as unusual.' His voice dipped slightly as he added, 'I guess when you love someone they always seem . . . special or different to you, and Jeannie could be . . . a force of nature, I suppose you could call her. Unpredictable and fascinating, like an undiscovered universe . . .'

Hoping not to sound rude, Cara said, 'If we could try to keep this a bit more – grounded?'

He smiled and said, 'I'm sorry. What I meant to say is that she's complex, driven in a professional sense, passionate about her books and authors, and she rarely suffers fools. She's also loyal and compassionate, believes strongly in listening to both sides of a story before coming to a judgement, and she's someone you'd definitely want on your side if things were to go wrong. Having said that, she can be horribly unforgiving if she feels someone has let her down or betrayed her.'

Knowing what her next question should be, Cara felt thankful when Andee, speaking for the first time since their initial hellos, asked it for her. 'Have *you* ever betrayed her, Guy?'

Cara clocked his surprise at the question, and the way he looked straight into the camera as he said, 'I have not.'

Well, he would say that, wouldn't he, she was thinking, although he'd sounded sincere enough.

'Do you know of anyone who has?' Andee prompted.

He regarded her helplessly. 'That's a better question for Maurice, her assistant. He'd be able to tell you about staff members, or authors who've jumped ship for another publisher. It happens in that world – and sometimes, from what I can tell, the scars go deep.'

Andee nodded and, taking it as her cue to continue, Cara quickly made a note to bring this up with Maurice Bisset when they spoke, and said,

'Has Jeannie been married before?'

'No,' he replied. 'There were a couple of long-term relationships, I believe, one in her twenties, the other in her late thirties, but as far as I'm aware she's not in touch with them now.'

Knowing they could check on that once the phone records came through, Cara said, 'OK, so you last spoke to her on January the fifth, and you came home to find she wasn't there on January the eighth. That's two days, give or take. Did you wonder where she was or feel worried at all during that time?'

He shrugged. 'I did and I didn't. You see, it's not unusual for us to go a couple of days without being in touch. I might have a hectic schedule and she's often busy with meetings; some don't finish until as late as midnight if she's on with someone in Australia or New Zealand. So, to be honest, I didn't think too much of it until I got home on the Friday and couldn't find her.'

'Which was at about four thirty?'

'That's right.'

'Could you describe what happened?'

'Of course. When I got to the house—'

'Did you notice whether or not Jeannie's car was there at that point?'

'No. I would have assumed it was in the garage, which is where she usually keeps it.'

'Had you called ahead to say you were on your way?'

'I had actually. It kept going to voicemail, so I assumed she was busy talking to an author or one of her team, or in a meeting. Anyway, she wasn't in her study when I went to look and her computer was off, which I found unusual for that time of day. She almost never finishes before six. Everything was tidy, put away or stacked neatly in piles, a sure sign that she'd clocked off for the weekend. So I went to the kitchen, assuming she was fixing herself an early drink or something to eat, but she wasn't there either. I tried the bedroom, bathroom, the gym. I went outside and called out for her, but it was already dark by then, so I didn't really expect her to answer.

'I tried ringing her again, obviously, but my calls were still going straight to voicemail. I thought she must have run to the supermarket, or maybe to fill up with petrol and that either she'd forgotten her phone, or it was out of battery. I'm not sure how worried I was at that point; I'd say probably more confused, and even slightly annoyed that she hadn't thought to leave a note. Then I had a call from the hospital where I work that had me tied up for about half an hour. By the time it was over and she still wasn't back, I started to feel more concerned. I went out to the garage and saw that her car had gone. I thought I must have forgotten something; that she'd told me she was going somewhere and for some reason it hadn't registered, or had slipped my mind.'

When she was sure he'd finished, Cara said, 'You mentioned to Andee that she's gone off without telling you before, so did you think that might have been what had happened this time?'

'Yes and no. We're in lockdown, so where would she go?'

Good question, although one she should be asking. 'Same place she went in the past?' she suggested. 'Do you know where that was?'

'Different places. She books herself into an Airbnb and "stays quiet" for a while, which means she wants to be off-radar, left alone until she's ready to come back.'

'Why does she do that?'

He sighed. 'Sometimes things get on top of her. Her job can be very stressful.'

'And how long is she gone for?'

'A couple of days.'

'And then what happens?'

'She comes home.'

'Is she ever in touch while she's gone?'

'Sometimes she texts to tell me not to worry, she's just getting her head together and will be back soon.'

'Does she ever give you any notice that she's going?'

'Not really. They're impulsive, almost irrational acts, which at times are probably designed to worry me.'

'Why would she want to do that?'

'It's just the kind of thing she does. It doesn't really mean anything.'

Finding it a bit hard to get her head around that, Cara said, 'Why do it, if it doesn't mean anything?'

His smile was sad. 'We often test or tease one another. I can't really explain why, it's just something we do.'

'So she could be teasing or testing you now?'

'I thought so, at first . . . Maybe she still is, I don't know.' He took a breath and sat back a little further in his chair. 'My biggest concern,' he said, 'and it's growing by the day, is that she's driven off the road somewhere and no one has noticed. She could be trapped, or . . .' He broke off, clearly not wanting to put the awful images into words.

Andee said, 'Guy and I have driven around the moor hoping to find something, but without knowing where to look, or exactly what we're looking for, or if we're even in the right place, we haven't been able to come up with anything.'

Cara's eyes went back to his as he said,

'I don't want to torment myself with that, at least I try not to . . .' Wiping a hand over his jaw, he said, 'This isn't much comfort, but something I've been thinking about lately . . . She's intimated a couple of times that she has a surprise for me . . .'

When he didn't continue, Cara said, 'Do you know what sort of surprise?'

He shook his head. 'On one occasion we were in her study, in the window seat, perhaps around September time . . . I forgot about it after, I guess she did too, because nothing ever came of it, or not that I can recall.'

'You said there were a couple of times?' Cara prompted.

'Yes, the other was on New Year's Eve, so relatively recently. I got the impression she was planning something, but when I asked what it was, she said it wouldn't be a surprise if she told me.' He swallowed. 'I've wondered since – I keep wondering now, if she was planning to go. Maybe it's been in her mind for some time.' He closed his eyes tightly and pressed his fingers to them. 'I guess all kinds of things are going round in my head right now,' he said, 'and that's just one of them. I honestly don't know if it has any relevance.'

Cara hesitated in case Andee wanted to speak first, then because she had no idea if it had any relevance either, she said, 'If we can go back to the Airbnb places – do you know where they were?'

He nodded and returned his eyes to the screen, his face paler now than it had been before. 'Yes. On one occasion she was in Bath,' he said, 'and another in Maidenhead. Once she was in Paris.'

'So she went abroad without telling you?'

'She did.'

'Any idea *why* she chose those particular places?'

'I'm not sure that the destination is as important as the need to clear her head for a while, and to keep me on my toes.'

Cara definitely wasn't finding an easy route into

Jeannie's way of thinking – or his, come to that. However, she was far from ready to give up. 'Have you checked her Airbnb account to see if she's made another booking?'

'Of course, but it's not possible to reserve accommodation at the moment unless you're a key worker.'

This was true, if you were playing by the rules. 'And her passport's at the house, so she can't have gone abroad,' Cara said. Nor would her car have driven itself off into the night, so they were obviously missing something, somewhere.

Bracing herself for the answer to her next question, Cara said, 'Has Jeannie ever tried to harm herself?'

Apparently understanding her meaning, he said, 'I don't think anyone who knows her would consider her in any way suicidal. She could get down at times, like most of us, but no, I can't see her deliberately hurting herself.'

'Can you rule it out?' Andee asked.

He splayed his hands. 'I would like to, obviously, but right now I'm not sure what can or can't be ruled out. Have any of her colleagues suggested anything like it to you? Maybe they wouldn't want to say it to me?'

'No, they haven't,' Andee admitted.

'I can tell you,' he said, 'that her absence is causing some chaos at Athene. Obviously that's not a concern for me, but it would be to her, which is why this isn't making any sense – and why I was so keen to get the police involved.'

Cara said, 'I've sent information requests to the phone and credit card companies. As for number plate recognition, there are no cameras up around your way, on the Heights, but we already knew that. So we've no idea which direction she turned in when she left the house. She could have gone across the moor – no cameras there either – or into town, but we'd be looking more at CCTV there. I've yet to get to that, and obviously we'll be checking main artery roads and motorways in the area. Is there anything else you can think of that I should be taking a look at?'

He shook his head slowly, his brow furrowed.

'OK, in that case I thought I'd make a start close to home by talking to the gardener and cleaner.'

His smile was wry as he said, 'We call them the landscaper and housekeeper, but same thing.'

Noting that for when she became posh, Cara said, 'And what about friends locally?'

'As I think I've mentioned before, we've never really got to know that many people around here, mostly because we only came for weekends before the lockdown. We've based ourselves here more permanently since July, or Jeannie has, but the restrictions still don't allow for much of an expansion to our social lives.'

The party on the lawn had looked pretty social to her, Cara mused, although the guests probably weren't locals. Cara was about to continue when she noticed him glance to the top corner of his screen.

'I'm sorry,' he said, 'but I'm due to take a Zoom call in the next few minutes. Can we pick this up later? I should only be about half an hour.'

'Yes, of course,' Cara replied. What else could she say? It might be a matter of life or death for one of his patients. 'Actually, we're probably OK for today,' she said. 'If you can sign the Statement of Witness and send it over, that would be great, and I'll call you again in the next day or so if I have more questions. Or you can call me at any time if you'd like to.'

'Thank you,' he smiled, and not for the first time Cara thought of how much her mum would like him. Being a nurse at the local health centre, she had a bit of a thing for surgeons, and this one had a really nice way with him.

After he'd left the call Andee said, 'Can you hold on there, Cara? I'll be right back.'

Guessing it might be a bathroom break, or gin and tonic time, Cara sat mulling the conversation as she waited, trying to sort through the instincts and questions it had kicked up, and making notes on both. She also pulled up Jeannie's Facebook page to scan the shots of last August's garden party to try and work out why it had stuck in her mind.

She abandoned it a few minutes later when Andee came back onscreen saying, 'Sorry to keep you. I had to take a call from my mother. So, tell me your first impressions after speaking to Guy.'

Ready for this, Cara said, 'OK, apart from the obvious worst-case scenario that he, or someone else, has done away with her, I reckon it's possible she's been having an affair and has taken off with whoever he or she is to start a completely new life. What do you think?'

With a smile, Andee said, 'Actually more or less the same as you at the outset, but now, as time has gone on . . . I keep asking myself why she'd give up on her marriage and her job just like that? I mean, even if she didn't want to be with Guy anymore and has met someone else, she's very well established at Athene. I haven't spoken to anyone who seemed to think she'd had enough of it.'

'Maybe she was just good at hiding it.'

Andee still looked troubled. 'I just don't think we're asking the right questions,' she said, almost to herself. 'Tell me now, what you thought of Guy himself.'

Cara didn't have to consider it for long. 'I'm not ruling out the fact that *he* might be having an affair and she's gone off to punish him, or to remind him of what he's missing, or something like that. From what he's told us, we know she has her own way of doing things.'

Andee nodded agreement.

'How about he's a serial abuser who she's terrified of so she had to get away?' Cara suggested.

'If that were the case, she'd surely have contacted at least one of her friends by now, and her office.'

Accepting the likelihood of that, Cara said, 'Someone who features quite a lot in her Facebook shots of the garden is Neil Roberts.'

'As the landscaper, he would.'

'They seem quite close in some of them, as if they really like one another. What did you think when you spoke to him?'

'Actually, I mostly left it to Guy, because I know Neil, so it's hard for me to have an unbiased opinion.'

'Does that mean you like him, or have doubts about him?'

'The former, but you need to speak to him yourself to see what you think. I should probably emphasize something here that you might have seen in my notes: he's married to Estelle Fields, the writer.'

Remembering, Cara said, 'And that matters because?'

'She and Jeannie have a history. I don't know much about it, only that Jeannie used to publish Estelle until there was some sort of falling out. From the little I've heard it was bitter, and as far as I know, they've never made up.'

Cara's eyebrows rose. 'And yet her husband still does Jeannie's garden? That seems a bit weird.'

Andee made no comment.

Cara started to puzzle it out. 'So he's working for someone his wife can't stand, and as far as we know he was the last one to see Jeannie on Wednesday the sixth. Big leaps, but have you spoken to Estelle Fields at all, asked if she's seen her?'

'No, I haven't, and I don't think Guy has either.'

'Then I'll make her next on my list.' She checked the time. 'It's a bit late to contact her today, so I'll try first thing tomorrow. Would you like to be in on it?'

'I'm afraid I can't join you tomorrow, I have other commitments, but please send me the recording when you're done and we can go over it together later.'

After Andee had disconnected, Cara searched for Estelle Fields's details in the original notes, read a brief paragraph about her, then went online to find more. It was only when she saw the book title, *A Crow Amongst Blackbirds,* that she remembered her mum raving about it back when it had come out. According to this website that had been five years ago, and yes, it was an Athene publication.

So it seemed Ms Fields – aka Mrs Neil Roberts – had been published by Jeannie back in 2015 but not again since . . . No, there was definitely no mention of any more books. Then, in 2018, Jeannie had bought a house in the same general area of where Ms Fields lived, and in that same year Ms Fields's husband had gone to work for Jeannie.

Right now, Cara had no idea how any of it could be connected to Jeannie's abrupt departure from Howarth Hall. To her it seemed to have no bearing on anything at all. However, the fact that there was no love lost between the two women, and that Neil Roberts had been the last person to see Jeannie – that they knew of – was at least something to start with.

CHAPTER SEVEN

ESTELLE

Tuesday 22 September 2020
Four months before Jeannie's disappearance

'I've found her,' Estelle whispered, hardly able to believe it, starting to shake with the sheer enormity of it. 'Oh my God, I've found her.'

She spun round, back pressed to the kitchen worktop, phone clasped so tightly in her hand her fingers were turning white. She hadn't realized it would happen quite so fast; had expected to be waiting weeks, even months – could only wonder now why she hadn't done this before.

She read the email again – and again. It contained just a few formal lines, straight to the point, and leaving no room for doubt. She hadn't misunderstood anything, or skimmed something crucial in a desperate bid to see only what she wanted to. It was there, the latest message in a thread that went back over several days.

The investigator had found her birth mother.

Her heart skipped several beats and she laughed.

Guy Symonds was a genius. She would never have done this if he hadn't encouraged it, assured her it was the right thing to do. He'd convinced her that she shouldn't wait any longer.

How could such a wonderful man be married to a monster like Jeannie Haines? (Estelle often like to think of Jeannie by her maiden name, simply because she knew how much Jeannie would hate it.)

She needed to calm down, take some ujjayi breaths, stay centred and come to a meaningful and rational decision on what to do next.

Eventually, as her heart rate calmed and her mind ceased to spin, she began pacing – not manically – around the kitchen's centre island. This was the centre of her exquisite Grand Design home (they hadn't actually filmed the build, but it was certainly worthy of an episode, everyone said so, including the photographer who'd come a few years back from *HELLO!*). Neil's landscaping business had seriously taken off after the feature. Well, to be fair, it had been doing really well before that, but the publicity certainly hadn't done him any harm. It was a pity Zac, her extremely handsome stepson, hadn't been around for the shoot. They made a beautiful family, everyone said so, even those who'd envied her the success of *A Crow Amongst Blackbirds*. (Amazing, shameful, how envious some people could be.) However, what really mattered was that Chloe, who'd been four at the time, had lit up just about every shot.

Suddenly needing to look at herself, to see how her own delight and nervousness was manifesting, she went to the dining-room mirror to study her reflection. She took great pride in her curly chestnut hair and olive-green eyes, her kittenish chin and slightly upturned nose. Her petite figure was trim and well-toned thanks to their basement gym and indoor pool, and she was always lightly tanned from sessions on the sunbed. She loved being able to swim and cycle and run without having to leave the house, although she'd started exercising outdoors lately. Since August, really – lovely, lengthy walks on the moor.

She also loved to jump, especially when she was happy. Not on a trampoline, just from the floor, as if her euphoria was simply too much for gravity. She jumped now, arms raised, feet kicked up behind her, lifting off effortlessly, playfully, and landing light as air.

Gosh, that felt good.

She jumped again and laughed. The children would groan if they could see her. Neil might too, although his eye-roll would be one of amused affection rather than embarrassment. He was good on affection. He was also good on knowing everyone, seeing everything and almost never gossiping. In other words, he could be as maddening as hell, and his son was just like him.

And don't get her started on Zac's mother, Felicity Roberts, who owned the Seafront Café . . . No, really don't!

Today was all about her, Estelle Fields, internationally bestselling author of *A Crow Amongst Blackbirds*, and the email she'd just received that could change so much.

Jump!

'Well take a look at you, leaping about like an old frog in search of a young princess.'

With a laugh Estelle spun round to greet Primrose Barnes, her large and trusty personal assistant, whose timing was, as usual, impeccable. 'Just the person,' she declared excitedly. 'Wait until I tell you what's happened.'

Attending to priorities, Primrose went to fix herself a

cup of tea from the boiling tap, saying, 'Sounds as though it's going to be good, so let me guess. You've finally finished the new book?'

Estelle instantly deflated. This was such a sore point for her, and wasn't it typical of Primrose to try to bring her down with a reminder of all that was wrong in her life? Sometimes she adored the woman, other times she detested her.

'OK, not that,' Primrose remarked dryly. 'So what's got you hopping about like an excited firework?' Then, glancing at the time, 'Are you ready? We don't want to be late.'

'Oh, don't worry about that,' Estelle scolded, waving her hands as though to brush their online commitment into oblivion. 'This is much more important, and I want to tell you before Neil comes in.'

'Are you expecting him? Isn't it a bit early?'

'He's picking up Chloe from school so he could be here soon.'

'OK, I'm all ears. But before we go there, am I sworn to secrecy, or can I send it to your publicist?'

Estelle deflated again. Her publicist! A young woman she'd never yet met in person, who worked for a publishing house she'd never visited thanks to lockdown – and a contract for two books she feared she'd never produce.

There was a time when Prim had been her publicist at Athene, but the world had changed for them both since those heady days. Prim had also suffered a horrible rejection, courtesy of Jeannie, when Jeannie had appointed a friend's Oxford-grad daughter to head up the publicity department. Everyone knew the job should have been Prim's. She'd worked hard enough for it, for God's sake, and she was damned good at what she did. It had caused outrage within the division. Prim's colleagues had all begged her not to resign over it, but she hadn't felt she had a choice.

To show how much she, at least, valued Primrose Barnes, Estelle, at the time still flush with the success of *A Crow Amongst Blackbirds,* had taken her on as her APP – all purpose-person. She'd even moved her out of London and into the two-up, two-down annexe right here, next to the house, after Neil's mother had passed so didn't need it anymore.

It could be said, therefore, that Prim was now one of the family.

'So, can I send it to the publicist?' Prim prompted, her warm, chocolate eyes behind their jolly round specs making her appear far more guileless than she really was.

'No! You absolutely cannot do that,' Estelle cried. 'At least not yet. It's an extremely delicate matter, and a very personal one, but I know I can trust you so I want you to read this email.'

As she called it up and handed the phone over, her insides were whirling off into another blizzard of nerves, making her feel light-headed and even faintly nauseous.

When Prim had finished reading she looked up, perplexed. 'So who's Serena Fellowes?' she asked.

Irritated, until she remembered Prim couldn't possibly know because she'd never confided any of this in her before, Estelle said, 'She's my *birth* mother.'

Prim frowned and looked at the message again. 'And who's Andrew Bailey?' she asked, referring to the email's sender.

With an impatient roll of her eyes in an effort to disguise her guilt, Estelle was about to reply when Prim said, 'He's the private investigator I found a couple of years back for you to talk to about a book?'

'That's right.' She wouldn't mention anything about Guy Symonds's involvement in this, or perhaps moral support was a better way of putting it; there was simply no need to. It would only end up complicating things.

Prim clearly wasn't happy. 'And you went to this investigator because?' she said coolly.

'Because,' Estelle replied, thinking fast, 'I didn't want to use your valuable research talents on a personal issue. I thought it would be too . . . distracting?'

Prim continued to stare at her.

'But I do need your help from here,' Estelle hurriedly assured her. 'I mean, there's a lot to decide about how I go forward, and I wouldn't dream of taking a single step without you.'

No response.

Estelle laughed awkwardly. 'Well, I can't just turn up on her doorstep, can I?' she ventured.

Still no reply.

'Or maybe I can?' *Could she? Hi, Serena, guess who I am?*

'Maybe you can ask Mr Bailey for his advice,' Prim suggested tartly.

Estelle's shoulders drooped. *Or Guy,* she was thinking, but didn't say. 'Oh please don't be like that,' she implored. 'You know I've always wanted to find her . . .'

'And I'd have done it for you . . .'

'Of course you would, but I decided to do it this way, OK? I have the right to make up my own mind about things, you know? Anyway, we're getting off the subject. Can't you see how big this is? *My mother,* Prim. The

woman who gave birth to me. Serena Fellowes is my
mother – it's a lovely name, isn't it? Serena? Makes her
seem . . .'

'Serene?'

'Very funny,' she said, although it was kind of what
she'd meant. 'Anyway, all the documents are attached to
prove our connection – I haven't actually been through
them yet, but I trust Andrew Bailey—'

'I'll check them,' Prim told her.

'Everything's fine. She's Serena Fellowes, née Serena
Jameson and she had me at St Thomas's Hospital in 1983.
Now please, put yourself to one side for a moment, important though you are, and try to imagine just how much
this means to me.'

Prim regarded her warily, seeming, to Estelle's mind,
more baffled than sympathetic. Either way, she was definitely not fully on board.

'Prim! Honestly,' she implored, tears starting in her eyes.
'It's all right for you. You come from a loving home with
two parents who adore each other and *you*. You know
without any doubt that they're yours, no adoption, no
different blood or DNA, no mystery at all . . .'

'You're starting to make me sound boring.'

Estelle had to laugh. 'That's the last thing you are, but
OK, I admit, being separated from my mother at birth,
as I was, adopted by a couple who ended up not actually
wanting me, and then making something of myself the
way I have, does, perhaps, in some people's eyes, make
me more interesting.'

'Certainly in yours.'

'I'll ignore that, because I know that deep down in that
great big generous heart of yours, you're as pleased for

me about this as I am for myself. I've just thrown you by bringing it up the way I have, and being thrown is often quite difficult for people on the spectrum—'

'I'll throw something at you in a minute.'

Delighted with her little joke, Estelle said, 'She lives in Kensington now – good address—'

'Depends on the post code—'

'And apparently she's a solicitor, so very respectable. She also helps run a charity for the bereaved, how sweet is that? Goes to show she's a caring and compassionate person who . . . No, stop, I know you're going to say that if she was that caring and compassionate, she wouldn't have given me up. And why, in all these years, hasn't she come looking for me?'

'Well?'

'Well, that's a part of what we're going to find out . . . Don't worry, I'm already bracing myself for a negative outcome.'

'Like her not knowing who your father is? And why she would walk away from a newborn baby in 1983? Not exactly the Dark Ages.'

'OK, there's a lot to discover, and they are questions I've carried with me for most of my life, so please try to understand how excited and nervous I am to have them answered. I need you by my side, Prim. You're the best friend I've ever had, and please don't say the only friend, because I'm feeling a bit too raw for any more of your teasing right now.'

Seeming to realize, finally, just how fragile her boss – and best friend – actually was, Prim came to take her hand. 'I'll always be there for you, Estie, you know that. And this really is fantastic news.'

Estelle looked up at the sound of the front door opening and closing. 'That'll be Neil with Chloe,' she said, not thrilled at the timing, but of course happy they were both home safely.

'Hey Mum, hey Prim,' Chloe murmured, eyes glued to her smartphone as she came to dump her bag on the kitchen island and make a show of washing her hands over the sink. With her tumbling dark waves and lovely big blue eyes, she was as cute as her new braces and sallow skin would allow, and way more confident than Estelle had been at any age, never mind such a tender one. (This was what came of having good parents, she'd decided long ago; they always made a difference, even with the teeth, so dear little Chloe wouldn't have to go through life with a gap at the front the way her mother had, and still did.)

'Hi sweetie, good day?' Estelle asked, glaring at the school bag as if it were a live virus (which it might be) while going to drop a kiss on her daughter's forehead.

Chloe glanced up, and seeming finally to connect with where she was, she broke into a smile that softened and opened Estelle's tetchy heart as if it were water on a sun-dried flower.

'Where's Dad?' Estelle asked.

'In the garage putting some stuff into the truck. Can I have something to eat?'

Going to the fridge, Prim took out a Babybel cheese and a pot of vanilla yoghurt, while Estelle's attention returned to Chloe's bag.

'Do you think we ought to be wiping that down?' she asked of no one in particular. 'You don't know what you might pick up at school these days. Are they taking enough care?'

Chloe rolled her eyes. 'It is totally mental,' she complained. 'We've got to follow one-way systems, make sure we don't touch one another, or get too close to the teacher. It sucks, but – sorry, Mum – it's a whole lot better than your home-schooling.'

Estelle laughed gaily. 'I did my best,' she replied, 'but really, I'm hardly cut out to be a teacher, now am I? Prim was much better at it, I'm sure.'

'Yeah, she was. And Dad was pretty cool.'

'I had to work,' Estelle pointed out irritably. 'My world didn't stop just because everyone else's did. Ah, darling, there you are.'

'Here I am,' Neil agreed, dropping a pile of mail onto the table and helping himself to Chloe's peeled cheese before she could get it to her mouth.

'Dad! You are so not funny,' she informed him, outraged. 'You can get me another now, and a drink.'

Going to do just that, he said, 'And where are you two ladies off to, looking your supermodel best?'

Thinking how sweet he was to include Prim in the compliment, Estelle began scrubbing Chloe's bag, and the mail, with Dettol wipes. 'We're still in dangerous times, Neil,' she reminded him. 'Everyone's very worried about what's going to happen now the children are back at school. Apart from you, apparently.'

Delivering a snack to Chloe, he said, 'Better eat that fast if you're coming back out with me.'

'Defo I am,' she assured him.

'Where are you going?' Estelle wanted to know.

'We're taking some things to Zac,' Chloe informed her, as Neil poured himself a juice. Estelle was watching him absently, her thoughts flitting around issues and scenarios that actually had no place in this kitchen. Quickly she shut them down as Prim said, 'We need to go to your study now, Estie, or we're going to miss the start.'

'Of what?' Neil wondered, checking his phone as a text arrived.

'Estie's doing a Q&A on Zoom for the South West Women's Institute,' Prim told him.

Estelle's heart sank. What had she been thinking, agreeing to do that? No one would turn up; they'd probably only asked her because someone who'd written a much more recent book had dropped out, or they just couldn't get anyone else.

Apparently only half-listening as he replied to the message, Neil said, 'Sounds good. You've always enjoyed doing events.'

Yes, back in the day when everyone was interested in what I had to say – when you were too, come to that. 'Where are you taking Chloe?' she asked again, needing to change the subject. 'Please don't tell me Zac's working at Jeannie Symonds's place today.' Her expression had turned sour, it offended her even to say the name.

'No, he isn't,' he replied coolly.

'And why hasn't she gone back to her London home yet? I thought she was only going to be here for the summer.' Of course it was the last thing she wanted, because if Jeannie went, Guy would go too, but it had slipped out before she'd thought it through.

His eyes were twinkling as he said, 'Maybe she's staying because she has a beautiful garden that she doesn't want to leave?'

'Don't do that,' she seethed. 'You know that woman

ruined my life, but still you had to go and work for her . . .'

'OK, let it go,' he said, doing the same with the light-hearted moment. 'I'm sorry I brought it up . . .'

'If she's flirting with you, I advise you not to consider yourself special. She has a reputation for it.'

Prim cocked her head in surprise. 'Really?'

Slanting her a look, Estelle said, 'That's what I've heard.'

Neil said, 'Ah, so that's what she was doing when she came outside in her see-through negligee the other day?'

Estelle's eyes popped, until she realized she was being baited, and said to Prim, 'Do you find him funny? Because I don't.'

Amused, Prim said, 'I'll go and set things up and start the intro. See you there.'

As she left, Estelle said to Neil, 'So where is Zac, and why couldn't he come and collect his own things?'

Appearing puzzled by the question, he said, 'Because he doesn't have a car?'

'He can drive his mother's.'

'She's probably using it herself.'

'Or maybe he doesn't want to come here?' Estelle challenged.

Choosing to ignore the comment he said, 'We have to go and repair a sprinkler system that's shooting water all over a client's back terrace,' and, turning to remove a sound bud from Chloe's ear, 'you'd better get yourself changed if you're coming with me—'

'She can't go out,' Estelle interrupted. 'It's not allowed.'

'It is if she's with me, and we're working outside.'

'Are we going to Fliss's to get Zac?' Chloe asked. 'Please

say yes. Please, please, please. I could stay there and help with some baking while you're working.'

Estelle stiffened with fury and hurt. She hated the fact that her daughter was so attached to Zac's mother, the woman whom everyone seemed to love, so she had to pretend to as well. One of these days she'd blurt out the real truth about Fliss Roberts; it would be interesting to see who thought so highly of her then.

Realizing she'd missed whatever answer Neil had given, she took a breath to try to rejoin the conversation. Apparently they'd forgotten she was there. Chloe was now texting and Neil was involved in the kitchen recycling. She wanted to tell him about her mother, to find out if he was pleased for her, if he'd want to help or advise in some way, be there when she met Serena Fellowes for the first time; but even as the thoughts descended, they brought a dark cloud with them. Of course he'd care, and there was no doubt he'd be there for her, he wouldn't be Neil if he didn't, but it still wouldn't change the fact that he was seeing much more of Fliss these days than he used to. It was Zac's fault, of course. If he hadn't decided, for no good reason, to go and spend lockdown with his mother rather than stay here where he'd mostly grown up and was safe from everything including viruses, there wouldn't be any need for Neil to go to the café so often.

She watched Chloe run off to her room as, seeming to sense her inner wrangling and loss of direction, Neil came to place his hands on her shoulders. He gazed knowingly into her eyes. 'Everything's going to be all right,' he told her gently. 'The next book will come as soon as you start to relax, and it's not as if you don't have a new publisher.'

Who paid me a fraction of what I'm worth, and who's

not in the least bit interested in helping me through this block, otherwise he'd ring, she wanted to shout in rage and frustration.

What came out was, 'Are you having an affair?'

His eyes widened in surprise. 'Where did that come from?' he asked, clearly not thrilled by the question.

'Just answer me,' she pressed.

'OK. No, I am not having an affair.' Then he added, 'Are you?'

She did a double-take. 'No!' she protested, choosing to ignore the contact she was having with Guy Symonds. That was entirely different. 'What made you say that?'

'What made you say it?'

'I don't know. I . . . So you're not sleeping with your ex-wife?'

'You know very well that I sleep here every night, with you.'

'Which isn't what I'm asking.'

Sighing he said, 'All that Fliss and I share is a good friendship, and our son. Now, before we end up down the rabbit hole of your over-developed imagination, why don't you go and do your Q&A?'

Starting off towards the hall, detesting the way he sometimes treated her like a child, she almost turned back to ask him about Jeannie Symonds and whether he might be sleeping with *her*. However, sensing it would be a step too far, she continued on her way.

CHAPTER EIGHT

Fliss = Felicity = Happiness.

It could even be intense happiness.

The name derives from the Latin – Felicitas – meaning good fortune.

It dates back to the sixteenth century when 'virtue' names were popular.

I don't think she's happy, or particularly virtuous, and fortune is not favouring her right now. I watch her as closely as I can and wonder about her life, how much she is hiding, who she really talks to. I wonder too how aware she is of me, of what I think and feel, of how she affects me. When she speaks to me, her eyes seem to sink into mine, but she's like that with everyone: open, attentive and caring. I don't know that she has any special feelings for me.

Is there anything I could do to change that? How would it be viewed by others if I tried?

How would it be viewed by her?

CHAPTER NINE

FLISS

Thursday 24 September 2020
Four months before Jeannie's disappearance

'Hello!' someone called out from the café door. 'Is it OK to bring him in?'

Fliss looked up from the egg and bacon rolls she was setting out for late breakfasts and broke into a smile to see Guy Symonds holding on to the lead of a very lively looking Jack Russell. 'Of course,' she said, beckoning them forward. 'Dogs are welcome here, but I didn't know you had one.'

'This is Fergus. He belongs to Magda, our housekeeper,' he explained as he was tugged to the counter. 'She's inundated at the moment, so Jeannie agreed he could stay with us for a week. He's quite a character.'

'He is indeed,' Fliss agreed, adjusting her visor as she dug a treat from a jar. 'We know little Fergus quite well, don't we, sweetie.' She passed the treat to Guy.

'Oh, my favourite,' he declared. He looked from the biscuit to the dog, to the biscuit and back to the dog who, taking the hint, sank onto his hind legs and raised his paws. 'Good boy,' Guy praised, 'but just the treat, OK? I need my fingers.'

Fliss was on the brink of laughter as she watched the careful transaction that ended with Guy's hand under one arm and Fergus practically grinning as he licked his chops.

'I love dogs,' Guy told her, 'and this one's no exception, but he really needs to learn some manners.'

'Are you walking him this morning?' she asked dubiously, for torrential rain was sweeping the Promenade and causing such a dense mist it wasn't even possible to see across the street.

'Apparently he loves the beach, which is why we're down this way, but it doesn't look as though this storm is going to let up any time soon. So, sorry, mate, it'll have to be another time.' As he finished he was declining a call on his phone. 'Not something I do often,' he said, 'but is it too much to ask for five minutes to get a coffee?'

'Absolutely not,' she assured him. She added teasingly, 'And we are honoured – this has to be the third time we've seen you here in as many weeks.'

Clearly amused, he said, 'It's your fault for serving such good coffee, and I have to admit my schedule's not too crowded right now, which makes a nice change.' He looked around. 'How are things going here? It seems quiet this morning.'

Making a start on his usual Americano with a dash of cold milk, she said, 'We had a few in for early breakfast, but we're still restricted to less than half capacity, and with the weather as miserable as this . . . Hopefully it'll pick up by lunchtime. Are you home for the weekend?' she asked, wanting to get off the subject of how difficult things actually were for her and the café.

'Until Tuesday,' he replied, 'so a nice long break.'

Aware of him watching her in a way that felt a little flattering, she gave a mischievous nod towards the flaky sausage rolls. 'I know how much you like them,' she said, 'and Annalind delivered them fresh about half an hour ago.'

'Then I'm definitely not saying no.'

Delighted, she reached for the tongs and a paper bag. 'Shall I pop one in for Jeannie?'

'Lovely. If she doesn't want it, it won't go to waste.'

Deciding to put in a third, just because it was small, she said, 'How is Jeannie? I haven't seen her in here for a while.'

With a sigh he said, 'She's working so hard that she barely has time to leave the house. It's only on the days Neil's there, she tells me, that she says, to hell with it, and allows herself to go out into the garden for a while. Not on a day like this, of course, although she assures me she's getting very good at braving all winds and weathers.'

Knowing only too well how persuasive and entertaining her ex could be when he wanted company, Fliss said, 'I still haven't seen what he's done for you up there. I know it's magnificent, spectacular, a veritable triumph of land-scape design, because he's told me.'

Laughing, Guy said, 'He's not wrong. We love it, and what he did last month when we had a party – it was sublime, to quote my wife. Have you seen any of the photos she posted on Facebook?'

'No, but I'll take a look some time. I'm sure they're all over Neil's page as well, but I'm afraid by the time I've cleared up here at the end of the day, and dealt with the café's social media accounts, I usually can't wait to get off the computer.'

'I completely understand. It's why I hardly bother with it. Now, how much do I owe you? Fergus is paying and he assures me he's a very big tipper.'

Enjoying his light-hearted banter, as she always did, she said, 'It comes to eight pounds thirty, but we can call it a round twenty if you're feeling generous, Fergus.'

Fergus wagged his tail and lifted his front paws, earning himself another treat from Fliss as Guy put a twenty-pound note on the counter and started to leave.

'I wasn't being serious,' she cried, waving it after him. 'You need some change.'

'Put it in the charity tin,' he said, nodding towards the one next to the till.

'It's too much—'

'Not at all,' he interrupted. 'By the way, do we have to book for breakfast if we want to eat inside?'

'I'm afraid so. Just let me know when you want to come.'

Whipping out a notebook and pencil he said, 'I don't think I have the number . . .'

'OK, I'll give you the café and my mobile, so if someone else answers here you can get hold of me direct.' After he'd jotted down both, he tucked the notebook back in his pocket saying, 'I'll talk to Jeannie, maybe we'll come on Sunday.'

'That would be lovely. We still have space at the moment, so just let me know.' They were actually fully booked, but if he did ring they'd work something out.

Only moments after he'd left via the back door, the front door opened and someone else came in, lowering an umbrella. 'Good morning,' she called cheerfully, not realizing until the hood was off that it was Estelle. 'Estie,' she said warmly. 'Have you just dropped Chloe at school?'

'I have,' Estelle confirmed, casting aside the umbrella as she dug around in her bag. 'Oh sod it, where's my mask?' she growled. Finding it, she popped it on and said, 'I'll have a decaff latte. And I probably ought to take something for Prim.'

'She usually has the same. Are you OK? You seem a bit . . . frazzled?'

Irritably, Estelle said, 'It's this weather, and worrying about how Chloe's doing at school, and . . . Oh, I don't know. I guess I've just got a lot on my mind.'

'Everyone's uptight at the moment,' Fliss sympathized, turning to start the coffees. 'The scientists' warnings about the way this virus is going to spread again is extremely worrying.'

Estelle wasn't listening. 'Was that Guy Symonds I saw in here just now?' she asked abruptly.

Praying this wasn't going to launch into something about Jeannie, Fliss stifled a sigh as she said, 'Yes, it was, with Fergus, his housekeeper's dog.'

'You seemed to be getting on very well with him.'

Bristling slightly, Fliss said, 'Is there a reason I shouldn't?'

'No, of course not. I just thought . . . Well, you know, if Jeannie saw you flirting with him—'

'I wasn't flirting,' Fliss protested crossly, while knowing she actually might have been. But why not? Everyone had their little fantasies.

'I'm just saying that Jeannie is very possessive, that's all.'

'Well, thanks for the heads-up.' It wasn't worth getting into anything with Estelle; she always liked to be right,

Susan Lewis

and Fliss had more important things to do with her time than try to prove her wrong.

'I can tell you don't believe me,' Estelle accused, 'but if you talked to the people she works with . . .'

'I'm really not going to do that,' Fliss informed her, and promptly set off the steamer to drown out the next few moments.

By the time she turned round with the lattes, it was as if Estelle had undergone some kind of personality change, or maybe the sun had come out. Whatever, it made Fliss blink, for Estie had clearly cheered up immensely. Eyes shining, skin glowing, she even gave one of her silly little jumps. Apparently the text she'd just received had contained good news.

Putting down the lattes, Fliss said, 'That'll be five pounds exactly, unless I can tempt you to some croissants or egg and bacon rolls?'

With an airy little laugh and another half-jump, Estie said, 'I'm afraid I have to be going. Thanks for the coffees – shall we settle up later?' and, grabbing the takeout mugs, she almost ran to the door, leaving her umbrella behind.

CHAPTER TEN

ESTELLE

Thursday 24 September 2020
Four months before Jeannie's disappearance

'I know we shouldn't,' Guy said as Estelle climbed into the passenger seat of his Range Rover and quickly closed the car door behind her before any more rain could get in. She'd already dumped her coffees in a street bin, and she must have left her umbrella in the café, because she no longer had it. She wasn't looking particularly good either, having left the house *sans* make-up and her hair in need of a wash, but this wasn't a date, she reminded herself. They didn't have that sort of relationship, although she'd still rather look her best for him.

'I thought it was you who went into the café after me,' he said. 'I was going to get in touch with you this weekend. If the rain eases off it would be lovely to walk, if you have the time.'

'Oh, I'm sure I will,' she insisted, knowing she'd sounded too keen, but she was so relieved to see him, and pleased that he wanted to see her, it was hard to hide it.

'Excuse me a second,' he said, holding up his phone.

She kept her eyes fixed on the streaming windscreen as

he sent a text to someone, or replied to an email. She didn't know what he was doing, but it hardly mattered. All that did was that she was here.

She breathed, and breathed again. Funny how simply being with him made her feel stronger and calmer.

'OK,' he said, putting his phone away. 'So a walk this weekend.'

'Just let me know when works for you,' she said. 'Neil and Chloe always have plans of some sort; it'll be good to have an excuse to get out of the house.'

He smiled and turned to check on the dog in the back seat.

'So how are you?' they asked in unison.

'You first,' she insisted, finally able to smile.

'I'm OK, thanks. Glad to get home last night. I'm interested to know, have you contacted your mother since hearing from the investigator?'

Her insides twisted. He only knew that much because she'd put it into a text. 'No, not yet,' she replied. 'I've composed an email, but I haven't sent it yet. Prim is helping me to find out more about her before we go any further.'

He nodded slowly, seeming to understand her reticence. 'It's perfectly natural to feel worried,' he said. 'It takes a lot of courage to open yourself up to being hurt, especially by someone so important in your life.'

She felt stiff with how hard she was resisting even the chance of it. 'I could just forget all about it,' she said, 'but then I'd probably end up feeling even worse.'

'It would just keep playing on your mind. Have you mentioned anything about it to Neil?'

Not sure whether it was guilt she felt that she hadn't, or resentment for feeling she should when she didn't want to, or a combination of the two, she swallowed her irritation. 'I know I ought, but he . . . We haven't seemed as close lately as we . . . I'm not sure he'd think it was a good idea.' She felt wretched for telling the lie, since she was sure Neil would be supportive if he knew, it was just that she'd rather not share this with him for now.

'I'd be surprised if he didn't, but you know him better.'

Before she could stop herself she said, 'Have you told Jeannie?'

His eyebrows rose in surprise. 'Would you like me to?' he asked carefully.

Feeling absurd and confused, she said, 'No, I'm – I don't know why I asked that. I'm sure you've got better things to talk about.'

Moving past it, he said, 'I'm sure, in the end, your mother will be happy to hear from you, but try to remember that your message, when you send it, will come out of the blue for her. There might be other family members she has to explain things to before she can be in touch.'

Estelle nodded, understanding that, and wishing it didn't matter, but at the moment it did. She wanted her mother to respond right away, to feel that her long-lost daughter being in touch was the best thing ever to happen to her.

'It was good to see you,' he said gently, 'but I probably ought to get Fergus home before Jeannie starts wondering what's happened to us. I'm around until Tuesday, so I'll contact you before that in the hope we'll be able to meet for a walk.'

'Where have you been?' Primrose demanded as Estelle breezed into her writer's room, all rosy cheeks and windswept hair.

Not much liking being reprimanded, even if she had kept Prim waiting for an hour, Estelle scowled as she tossed her bag onto an empty sofa and unbuttoned her collar. She wasn't going to mention Guy, although she'd really like to.

'And what happened to the coffee?' Prim asked, wheeling away from the computer where she'd been working during Estelle's absence.

'Oh, yes, sorry. I . . . It got cold so I threw it away,' and she sank into the chair Prim had just vacated. 'So how far have we got?' she asked, feeling her nerves and excitement building in equal measure as she prepared to take in more information about her birth mother.

With a sympathetic smile, Prim said, 'Don't worry, none of it's bad. We already know that she lives in Kensington – the address is on the right side of the borough – and she's on a second marriage to Sir Jerome Fellowes . . .'

Estelle's eyes rounded; a knight! If she hadn't been sitting down she might have jumped. Even Jeannie Symonds would have to agree that a knight was impressive. She could hardly wait to tell Guy.

'Her first marriage,' Prim continued, 'ended when her husband of eighteen years died of a heart attack. He was the father of both her children – sorry, that doesn't include you—'

'We know that,' Estelle interrupted irritably. 'How old are the children now?'

Prim checked her notes. 'The eldest, Aubyn, is twenty-seven, and the youngest, Talia, is twenty-five. He works in the City – single, possibly gay judging by his Instagram account; she does PR for a major fashion house, also unmarried but in a relationship with a human rights

98

lawyer. There are photos, plus more background and addresses.'

Not wanting to look at it now, much less admit to how unnerved she felt by the idea of having siblings, people who might not want her in their lives, and who undoubtedly meant more to her mother than she ever had, Estelle said, 'Have you put it all into a special file for me?'

'Of course.'

'Then I'll go over it later. Just tell me: does anything stand out for you that makes you uneasy about me doing this?'

Prim's expression was kind as she said, 'Not really, but it's a big thing and it's a good idea for you to be fully prepared before you get in touch.'

'You mean for it all to go wrong?'

'I'm sure it won't, but I can't help being concerned about the fact that she hasn't tried to contact you . . .'

'Unless she has, and my ever-so-*not*-sweet adoptive parents never told me.'

'But it's been a long time since you left home . . .'

'So what you're saying is that my real mother probably isn't interested, so I should . . .'

'That is *not* what I'm saying. I've no idea what she thinks, or how she feels about anything. But how much consideration have you given to what you hope to gain from being in touch with her?'

'A mother would be the obvious answer,' Estelle replied snappishly, while knowing it was so much more than that, far more than she could put into words even to herself, except it had to do with validation and worth and belonging. 'Actually, if you must know,' she said, 'I want her to know who I am and feel proud of what I've achieved.

OK, I know that sounds pathetic, and that it's mostly in the past . . .'

'It doesn't sound pathetic. It's perfectly understandable.'

'Maybe I should attach a link to my website to the email. Once she realizes that her daughter wrote *A Crow Amongst Blackbirds*, I'm sure she'll want to be in touch.'

'If she wants to see you just because you wrote a best-seller and not because you're—'

'Oh, stop! It's so typical of you to misunderstand what I'm saying.'

'And it's typical of you to accuse me of that when I say something you don't want to hear.'

Estelle rolled her eyes impatiently.

'Listen, I just want us – *you* – to be clear about everything in your mind before you go any further. So, have a read of the file I've put together, and then we can discuss—'

'I don't have to discuss *everything* with you,' Estelle reminded her.

Prim's face flooded with colour.

'Oh God, I'm sorry,' Estelle groaned, going to her. 'I'm so on edge about it all that things just aren't coming out the right way.'

'They rarely do with you,' Prim said wryly, 'and you don't have to kiss me, for God's sake . . .'

Estelle laughed. 'Sorry, letting go! And thanks for all you're doing. You know I couldn't manage without you.'

'Yeah, yeah, we'll get the violins out, shall we?'

Going back to the computer, Estelle said, 'Are there pictures of my mother in the file? Is she beautiful?'

With a smile, Prim said, 'I'd say she is, yes, even at fifty-one.'

Estelle's heart contracted with shock. 'So she was . . . fourteen or fifteen when she had me?'

Prim nodded.

'Well, that explains why she gave me up. She was under age. Maybe she was forced to.'

Prim didn't argue with that.

Estelle gave a little jump without quite knowing why.

'I wonder if that's in the genes,' Prim remarked dryly.

Estelle laughed. 'It would be funny if it was, wouldn't it?' she said and, steeling herself for more, she opened the file Prim had created to start getting to know her mother better, while wondering if it would be a good idea to send a copy to Guy. Maybe she would if she had his email address; on the other hand, she could always show him the photos on her phone when they walked some time before next Tuesday.

CHAPTER ELEVEN
CARA AND ANDEE

Tuesday 19 January 2021
Thirteen days since Jeannie's disappearance

It wasn't even seven o'clock on a freezing cold January morning, but Cara was already battling through the sleety snow in her trusty Fiat en route to the station. She'd dropped her mum at the health centre a few minutes ago, before detouring slightly to Tesco where her sister, Kayleigh, had run inside to start her shift as a delivery driver. Really Kayleigh should be at uni studying to be a paramedic, but her lectures were all online at the minute, so she was using her time at home to earn some extra cash.

They were a diligent and close little family, all of them key workers now that Cara had joined the police, and all of them quite happy with their lot living on the right side of the Temple Fields estate. However, both girls missed their dad desperately, as did their mum – he used to be a manager at the Infirmary before he'd gone and got Covid back last April and not recovered. What a terrible, horrible time that had been, and neither of them were even close to getting over it.

He'd be so proud if he could see her now, Cara was

thinking as she reached the outskirts of town, eager to get to work. And maybe he could. She liked to think so, and why not – no one ever knew what came after. She just hoped it was as good as her lovely dad deserved.

Seeing Andee's name come up on her Apple CarPlay, she quickly clicked on saying, 'You're early. Has something happened?'

'Not that I know of,' Andee replied. 'I just wanted to touch base with you before the rest of the day takes over.'

'Actually, that's great, because I was going to call when I got to the station. Have you read Estelle Fields's book, *A Crow Amongst Blackbirds*?'

'No, I can't say I have. Why do you ask?'

'I was up late reading it last night. It's pretty dark stuff about a girl who was adopted as a baby by a couple who treat her badly, and when she's in her teens she ends up offing them, quite violently, and getting away with it.'

'Lovely,' Andee commented dryly.

'It sent chills through me, I can tell you. Talk about gruesome. Anyway, something I noticed in the acknowledgements at the back of the book was how she goes on about Jeannie Symonds, the world's best publisher, and how she'd never have been able to do it without her. Apparently she couldn't have asked for a more sensitive mentor, and she'll always be grateful to Jeannie for showing her what true friendship is all about. Seems like she's had a change of heart since then.'

'Well, hopefully you'll get the chance to ask her about that when you talk to her,' Andee replied. 'Have you set it up yet?'

'It's top of my list when I get in. Have you ever asked Guy why Jeannie and Estelle fell out?'

'Actually, I haven't. Her name has barely been mentioned

until now, other than in an abstract, historical sense. Also because she's married to Neil Roberts.'

'He's someone else I'd like to connect with today if I can. Will you be available to talk to, if need be, or are you completely off radar for the rest of the day?'

Andee laughed. 'I'm only helping to deliver food parcels from the Seafront Café to those in need, so my phone will be on.'

'Oh, cool.' Actually, it really was cool; she'd be offering to help with those deliveries if she wasn't all tied up in this case.

By nine o'clock she'd managed a quick meet with DS Rundle to update her on progress so far and on how today might pan out; then, after downing a quick coffee with Leo Johnson, one of the DCs, she brought her incident room to life and made contact with Estelle Fields. Luckily the woman rang back within minutes, and though she didn't sound happy about signing a Statement of Witness and reconnecting via video-link to talk about Jeannie, at least she didn't refuse.

The chat started out well enough, with the usual stuff about the weather and lockdown, and how much Cara had enjoyed the book (definitely not the right word, but she had to admit it was gripping). If she'd expected Estelle to be chuffed with the praise, she was disappointed. If anything the solemn, pixie-faced woman seemed uncomfortable about having it mentioned.

Awkward, since her writing career was something Cara was hoping to delve into further. However, she could always work round to it another way if need be, so she began by asking how long Estelle had lived in the area.

Instead of answering, Estelle came straight to the point. 'This is obviously about Jeannie, so I can tell you that I don't care where she is. As far as I'm concerned, I hope she never comes back. We'd all be a lot better off without her.' She seemed slightly twitchy and it was over the top; however, she clearly didn't feel the need to hide her dislike.

Cara frowned. 'Why do you say that?'

'The woman's an arch bitch, who doesn't think twice about making other people's lives a misery.'

'In what way?'

'In any way she can. She ruined my life once, but don't you worry, I'll never let her do it again.'

Cara could see her fists were clenched on the desk in front of her, small and delicate, turning white at the knuckles, and she was obviously watching herself on the screen, for she wasn't looking at the camera as she spoke.

Opening *A Crow Amongst Blackbirds* to the acknowledgements page, Cara said, 'From what I've read in your book it seems you two were good friends once. Can I ask what happened to change that?'

'You can ask whatever you like, but I can assure you that what went on between me and Jeannie back then has nothing to do with where she is now. OK? Nothing. It was six years ago, for God's sake. I haven't seen the woman since, apart from at a distance, so really you're asking the wrong person if you're hoping to find her.'

Taken aback by the sharpness of her tone, Cara said, 'So she didn't contact you when she moved to the area?'

'No.' Clipped and sour.

'Did you try contacting her?'

'Actually, I sent a house-warming card, but she never bothered to respond.'

Did people respond to those sorts of cards? Maybe they ought if it was a kind of olive branch. 'She did get in touch with your husband though, to ask him to sort out her garden?' Was he the other person in the room, listening to this?

'She did, and I'm sure it was to spite me, as he's not the only landscaper in the area. In fact, knowing her, I'd have expected her to bring someone from London.'

'Why would she want to spite you?'

'Because she's that sort of person. You don't cross Jeannie Symonds and get away with it.'

'So you crossed her?'

'Not intentionally, no, but she suddenly decided one day that she didn't want to publish me anymore. I'd delivered another book and she said it wasn't for her, or not as it stood. We argued, she started to block my calls, and in the end I pushed my way into her office to confront her.' Her colour was greatly heightened now, and angry tears shone in her eyes; it was almost as if she was right back there in the moment. 'That was when I realized what it was really about,' she spat. 'She was jealous of my success. It was great for the company, of course, for her bottom line, but on a personal level she resented all the attention I was getting and the money I made. She likes to be the centre of attention, the great builder of careers, the goddess of fiction, then when someone gets to the top she turns on them. Or she did on me. I'll never be able to forgive some of the things she said. They were beyond cruel, they completely devastated me. Yes, I said things too, but I was angry, fighting back, and I wasn't the only one saying them.'

'Saying what?'

Estelle raised a hand and shook her head. 'It's in the past now. I apologized after, which is more than I can say for her. In fact, if it weren't for . . .' She stopped and looked away.

'Weren't for what?'

'It doesn't matter. Like I said, it's in the past, and none of it's going to help you find out where she is now.'

'How do you know that?'

She gave an incredulous laugh. 'Because I have nothing to do with her. I've no idea who her friends are, what she's working on . . . I don't even know what kind of car she drives, or whether she's glad she moved to that monstrosity of a house.'

Still so much bitterness over something that's supposed to be in the past. Cara was about to move on when Estelle turned and spoke to someone off screen. 'Would you believe, it's the police,' she declared irritably. 'They want to know if I can throw any light on where *Jeannie* might be.'

Cara couldn't hear the reply, although it was definitely a woman.

'That's true,' Estelle said, and looked at the screen again. 'I think you've probably realized by now that you're speaking to the wrong person. I'm sorry I can't help—'

'Actually you can,' Cara said quickly, sensing she was about to cut the connection. 'Can you tell me where you were on January the sixth this year? That's just under two weeks ago.'

Estelle's mouth tightened with rancour. 'Are you trying to suggest . . . ?'

'I'm just asking the question. It would be helpful to know.'

107

'I was here, at home. We're in lockdown again, remember? Now I'm afraid I have to go. I hope you find her; after all, we wouldn't want anything bad happening to *her*, would we?'

With the unbridled insincerity still ringing in her ears, Cara sat back in her chair to go over the last few minutes in her mind, trying to work out how much she'd learned of any real value. It was hard to say, although it was clear time had been no healer where Estelle Fields's loathing of Jeannie was concerned. She could only assume the feeling had remained mutual – something to check with Guy – but, on the face of it, it wasn't offering any answers as to where Jeannie was now.

She wondered who had come into the room during the call. Whoever, whatever, Neil Roberts appeared to be the only link between Estelle and Jeannie these days, which led Cara to wondering what his relationship actually was with Jeannie. Maybe it had been a bit closer than landscaper/client.

Deciding it could be a good idea to read back through Andee's earliest interviews, she called them up on the screen. The first was obviously with Guy himself, and the next was with Fliss, who, Cara had learned from her mum, was Neil Roberts's ex-wife.

Was there anything to be read into that?

'I don't think so,' Andee said, when Cara put the question to her at lunch time over a bowl of delicious chicken soup that Fliss had sent over from the café, 'but they are still good friends and see each other regularly. I think your other question about the relationship between Neil Roberts and Jeannie could be more relevant.'

Glad that Andee agreed, Cara said, 'We still don't have

her phone records, so there's no way yet we can be certain she actually left on the sixth, after Neil says he saw her. It might have been the seventh, or early on the eighth.'

'True, but the fact that she wasn't in touch with anyone we've spoken to after the sixth, not even Guy, still leads me to think she went on that day. We know she took her car and has her phone and credit cards with her. We can probably also safely assume that she took clothes and toiletries – I'm sure I could leave the house for a month or more without Graeme knowing what I had or hadn't taken from my wardrobe or bathroom.'

'Apart from a toothbrush?'

'I have several that I keep in a bag for when I travel. Jeannie's electric toothbrush is still there, apparently, so maybe she has a similar travel bag. So, apart from asking the question where is she, we also need to ask who is she with? Or could this all be some sort of publicity stunt that she's cooked up with an author?'

Cara wrinkled her nose. 'Would they actually do something like that?'

'I've no idea, I'm not a part of that world, so I don't know how extreme or not it can be.'

'You've talked to all her authors though, haven't you?'

'And so has Guy. They all seem as concerned and baffled about Jeannie's whereabouts as the rest of us, but they're authors, they're good at telling stories.'

'Well, obviously someone has to know where she is,' Cara stated in frustration.

Not arguing with that, Andee said, 'What have you taken away from the interview with Estelle Fields?'

Voicing her thoughts as they came, Cara said, 'Well, she didn't try to hide the fact that she can't stand Jeannie, and she obviously wouldn't mind if she never came back. She seems quite highly strung, bitter. As for whether she knows where Jeannie is . . .' She shook her head. 'She's hardly Jeannie's closest confidante, so it doesn't seem very likely, based on what we know so far. On the other hand, maybe her husband's told her something . . .'

'Did you get the impression he might have?'

Cara grimaced. 'I might find that easier to answer once I've spoken to him.'

CHAPTER TWELVE

FLISS

Thursday 24 September 2020
Four months before Jeannie's disappearance

'Hello you,' Fliss said, looking up as Neil came into the café fifteen minutes after she'd closed. She'd deliberately left the door unlocked, just in case he turned up, as he seemed to be calling in after-hours quite often lately, with or without Zac.

'Hi,' he said, sounding slightly distracted, although when his eyes came to hers to find her regarding him quizzically, he seemed to relax a little. 'How's your day been?' he asked, perching on a stool and putting his phone aside.

'At least people are still coming,' she replied, 'but not many tourists around now. By the way, Estie left her umbrella this morning, if you'd like to take it home with you.'

'No problem.'

As she went to get it she said over her shoulder, 'I hear Jeannie Symonds has posted a lot of shots of their garden on Facebook. I'd love to see them.'

Surprised, he said, 'For sure. Was she here today then?'

'No, Guy came in. He brought the housekeeper's dog,

Fergus. A proper little cutie, he is. Actually, he mentioned that you're quite good at getting Jeannie to take a break now and again.'

His eyes twinkled. 'You know me, I do my best.'

'And do you recite poetry for her as you go around the gardens?' It was meant to be a tease, but she saw the laughter fade in his eyes as it did in her own as the memories crowded in. They used to call it his party trick, the way he could recall just about any poem he'd ever read and perform it; it was just one of the many contradictions and complexities she'd always loved about him. As her mum had once said, 'He's not all plants, diggers and muck. There's Shakespeare in that soul of his.'

'You know I could still be reciting it for you,' he said quietly.

Avoiding his eyes, and sorry now that she'd mentioned it when she'd love nothing more than to share those special moments with him again, she turned to the door as it opened and Zac came in.

'I'll have one of those,' he said as Fliss put a cold beer on the counter for Neil. 'Can I have the car tomorrow, Mum? A few of us are going surfing down at Croyde. Do you want to come, Dad? We can take your truck if you do. And what about Guy, we could ask if he wants to join us. He keeps threatening to.'

Checking his phone as it rang, Neil held up a hand for Zac to wait as he took the call. 'Hi Estie. Everything OK?' He listened, and sounded surprised as he said, 'Of course it's all right if you go for a walk tomorrow. I don't understand why you need to . . . Sure, if Prim's going to see her parents, I was planning on spending time with Chloe anyway. Did Bob Lowe come and repair the pool heater?

Great . . .' He started to frown as he said, 'No, I'm not at Howarth Hall. No, I haven't been there today. What does it matter where I am? All right, all right, I'm on my way home. I should be there in half an hour.'

Sighing as he rang off, he pushed his freshly opened beer to Zac. 'Here, take that one and call me tomorrow. There are a few jobs next week you can probably tackle on your own.' Looking regretfully at Fliss he said, 'Short and sweet, but always lovely to see you. Have a great evening, you guys,' and a few moments later he'd gone.

Picking up the beer, Zac tipped the bottle up and downed half of it swiftly, before wiping his mouth with the back of his hand. 'Is he OK?' he asked, swallowing a burp.

'I think so,' Fliss replied. 'What makes you ask?'

He shrugged. 'He just seems . . . I don't know, kind of not himself lately.'

Concerned that she might have missed something, Fliss said, 'I expect he's just tired. It's the end of the week and he was about to relax for half an hour.' What else could she say? She didn't want to worry Zac when there might actually be nothing to worry about.

Taking another swig of beer, he said, 'I wonder who Estie's going for a walk with if Prim's not going to be around. She never seems to have any friends.'

'Oh, I'm sure she has some,' Fliss responded, having no idea who they were if she did. 'Anyway, it's fine for you to take the car tomorrow if Dad can't go surfing, and it doesn't sound as though he can, unless you want to take Chloe.'

Zac grinned. 'She'd love it if we did, so hey, why not, and if you weren't working I'd be on your case to come too – except we know that you in a wetsuit can be a bit too much for some of my mates.'

Throwing a dish towel at him, Fliss laughed and went to make sure the door was locked before going upstairs to take more painkillers to soothe her back. It had played her up a lot today, long, burning aches curling like claws around the bottom of her spine. It wasn't something she ever mentioned to Neil or Zac – no one wanted the reminder of why she suffered like this – and nor did she want them knowing how much more often these days she was having to take something to help her to sleep.

CHAPTER THIRTEEN

JEANNIE

Friday 25 September 2020
Four months before Jeannie's disappearance

Jeannie was in a Teams meeting with Hunter, her American counterpart, when Guy came into her study with a surprise gin and tonic – surprise, because it wasn't even five o'clock yet. The towel around his neck, sweat-stained T-shirt and shorts told her he'd already taken the dog back to Magda, and had just completed a vigorous session on the Peleton.

'Hey Guy,' Hunter called out from the screen as Guy came to stand behind Jeannie. 'Don't worry, I'm taking the hint. I know it's Friday and time to pack up for the weekend over there. How are you, my friend?'

'Staying sane,' Guy responded, raising his glass. 'How about you?'

'It's crazy time over here with the election coming up. I expect you're catching the news.'

'We are,' Guy assured him.

'Whatever the outcome, don't let it put you guys off coming here when this virus is finally in the rearview mirror. We miss you. It's been too long.'

'It certainly has,' Guy agreed. 'Now I'm going to let you finish up here. Stay safe and have a good weekend.'

It was another half an hour before Jeannie was finally able to close down her computer, by which time all she really wanted was to shower, dress in something casual, and go out for a pub dinner. It might be possible, if they were able to get a table at The Notley Arms or maybe The Mermaid. The Eat Out to Help Out scheme might be over now, but at least it had kept some of their favourite local places going.

'At last,' Guy commented as she appeared in the doorway of his study where he was sitting at his desk, making notes from an enormous textbook. This room was nothing like his study in London; there were no models of human brains or skeletons, in fact no anatomical equipment at all, and only a few medical tomes. Howarth Hall was where he came to relax, so it was actually more like a den, or a man-cave as she called it, than a place to work.

'Shall we go out to eat?' she said, spotting a pile of mail on the corner of his desk and pulling a face. 'Please tell me none of that is for me,' she implored.

'I'm afraid it's all for you,' he replied, 'and I'm wondering if I'm the only one who ever checks the box?'

'Probably,' she admitted. 'If it's urgent it usually comes by courier. So what do you say to trying The Notley?'

'I've already rung and they're full. Same goes for everywhere else, so it looks like we're stuck with a pizza from the freezer, or sandwiches?'

With a laugh she said, 'Am I the worst wife you've ever had?'

'You're definitely the best,' he assured her, which was always good to hear, in spite of his first marriage being

116

ancient history by now. And what a piece of work *she'd* been.

'Incidentally,' he said, putting aside his reading matter and picking up his drink, 'I forget to mention I ran into Estelle Fields while I was at the café yesterday morning.'

Jeannie was stony. If she'd remembered when they'd bought this place three years ago that Estelle Fields lived in the vicinity, she might never have entertained the idea. Had she known that the awful woman was Neil Roberts's wife, she definitely wouldn't have given him the landscaping contract. She couldn't regret that, however, given what a fantastic job he'd done and how attached she'd become to him. And thankfully, even after she'd found out who his wife was, he'd never once tried to get Jeannie to meet her, or to talk about her. Jeannie was in no doubt that Estelle had wanted her husband to create a kind of bridge between them, but it was never going to happen.

'I'd rather talk about Fliss,' she told him archly.

He merely looked at her, but his expression made it clear that he didn't want to change the subject.

Sourly, she said, 'I take it you spoke to Estelle.'

'Of course I did. Why wouldn't I?'

'Because you know I can't stand her and, by the way, you don't have to be nice to everyone. I guess you understand that, don't you?'

Not backing down, he said, 'You gave her a rough deal, Jeannie, and you know it.'

'That might be true, but let's not forget what she said to me.'

'I haven't,' he assured her, 'and it was terrible, I'm the first to admit it, but she apologized – and it was only words, it wasn't as if—'

'*Don't* defend her to me,' she cut in fiercely. 'Let's just remember that it happened a long time ago. It's over now . . .'

'It might be over for you, but it clearly isn't for her. In fact, I'm sure that all she really wants is to let bygones be bygones so you can be friends again.'

'Yeah, and that is going to happen over my dead body. So, end of conversation. Let's go fix ourselves another drink and decide what we're going to eat.'

CHAPTER FOURTEEN

CARA

Tuesday 19 January 2021
Thirteen days since Jeannie's disappearance

Cara was unable to make up her mind which was worse, interviewing someone by video-link when there was never any knowing who else might be in the room at their end, or in person behind masks. Eyes, she had discovered, were not quite the giveaways some people claimed; they could be dead flat even when a person was laughing. That was really spooky. Anyway, the mouth mattered, she'd decided, because it went about its business in some extremely telling ways, so a whole world of unspoken communication could be going on behind a piece of cloth that she was left merely to guess at. Of course, tone of voice helped, a lot could be told from that, but it was perfectly possible for someone to utter the sweetest of words while grimacing fit to vomit.

Not that she thought Neil Roberts was about to try in any way to deceive or ridicule her – none of her chats with colleagues during the past hour (Roberts was well known in the community) had suggested he was that sort of bloke. However, who could be totally sure about anyone, even their own families when push came to shove, so for the moment she was going to keep an open mind.

'Thank you for coming in,' she said as they sat down opposite one another in a soft interview room on the ground floor of the station. She noted the nice smell of cold air and damp earth that he'd brought in with him. His eyes, above the black face covering, definitely weren't flat; in fact they reminded her a bit of her dad's, gentle and blue and as though they did a lot of laughing. Swallowing her sadness, she said, 'I didn't realize you were so close by when I rang,' she added.

'Just out on the Quadrant,' he confirmed. 'We have a contract with the local authority, so I was checking out the crocus and snowdrop displays. They're coming through; I expect you've noticed.'

Actually she had, and was happy to say so. After all, who didn't love winter flowers? Before too much longer, she guessed Kesterly-on-Sea was going to be spelled out in lovely yellow daffs right outside the station. She always felt uplifted when she saw that. 'So, like I told you on the phone,' she continued, 'I'd like to talk to you about Jeannie Symonds.'

'Of course,' he replied, unbuttoning his waxed jacket and sitting more comfortably on the mock leather sofa. 'I'm happy to help in any way I can.'

She smiled her thanks, even though he couldn't actually see it. 'It's all a bit of a mystery,' she said chattily, 'and no one seems to know what to make of it so far. So I was wondering, as someone who knew her, if you happened to have any theories?'

His eyebrows arched in surprise. 'You mean about where she might have gone? I'm afraid I'm not familiar enough with her personal or professional life to be able to answer that. All I can tell you is what you probably already know, that I saw her on Wednesday the sixth of January at the Hall. She was in her study, walking up and down in front of the window, talking to someone on the phone. She saw me outside and waved, so I waved back and,' he shrugged, 'that was it.'

'Did she seem upset about anything, or distressed in any way while she was talking?'

'Not that I could tell.'

'How close were you to the house?'

He frowned. 'I guess about twelve feet away. I was tying fleeces around some of the larger pots in front of the terrace.'

'And this was at what time?'

'Same as I told Guy, about one.'

'How long did you stay?'

'No more than fifteen or twenty minutes. Half an hour, tops.'

'Did you see anyone else while you were there?'

'Not outside. I guess there could have been someone inside, but I wouldn't know about that.'

'Any cars?'

'Not that I recall. Jeannie usually parks in the garage and, as we know, Guy was in London.'

'So you didn't go into the house at all?'

'No, I just finished off with the fleeces and left.'

'And where did you go then?'

'To my nurseries out on the Old Moor Road, just past the cider apple orchards.'

'Any idea what time you got there?'

'I guess around two, two fifteen.'

'Was anyone else there?'

'No. We're closed to the public on Wednesdays, and at this time of year there's not much to do, so the other chaps take the day off.'

'How long did you stay?'

'A couple of hours. I had a lot of paperwork to catch up on, and it's a good time when things are quiet.'

'Did you see anyone at all while you were there?'

He frowned as he thought. 'I don't think so.'

'Did you make or receive any calls?'

'Not that I remember, but I can check.'

Nodding for him to go ahead, she waited until he brought up the log for that day and held out the mobile so she could read it.

'Two calls from my son,' he said, 'and one from Jeff Barber, a client who lives on the moor.'

'What about this one?' she asked, pointing to a number with no name.

'Your guess would be as good as mine, but here, let's give it a try,' and with a tap he made the connection. The phone rang seven times and was followed by an automated recording saying, 'The number you are calling is unavailable.' He shrugged, and clicked off. 'I'd say a telemarketer, wouldn't you?' he said.

Making a quick note of this, Cara asked him to check his text messages for the same day and, though he complied, she wasn't surprised when he said, 'Are you suspecting me of something here, because if you are—'

'I'm just trying to be thorough,' she assured him. 'So, any texts?'

He showed her his phone again, and since nothing stood

out in any way, she said, 'What time did you leave the nursery?'

He shrugged. 'I guess around five. It was dark anyway, and from there I went straight home. Before you ask, I'd have got there around five thirty.'

'Was anyone else there?'

Clearly not appreciating the way this was going, he said, 'I honestly don't remember, but I can tell you this, I have no idea where Jeannie is. If I did I'd have told Guy right away.'

Well, he would say that, wouldn't he; it still didn't mean he wasn't more involved than he was admitting to, or hiding some secret that Jeannie had trusted him with.

'Can I ask how well you get along with Jeannie?' she said. 'I mean on a personal level.'

He sat back in his chair and regarded her for a long moment before answering. 'If you're asking if there's something going on . . .' He stopped and started again. 'I know you've spoken to my wife,' he said, 'and if she told you that Jeannie and I are involved . . . Did she tell you that?'

Deciding not to admit that she hadn't, Cara held her silence.

Sighing, he said, 'Estie is not in a good place at the moment. Her career hasn't been going well for some time, and she has a family issue that came up back before Christmas with her birth mother . . . Frankly, she's long had a problem with self-esteem, and because of it she can get things into her head that simply aren't true.'

'But she does have a history with Jeannie?'

'Yes, but it was a long time ago, and I can tell you that she has no more of an idea where Jeannie is than I do.'

Wondering how he could be so certain, she said, 'Has Jeannie ever discussed the situation with you?'

'You mean the reason she and Estie fell out? No, never. It was all to do with a second book, anyway.'

'Has your wife had any contact with Jeannie since the Symondses moved into Howarth Hall?'

'Not that I'm aware of.'

'Would she tell you if she had?'

'To be honest, I'm not sure.'

Finding that interesting, Cara said, 'So you're not aware that she sent a house-warming card?'

He frowned. 'No, I didn't know that.' After a beat, he added, 'I think, deep down, Estie is desperate to be friends with Jeannie again, but I'm afraid . . . Well, I don't think it's what Jeannie wants.'

Going out on a short limb, she said, 'Do you think your wife might be jealous of your relationship with Jeannie?'

His eyes seemed to darken a little. 'I don't have a relationship with Jeannie in the sense you seem to mean it.'

'Has she ever confided anything in you to make you think something might not be right with her?'

'You mean Jeannie? Like what?'

'Like she's worried about something, or someone?'

'No, but why would she tell me if she was? I'm just the gardener.'

Landscaper, she didn't say, while wondering if she was being overly suspicious, or was she right to think he was becoming defensive? 'Do you get the impression she's happily married?' she asked bluntly.

He pulled back, as if not wanting to touch that. However, he said, 'I'm not someone who pokes around in other people's business, but I'll tell you this, if there's anything wrong in the marriage, I know nothing about it.'

Or you're just not going to tell me. 'I understand,' she said, 'that you and Mr Symonds searched the woods near Howarth Hall after Jeannie disappeared. Is there a reason why you did that when you knew that her car had gone?'

He threw out his hands in a helpless gesture. 'I guess he was getting desperate by then. No one seemed to know where she was and I think he just needed to do something, so I helped. What else was I supposed to do, tell him to look on his own? Great sort of bloke that would make me.'

'And you didn't find anything?'

'If we had, I think you'd know about it by now.'

Looking down at her notes for where to go next, she alighted on a question that she wasn't sure about, until she decided just to go for it. 'Have you ever had affairs with any of your clients?' she asked.

He got to his feet. 'This has gone far enough,' he growled. 'I came here because I thought I might be able to help in some way, but the way you're going about it . . . Sorry, this is over.'

She watched him go, starting slightly as the door slammed behind him, and having to admit that the question had been a bit clunky. However, it seemed to have rattled him.

Removing her mask, she began compiling notes and observations to go along with the recording, but broke off as DS Rundle let herself into the room.

'How's it going?' she asked, coming to sit on the sofa Neil Roberts had vacated.

'Slowly,' Cara admitted with a sigh, 'but I'm making some interesting . . . discoveries.'

'Such as?'

'Well, Neil Roberts didn't like being asked if he had affairs. How well do you know him, ma'am?'

'Not at all, really. Remember, I only started here myself a year ago, and I don't even have a window box. So are you saying he and Jeannie . . . ?'

'I'm not ruling it out. No one else seems to have seen her since Neil Roberts did on Wednesday the sixth at the house. He says he went to his nurseries on the Old Moor Road after that, and from there he went home, but I didn't get a sense of anyone seeing him. So, it's possible he was with Jeannie for a lot longer than he's saying on that day. We know her husband was in London, so a perfect opportunity for some time together without interruption?'

Rundle nodded slowly, as she said, 'You could be right, but even if you are, has it brought us any closer to where Jeannie might be now, because she's obviously not with him?'

'True, but maybe she went first and he's going to follow?'

'Do you have anything to support that?'

Cara had to admit that she did not. 'But I've only been on the case for twenty-four hours,' she pointed out. 'I'm still at the theory stage.'

DS Rundle smiled, then said, 'You understand that what we're really about here is finding out if a crime has been committed, and what you've just described – Jeannie going first and Roberts following at some later date – might be a crime in the eyes of their loved ones, but not in the eyes of the law.' She stood up. 'Keep going,' she said, 'talk this interview with Roberts over with Andee and then send me what you have so far. Oh, and don't forget to follow up with some of Jeannie's colleagues. She could have got a very long way from Kesterly by the time Guy Symonds realized she was missing, so it's quite possible we're not casting our nets wide enough by focusing on the more immediate area. It could even be that the case belongs to another Force.'

CHAPTER FIFTEEN

JEANNIE

October 2020
Three months before Jeannie's disappearance

'Are we lost?'

Jeannie breathed out a laugh, the sound of it floating up into the autumnal trees all around them like a warm breeze. 'I've come to know these woods like the back of my hand,' she assured Maurice, her town-loving, exquisitely dressed and loyal assistant who'd been very happy to enjoy lunch beside the chiminea on the terrace, but wasn't quite so thrilled to be trudging through such rugged nature with his boss. 'Would you like to turn back?' she offered. *Please say no*, she didn't add. These woods that bordered the grounds of Howarth Hall were one of her favourite places in the world right now and, thanks to Neil, who'd lately taken to walking with her, she was coming to know them better by the day.

His way of talking about trees was fascinating, mesmerizing even, and delightfully droll when he explained how useful ash could be as a cure for obesity or bladder stones or flatulence. Willow bark was a painkiller, oak leaves could be used to make wine, and hornbeam was great for the blues. She'd watch his large hands smoothing furrowed bark, and his closed eyes as he inhaled the heady scent of linden leaves, shaped like hearts.

Best of all was when he broke into poetry, reciting long, mellifluous verses from Longfellow, Keats, Frost, Dickinson, Walt Whitman; he seemed to know them all.

'Just name me one you want to hear,' he'd challenged the last time they'd walked. 'You won't be disappointed.'

She'd said, '*Albertus*, by Théophile Gautier.'

'I don't know that one,' he'd replied, deadpan, and she'd laughed so hard she could barely catch her breath. Quite why she'd found it so funny, she truly didn't know, it must have been the way he'd said it.

Maurice was saying, 'I want what makes you happy, darling,' and coming back to the present she smiled, for Maurice always wanted to make her happy. They'd worked together for so long now – first in marketing, then editorial, and all the way up to Jeannie's directorship of the Athene brand – that sometimes he felt more like a brother than a PA. She and Guy had even spent holidays with Maurice and his partner, Etienne, at their villa near Cannes. And if Guy couldn't make a party, or dinner, or a ball, Maurice was always there to stand in for him. 'Just don't have a heart attack on me, will you,' he added wryly, 'because I've lost all my bearings.'

'Actually, we're only about half a mile from the house,' she told him, reaching out to catch a yellowing oak leaf as it fell. She only knew what it was because Neil had told her, and she was pleased by how quickly she'd recognized it.

'Hah! So you've been walking me around in circles this past hour?' Maurice asked archly.

'Kind of,' she confessed, letting go of the leaf as if it were a passing thought. 'The paths are all interconnected, like a maze, but most are clearly marked, provided you know what you're looking for.'

He glanced over at her, but it was a while before he said, 'Are you OK, Jeannie?'

Surprised, she said, 'I'm fine. Why do you ask?'

He shrugged. 'You seem a little – *distrait*.' Since he often peppered his speech with his native tongue, Jeannie simply smiled – as a French speaker herself, she never had a problem understanding him. 'Is something bothering you?' he asked.

How well he knew her. Letting her head fall back to take in the canopy of gold and russet leaves above, and glimpses of blue sky beyond, she said, 'Do you think I was too harsh on Estelle Fields?'

'*Mon Dieu!*' he exclaimed in astonishment. 'Why on earth are you asking that? It was so long ago – and we hated her.'

'I know, but—'

'Has her husband said something?'

Jeannie smiled. 'No, he never mentions her.' She was glad about that, for she liked having a small part of Neil all to herself, and certainly didn't want to be reminded of who he went home to each night. 'I wonder what it's like for him, being married to her,' she mused. 'You know how self-involved she is – unless she's changed, but I doubt it.'

'Self-involved, way too pleased with herself . . . I could go on, but why is she even on your mind?'

Annoyed that she was, she said, 'Guy thinks that we should put it all in the past and let her come here. I know she'd love to be invited, but could we actually bear it?'

'After what she said to you, no way. You should have sued her for slander, enough of us heard it, we'd have backed you up. So no, I'm sorry, Jeannie, you just can't go there again.'

'I swear, I don't want to, but we both know I was pretty mean to her too.'

'Like she didn't deserve it? You can't deliver a pile of crap the way she did and not expect to be told it's anything but a pile of crap. I wonder if she remembers me handing her a toilet roll on the way out.'

Jeannie couldn't help but laugh. 'That was so bad of you, Maurice,' she scolded.

He shrugged. 'You do what you have to do. Anyway, lucky for you it's looking like we're heading into a second lockdown, so you have the best excuse in the world to carry on ignoring her.'

Jeannie felt relieved, glad to be able to dismiss the thought of having to socialize with Estelle, to listen to her and be polite, interested in whatever new book she might be writing now, when she'd far rather be in the garden or the woods with Neil.

'Enough about her,' Maurice declared with a flap of his hand. 'Let's talk about *Monsieur le Prof.*' His name for Guy. 'How is he? And why isn't he here today?'

'Because he's working, as usual. Don't worry, I get it, people don't stop falling ill just because there's a virus running riot in the world.' She smiled at the absurdity of her own words. A moment or two later, she said, 'Actually, I'm worried, Maurice.'

She felt his concern almost as if it were a current coming across the trail. Now that Guy's name had been mentioned, she didn't have to tell him what she was worried about;

in fact, she could almost hear him saying, *Oh my God, please tell me I'm wrong, but at the same time please don't.* He couldn't help it, he thrived on gossip, loved nothing more than a scandal, although she'd never known him to break a confidence of hers.

'You've caught him out again,' he declared, in a heart-felt whisper.

Keeping her eyes straight ahead, she said, 'I'm not convinced, but it's possible.'

'Do you have any idea who it might be?'

Although she had a suspicion, she simply walked on, picking a path over exposed tree roots and snaking brambles, watching out for untrustworthy stones and hidden burrows. Her marriage was a little the same, she thought, not always the smoothest of journeys. But would she have it any other way?

A deer suddenly skittered across the trail in front of them, causing them both to gasp.

After stilling his heart, Maurice said, 'Have you brought it up with him?'

With an arched brow, she said, 'Of course, but he just says I like to fantasize about him with other women, and actually, he's not entirely wrong about that.'

'*Oh, là, là,*' Maurice muttered. 'Are you still doing that?'

She smiled and stopped for a moment to watch a squirrel scamper along a low hanging branch, the same branch she'd climbed onto a week ago to prove to Neil that she could. How he'd laughed, and how she had too. It had been a wonderful, joyous moment, so unexpected and enlivening.

'It's one of my little . . . indulgences,' she said, 'but I

think we both know there have been other women, in the past.'

'So you say, and anyway, you dealt with them.'

She nodded as she recalled it. 'Rather well, I'd say, wouldn't you?'

When he didn't reply she turned to look at him and smiled. 'I don't want you to worry yourself about this,' she said. 'It's not a problem, it really isn't. He's a good man, you know that, and I know he loves me.'

'He does.'

Glad to have it confirmed, she decided to change the subject. 'Have you finished reading Dylan Frank's new manuscript yet?'

'No, I have it set aside for this weekend. Have you?'

'I've almost finished. I love the way he talks about story-scapes as if they were landscapes or seascapes, don't you? And he certainly has a gift for painting pictures with words. However, the scenes in nineteenth-century Vienna aren't quite working for me. Not being able to go to Austria is hampering his ability to bring the palaces and parks to life.'

'You know Vienna well, so you will help him?'

Thinking of the wonderful weekends she'd spent in that city with Guy, and before, she said, 'Of course. I'm already looking forward to it.'

'Great. Just let me know when you're going to brain-storm with him and I'll make sure to blank out your diary. Hang on, are we . . .? Is that . . . ? We're back,' he stated with a jolt of surprise and relief as they left the woods by passing through a kissing gate into a grassy meadow. 'And there was I thinking we were about to walk off the edge of the world into the sea.'

'You could if you didn't know these woods well enough,' she cautioned. 'If you get as far as the moor where the trees dip into a leafy dell, there's a place known as the Devil's Scoop. It's right on the cliff edge; one wrong foot and you'd be dashed about on the rocks below like a useless piece of flotsam.'

Shuddering he said, 'Then I'm glad we didn't go there. Now tell me, who is *that*?'

Following the direction of his gaze she exhaled an amused sigh. 'That, my darling, is Neil Roberts's son, Zac.'

Maurice's eyes flew open. 'He's Estie's?' he protested, clearly not wanting to believe it.

'No, his mother is Fliss, who owns the Seafront Café. You've met her a few times when we've been for Sunday breakfasts. Actually, Fliss made the shepherd's pie we had for lunch. Or someone at the café did.'

Still watching Zac, Maurice said, 'I had no idea Fliss was related to Neil.'

'She isn't, they're divorced,' but she was no longer really listening. She'd just spotted Guy in the drive and with him was . . . 'Oh my God,' she murmured, as her darling niece turned and waved.

'*Mon dieu*,' Maurice muttered, recognizing Mallory too. 'Did you know she was coming?'

'Of course.' Jeannie was already starting to run. 'She's been quarantining at the house in London, I just didn't know Guy was bringing her today.'

When she was close enough to be heard, she cried, 'Why didn't you tell me you were coming?'

'We wanted it to be a surprise,' Mallory laughed, bouncing up and down with the frustration of not being able to get any closer to her aunt. 'Guy said it was OK to come now. Oh God, it's so wonderful to see you.'

'And to see you,' Jeannie replied, unable to stop looking at her, bunching her hands to her throat to stop them reaching for her darling girl. She was so beautiful, and lively and happy – and *here*. Her lovely chestnut hair had grown so long, spilling over her shoulders in glossy, random curls, and there was a new radiance to her now she was nineteen that made her seem more confident and sophisticated and doubly adorable.

Guy said, 'She's done the quarantine, her test is negative, so there's no reason for you to hold back.'

Jeannie immediately wrapped Mallory tightly in her arms, loving the feel of her long, slender limbs and answering embrace. Catching Guy's eye she mouthed, 'Thank you,' and loved him so much for this surprise that she was ready to forgive anything.

He smiled and raised an eyebrow. 'I think this calls for champagne,' he suggested as Maurice joined them.

'Hello, Maurice,' Mallory beamed. 'It's lovely to see you, and if you're wondering if Dad's with me, the answer is very definitely no. I didn't even tell him I was coming until I'd already arrived.'

'Oh God,' Jeannie muttered, knowing how well that would have gone down with her brother. But what the hell did he matter? Mallory was here because she was going to serve an internship with Athene for a while, and with Paul so far away and so much to catch up on, they wouldn't even have to think about him.

A few hours later, Jeannie and Guy were in the spacious, wood-panelled drawing room that overlooked the garden and bay beyond, relaxing in front of the first indoor log fire of the season. He was in his favourite armchair, feet propped on the fender as he wrote in his notebook, while she was curled into one of the sofas checking emails on her laptop. Maurice had left a couple of hours ago, and Mallory was upstairs in her room FaceTiming her mum, Yolanda.

Dear sweet, generous Yolanda, a woman who didn't even seem to know the meaning of jealousy or possessiveness, who loved anyone who loved her daughter, and who'd passed on all her blessings to her only child. She'd always been ready to assure Jeannie that she shared none of her ex-husband's views about the way his and Jeannie's parents had died. She'd even stood up to him when he'd lost his mind to rage and recrimination following the tragedy, and Mallory had sworn never to see him again if he didn't stop. That had helped bring him to his senses – he adored his daughter and couldn't bear not seeing her – so he'd backed off the attacks on his sister.

Sighing to herself, she watched Guy stack another log onto the fire and felt a swell of happiness wash over all the doubts in her heart. Trust was an issue that shifted like sands beneath them. She didn't know for certain if he'd ever actually been unfaithful, and was sure he had no idea if she had been either, but she had no doubt there had been attractions, temptations even, and once or twice she'd had a word with the women concerned to make sure they didn't come too close.

Would Guy ever think about having a similar chat with Neil? He knew very well she was attracted to him, but was he aware of how much more often Neil was coming to the Hall these days?

He sat down again and she watched his elegant hands as he continued to write, wondering if his notes concerned a certain surgery, or diagnosis, or maybe they were thoughts for a paper he was writing, or one of the online lectures he gave each month. His scribblings and diagrams, decipherable usually only by him, could fill many pages when he was sitting quietly like this, so she decided not to interrupt and returned to her emails. Now wasn't the time anyway to ask him how come he had Fliss Roberts's personal mobile number written into his very important book, not when Mallory was likely to come down at any minute.

Eventually he looked up and, feeling his eyes on her, she put aside her laptop. 'You haven't told me about your week,' she reminded him.

'Do you really want to know?' he asked.

'I do if you want to tell me.'

A shadow seemed to pass through his eyes as he said, 'I'm getting more and more patients with Covid-related issues, and there's still so much to learn about the disease. However, you know how much I like to switch off while I'm here.'

'Even though you're thinking about it all the time?'

He smiled. 'Not the entire time,' he corrected. His eyes remained on hers and she felt their connection deepening as the mood subtly changed. 'Are you happy?' he asked quietly.

She nodded and smiled. 'How could I not be when you've just given me such a special gift?'

'I'm glad she's here.'

'Because you don't like to think of me alone all week?'

'That, and because I know how special she is to you.'

Sighing, she said, 'We should take her out while we can, just in case another lockdown happens. Do you think it will?'

'It seems inevitable, which makes me doubly glad she's here, because you probably won't be able to go anywhere for a while. Apart from on your walks with Neil, of course.'

As their eyes met again, she could sense the unspoken challenge in his words, the playful dare to tell him more. She wouldn't, and nor would she ask if he was jealous – it would seem petty and banal somehow – so instead she countered with, 'Maybe we should take Mallory to the Seafront for breakfast in the morning?' Would he pick up on her own provocation, or just move past it?

'Great idea,' he said, 'only I won't be able to join you, I'm afraid. Neil and I have arranged to go surfing.'

Her eyes widened with the unexpectedness of that. 'You're going surfing with Neil?' she repeated, as though it was the most extraordinary thing.

He shrugged. 'We keep talking about it, and now we've finally arranged to do it. We're meeting tomorrow at six to drive to a beach he knows just south of Croyde. I thought it would give you some time to settle in with Mallory without me getting in the way.'

With a laugh she said, 'You are never in the way, my darling. The reverse, we'll miss you, and I'm sure Fliss will be sorry not to see you when we go to the café.' *Would he grasp the nettle this time?*

'Tell her hi from me,' he said, and turned as Mallory came into the room, lighting it up with her youth and natural beauty. 'Everything OK?' he asked as she went to settle into the sofa adjacent to Jeannie's, mobile cradled between her hands.

'Everything's great,' she assured him. 'Mum sends her love.'

'How is she?' Jeannie smiled. 'Missing you like mad, I expect.'

Mallory laughed. 'I don't know about that, but she's glad I'm here at last. Apparently Dad wants me to get in touch, but I'll leave that for a couple of days.' To Guy she said, 'Did I hear you say something about surfing just now?'

'You did,' he confirmed. 'Why? Do you want to come?'

'I'd love to. When are you going?'

'In the morning.'

'Oh, that soon,' she grimaced. 'I need to get some gear. I didn't think to bring any. Maybe the next time you go?'

'Whenever it suits you. Just say the word. Zac will almost certainly come too. You met him earlier, just after you got here.'

Her eyes shone wickedly.

Guy laughed. 'Apparently surfing is just one of his many talents.'

'Should I ask what the others are?' she said mischievously.

It was Jeannie's turn to laugh. 'Maybe you'll be able to tell us before you leave.'

Accepting the challenge with comically batting eyelids, Mallory said, 'But don't worry, my internship definitely comes first. I can hardly wait to get started. Maurice has already sent me loads of stuff to read up on, so I'm good to go whenever you are.'

Checking his phone as it rang, Guy looked at Jeannie as he said, 'Hi Jodi. No, don't worry, it's not too late. What is it?' He rolled his eyes as he prepared to listen.

'OK, hang on,' he said, 'I'll go to my study and look at it online.'

As he left the room Jeannie said, 'His secretary.'

'Oh yes, I spoke to her a couple of times last week. She seems really nice.'

Going to pick up the notebook he'd left on the arm of his chair, Jeannie said, 'She and Guy were an item once, before I came on the scene.'

Mallory frowned. 'And she still works for him?'

'Personally, I think he should have replaced her as soon as we decided to get married, but he's always refused to.'

Seeming worried now, Mallory said, 'Do you think they're still involved? I swear I never saw anything to say they were while I was in London.'

Jeannie smiled. 'She works from home these days, in Hampshire, so he probably doesn't see her at all, unless he goes out of his way to, and I don't think he does.'

Mallory seemed unsure what to say to that.

'I had a word with her,' Jeannie confided. 'It was a while ago now, but I made it clear that things wouldn't go well for her, or Guy, if I ever found out they were still seeing one another.'

Mallory's eyes widened. 'Does Guy know that?' she murmured.

Amused, Jeannie said, 'Of course he does. We don't have any secrets, although it's true we don't always tell each other everything straight away. Now, that's enough about us, come and help me prepare some dinner. I want to hear all about you, and make plans for the wonderful time we're going to have while you're here.'

Mallory glowed. 'I just want to be as helpful as I can

in any way I can,' she said, 'without doing Maurice out of a job.'

'Did he say that?' Jeannie laughed. 'He would, but don't worry about him, he adores you as much as I do. Once this ghastly virus is over, whether it's a few months from now, or even a year from now, we'll all go to his villa in France to celebrate our freedom.'

CHAPTER SIXTEEN

ESTELLE

Early October 2020
Three months before Jeannie's disappearance

Estelle knew exactly where she was. There were no doubts in her mind. What had just happened was all part of a nightmare. It wasn't real. She was awake now and in bed at home. Her breathing was unsteady and her head in chaos, but Neil was fast asleep beside her; Chloe was safely tucked up in her own room and Prim was right next door in the annexe. The terrible, twisted dream she'd just broken out of had been no more than a cluster of tricks in her mind with cruel neural reconfigurings of people's faces, and recastings of bad memories into a hellish new form of torment.

It wasn't a part of her life and never would be, not the way she'd just seen it.

It was all from the past.

Her adoptive parents were history now.

The scene with Jeannie had happened five years ago.

There had been no scene at all with Serena Fellowes, her birth mother, because she hadn't even contacted her yet. And she had no reason to think that she would ever treat her as callously or damagingly as her adoptive mother had – or as Jeannie had. She had to stop seeing Jeannie and Serena as the same person; they didn't even look alike, apart from in that horrendous dream, when they'd morphed in and out of one another's features.

Slipping out of bed, she wrapped herself in a robe and made her way in the dark to her writer's room. Only when the door was closed behind her did she put on the light. She didn't want to wake anyone, didn't want to have to explain why she was shaking and crying and then staring at a picture of a woman called Serena Fellowes as she pulled it up on her screen. It was the only way she could think of to erase Jeannie's face from her mind, to stop it ghosting itself onto Serena's again.

She wished she could call Prim. Prim would understand, would know how to calm her, but it was three in the morning and right now she wasn't sure she could actually speak to anyone anyway. She was still numb with the horror of it all. It felt so real; she was still hearing Jeannie's voice as she shouted and snarled at her, except it was Serena who was saying, 'What the hell are you doing barging into my life like this?'

It was all so mixed up, so true to memory and yet warped by the bizarre disturbances of her unconscious mind.

She stared harder and harder at the picture of Serena, taking in each and every detail of her soft brown eyes, the small uptilt of her nose, the wide, generous mouth and shoulder-length hair. She was nothing like Jeannie; they could hardly be more different in colouring, looks, even in the air they exuded. Her birth mother's was one of refinement and gentility; Jeannie's was all confidence and arrogance. They were the same age, but that was never going to mean that Serena Fellowes's character was in any way the same as Jeannie's.

Except she'd rejected her own baby, given her up and never tried to see her again.

Wasn't that even worse than what Jeannie had done to an author she wanted to be rid of?

'What the hell are you doing barging into my office like this?' Jeannie had yelled as Estelle had pushed past Maurice and flung open the door. 'You don't have an appointment. I don't want to see you, so please go.'

'You have to listen to me,' Estelle had shouted back, barely noticing how haggard and stressed Jeannie looked. 'There's nothing wrong with my new book. It's only you who has the problem—'

'No, Estelle, *you* are the one with the problem. Just be thankful you had one book in you, most people don't even have that. Now please go away, I don't have time for this.'

'Really? You had plenty of time for me when I was top of the bestseller list. Nothing was too much trouble for me then, and I never minded you taking the credit, telling everyone how much editing it had needed . . .'

'Because it did. Because you can't really write, Estelle. You had a good story to tell, I'll grant you that, but without my input and Maurice's it would never have made it. You need to get to grips with that and accept that what you're trying to land me with now is never going to fly. I'm sorry it's not what you want to hear, but I tried to be tactful about it, I sent you a very long email . . .'

'Which proved that you simply don't get it. If we could talk it through . . .'

'It's not going to happen, Estelle. It will never make it onto the Athene list and I wouldn't be doing you any favours if I tried to pretend otherwise.'

'I can take it to another publisher . . .'

'No one's stopping you.'

'I don't understand why you're being like this. I know you're going through a difficult time . . .'

'You're right, I am. My parents' funeral was less than a month ago, and here you are getting hysterical with me over a book that could hardly matter less.'

'You're just not thinking straight after what happened. I understand . . .'

'No, you don't. You're making everything about you, as usual, and I've had enough of it. I don't want you in my office, I don't even want you in my life.'

Suddenly exploding, Estelle yelled, 'Everyone's right what they say about you, aren't they? You're a monster. Did you know that's what they say? I always tried to defend you, I even felt sorry for you when I heard you'd lost your parents the way you did. I couldn't think of anything worse, but now, seeing what a bitch you really are, I have no problem believing that you killed them. Even your own brother thinks that you left that candle burning on purpose—'

'Get of here *now*!' Jeannie screamed. 'Maurice, remove her from my sight before I do something we'll all regret.'

'Don't you dare touch me,' Estelle hissed, as Maurice tried to grab her. 'You're the one who poisoned her against me . . .'

'I've never been able to stand you,' Jeannie cried. 'Even when you were at number one, I detested you. You're a whiny, self-important, jumped-up, talentless nobody who's trying to deliver me a pile of crap and it's not going to happen. So get out of here now or I'll call security.'

'That,' Maurice said, muscling her to the door, 'is what's called getting your ass handed to you on a plate, so take this, sweetie, and don't even think about coming back.'

It wasn't until she was outside on the street that Estelle realized she was clutching a toilet roll, and because she had nothing else to hand, she used it to dry her tears.

She was using a proper Kleenex now, but she barely needed it, for the tears had more or less stopped, and so, thank God, had the grotesque image shifting between Serena and Jeannie. She was seeing only her mother on the screen now, and was even, in an other-worldly sort of way, hearing her voice, soft and soothing, reminding her of how she'd written to Jeannie to apologize after that terrible day, several pages of deeply heartfelt words saying how much she hated herself for what she'd said, how very sorry she was, that she didn't believe any such thing, that Jeannie really meant the world to her. *It was only because I was so afraid of losing your friendship that I kicked out the way I did, and as we all know fear can make people say and do terrible things. And you were in a terrible place. I should have been more sensitive to that, I truly wish I had been. I'm ready to do anything to make it up to you, Jeannie. Please say you forgive me. I won't be able to bear it if you don't.*

Jeannie had never written back; hadn't even acknowledged the email Estelle had sent asking if she'd received the letter.

'The fact that I apologized makes me the better person,'

she whispered aloud to her mother on the screen. 'Don't you agree?'

'Estie, what are you doing in here?'

Starting as Neil came into the room, she quickly closed down her computer and said, 'Sorry, I didn't mean to wake you. I had a bad dream, that's all. I'm fine now.'

Coming to her, he pulled her up to her feet and held her close. 'Shall I make you a hot drink?' he offered.

Finding herself leaning into him, and warming to the feel of him holding her with such tenderness, she said, 'That would be nice.'

'Then go on back to bed and I'll bring it up. Tea or chocolate?'

'Tea. Thanks.'

As they reached the landing, he pulled her into another hug and kissed the top of her head. 'Did it upset you that I went surfing with Guy Symonds today?' he asked. 'Is that why you wouldn't speak to me earlier?'

'Maybe,' she said, knowing that it was the reason she'd turned her back on him when he'd come in. She'd been unable to think about anything else all day and all evening, the two of them out there on the waves when Guy could have been with her.

'Did you see Jeannie? Did she go too?' she asked. She'd want to die if the answer was yes, if her imaginings of everyone together, riding the surf, shouting and laughing, shivering with cold and bursting with exhilaration turned out to be true.

'No, she didn't come,' he said, 'and I didn't go to the Hall so I haven't seen her. Zac and I met Guy on the way there and we went in convoy.'

'Oh, I see,' she said, wondering why Guy had chosen

to see Neil today and not her. When they'd walked last Saturday, he'd said he would be in touch again this weekend. Maybe he'd text tomorrow.

'Let's do something tomorrow,' Neil said, 'just the three of us.'

She tensed. 'You mean with Guy?'

He laughed. 'I was talking about Chloe. Zac's helping his mother at the café, but Prim might be up for a day out somewhere.'

She forced a smile as she nodded. She could always make an excuse if Guy got in touch and suggested a walk.

'We could start with a lovely big breakfast at the Seafront,' he said, walking her to the stairs, 'and from there how about a stroll around the Botanical Gardens if the weather holds up?'

'Sounds good,' she replied, barely listening now. She wanted him to go down to the kitchen so she could sneak back into her writer's room and send the email to her mother. She'd suddenly decided that it needed to be done now, tonight. She didn't want to hold on any longer.

CHAPTER SEVENTEEN
CARA AND ANDEE

Wednesday 20 January 2021
Fourteen days since Jeannie's disappearance

Putting a coffee down in front of Andee, Cara carried hers to an open window and removed her mask. It was trying to snow outside, and the wind was blowing a hooley across the bay, but they couldn't drink with masks on, so while they were off fresh air had to flow in the interests of staying safe. She only wished she'd got in earlier to put the heating on in here.

'I've listened to your interview with Neil Roberts,' Andee said, her breath mingling with the steam of her Americano as she spoke, her half-gloved hands circled around the mug for warmth. 'You did a great job.'

Pleased by that, Cara said, 'So do you think he and Jeannie might be having an affair?'

Andee looked pensive. 'We can't rule it out,' she replied. 'He was quite defensive when you brought it up. I just wouldn't have thought . . .' She broke off and began to shake her head.

'What?' Cara prompted.

'This is the trouble when it's people you know,' Andee

explained. 'It's hard to be objective. Anyway, he doesn't seem to have an alibi for the rest of the day, at least up until five thirty when he says he got home. And that's not good.'

'We only have his word for it that he didn't go into the Hall,' Cara pointed out. 'He could have been there all afternoon. There's no proof he went near the nurseries.'

'It's possible he was helping her to pack up her car,' Andee suggested, going with the theme. 'If that's the case, then he quite likely knows where she went and is respecting her wishes to keep it from Guy.'

'Which means lying to the police – and to you?'

Wryly, Andee said, 'It certainly wouldn't be a first. Have you had any luck with number plate recognition yet?'

Cara shook her head. ''Fraid not, but I'm still on it.'

'OK. Well, working on the assumption that she hasn't gone off the side of the road somewhere, we know that her car isn't at the railway station because Guy and I have already checked, so she didn't leave the area by train. Maybe I'll take a drive out to Neil's nurseries later. I can't imagine I'll find the car there, but there's no harm in looking I guess.'

Cara said, 'You mean he might be keeping it for her and has loaned her another meanwhile?'

Andee didn't look convinced.

After finishing her coffee, Cara put the mug down and tugged her scarf up around her mouth. 'His wife seems to think there could be an affair,' she stated. 'Estelle Fields didn't mention it herself when I spoke to her; it was he who brought up that she suspected there might be something going on. Weird that, isn't it?'

Andee nodded. 'Have you been in touch with Primrose

Barnes yet? She's Estelle's PA and lives in the house next door.'

'No, but I've sent an email asking her to contact me. I'm still waiting for a response.'

Andee was quiet for a while as she thought it all through. In the end, she said, 'I guess there's nothing from Vodafone yet, or the credit card companies? No, because this isn't a priority case so we'll be lucky to hear back before the end of the week.'

Cara grimaced. 'My name doesn't carry much clout, I'm afraid.'

With a smile, Andee said, 'It will if Natalie Rundle gets behind you, but she's not going to do that until we have a good reason for her to.'

'You mean until we have some evidence of a crime? Do you think there's been one?'

Andee inhaled deeply. 'What I think,' she said, 'is that it's more credible than her going into hiding, or running off with a lover who even her closest friends and family seem to know nothing about. However, I'll be interested to see how you get on with her assistant, Maurice Bisset. When are you talking to him?'

'We've got a video-link set up for half four this afternoon.'

'Good. I wasn't entirely sure what to make of him myself when we spoke.'

'You put in your notes that you reckon he'd go to the ends of the earth for Jeannie, and you don't believe he knows where she is.'

'I don't, but that doesn't mean I'm right, or that he's being completely honest with us. It's always interesting to see how much people start to remember as time goes on.

In my experience, as dynamics shift and other suspicions kick in, it can be quite a lot.'

At four thirty on the dot, Maurice Bisset came onto Cara's screen, looking as though he hadn't been sleeping too well judging by the sallow cheeks and dark circles under his eyes.

'Do you have any news?' he asked before Cara could begin.

'No, I'm sorry,' she replied, 'but as soon as there's anything we'll be sure to let you know.'

He nodded, almost curtly, and picked up a mug that had the string of a tea bag hanging over the edge. 'Poor Guy,' he said wretchedly, 'he must be going out of his mind by now. I wish she'd just get in touch to let us know she's all right.'

Interested that he seemed to think that was possible, Cara got down to business with her opening question. 'I believe the last time you saw her was when you went to her home back in October?' she said.

'In person, yes,' he replied. 'God, it seems so long ago now. This damned virus. When are we ever going to get back to normal? Anyway, we've spoken most days since, usually on Teams or Zoom, so I see her then, but it's not the same.'

'Were you on a video call when you spoke to her on January the sixth?'

He shook his head. 'No, but I wish we had been, I might have got some sense of what was going on with her if I'd actually been able to see her.'

'Did you get the impression something was going on?'

'Not really. I guess she was a little distracted, but that's not unusual, she's always got a hundred and one things going on all at the same time.'

'Do you think anyone might have been with her?'

He shrugged. 'Mallory, her niece, had gone by then, she left just before Christmas, so as far as I knew Jeannie was alone when Guy was in London.'

'Did she mention anything about going away somewhere?'

'If she had, you can be sure I'd have already told Guy, but remember, this current lockdown began on January the sixth, so she couldn't go anywhere even if she wanted to.'

'Except her car's gone, along with her phone and credit cards.'

His shoulders drooped. 'I can't explain that,' he said woefully. 'She doesn't usually go anywhere without telling me, but it seems she has this time.'

Cara said, 'Her husband says that, in the past, she's booked herself into an Airbnb without telling anyone where she was going, or when she'd be back. Did you know where she was on any of those occasions?'

'Yes, I did. I had to know in case any emergencies cropped up at the office.'

'But you never told her husband?'

'It wasn't my place to. If she doesn't want to tell Guy everything, that's her business, not mine.'

'Was she ever with another man? Or woman?'

'Not that I know of – and it would have been a man if we're talking affairs.'

'So she could have been with someone?'

'I don't think so. I'm sure she'd have told me if she was.'

'Have you ever known her to have an affair?'

'No.'

Unable to tell if he was being entirely truthful, she stared at him for a moment, hoping he might say more, but he didn't. 'Why did she go away without telling her husband where she was?' she asked.

'I'm afraid you'd have to ask her that.'

If I could, I would, she didn't remind him. 'Do you actually know where she is right now?' she challenged.

Clearly annoyed he said, 'If I did, we wouldn't be going through all this.'

'Then if you want us to find her, you need to tell me what you know.'

Huffing a sigh, he fanned a hand as he said, 'You really need to talk to Guy about this, not me. All I can tell you is that she likes to worry him sometimes. And frankly, he probably does the same to her, although don't ask me how because I don't even know if I'm right.'

Confused, in spite of having heard much the same from Guy, Cara said, 'Why do they want to worry one another?'

'I've no idea. Maybe it's a power thing, who's controlling the relationship and who isn't. That's my best guess.'

'So would you say she's controlling it now?'

He regarded her helplessly. 'You could think that, but even if you're right I've no idea where you'd go with it.'

Having no idea either, she said, 'Do you think they're happily married?'

'Yes, I think so. They just have their own . . . ways of doing things.'

'Like taking off without telling one another where they're going. Does he do the same?'

'Not as far as I know.'

154

'Are they faithful to one another?'

'That would depend on how you define faithful.'

She blinked.

'They're in love,' he explained, 'but are they exclusive? I'm not sure, you'd have to ask them.'

'You said just now that you didn't think she had affairs.'

'Because affair connotes something deliberate and committed.'

'So are you saying they have casual relationships with other people?'

He shrugged. 'You know what they say, the only people who really know what goes on inside a marriage are those who are in it.'

Starting to feel a bit out of her depth with all this, Cara said, 'So it's possible she could be with another man now?'

He looked doubtful. 'Not unless Neil, her landscaper, has also disappeared. He's the last "crush" that I know about.'

Seizing it, perhaps too quickly, Cara said, 'So you think they could be sleeping together?'

'That's not what I said, but I guess it's possible.'

Wishing Andee was there to take this over now, Cara went out on a limb and said, 'Do you think something might have gone wrong in that relationship and Neil Roberts has . . . Well, done her some harm?'

He sat with that for a moment then began slowly shaking his head. 'I guess there's a chance he might know where she is, you'd have to ask him that, but would he want to harm her? Sorry, I just can't see it. If you were asking about his wife, Estelle Fields, I'd say she'd like nothing more than to stick a knife into Jeannie. I speak metaphorically, you understand, at least I think I do. There's no telling what that little psycho might do.'

155

Going with it, Cara said, 'I've heard about the falling out between them—'

'Oh yes, and some. That nasty little bitch actually accused Jeannie of killing her own parents, can you believe that? How can anyone even think it, much less shout it into someone's face only weeks after the funeral, for God's sake! Then she had the gall to try and apologize. No way was Jeannie ever going to accept. We never could stand her anyway, so we were glad to be rid of her.'

Not at all sure about the logic of her next question, but deciding to ask it anyway, Cara said, 'Do you think Jeannie might have got involved with Neil Roberts to spite Estelle Fields?'

Bisset scoffed a laugh. 'Have you seen the man? I mean, please! Jeannie's attraction to him would have nothing to do with his wife, I can assure you of that. Frankly, Estelle isn't important enough for Jeannie even to want to get some sort of payback.'

Cara looked down at her notes again, giving herself some time to think. This wasn't going very well, at least she didn't think it was, she certainly didn't seem to have a proper handle on it, and she wasn't entirely sure how to continue.

'Listen, I want to help find her,' he said, 'so I'm going to tell you this . . . I've no idea if it'll . . . Well, I touched on it just now, the way she and Guy sometimes kind of bait one another. I don't know how real things actually get, but there have been at least a couple of occasions when Jeannie decided to pay the other woman a visit.'

So Guy Symonds had been involved with other women? Cara waited for him to go on.

'One was Guy's ex-wife. I don't know what happened

when Jeannie went to see her, but I do know, or at least I'm pretty sure, that she – Kate – and Guy have never seen one another again.'

'Does Guy know Jeannie went to talk to his ex?'

'Probably, I'd say almost definitely, but he's pretty chilled about most things. Not this, obviously, whatever *this* is. She's definitely going too far this time.'

Cara said, 'How long ago did she confront the ex-wife?'

'Three or four years ago. Maybe longer. If Jeannie wants someone out of the picture, she makes it happen. She's the same at work. If she doesn't rate you, or you've crossed the line somehow, you can start packing your plants.'

'Could she have gone to confront another woman now? Someone she suspects her husband of sleeping with?'

'Anything's possible, but you'll have seen for yourself how worried Guy is. If he was involved with someone else, he'd presumably have started his search right there.'

Knowing already that she was going to be in touch with Guy Symonds as soon as this call was over, Cara said, 'You seem pretty certain that Jeannie is OK, wherever she is.'

He shrugged. 'It's just a feeling I have. I think I'd know if anything had happened to her. You do with people who are close, don't you?'

Not too sure about that, she said, 'Do you think she's still somewhere in this area, or in London?'

He frowned as he gave it some thought. 'I honestly have no idea,' he finally replied. 'With her car gone, I guess anything's possible.'

'What about one of your colleagues, or an author, or a personal friend of hers? Could she be with one of them?'

'I've spoken to just about everyone, so has Guy. I don't

think she's with anyone we know. However, something that 'has occurred to me recently is that at least half the people in her set have second homes. I have one myself, in the South of France, but we know she's not there because we've already asked our letting agent to check. Anyway, she didn't take her passport, did she? And only essential travel is allowed. So if she is using someone's place, it would have to be in this country, and one person who comes to mind is Dylan Frank. He's an author she's been working with for the past few months on his latest book. He lives in the next street to me, here in Wandsworth, and I know he's spending this lockdown there because I see him out walking most mornings. But he also has a cottage in Norfolk. I guess she could have gone there. I'll call him when we're done here to check if you like. Or I'm happy to give you his number if you'd prefer to do it yourself.'

'Thanks, that would be good.'

'The book is interesting,' he continued, after she'd jotted down Dylan Frank's number, 'because it's one of those time-slip stories that can either be brilliant or a disaster. This one has great potential of being the former, and the reason Jeannie's so keen to be involved is because of its historical setting in Vienna. Believe me, if times were different, she and Dylan would probably be there right now.'

After reminding him about the passport, Cara decided she needed to ring off before she went into weird-information overload, so she said, 'Thanks very much for talking to me, Mr Bissell.' She saw him wince and realized she'd got the name wrong and had probably just made him sound like her old nan's carpet sweeper. 'If anything else comes to mind, or if you hear from Jeannie, please let us know.'

As the screen darkened, she immediately went to the email Guy Symonds had sent with his work schedule attached. A quick glance told her that he was in surgery right now, carrying out a VS – whatever that was – on someone called Jacob Hartley. Nevertheless, she reached for the phone and left a message on his mobile for him to call as soon as he could.

Next she rang Andee and had to leave a message for her too. 'I've just finished speaking to Maurice the PA,' she said. 'You need to listen to the recording, because he's said some interesting stuff, including the fact that there *might* be something between Jeannie and Neil Roberts. Anyway, there definitely seems to have been some strange stuff in the Symondses' marriage, or in Jeannie's headspace, or possibly both. Oh, and apparently he once cheated on her with his ex-wife, or Jeannie thought he did, I couldn't quite make out whether or not it was real. Anyway, please call me when you can. I need advice.'

Several minutes later the phone rang; to her surprise it was Guy Symonds. 'Thanks for getting back to me so quickly,' she said. 'I hope I wasn't interrupting anything.'

'Not at all. I'd already left theatre by the time I got your message. Do you have some news? Please tell me it's good.'

'Oh, uh, I'm sorry, it's . . . I should have been clearer. It's just that I have a few questions I was hoping you could help with.'

His disappointment was audible as he said, 'Of course. Go ahead.'

Grabbing her notes, she braced herself and said, 'I've just learned that sometimes Jeannie goes to visit women she suspects you of being involved with, so I have to ask if there's anyone you haven't yet told us about?'

Sounding patient, he said, 'If the question is, am I having an affair, I thought we'd already cleared that up: no, I am not. However, Jeannie has been known to convince herself otherwise at times. It's more of a game with her, though, than a real suspicion.'

Cara was silent as she tried to puzzle that out.

'I'm sorry,' he said, 'I don't expect you to understand that. I'm not sure I always do myself, but I can assure you I'm not involved with another woman.'

'But Jeannie might think you are?'

'It's possible, I guess.'

'Could it be your ex-wife?'

'Kate? I shouldn't think so. We haven't seen one another for a long time, although I know she's someone Jeannie visited a few years ago.'

'So were you and Kate having an affair?' She really needed some clarity on this.

'No, we weren't. I can give you her number if you'd like to speak to her, but I strongly doubt she'll be able to tell you where Jeannie is.'

After taking the number down, Cara felt slightly light-headed as she launched into her next questions. 'What about Neil Roberts?' she asked. 'Have you ever thought Jeannie might be involved with him?'

Sounding slightly weary he said, 'She was certainly attracted to him, but as far as I'm aware . . . Has Neil said something to make you think it was more than a mild flirtation?'

'No, but I've just spoken to Jeannie's assistant, Maurice, and he told me there might be something.'

'Really? Jeannie talked to Maurice about Neil?'

'It would seem so.'

'And have you asked Neil about it?'

Deciding not to answer that, she said, 'Did Jeannie ever mention anything to you about Neil?'

'Well, she's teased me with the attraction at times, but it's something she does when she finds another man . . . appealing. I never really take it seriously, although I have to confess I'll act jealous if I think that's what she wants.'

'What do you mean by acting jealous?'

'What I said. I certainly don't take it to extremes, if that's what you're thinking.'

Not entirely sure what was really in her head she said, 'Do you have anything to say about Neil Roberts being the last person to see Jeannie before she left? I mean, that we know of.'

'No, I don't think so. Should I have?'

'I just wondered, that was all.'

He fell silent.

So did she.

'And that leaves us where?' he asked.

Wishing she had a better answer, she said, 'I'm going to talk things over with Andee and we'll get back to you.'

CHAPTER EIGHTEEN

I saw her again today, and was moved by the sadness and worry in her eyes. I understand her pain and what she has suffered, and her dread of what might be to come, but I have no idea how to make things better.

The suddenness of her beauty when she laughs affects everyone around her, lighting them up, making them glad to know her, but I don't think she realizes that. She clearly enjoys being with her friends who help out at the café. It's when they're not there that she seems lonely, gazing at nothing, dreaming of only she knows what. I wish I could do something to help her.

CHAPTER NINETEEN

FLISS

Early November 2020
Two months before Jeannie's disappearance

'Mum! *Mum!*'

Fliss started out of her reverie and turned to look up at her son, towering over her like a worried parent as she sat curled up in an armchair in front of the window. For a fleeting moment she thought he was part of a dream, that he wasn't really there and nor was she; that they weren't in the flat above the café, they were somewhere else entirely. Then she smiled and pressed her hands to her cheeks. 'Sorry, I was miles away,' she said, not sure anymore where the miles had taken her.

'You're not kidding,' he replied. 'You had me spooked there for a minute, sitting staring at nothing and not even hearing me come in. Are you OK?'

'I'm fine. Have you been working with Dad today?'

'Duh! I've been delivering food parcels for you,' he reminded her. He dropped his jacket on the sofa, then checked the messages on his phone, thumbed off a few texts and took a call. 'Hi Matt, how are you? Yeah good, thanks. I'm at home.'

He turned and grinned at his mother as he said, 'Sure, the MILF is here. She sends her love.'

Fliss shot him a meaningful look, although she couldn't deny it was a small confidence boost in its way, and these days she took them where she could.

As she listened to him continue to joke and laugh, she enjoyed the sense of him growing into a confident and carefree young man, with more friends than he'd probably ever need, and, so she'd been told, his pick of the girls. He didn't have a steady one right now – a 'Mrs', as he and his mates called their partners – but it was hardly the time for serious relationships when he was still so young, and barely able to go out anyway.

'You're kidding me, man,' he cried, clapping a hand to his head. 'She's binned him twice already . . . Tell you what, she's carrying his *cojones* round in her handbag . . .' He laughed, and said, 'Sure, catch you later,' and as he rang off he glanced at Fliss in surprise.

Realizing she still hadn't moved she made to, but stopped as he said, 'You know what, you don't look too good. How about I make you a nice cup of tea?'

'That'll be better than a horrible one,' she said, repeating an old joke of her mother's that she and Zac had long enjoyed. 'Just what I need.'

She'd have preferred a glass of wine, but she didn't drink when Zac was around, or not at this time of day anyway. 'Is Andee still downstairs?' she asked, following him into the kitchen and checking to make sure she'd put her latest delivery of painkillers out of sight. If he saw them he'd realize her back was playing up, and she didn't want him worrying or telling Neil. And actually, it wasn't that bad. It just helped to know that relief was at hand if she needed it.

'Yep,' he replied, 'and the rest of the Corona Girls.'

Andee, Leanne, Wilkie, Claudia, Marcy and Angie. Six of the best friends anyone could wish for. Sometimes, like now, Fliss could feel quite emotional simply to think of them and how loyal and supportive they were continuing to be during this second lockdown. She hadn't yet found the courage to tell them that before too long she would not be able to pay any of her kitchen team, and as for her major suppliers . . . Her credit had already run out with some and was very close to the end with others, and with no sign of this virus going away . . . The mere thought of it made her want to scream with dread of where it was all going to end.

'Here you go,' Zac declared, putting a mug of tea on the table in front of her. 'You remember we're going to Dad and Estelle's tonight, yeah?'

Fliss smiled. 'Of course I do,' she lied. In fact, she'd forgotten all about it, and now she was already trying to think of a way to get out of it – the obvious excuse – that according to the rules they were unable to visit anyone for the next four weeks – wasn't going to fly. As far as Zac and Neil were concerned, their two households were bubbled and, anyway, she didn't want to deprive Zac of a family dinner, or Chloe of some time with her big brother.

'So how come you're up here all on your own?' he asked, breaking out a packet of biscuits and practically inhaling the first. 'Don't tell me, you've put yourself on furlough.'

She smiled, but didn't want to admit that Andee had insisted she take a few minutes upstairs before she dropped, so she said, 'I had some phone calls to make and Leanne and Wilkie were packing boxes in the office. Did they talk to you about the Facebook page, by the way?'

'They did and I'm on it. Or I will be first thing tomorrow.' Down went another biscuit before he said, 'I thought I'd go to Dad's early, if it's OK with you, so I can use the gym. It'll mean me taking the Seafront van—'

'That's fine,' she interrupted, knowing how much physical fitness meant to him, and wishing she had a gym herself that he could use. She wanted to give him the world so he'd never want for anything, ever, but of course she couldn't. She wondered if she should tell him she wouldn't mind if he moved back to his dad's, that she'd understand perfectly when there was so much more there for him. She didn't say it, for she simply couldn't bear to think of him leaving now she'd got used to him being here.

Not yet anyway.

'Mum?'

She looked up and felt her heart contract at the mere sight of him standing there safe, alive and healthy . . .

'Oh God, Mum, you're crying,' he said, and quickly he came round the table to kneel in front of her. 'What is it? What's upset you?' he insisted, taking her hands in his.

'Nothing,' she laughed, smoothing her fingers over his stubbly cheek. 'I was just . . . You know me, always too emotional and with all that we're going through, as a country . . . Everything's so . . .' She shook her head, not sure of the right words to say; certainly she'd never tell him how much she longed to be with his father, that sometimes she almost couldn't bear it. 'What's important to me is that you're all right,' she said, turning it into a playful scold. 'You are, aren't you?'

He rolled his eyes in a way that made her smile. 'I swear I'm not depressed, or feeling suicidal . . . I know some guys my age are, but I'm not one of them.'

'That's good, and you'd tell me if anything was worrying you?'

He seemed to consider that for a moment, then said, 'Actually, I would, so here goes, you're what's worrying me, so come on, cough. What's really going on with you? I know something is, and I want to help.'

Loving him for being so intuitive and sensitive, so very like Neil in fact, she found herself wanting to tell him the truth, to let it all come pouring out, but there was so much, too much, starting with why she'd left him when he was only four, right through to today, and how much it meant to her that he was with her. He didn't need to hear it, it was too big a burden for his young shoulders, so staying with the moment and going for as much honesty as she could, she said, 'This new lockdown . . . Money's already tight. There are bills that need paying and I'm not sure I can meet them.'

'Then we'll talk to Dad. He'll—'

'No! Zac, please don't mention it to him. He has enough on his plate with half his clients being unable to pay him. I'll work it out, I promise. It's not really as bad as I'm making it sound. I just feel a bit overwhelmed now and again. We'll get through it. You know me.'

Pulling her into a hug he said, 'I think everyone's feeling the same way, you know, trying to be optimistic when everything around us is going to shit. This is a really crap time, but it'll get better, you wait and see.'

'Of course it will.' She smiled, and pulled back to look at him again. Sometimes she just couldn't get enough of looking at him, and because he understood why, he often just let her get on with it.

'Fancy starting a new series when we come back tonight?' he suggested, making it sound like an extra-special treat.

Did he realize that, for her, watching anything with him was exactly that? 'Definitely,' she agreed. 'You can choose.'

Ten minutes later he'd left the flat, taking laptop and keyboard with him (this meant they were in for a musical evening at Neil and Estelle's), and Fliss was downstairs in the café boxing up a delicious strawberry gateau for Guy Symonds, the last customer of the day.

'Is it someone's birthday?' she asked as she placed the finished parcel on the counter.

Wryly he said, 'Actually it's mine, and Jeannie insisted I pick up a cake on my way home. She meant to order one, apparently, but she's so busy all the time, and now her niece is staying for a while . . .' He laughed. 'You don't need to hear all that. How much do I owe you?'

Wishing she could say it was on the house as a birthday gift, Fliss said, 'Let's just make it ten pounds and I'll throw in these roses . . .'

'No, you won't,' Andee protested from where she was cleaning the coffee machine. 'Chloe brought them in earlier, for you.'

Surprised and pleased, Fliss said, 'I didn't know she'd been in. She should have come up to find me.'

'I think Estelle was in a hurry.'

Turning back to Guy, Fliss grimaced an apology as she said, 'Well, the thought was there.'

'And much appreciated,' he assured her. 'Here's your ten pounds, and another five for the charity box.'

'Again,' she laughed. 'That's very kind of you,' and she watched him take the money from his wallet while thinking that his hands actually looked like a surgeon's, or how she'd want a surgeon's to look if she was ever in need of one. 'Are you on your way back from London?' she asked, chattily.

'Bristol, actually,' he replied. 'I was at a meeting at the university there today, and again tomorrow, which means I can come home for the night *in the middle of the week.*'

'Lucky you're not spending your birthday alone then,' she commented dryly.

Although she couldn't see his smile behind the mask, she knew it was there from the way his eyes crinkled at the corners. And he could see her face, because she was wearing her transparent visor.

After pocketing his wallet, he lifted the cake by the bow strings and said, 'Have a good evening, ladies.' His warm grey eyes were on Fliss, and ludicrously she felt herself blush.

A moment later he'd gone, and once she was certain he could no longer hear, Fliss said, 'He's such a nice man, isn't he?'

Andee said, 'Just a shame he's married.'

Feigning shock at such an outrageous remark, or at having her thoughts read, Fliss laughed as she went to lock the front door before anyone else tried to come in. Too late, Detective Sergeant Natalie Rundle was already there. 'I'm sorry,' Fliss told her, 'there're no more hot drinks. We've turned everything off.'

'Just give me food,' the detective implored. 'I don't care what it is, I need to eat something. I haven't had a crumb since breakfast.'

'Busy day?' Andee asked, starting to parcel up the last remaining slice of stilton and broccoli quiche and a large apple turnover as Rundle came to the counter.

'Manic, and every day's like it now, with half the team isolating and the other half breaking up raves, or street parties or weddings. What a world we're in where we can't let people get married in peace.' She checked her phone as it rang and gave a painful groan. 'I'd better take it,' she said, clearly wishing it to hell, and after throwing a ten-pound note on the counter, she picked up her hastily packed meal and headed out to her illegally parked car.

Finally locking the doors, Fliss went through to the kitchen where the rest of the Corona Girls were already cleaning and disinfecting and chattering in their usual light-hearted way, and she was soon laughing along with them as Wilkie, aged seventy-two, filled them in on the farcical world of oldies' online dating during a pandemic.

No one, to Fliss's relief, ever suggested that she, as the only other singleton amongst them, should give it a try; they all seemed instinctively to know that it wasn't for her. However, she had to admit, if only to herself, that she often wished she could meet someone and fall in love. If nothing else it would prove, after all these years, that she was finally over Neil.

Time sped by as three of them moved into the café to clean, leaving the others to load up with leftover food for the night shelter, until eventually they all elbow-bumped a farewell at the door. It was a nonsense really, for they were working so closely together most of the time that it was impossible to stick to the rules, but at least these small gestures showed some effort to recognize them.

'Can you spare me a few minutes?' Andee asked, as the others headed off to their cars.

'Yes, of course,' Fliss replied, feeling both anxious and glad that Andee apparently wanted to chat. People often said that when Andee was around, things never felt so bad, and she was one of them, for there was something about this beautiful and capable ex-detective that seemed to make even the most daunting challenge feel not entirely impossible.

Andee went to perch on one of the bar stools and, as Fliss took another six feet away, she glanced outside to see if Neil was around. He hadn't been in after hours for the past couple of weeks, and despondently she realized he probably wouldn't be this evening, given that she and Zac would be seeing him later.

Turning to Andee, she felt her heart flip to see the seriousness of Andee's expression. 'Please don't tell me someone else has died,' she implored.

Andee's exquisite aquamarine eyes showed her understanding of the question; they'd lost too many friends and neighbours these past few months ever to take life for granted again. 'No, it's not that,' she assured her with a small smile. 'It's about Becky Farmer, on Temple Road. She was expecting you earlier with her prescription. Apparently you said you'd pick it up for her and—'

Guilt flared in Fliss's chest as she cried, 'Oh God, it went completely out of my mind. Is the pharmacy still open? I can do it now.'

'It's OK, she called me so everything's fine. Except, you obviously aren't, Fliss. I don't know what's going on with you, but I'd like you to tell me if there's anything I can help with.'

First Zac, now Andee.

Fliss's defences were already up, damming her emotions, creating a fierce wall of self-protection that she always called on at times like this. She didn't want anyone's pity, or to feel a burden in some way, even though she already was one, considering all the help she was accepting from the Corona Girls.

'Come on,' Andee coaxed gently. 'You know I'll get it out of you sooner or later, so why don't we do it now?'

Funny how that bullying sort of kindness always got through, fracturing her resolve, pushing tears to her eyes, and doing more to melt her defences than any amount of actual force. So why not tell Andee? There was no one she trusted more. 'OK, it's my finances,' she admitted. 'In fact, I've messed up so badly that I hardly know whether I'm coming or going. I realize that's a horrible excuse when an old lady needs her medicine, but it's like my own dire situation is all I can think about. And please, please don't start offering me a loan, because I won't be able to pay it back so I couldn't possibly take it.'

Andee was watching her closely, appearing – as she often did – to see past what was being said to other, deeper truths. How did she have that knack? What made her so intuitive, so understanding of a situation before even knowing all the facts? 'I'm aware that your accountant died back in April,' she said softly, 'which tells me you've already been struggling with this for too long . . .'

'Believe me, I've tried the government loan scheme and talked to the bank—'

Andee held up a hand. 'Let me ask my accountant to take a look at your books. It won't cost you anything, he owes me plenty of favours, so he'll be happy to repay one.'

Fliss's pride was all ready to point out that favours owed to Andee didn't belong to her, but common sense was doing its best to remind her that not only would it seem ungrateful, it would be worse than foolish to turn down free help. 'Thanks,' she said with an awkward glance away. 'I'll get something together and hope he doesn't scream in horror when he sees it.'

Andee smiled. 'He's made of stern stuff, so I don't think we need to worry about that. Now, let's get to what else you're keeping to yourself.'

Fliss tensed with surprise and wariness. 'What do you mean?' she asked, stepping back from it.

Andee didn't reply, simply waited for an answer.

Fliss wanted to swear that her financial chaos was the extent of it, that Andee was imagining things if she thought there was anything else; after all, wasn't that bad enough? But in spite of knowing there were no solutions to her biggest problem, she decided to open up anyway.

'It's Zac,' she confessed, dabbing at her eyes. 'I could never tell him this, obviously I couldn't, but since he moved in . . . Well, the truth is, I find it difficult having him here. Not that I want him to go, if I had my way he'd never leave, but seeing him every day, watching him grow into a man, it's like a constant reminder of what happened . . . Of why I had to give him up—'

'But you didn't give him up,' Andee interrupted, gently. 'You've always played a very big part in his life. OK, he might not have lived with you, but you've been there for him in every way possible. He knows it and so do you.'

Fliss took a breath as she nodded. It was true, after being released from prison she hadn't missed a single parents' evening, football game, pantomime, musical event – she'd even been there for high days and holidays thanks to Neil and Estelle allowing it. She wondered if she could have been so generous in Estelle shoes, and doubted it.

Andee said, 'Tell me, are you still taking something to help you sleep?'

Fliss felt heat spread through her. She should have seen this coming, and already knew where it was going, which wasn't anywhere she wanted to be. 'Now and again,' she admitted, although it was every night and sometimes more than one a night. 'I have to,' she explained, 'I'd go mad otherwise. All the worry about the café, the guilt over not being a proper parent, losing so many people we care about . . .'

'It's OK,' Andee soothed. 'I'm not judging you. A lot of people need that sort of help right now, but please tell me it's coming from the doctor.'

'It is,' Fliss lied. Dr Gorman had refused her last two prescription requests unless she agreed to counselling. She didn't want counselling, she just wanted peace of mind and an end to the back pain and wakeful nights. Diazepam, lorazepam, tramadol, fentanyl, temazepam. She'd tried it all, but at least she wasn't buying it on the streets. She'd found a good and reliable online supplier who didn't even charge very much.

'I don't want Zac to know how hard I find it to sleep,' she said, 'so if I take a pill it's not an issue for either of us.' How was this sounding to Andee? It seemed to make sense to her, and why not when it was true? 'I promise you, I have it under control,' she said. 'The doctor wouldn't let me have them if he was worried, would he?' Why had she added that? Lying to Andee was even worse than lying to herself.

'Perhaps you should talk to the doctor again and get some proper direction on dosage,' Andee suggested.

'Of course,' Fliss agreed. 'Good idea.'

Andee got to her feet – and once again Fliss found herself thinking of how comfortingly safe and less afraid of things she felt when Andee was around, as though all her problems were solvable and even her pain might be persuaded to go away. It was extraordinary for someone to have such a profound and consoling effect on someone else without actually doing very much.

As they reached the door, Andee made a gentle fist and touched it to Fliss's elbow. 'I'll get my accountant to call you tomorrow,' she promised, 'and I understand that you don't want to talk about Neil, but I'm here if you need to, OK?'

As Fliss watched her go, heading towards her car on the other side of the Promenade, she found herself starting to drift, thinking of nothing at all, simply staring out into the street, no longer connecting with what had been said, only vaguely aware that the last few minutes had even happened. It would come back to her, it always did, perhaps not right now but later. Thoughts, reminders, memories were like that, weren't they? They materialized and faded, tangled and tricked in a way that didn't always conform to time, logic or reason; they just came and went with their own baffling agenda and unsettling ways of making regrets bigger instead of smaller, and longings greater than reality could deliver.

She was glad Andee understood about Neil. She wasn't sure why, but somehow it made it easier to bear.

Later, she was sitting around a firepit with Neil, Estie and Prim, watching Zac on the keyboard as he accompanied Chloe. She was singing 'Morning Has Broken' with all the sweetness her lovely young voice could muster. She had a true gift and was such a beautiful little girl in looks and spirit; it was no wonder Neil adored her. What father wouldn't? Fliss loved her too, not quite as if she were her own, but she'd known her since birth and over the years had shared in the pride and joy she brought to her parents. Always careful to keep at arm's length, of course; Chloe didn't need two mothers and nor did Estelle need to feel they were in any kind of competition.

As she listened to the words of the song and watched the others in the firelight, she felt a swell of love for Neil that was far bigger than it ought to be; much deeper and more consuming than ever. It could so easily become all that the world and her life was about, but thankfully she usually had enough self-control to make sure it didn't. She wasn't looking at him, but could feel his eyes on her, and when she glanced up he seemed to be asking how she was, saying sorry for not coming to see her lately, but that sometimes it was too hard for him too.

Of course, he might not be thinking about her at all, was probably caught up in his own concerns – being married to Estelle didn't come without challenges. It wasn't possible to tell whether or not he actually loved Estie. He never spoke ill of her, nor had Fliss ever detected any animosity towards her, and she knew it was despicable of her to wish that he would. She couldn't help it though; sometimes it was as if Estelle had everything that should have been hers – apart from Chloe, of course. But it wasn't true, obviously, for she really wouldn't want to live in this house, or be a bestselling author who was struggling now; or someone who frequently offended others without actually meaning to. Estie had done it again earlier this evening when Neil had asked about the Corona Girls.

'I've always wondered, why do you call yourselves that?' Estie had laughed. 'You make yourselves sound like a virus, and that's the last thing any of us needs any more of right now.'

An instant later she was apologizing, saying it had come out all wrong and that she was actually terribly impressed by how many friends Fliss had. 'I've never been very good at friendships,' she'd grumbled. 'Apart from with Prim, but that doesn't really count, does it?' And there she went again, hurting someone's feelings, although Prim was clearly used to it by now and had her own way of dealing with it that often made them all laugh.

For some bizarre reason, Fliss felt a sudden urge to cry. She mustn't, of course. God forbid she should draw attention to herself that way. They'd all want to know what had upset her, and the last thing in the world she'd ever be able to admit was how unbearably lonely she felt when she was with them. She had no proper family of her own anymore, and maybe it was time for her to stop pushing her way into this one.

I have to throw away all the meds; they might help with the pain and insomnia, but they're making me so bleak.

She really must stop coming here, make more of an effort to move on.

As soon as the pandemic was over – dear God let that be soon – Zac would either go travelling or straight to uni, and there would be no reason for her to see his father anymore. They could finally go their separate ways, and maybe, with any luck, by some miracle in fact, she wouldn't only save the café, but she'd meet someone else to love.

CHAPTER TWENTY

JEANNIE

November 2020
Two months before Jeannie's disappearance

It was cold around the bay, but bright and sunny as Jeannie parked her Lexus opposite the Seafront Café and turned off the engine. Beside her Mallory was busy replying to an email from Maurice who was overseeing her internship, so as Jeannie waited she surveyed the short, socially distanced queue that snaked from the café's main entrance around to the Promenade. There would be no opportunity to have a quiet word with Fliss this morning, she realized, not that she'd expected there to be, especially with Mallory there and other staff around. But it didn't matter; she could always come back another time, if necessary.

It was important for Fliss to know that the little attraction she and Guy were sharing would never go any further.

'OK, done,' Mallory declared, putting away her phone. 'I have my orders for the day, so let's get some coffee.'

Smiling, Jeannie slotted her phone into a side pocket of her voluminous bag and got out of the car. 'I really should have brought you here before today,' she said as they linked arms to cross the road. 'I guess we're always so busy. I've told you, I'm sure, that the owner is Zac's mother?'

'Zac did,' Mallory replied, and added a romantic sigh. 'He is totally drop-dead, isn't he? And he so makes me laugh. He was teaching me how to imitate bird calls yesterday, it was hilarious.'

Having noticed them larking about in the garden, Jeannie said, 'You're seeing quite a bit of him now you've joined the surf parties as well. Are you going again this weekend?'

'I think so, and it might be just the two of us because his dad's got other things on, and so has Guy, apparently. Do you think Guy enjoyed his birthday dinner last night?'

'Are you kidding?' Jeannie cried. 'It was probably the best meal he's had since we were last at a Michelin-starred restaurant. You're spoiling us with your gourmet skills. We might have to keep you.'

Laughing delightedly, Mallory checked her phone as another message arrived. She was still reading it as they joined the queue. 'Maurice again,' she explained, 'with more instructions, and one of them is to make sure I don't distract you from the meetings you have lined up for the afternoon.'

'He's so bossy,' Jeannie remarked, watching Fliss through the window as she served an old couple with a dog in a buggy. She was always so friendly with people, seemed to know the right things to say and how to laugh even if something wasn't funny. And apparently she had treats for pets.

Peering through the window too, Mallory said, 'It looks as though they've made a start on their Christmas decorations already.'

'Pretty, aren't they?' Jeannie commented.

'Is that Fliss?'

'You mean your future mother-in-law?' Jeannie whispered.

Mallory's eyes were shining as she drew back to look at her aunt. 'You're so bad,' she scolded.

Jeannie laughed and stepped up to the café's door as the customer in front of them went in. 'Everyone seems to be getting a tree early this year,' she said, 'so maybe we should too. It would be good to have one before you go back.'

'Oh, don't remind me,' Mallory groaned. 'I wish I could stay with you forever, or at least for Christmas. I would, if I hadn't already promised Mum I'd spend it with her.'

'And you can't let her down.'

'You're right, I definitely can't. Nor Dad. I usually spend Boxing Day with him, and he's already talking about what we're going to do this year.'

Not enjoying the thought of Mallory spending any time at all with her father, Jeannie said, 'Have you made up your mind about when you're going back yet?'

'I haven't even looked at flights, but I probably should. I told Dad I was only going to be away for a month . . . OK, I shouldn't have lied about it, but you know what he's like. He can be so *stifling* at times, and every time I talk to him he goes on about what happened when Granny and Grandpa died—'

'We all still find it hard,' Jeannie interrupted, guessing what Mallory's next words would be and not wanting to hear them. It was enough to know that Paul still blamed her, and in truth she preferred her parents' death never to be mentioned. It almost never was between her and

181

Guy, and she'd hoped, since Mallory hadn't brought it up before, that she'd understood that it was best not to. However, she didn't want to make the dear girl feel bad for something that wasn't her fault, so she put a hand on her beautiful creamy cheek and said, 'I think the chap in front of us is about to leave, so masks on.'

Moments later they were inside the door and Jeannie was saying, 'We're bubbled, so I hope it's all right for us to come in together.'

'Of course,' Fliss said, beckoning them to the counter. 'And I'm guessing you're Mallory,' she smiled from behind her transparent visor.

She really is lovely, Jeannie noted.

Mallory said, 'That's me.'

'Yes, I've been hearing all about you from Zac. He's even admitted that you might be a better surfer than he is.'

'Only *might*?' Mallory objected.

Fliss laughed. 'He's also quite envious that you're able to travel at this time when he's had to postpone his gap year.'

As Mallory replied, Jeannie was still watching Fliss thinking: *She looks tired, but even the dark circles under her eyes don't take away from the radiance of that smile.*

Joining in the conversation, she said with a playful roll of her eyes, 'Lucky Kiwis having the right prime minister.'

'Isn't that the truth?' Fliss groaned. 'But she's a woman, so of course she's getting it right.'

As they laughed, Fliss winced at the sound of something smashing in the kitchen and said, comically, 'So what can I get you, ladies?'

'Cappuccino for me,' Mallory replied.

'And a flat white for me,' Jeannie added.

Turning to prepare the order, Fliss said chattily, 'So how did the birthday celebrations go last night?'

'Very well,' Jeannie assured her. 'We have a gourmet chef in my niece, and please tell whoever made the cake that it was exceptional.' She gave a playful grimace. 'I should have thought about one sooner, of course. Poor man, neglected by his wife. Lucky you had one here or he'd have had to go without.'

'We had twelve candles though,' Mallory put in, 'you know the type that you can't blow out? You should have seen him until he caught on to what was happening. We couldn't stop laughing.'

Eyes shining, Fliss put a flat white on the counter and sealed it with a lid. How different and uncomplicated and enjoyable their evening sounded, in comparison to the awful emotional turmoil she'd experienced at Neil and Estie's. 'Which part of New Zealand are you from?' she asked Mallory.

'Oh, the Bay of Islands. My mum has a small hotel near Kerikeri, and my dad runs a sailing school near Opua. They're not together anymore – but, believe me, that's a good thing. I'm at uni in Auckland, transferring to Melbourne next year. Have you ever been Down Under?'

Fliss's back was turned for a moment as she said, 'Actually, it's where Neil and I went for our honeymoon. Sydney, Melbourne, Auckland, Wellington and Christchurch. It was wonderful, we even talked about moving there for a while, but you know dreams, they always seem possible at the time, but then life catches up with you.'

Wondering, not for the first time, exactly what had

happened to change the dreams and break up the marriage, Jeannie said, 'Let's hope we can all get to visit again before we go nuts on this highly infected little island of ours.'

With a roll of her eyes, Fliss said, 'I'll second that, but we're getting good news about a vaccine, aren't we?' and, putting a cappuccino on the counter, she picked up a chocolate shaker.

'Lashings,' Mallory instructed. 'Oh, and what was it Neil told us we should order to eat?' she asked Jeannie.

'The minced pie turnovers,' Jeannie reminded her. 'He said you made them yourself?' she asked Fliss.

'I'm afraid I did,' Fliss confessed. 'Our usual baker is a bit behind at the moment, so I've been doing my best, and I'm pretty sure it's only Neil who's rated my little efforts so far. Probably because he felt he had to.'

'Well, we're definitely going to give them a try,' Mallory informed her, 'and we should take one for Guy?'

'Oh, he isn't in Bristol today?' Fliss asked, sealing the cappuccino.

'His meeting got cancelled,' Jeannie replied, interested that Fliss knew about his schedule, 'so we've just left him collecting kindling in the woods with Neil.'

With another playful roll of her eyes, Fliss said, 'It's a nice life for some.'

Mischievously, Jeannie added, 'I can't help wondering if Neil's reciting Longfellow or Frost to my husband the way he does to me when we walk in the woods. He has an amazing repertoire, doesn't he? Very impressive.'

A small amount of light seemed to drain from Fliss's smile as she said, 'Yes, he does. It used to be a bit of a party trick of his, back in the day.'

'I wonder what Zac's is?' Mallory mused, and quickly

added, 'Please forget I said that. I don't really want to know, unless it's poetry, of course. That would be cool.'

'Well, I'm afraid it's not that,' Fliss told her wryly. 'But he's a good musician. He can sing, play piano and guitar, quite unlike his father, who is completely tone deaf, but you didn't hear that from me.'

Laughing, Jeannie paid for their coffees and pies while Mallory loaded up ready to leave.

'It's been lovely meeting you,' Mallory said warmly to Fliss.

'And lovely meeting you,' Fliss replied. To Jeannie she added, 'Thanks for coming in. It's always good to see you. Please say hello to Guy from me, and I hope he enjoys the turnovers.'

As they exited through the back door onto the service road, Jeannie couldn't help wondering just how pointed Fliss's parting remark had been. It hadn't seemed to have a particular edge to it, Fliss didn't actually strike her as a double-speak sort of person, so maybe she, Jeannie, shouldn't judge everyone else's behaviour by her own. She'd pass the message on, of course, and was already imagining Guy's response. He'd treat her to one of his knowing stares, she was sure of it, which she'd meet with a similar one of her own. It made her want to laugh simply to think of it.

'Do you know that woman over there?' Mallory asked as they crossed back over the Promenade towards the car. 'She seems to be looking this way.'

Turning around, Jeannie spotted a lone figure about fifty metres away at the top of some steps leading down to the beach. Frowning, she said, 'I'm not sure, but I think it's . . . Yes, it looks like Primrose Barnes.'

'Who?'

'She's Estelle Fields's PA.'

'Oh.' Mallory knew all about the one-book wonder. 'Are you going to go over?' she asked.

'No. I'm afraid I upset her a few years ago when I promoted someone over her head.'

Sighing sympathetically, Mallory said, 'It must be hard making decisions that you know someone isn't going to like.'

With a certain amount of dryness, Jeannie said, 'Unfortunately I'm having to do it all the time, but luckily some take it better than others. The worst are always the authors, but these days my wonderful editorial team is far more hands-on with them than I am, so the grisly business is all theirs. Now, the sun's come out so shall we stroll on the beach over to the marina to check on the apartment?'

Clearly happy to do so, Mallory glanced back at Primrose Barnes, who was crossing over to the café now, and asked, 'So who does the apartment belong to?'

'A good friend of ours, Val Clayburne. She lives in London, and comes here for weekends and summer breaks. She hasn't been able to make it since August, so Guy and I pop in to check on the place now and again.'

Following her aunt down a ramp onto the damp, shingly sand where other walkers, dogs and even a couple of horse-riders were taking advantage of their permitted hour of outdoor exercise, Mallory let her head fall back for a moment to feel the late autumnal sun on her face.

'I have to tell you,' Jeannie said, inhaling the tangy scent of salt air mixed with horse dung and a passing jogger's potent perfume, 'that during the month you've been here you've made quite an impression on my publishing team with your readiness to learn and willing-ness to help in any way you can – and that includes me. You've been invaluable at times, although I know we haven't worked together as often as I'd have liked. It's mostly the confidential nature of what I do that prevents it, but it's more interesting for you to work with the editors whenever you can.'

'I absolutely love it,' Mallory enthused. 'The whole process fascinates me, from first read right through to collating the page proofs.'

With a tender smile, Jeannie said, 'I've put some time aside this weekend to go through Dylan Frank's edit of the Vienna book. Why don't you read it first and let me know your thoughts? I'm particularly keen to find out if the city is coming alive for you, and what sort of sense you have of Empress Elisabeth.' With a playful laugh, she said, 'If he's got it right, we should feel as though we're time-travellers, and wouldn't that be a wonderful way to escape this infernal lockdown?'

Later in the day, taking a few minutes between meetings, Jeannie went to stand in the doorway of Guy's study, watching him quietly as he spoke to someone on the phone. He was clearly explaining an upcoming procedure, and Jeannie knew better than to interrupt a call to a patient, so she simply kept her gaze on him and listened until eventually he rang off.

After finishing the notes he was making, he looked up. 'Have you come to apologize?' he asked mildly.

She smiled. They'd argued last night, after Mallory had gone to bed, and this was the first chance they'd had to

speak since. 'I have,' she admitted. It hadn't been a particularly serious falling out, and she knew it was her own
tetchiness that had caused him to say, 'I'm sorry this new
lockdown has you out of sorts, but try to remember, if
you can, that a lot of people are truly suffering out there,
not only from the disease, but from losing their jobs—'

'Don't patronize me,' she'd cut in angrily. 'I'm fully
aware of what's going on in the world. What I don't
always know is what's going on in yours.'

'Then I'll email you my diary each morning. Will that
keep you happy? Maybe having it to hand will feed your
possessive nature adequately,' and with that he'd gone
into the bathroom and closed the door behind him.

They might have made up as soon as he'd got into bed
had Jeannie not already been asleep by then.

'So,' he said now, 'will you be requiring regular updates
of my diary?'

'To satisfy my possessive nature?' With a sigh she went
to sink into his deeply cushioned sofa. 'No, I don't need
to see your schedule, unless you want me to have it.'

He shrugged. 'It's your choice.'

'You still seem cross,' she told him.

He shook his head in denial. 'Not at all, just a lot on
my mind and not a terribly clear head. I'm afraid we'd
both had too much to drink, and it was a shame to end
a lovely evening on a bad note.'

'It was,' she agreed and, deciding they'd discussed this
enough for now, she changed the subject. 'Did you happen
to run into Estelle Fields when you were in the woods
earlier with Neil?' she asked.

He looked at her sharply. 'No. Why? Was she there?'

'I spotted her car in the layby when Mallory and I came

back from the café. She drives one of those Mazda sports cars, doesn't she? A blue one. I thought she might be spying on Neil, if she'd heard that he sometimes walks in the woods with me.'

He appeared amused by that. 'Then it would have been quite a disappointment for her to find him with me, wouldn't it? She could have just stopped to take a call. People do in that layby.'

She waved a dismissive hand. What did she care about Estelle Fields and her little espionage missions? If she came across something she didn't like, it would be her own fault. 'Did you try the turnovers we brought back from the Seafront?' she asked. 'Fliss wanted me to say hi, by the way.'

'That's nice of her. I hope you told her we enjoyed the cake last night.'

'I did.'

'And Neil was right about the turnovers, they were delicious. Have you tried one?'

'Mallory and I shared one for lunch.' After a beat she added, 'I can see why you're attracted to Fliss. She's definitely got something about her.'

His eyebrows rose and she smiled as he treated her to the look she'd been expecting. Then he surprised her by saying, 'Please don't feel you have to have a word with her.'

She gave a laugh and said, 'Has Neil ever told you why they broke up?'

'No, but I think that's the kind of conversation he's more likely to have with you than with me.'

Conceding the point, she checked the time on her phone and said, 'I need to go and join a budget meeting. Shall we meet upstairs in an hour?'

His eyes darkened as he read the suggestion and, getting up from his chair, he came to pull her to her feet. Slipping a hand between her legs, he murmured, 'If you're sure it's me you want.'

Eyes half closed as pleasure surged gently through her, she said, 'It's always you, my darling, you know that.'

'Do I?'

'If you don't, then you should,' and after a lingering kiss she left him clearly wanting more; how she loved him to feel that way.

CHAPTER TWENTY-ONE

CARA

Thursday 21 January 2021
Fifteen days since Jeannie's disappearance

It might be proper brass-monkey weather out here in the town, and the sky as grey as an old gravestone, but after spending the entire day yesterday in the incident room, Cara was glad to be off the phone and out in the fresh air. Better still was this unexpected visit to the marina at the far end of the Promenade. The entire complex might be dead now, in the middle of January and during a pandemic, but in summer and better times it was always humming with life. Not her sort of life, it had to be said, since there was no way she could ever have afforded a boat, or one of the luxury apartments, or to eat in one of the swanky restaurants or cafés. With its gated entrance, smart flower beds and upmarket everything, it was – according to her estate-agent friend – Britain's answer to the French Riviera. Cara had never been to France, but even she knew that this had to be over-egging it. However, it wouldn't be all that surprising if it became stayca-tion-central now Brexit had happened and the virus had put paid to a lot of foreign travel. It was what all the investors were banking on, and though she'd never make anything from it herself, it still made her feel sad to see everything all closed up the way it was now. It was a bit end-of-the-worldish, she thought, and felt quite glad when Colin Cutler, a security guard and old school friend who was on duty in the reception of the biggest apartment block, offered to accompany her to the third-floor flat she'd come to check out.

Apparently Guy and Andee had already scoped the place back when they'd started the search, but Andee had thought it might be a good idea for Cara to visit it again, just in case Jeannie had been there since.

'I didn't know you were with the police now,' Colin Cutler remarked as he checked her ID without touching it. 'Can I ask what you're working on?'

Cara shrugged. 'Nothing major,' she said, thinking it might be best to avoid any detail at this stage. 'I just need to have a look round this apartment, that's all, to see if anyone's there.'

'Do you want me to ring up first?'

'Yes, good idea.'

A few minutes later, having received no reply from the flat, Colin took the lift first, in order to maintain social distancing. He was waiting in the lobby of the third floor when Cara stepped out to follow him along a subtly lit marble hallway with cascades of water running down one wall into pebbly troughs filled with plants. She experienced a clench of unease as they approached the door to Flat 3C. No one was really expecting Jeannie to be here, not even Guy, who was in London at the moment; he'd asked Andee to go to Howarth Hall last night to get the apartment's key. This was just one of those box-ticking exercises, so there was nothing to be worried about.

When they reached the door, Cara knocked and listened out for anyone inside.

'Let me,' Colin said after a minute or two, and bunching a meaty fist he gave the solid wood a tidy rap.

Still no response.

Cara took out the key, inserted it in the lock and turned. Before pushing the door open she said, 'Is there likely to be an alarm?' Why hadn't she thought about that before?

'Dunno,' Colin replied. 'I guess there's only one way to find out.'

Bracing herself for a screeching, she pushed hard on the heavy door and heard only the quiet swish of it brushing over carpet.

They waited, counted to ten, and – once satisfied they hadn't triggered some sort of armed response – Cara shouted,

'Hello? Is anyone here?'

Silence.

Reminding herself that absolutely no one had said Jeannie was suicidal, so there wasn't too big a chance of a dead body, or a mutilated one she hoped, she went a little further, listening for any sounds that might suggest someone was behind one of the closed doors.

There was nothing, so she moved on, calling out again just in case she hadn't been heard the first time, and led the way into a large room where the curtains were closed. It turned out to be a kitchen-cum-living room with three cushy sofas around a coffee table, a giant TV and sliding patio doors out onto a balcony.

Definitely no one there, although in the kitchen she found two wine glasses on the draining board. Both were perfectly dry, so they could have been there for hours, days or months.

After taking a few shots with her phone, she returned to the hall, where Colin was standing on the threshold of a bedroom, staring in as if he didn't want to go any further.

Dread buzzed in her head. *Please God, don't let there be blood.* She really couldn't stand blood. 'What is it?' she asked.

He stepped into the room and, after a beat, she gingerly followed.

'Do you reckon someone's slept in it?' he said.

Taking a closer look at the rumpled duvet, not quite covering the pillows, she said, 'They might have.' There was a small, half-empty bottle of Evian on one of the nightstands, and a group photograph of half-a-dozen middle-agers in yachting gear on a chest of drawers.

Still no way of telling when anyone had last been here – could have been last night or last year.

She took more shots and went to inspect the bathroom. The cabinets were full of shampoos, soaps, body lotions and various cosmetics, and the washbasin was dry. So were the bath and shower, and the towels stuffed onto a rail had clearly been used at some point, but heaven only knew when. The dust suggested a while ago.

After photographing this too, she returned to the hall, and heard Colin opening and closing cupboard doors in another room. When she joined him he was checking under a narrow, neatly made bed, as if someone might be hiding there.

No one was.

'I guess it's safe to say that whoever you're looking for isn't here,' he stated as they let themselves out into the hall and locked up again.

'Do people sign in and out of the building?' she asked.

He shook his head. 'No, but there's CCTV in the lobby for when visitors come and go. The residents mostly use the side door that opens direct onto the parking area for this block.'

'Any chance I can take a look at the CCTV?'

'Sure. It's a bit squashed in there though, so it won't be easy to distance.'

He was right about the size of the room, it wasn't much bigger than a cupboard, so she held back in the open door as he whizzed through the past two weeks of recordings, stopping only when someone came or went.

No sign of Jeannie, or anyone who looked like her; however, Guy had come in a few times, presumably to check on the apartment and maybe to let Andee in the side door, given she wasn't on any of this footage.

'Is there CCTV out there in the car park?' she asked.

He shook his head. 'They've been talking about putting it in, but no one's got round to it yet.'

Deciding she was done for now, she said, 'Thanks for helping me with this. I'll be in touch if there's anything else.'

Once clear of the marina, she sent her photos to Andee with the message: *Looks like someone's been in the flat, but not possible to tell who or when. Could just have been Guy when he went in to check the place. Did you and he have a drink while you were there? See photo of two glasses.*

A few minutes later, as she turned from the Promenade towards the station, Andee rang.

'No, we didn't have a drink,' she said, 'and I didn't notice the glasses when we went in, which isn't necessarily to say they weren't there, although I'm sure I'd have spotted them if they were.'

Checking the notes she'd made from the CCTV footage, Cara said, 'Guy Symonds has been into the building three times since Jeannie disappeared. The first was on January the ninth, the second on January the fourteenth—'

'That's when I was with him.'

'And the third was just a couple of days ago, on January the nineteenth.'

'That's the day after we first spoke to you. He told me he might go again, just in case she'd turned up there, but obviously she hadn't. The owner's name is Valerie Clayburne. It would be a good idea to get in touch with her to find out exactly when she was last there. Maybe she met Guy there and the glasses are theirs? I'll speak to him and text you with her number.'

'OK, I'll call her as soon as I get back.'

'Also ask if she's let anyone use the place recently, besides Jeannie and Guy keeping an eye on it. Did you see anyone at all while you were over that way?'

'No, it's pretty much a ghost town. Shame when you think of all those people out there losing their homes, and there are four blocks of apartments mostly standing empty. The only people I saw was a couple walking a dog along by the boats and the security guard. He came in with me.'

'Did you ask if he'd seen Jeannie coming or going?'

Cara felt herself turn a little hot. 'I wasn't sure if I was supposed to say exactly why I was there,' she replied, realizing now how dim that was, 'but I'll go back right away and show him her picture.' What an idiot: how could she have thought it was the wrong thing to do when the local paper was running the story on their website. 'Sorry.'

'There's nothing to be sorry for. Just let me know if he has seen her. I'm taking food parcels to the residential caravan parks over at Paradise Cove today, but my phone will be on.'

Retracing her steps to the marina, Cara found Colin back at his desk, showed him the picture of Jeannie, and a few minutes later she was talking to Andee again.

'He said he knows who she is and he has seen her, but he's pretty sure not in the last couple of weeks.' She still hadn't cheered up after her stupid mistake, but at least it had been rectified now, and luckily Andee didn't seem especially worked up about it.

'Shame,' Andee sighed. 'It would be good if at least one person had seen or spoken to her, or had a single idea about where she might be. I'm afraid it's looking more and more likely that she has gone off the road somewhere and still hasn't been found.'

'I know what you mean,' Cara responded, thinking of how awful that would be. She hesitated for a moment, then decided just to go for it. 'Have you ever seen the film, *The Mysterious Case of Agatha Christie*? I watched it with my mum over Christmas. Apparently she went missing for eleven days – Agatha Christie, I mean, not my mum – and no one knows, even now, where she was.'

Instead of sounding surprised or even sceptical about the story, Andee said, 'I have a sister who disappeared at the age of fourteen. We didn't see her again for thirty years.'

Cara almost gasped. *Thirty years?* That was longer than

her entire lifetime. She couldn't imagine how a family lived through something like that, and yet somehow Andee's apparently had.

'By then,' Andee continued, 'we'd long assumed she was dead, but it turned out she wasn't.'

Cara hardly knew what to say. *Andee's sister had actually turned up alive after all that time.* 'Where is she now?' she dared to asked.

'She lives in Sweden. We're in touch regularly. Obviously we haven't been able to see her for a while, but thankfully she's very definitely a part of our family again.' She was quiet for a moment, then said: 'People go missing for all sorts of reasons, and when we don't find them right away, we make all sorts of assumptions about why they went and where they might be. We also do the same about those closest to them, wondering where to apportion blame, if someone's hiding something from us . . . My family didn't know anything at all about where my sister could be, but it didn't stop the police, or the press – or even our friends and neighbours – from doubting us; some even turned against us. It taught me a long time ago that in these situations we can as easily be right in our thinking as we can be very, very wrong, and jumping to conclusions helps no one. I've no idea right now where we are with Jeannie, but we have to keep in mind, putting accidents aside, that she's someone who'd find it easier than most to disappear if she wants to.'

Cara didn't have anything to say to that, couldn't actually imagine why Jeannie would want to go, although the more she found out about her, the less she seemed to understand her.

'Who are you talking to next?' Andee asked.

Glad to be back on this more predictable ground, Cara said, 'Primrose Barnes. She finally got back to me.'

'That's good. I'll be interested to hear what she has to say about Jeannie, and about Estelle. Is she coming into the station?'

'No, she didn't want to, so we've arranged a video-chat at half past three,' and though she was still feeling slightly dazed by the thought of Andee's sister disappearing for all those years, and the fact that Jeannie really might not want to be found, she began mentally preparing herself for her chat with Primrose Barnes.

CHAPTER TWENTY-TWO

ESTELLE

Early December 2020
Four weeks before Jeannie's disappearance

Estelle hurried into the bedroom, already tugging a sweater dress up over her head to reveal a half-cup bra, matching thong and lacy-top hold-ups. She came to a sudden stop as she realized Neil was coming out of the dressing room.

'Gosh, what are you doing here?' she gasped as he looked up in equal surprise. 'It's the middle of the day. And why are you dressed like that?'

He continued knotting his tie as he said, 'It's Sam Long's funeral today. I don't want to miss it and I thought I should dress appropriately.'

Remembering that one of his oldest friends had recently succumbed to the virus, she immediately felt sad for him and searched for the right thing to say, but what was there when it was all so senseless? 'Can you go?' she asked. 'I thought it was only family these days.'

'It is, but I'm going to drive to the crematorium to pay my respects from a distance.'

Covering herself in a rose silk wrap, she went to put her arms around him. 'You were always a good friend to him,' she murmured. It didn't seem right to kiss him when he was about to go to a funeral, and when she'd just come from seeing Guy. Not that anything had happened between them, it never did; it just made her feel good to wear nice lingerie for the times they met. She wasn't even sure she wanted anything to happen. Well, yes she did, it would be the sweetest revenge on Jeannie to have an affair with her beloved husband. Who could say, he might even end up leaving her to be with Estelle.

What a victory that would be.

Except where would that leave Neil?

With Fliss, of course, because that was where he'd always wanted to be.

Before Neil could move away from their embrace, she let him go first saying, 'I'd better rush or I'll be late for Chloe. Will you come straight back from the crematorium? Don't forget Fliss and Zac are joining us for dinner tonight.' She didn't add *again*; it would seem unfriendly.

'I hadn't forgotten,' he assured her. 'What time are we expecting them?'

'Seven. Fliss couldn't make it any earlier. She's always so busy with the café and all her good deeds. Frankly, I'm surprised she can manage to fit us in.'

He said darkly, 'I hope you're not going to take any snipes at her later. I think she's finding things more difficult than she's admitting to . . .'

'Don't worry, I'll be my usual sparkly self, the way I always am when we're playing happy families.'

Coming to stand in the doorway of her dressing room, he watched her discarding her fancy lingerie and slip into a far less glamorous set. 'I could ask,' he said, 'where you've been this afternoon, but probably best that I don't?'

Feigning astonishment, she said, 'You can ask if you like, but the answer isn't very interesting.'

Apparently taking her word for it, he turned back into the bedroom, picked up his wallet and left.

She stood where she was, staring at the door, not sure whether to feel angry or abandoned or relieved that he hadn't pressed her for an answer. Of course she wouldn't have told him she'd been with Guy, she'd have made up some other excuse, for she didn't even want to think about how confused and horribly judgemental he'd be if he knew she was seeing Jeannie's husband. But he hadn't asked, probably because he just didn't care.

Today she and Guy had simply sat together in his car over near Lynmouth, listening to music and holding hands as she'd learned to breathe deeply and softly through the worst of her anxieties. It was always so calming to be with him; he seemed to understand better than anyone how hard she was finding it to have received no reply from her mother.

'It'll come,' he'd soothed. 'It still hasn't been very long and she needs time to process all that it's going to mean for her to reunite with you.' He made it sound so rational, so easy to cope with, and certain of a positive outcome that when she was with him it was what she believed.

In the end he'd raised their joined hands and, as he'd settled them into her lap to let hers go he'd said, 'I think you'll be fine now, and it was good to see you, but please try not to ring again when I'm at home. I don't want Jeannie to misunderstand anything, and in this instance I'm sure she would.'

As she got out of the car, Estelle swallowed the hurt. She'd felt so much loneliness and yearning in her heart that it had been hard to keep it in.

'Hey,' he said softly.

She turned around.

'That doesn't mean I don't want to see you again,' and she'd felt the energizing lift of his smile course through her like an elixir.

It would all come good, she knew it would, she just had to be patient and keep believing.

An hour later, in jeans and a sweatshirt, she was standing next to her Mazda outside the school, smiling as Chloe came out of the gates. She went up on tiptoe to plant a quick kiss on her cheek.

'How was your day?' Estelle asked as they got into the car.

'Yeah, cool. Still loads of rubbishy rules and stuff, but hey! Can we go to the café for hot chocolate?'

Estelle was checking her emails, as she did every few minutes, so barely registered Chloe's words.

Oh God, oh God, oh God.

'What is it?' Chloe asked, when they didn't drive away.

Estelle didn't know what to say. She couldn't simply blurt it out – I've just had a message from your grandmother, the one who gave me away as a baby – when she hadn't actually read it yet. And she couldn't look at it now with Chloe right there in case it was bad. She needed to be alone when she opened it, or maybe with Prim. She'd prefer it to be Guy but she couldn't call him at home again, not even for this.

'Yes, let's go to the café,' she mumbled, putting her phone away.

'Yay! And shall we take Fliss some flowers again? Dad says she's been a bit stressed lately and the last ones really cheered her up.'

'Yes, let's do that,' Estelle agreed, hoping that if she did something nice for someone else, the Universe would find its way to rewarding her.

My dear Estelle,
Such a pretty name they gave you.

As you can probably imagine, it was a surprise to hear from you and I'm sorry it's taken me a while to reply. Your email gave me a lot to think about, which might sound as though I haven't thought about you over the years. Naturally, I have, and often. It was good to hear of your success as a writer. I'm afraid I haven't read your book, but of course I shall do so now. How clever you are.

I understand how important it is to you for us to meet, and it's important to me too. These wretched restrictions on travel and keeping at a distance make things difficult, but I fear waiting any longer will not be good for either of us. So, now that the second lockdown is over, allowing us a little more freedom in the run-up to Christmas, at least for the moment, shall we bend the rules that remain in place and settle on a time and location that will work for us both? I have put some suggestions below, but I am open to others you might have. Let us hope that the weather will be on our side, as naturally it will have to be outdoors.

I shall look forward to seeing you.
With affection,
Serena Fellowes

*   *   *

By now Estelle had read the email at least fifty times, trying to take as much hope from it as she could, and for minutes at a time she managed to. But then she'd come crashing back down again, daunted by how formal and reticent the wording seemed. Serena had said she was surprised to get the email, but not that it was a good or lovely surprise. Maybe she was just one of those dignified and undemonstrative types who thought it vulgar to share their feelings with someone they didn't really know. And at the end she'd said she was looking forward to them meeting, had even expressed affection, so that had to be good, didn't it? Prim thought so, but Prim would, for no other reason than she saw the good in everything.

Thank God Guy had rung this morning to find out how she was. She hadn't mentioned her near sleepless night, going over and over the message until she was half out of her mind. Instead, she'd simply read the email out to him and asked, 'Do you think it's cold and dismissive?'

Sounding amused he'd said, 'No. What I think is that she obviously wants to meet and you are over-analysing every word.'

He was right, of course, on both counts, and what really mattered was that Serena did want to get together, was even willing to break – or bend – the travel rules to make it happen.

Now, looking down from her study window to where Prim was pottering about in her little garden next door, putting up even more Christmas lights, while counting the birds for a local project, Estie tried to tell herself that it was going to be all right. She'd meet her mother tomorrow in Wiltshire and, even if they didn't run into each other's arms (because they couldn't), they'd want to. They'd probably cry and laugh and want to know everything about one another all at once, and get things so jumbled up that they'd have to start all over again the next time they met. Or when they FaceTimed, or emailed, or spoke on the phone each day – the way most mothers and daughters did – to talk about nothing and everything. They'd have to decide when was the right time for Serena to meet Chloe and Neil. Estelle still hadn't told them anything about it. Although she wanted to, desperately, she was just too afraid that it would all go wrong and she'd end up humiliated and heartbroken, and she didn't want them to see that.

What was she going to do if it did go wrong? If her mother said she was sorry, but she never wanted them to be in contact again?

She'd stop caring, that was what she'd do. She'd cut everything about the woman out of her life and write her into a psychological thriller that ended in her terrible death. The same as she had with her adoptive parents.

CHAPTER TWENTY-THREE

CARA

Thursday 21 January 2021
Fifteen days since Jeannie's disappearance

As soon as she'd returned to the station, Cara had called Valerie Clayburne, owner of the third-floor flat, only to be told that Ms Clayburne hadn't visited Kesterly since last August. Nor had anyone else, to the best of her knowledge, apart from Jeannie and Guy. She couldn't remember exactly how she'd left the place, but was ready to accept that she might well not have made the bed or put glasses away, and she wouldn't have expected her friends to tidy up after her.

Next on Cara's list was Primrose Barnes, who connected right on time at three thirty from what looked like her kitchen. She had a nice face, Cara thought, round and friendly, and her eyes seemed abnormally large behind their wire-framed lenses.

'Thanks for agreeing to talk to me, Ms Barnes,' she began, making sure the record light was on.

'Call me, Prim, please, everyone does. And I'm sorry I didn't get back to you sooner. Life's been a bit hectic lately, but I'm happy to help in any way I can.'

Wondering what made life hectic during a lockdown, Cara said, 'You told me in your email that you don't ever see Jeannie Symonds these days, but you worked for her up until about five years ago, is that right?'

'Yes, she was my boss at Athene.'

'And you left because?'

Prim's open and friendly face seemed to close down a bit. 'Jeannie promoted an outsider to a position I thought should have been mine.'

Cara grimaced. 'I bet that stung.'

'It wasn't the best experience I've ever had.'

'Were you angry? Feeling like you wanted to get your own back in some way?' *Not very subtle, but she hadn't learned the fine art of that yet.*

'Actually, I was more hurt than angry, but I had a good job to go on to, with Estelle Fields, so I put it behind me.'

'Have you seen her since she bought the house on Westleigh Heights?'

'Not socially, no. I mean, I sometimes see her in town, or driving to and from the Hall – more often before the lockdowns, obviously – but we don't get together or anything.'

'Was it a problem for you when she moved to the area more permanently last summer?'

Prim frowned. 'No. Why would it be? It makes no difference to me where she is.'

Someone else who really doesn't like Jeannie, no matter how uninterested she's trying to sound. 'You obviously know that Neil Roberts, Estelle Fields's husband, works at Howarth Hall.'

'Of course.'

'Does he ever talk about Jeannie?'

Prim shrugged. 'I'd say no more than any other of his clients.'

'Does he give the impression that he gets along well with her?'

'Neil gets along well with everyone.'

Cara waited for more, but none was forthcoming, so she said, 'What exactly happened between Jeannie and Estelle at the time you and Estelle left Athene?'

With a sigh that suggested exasperation rather than reluctance, Prim said, 'All I can tell you is that Jeannie never liked Estie as a person, only as someone whose book would enhance her own reputation for spotting a new talent. And that's what *A Crow Amongst Blackbirds* did. You wouldn't have seen anything in the mainstream press, but in the trade press it was much more about Jeannie's success than it was about Estie's. Then Estie delivered the next book, Jeannie decided it wasn't going to serve her, so she was happy to be rid of it and its author.'

'Why didn't Jeannie like Estelle?'

Prim shrugged again and seemed a little defensive as she said, 'Estie isn't everyone's cup of tea . . . She sometimes speaks before thinking and it can cause offence when she really doesn't mean to. You have to know her to realize that – underneath it all – she's very sweet and actually quite fragile. So it wasn't hard for Jeannie to crush her, and that's what she did.'

Cara watched Prim's unblinking eyes.

'Coming back from it all has been a long and painful journey for Estie,' Prim continued, 'and, to be honest, I think the worst part of it for her has always been more about losing Jeannie than a contract for a new book.'

Cara's eyes widened. 'Why do you say that?' she prompted.

Taking a breath, Prim said, 'Estie didn't have an easy childhood. She was adopted by parents who didn't show her much love, so she's always lacked a mother figure, someone to feel proud of her, to share in her achievements, big or small, to be there for her when things go wrong . . . I doubt she'd ever admit to this, but I think Jeannie was that person for a while; someone she looked up to, wanted to impress and be close to.'

Understanding now why the rejection had been so hard for Estelle, Cara said, 'Do you think she's ever intended any harm towards Jeannie, as some kind of revenge for being . . . let go?'

Prim shook her head. 'She was very angry with Jeannie when it happened, but it was a long time ago now.'

'Has she mentioned anything about it lately?'

'No, but I can tell you she was deeply hurt about not being invited to any of Jeannie's parties. If you ask her, she might tell you differently, but that would be pride speaking, because I know it would mean the world to her to be included.'

'Do you know if she's ever tried to make contact with Jeannie?'

'She sent a house-warming card about three years ago, but I don't think she's tried again since.'

'Has she mentioned her at all recently, since she disappeared?'

'Only to wonder where she might be. Actually, we're a lot less focused on Jeannie right now than on other issues closer to home.'

Unable to resist it, Cara said, 'Such as?'

Prim shook her head. 'They're to do with Estie's birth mother so not related to this. Can we leave it there now?'

CHAPTER TWENTY-FOUR

ESTELLE

Early December 2020
One month before Jeannie's disappearance

To Estelle's relief, Prim had insisted on driving them to Wiltshire; she wasn't sure she could have done it herself, she was too anxious and excited and distracted by the thousand and one scenarios that kept flashing into her head of how things were going to turn out. Worst of all was that once again, every time she tried to picture her mother, she kept seeing Jeannie Symonds.

Still, at least the weather was good, and receiving an email from Serena first thing, confirming she'd be there and hoping it was still convenient for Estelle, had boosted her no end.

'You see, she's looking forward to it,' Prim had commented when Estelle had shown her the message.

'That's not what she said,' Estelle pointed out.

'You're just afraid to be positive, and I guess no one can blame you for that. It's a big deal, meeting your real mother for the first time . . .'

'OK, OK, don't let's make it any harder than it already is.'

Now, as they left the M4 and began heading towards the medieval village of Lacock, Estelle felt grateful to Prim all over again for the idea she'd had yesterday of sorting out some photographs of Estie as a child, and of Chloe, to give to Serena. She'd even managed to buy a little wallet to put them in. Prim was so thoughtful and kind, and always seemed to know the right thing to do in a way Estelle rarely did.

'Do you think one of her children might be with her?' she asked, fearfully, as they sped along the dual carriageway past Chippenham. Estie saw the sign for the station and fleetingly wondered if Serena might come by train. But no, that didn't make any sense, how would she get from there to the meeting spot?

'I'm sure she'd have told you if she was bringing someone,' Prim replied comfortingly.

'Why? I didn't tell her about you.'

'But I'm not going to meet her, am I? I'll wait in the car, as arranged. She probably wouldn't expect one of her children to do that.'

'If they are there, I think you need to be too. I don't want to be outnumbered.'

Throwing her a look of fond despair, Prim said, 'You know I'm always there for you, but let's see what happens when we arrive.'

Fifteen minutes later they were driving past the quaint old village and its thirteenth-century abbey, across a small bridge and up a meandering hill, until they reached a pub called The Rising Sun where they pulled into the car park. There were only a handful of other vehicles around and no sign of anyone, although what held Estelle's attention was the unexpectedness of the view that opened up before them, all the way down over the countryside below, right across to Bath. It was spectacular, breathtaking even, and enormous.

'She certainly chose a lovely spot,' Prim said as they came to a stop.

'I wonder how she knows it?' Estelle replied, taking heart from it not being somewhere awful. She was still staring at the view, almost afraid to take her eyes from it and look around to check if someone who might be her mother was already here.

'I think that must be her,' Prim said quietly.

Estelle turned to look and felt her heart twist with unease when she saw a smartly dressed woman sitting on a picnic bench about twenty metres away. She appeared to be alone, quietly taking in the view as she waited, hands folded in her lap, a handbag beside her.

Taking in several steadying breaths, Estelle started to get out of the car. 'Wish me luck,' she whispered and, mustering all her courage, she walked towards her mother, tears of hope and dread already filling her eyes. This must be one of the biggest moments of her life, and here it was, happening in a pub car park that seemed to be on top of the world.

'Hello,' she said, as she reached the side of the bench.

The woman looked up and Estelle felt an overwhelming rush of emotion. It was Serena from the photographs, Serena from the dreams she'd created since, and she was nothing like Jeannie Symonds. She was lovely, with thick, expensively highlighted shoulder-length hair held in place by a navy Alice band, clear, gentle features and wide, lustrous eyes, the same colour as Estelle's. She looked to be the kind of mother Estelle had always dreamed of having: refined, elegant and compassionate to her core.

'I'm Estelle,' she said, holding out a hand to shake

214

before remembering they weren't allowed to touch. She pulled back and watched Serena get to her feet, her moss green eyes searching Estelle's face, taking in every contour and feature, every nuance of expression. It was as though she was trying to memorize her, or perhaps she was seeking herself in Estelle's dainty features.

'Hello,' she said. Her voice was softly throaty and a little plummy. 'I was . . .' She swallowed and started again, 'I-I'm sorry, but I was afraid you'd look like him.'

Estelle's throat dried as she realized they were talking about her father, a man she'd hardly allowed herself to think about in the need to know her mother. 'Do I?' she asked, sensing it might not be good if she did.

Serena shook head. 'No, you don't.' Then seeming to collect herself, she said, 'Thank you for coming . . .'

'No, thank you. It must have been a shock when you heard from me.'

Serena smiled and nodded. 'Shall we sit down? I think this bench is about two metres long so we'd be within the rules.'

Estelle tucked herself into one corner and watched as Serena took the other. *This was her mother, her actual mother*, she was telling herself, trying to take in the reality of it, but the shock was disorienting, as though she was just waking from a dream. She remembered someone saying once that families were like pieces of a jigsaw puzzle, they were all different, but equally important, and were only complete when they came together. Serena had always been missing from her family puzzle, as she had from Serena's. Please let today be the beginning of filling the empty spaces, of completing the picture and making everything whole.

As they regarded one another, it finally dawned on Estelle that her mother was as nervous as she was, and she wondered if now would be a good time to show her the photographs to try to break the ice. But then she realized she'd left the album in the car, along with a signed hardback copy of *A Crow Amongst Blackbirds*. 'How was your drive?' she asked, for want of anything else to say.

'Yes, fine,' Serena answered. 'Not much traffic. Yours?'

'The same.' Estelle attempted a smile that didn't quite make it. She felt out of her depth, unable to set things on a right path, or even a wrong one.

She watched as Serena stared at the view, strands of her glossy hair lifting in the breeze, her skin seeming pale with cold. *We have the same nose*, Estelle thought, noticing the slight uptilt of Serena's. Maybe they were similar in other ways, such as how they laughed or cried or frowned when they thought. She'd heard that a parent didn't need to bring up a child to pass on certain characteristics, like the sound of their voices, an oft-repeated gesture, or perhaps a quickness of temper. She couldn't imagine Serena was hot-headed or impulsive the way she was. She couldn't see her doing Estie's funny little jump either; it would seem ludicrous for a woman like her to fling herself randomly into the air.

Estelle resolved there and then not to do it again.

As the silence rolled on, she struggled for a sense of connection, an early awakening of the bond they surely shared, but all she felt was a small, pathetic urge to cry.

Swallowing hard she said, 'It's lucky the weather's good.'

Serena continued to gaze into the distance, and Estelle had no idea whether it was because she couldn't bear to look at her, or because she was trying to control her own emotions.

In the end Serena said, 'I had to see you. I knew it the minute I read your email.' She glanced at Estelle and away again. 'You deserve answers, explanations for why I've never been in touch. For why I gave you up when you were born.' When her eyes returned to Estelle's face, they were sad and watchful, and something else that Estelle couldn't read. 'Have you told your adoptive parents that we're meeting?' she asked.

Estelle shook her head. She really didn't want her adoptive parents to be a part of this. They belonged to a different puzzle, one that they'd barely tried to fit her into. 'Do you know them?' she asked.

'No, we never met. I don't even know their names.' Estelle told her.

'Fields?' she repeated. 'So you're not married? You're wearing a ring.'

Glancing down at her wedding band, Estelle said, 'My husband was married before and his first wife still uses his name, so I decided to hang onto mine.'

Serena nodded as if this made sense, although it was impossible to know what she was really thinking.

Estelle continued to flounder, not knowing what to do or say. This woman seemed unreachable, so shrouded in her own world that Estelle was unable to break through. She thought about her half-brother and -sister and what it must have been like for them over the years, having this woman's love, feeling safe in her arms, and knowing she'd always be there for them. There would have been parties and holidays, magical Christmases and school plays, their mother clapping hard and laughing in the front row. Should Estelle ask about them, or their stepfather, or Serena's work as a solicitor, or at the charity . . . 'I have a daughter,' she said. 'Her name's Chloe. She's almost ten and she's adorable. Very clever. Everyone loves her.'

Serena smiled for the first time, and it was so lovely that Estelle felt her emotions rising as she smiled too.

Encouraged, she said, 'I brought some photos of her, in case you wanted to see them. They're in the car—'

'No, please don't get them.'

Estelle stopped, sat back into the bench, and tried not to feel as though she'd been slapped.

'I'm sure she's lovely,' Serena said, 'but we need to talk . . . *I* need to talk, to tell you what you really want to know.'

For a moment Estelle felt a desperate urge to run, to get as far away from this woman as possible before she said something to shatter every part of her hopes and dreams. Without thinking she suddenly said, 'Did you ever hold me? When I was born? Did you even see me?'

Serena's eyes seemed to dull as she said, 'The truth, Estelle, is that I didn't want to hold you or see you, not because—'

Estelle came in quickly, her heart starting to break. 'It's OK, you don't need to say any more. I'm sorry I've forced it on you now . . .'

'You didn't force it. I came of my own free will, because you matter to me and you always will. You're my daughter, my firstborn, and I've never forgotten that. I admit it wasn't always at the forefront of my mind, especially not at the start, but I prayed you were safe and with good people, parents who could give you the kind of life I never could.'

That isn't true, Estelle wanted to shout, but instead she chose to feel reassured that she'd mattered. 'I know you were very young when you had me . . .'

'Yes, I was. Fifteen. Still a child in fact.'

'Is that why you couldn't keep me?'

Serena gave a small shake of her head. 'Yes – and no. Had things been different . . . Had your father not been who he was . . .'

Estelle's heart turned over. So, who was he? A politician? A married man? A criminal? She willed Serena to keep talking, to tell her about him, perhaps even where he was, but she said no more. 'You can't stop there,' Estelle implored. 'I need to know. You said yourself . . .'

Serena's eyes came back to her and seemed to look right into her as she said, 'I never wanted to tell you any of this, in spite of knowing that one day I'd probably have to. You're an innocent in it all, how could you be anything else, but you're a living, breathing reminder . . .' She swallowed and started again. 'It's not that I didn't get over it, I think I did, in time . . .'

'Oh God, you were raped,' Estelle cried wretchedly.

Serena didn't deny it. 'If it had been a stranger,' she said, 'I think I could probably have kept you, but it wasn't. The man who . . . impregnated me, was my uncle, my mother's brother.'

Estelle was aghast. *Incest!* This horrible, vile possibility had never once crossed her mind.

'He was more than twice my age,' Serena continued, 'someone who was used to getting what he wanted, and at that time what he wanted was me. I wasn't a willing partner, far from it, but I think that just excited him more. I never told my parents what was happening, and until they died they thought your father was someone who'd assaulted me in a park near to our home. But he knew, he always knew, and he held it over me as if I were to blame, and I was the one who'd be spurned by my family if I ever told.

'A week before you were born, he got married. The wedding was a society affair, quite lavish, and everyone was there, even me. My parents made me go and he showed no shame. Worse, he told me, with his bride no more than a few feet away, that we could start again as soon as there was no longer a baby filling me up. I hated him more than I can put into words. He's the reason I couldn't keep you. I didn't want you because you were his. I know I should have seen you only as mine, as a child in your own right, deserving of love, but I was young, and angry and frightened. I suppose I was vengeful too. I thought by getting rid of you I'd get rid of him.'

Estelle was so tense and appalled she was barely breathing. She hardly knew what to say, or even how to feel, apart from sickened by who she was – an incest child – and guilty, ashamed even, that she'd now pushed her way back into Serena's life. She wasn't wanted and never had been.

'If you're wondering where he is now,' Serena continued, 'he died just over a year ago.'

Feeling only relief that she'd never have to meet him, Estelle searched for the right words, but as soon as they came she knew they were wrong. 'Did he ever ask about me?'

Serena seemed to flinch as she shook her head.

No, of course he hadn't, and how could she feel anything but loathing for the man who'd fathered her, the child-rapist who'd stood between her and her mother for all these years and, as far as she could tell, still did? She became aware of a primal need rising up inside her, urging her to throw her arms around Serena and beg her to forget the past and think only of the daughter who needed her so much.

She stayed where she was, unable to move.

'I tried never to speak to him,' Serena said. 'Sometimes, at family gatherings, it was unavoidable, but I made sure I was never alone with him and that he never touched me again. I think my mother might have guessed, but if she did she said nothing. Her brother was very precious to her. Everyone loved him.'

Wishing Prim was here on the bench, helping her to find the right responses, Estelle simply stared at her mother, unable to imagine where they could go from here. Was she really going to keep her shut out? Was this the only time in her life she'd ever see her? The fear and certainty of it was growing by the minute.

Turning to her Serena said, 'I understand that no one wants to hear the kind of truth I've just given you. I wish there was something I could do to change it, to rewrite the way you were conceived and what happened after, but I'm afraid there isn't.'

Somewhere, deep down inside, Estelle was still managing to hope that the very next thing she said was going to make everything all right.

'I'm glad for you,' Serena went on, 'that you have a lovely family now, and that you're a success in your chosen profession. You have much to be proud of . . .'

'It's not all it seems,' Estelle protested.

Serena's smile was small. 'Nothing ever is,' she replied.

Estelle fought back a rising panic. The little flame of hope that had been leaping around deep inside her was all but gone now. It had no air, no oxygen to aid its survival. 'Are we going to meet again?' she asked, desperate for something to cling to.

Serena's voice was cracked with sadness as she said,

'I'm afraid I can't tell my family about you. I'd have to explain things they don't need to know. My uncle, your father, has children, my cousins, who adored him. My own children did too. No one ever knew what he was really like, and there's no good reason for them to know now. I talked it over with my husband before coming here, and he agreed that I should tell you what I just have, and that after today we should go back to the way we were and no longer be in touch.' She got to her feet. 'I'm sorry, Estelle, I really am. If things had been different . . . Well, we wouldn't be here if they had, would we? I shall look out for your future books and read them. Good luck, my dear,' and pulling her coat more tightly around her, she half-lifted a hand in farewell and walked away.

Estelle stayed where she was, watching her go to her car, hardly able to believe it was ending like this, not knowing how to stop it. She wanted to run after her, to beg her to stay so they could talk some more, or to make her promise they'd meet again sometime after Christmas. There was still so much to say, so many dreams to fulfil – surely she knew that? This, today, couldn't be all there was. It just couldn't. She wouldn't let it be.

She was still on the bench, cold and motionless, as her mother drove away and Prim came to sit with her.

After a while she turned to Prim and said, wretchedly, 'This is worse than what happened with Jeannie. *She* is worse than Jeannie.'

Prim squeezed her hand. 'Come on,' she said softly, 'let me take you home.'

CHAPTER TWENTY-FIVE
CARA AND ANDEE

Thursday 21 January 2021
Fifteen days since Jeannie's disappearance

Cara looked up from her laptop as Andee came into the incident room. It was late in the afternoon by now, and inky dark outside, with a fine silvery rain coasting past the lampposts.

'Where is everyone?' Andee asked, taking off her coat. 'CID's deserted.'

'A stabbing over on one of the estates,' Cara told her. 'You got my texts about Valerie Clayburne, the marina flat-owner, and Primrose Barnes?'

Yawning, Andee said, 'Sorry. Yes, I did, thanks. I'll watch the Primrose interview later, but nothing really stood out for you?'

Cara shook her head. 'Something about issues at home – unrelated – but otherwise more or less what we'd expected.'

'OK. Who else have you spoken to today?'

'Well, I've just got off the line with Maurice Bisset. He's quite definite that it's not some kind of publicity stunt.'

'That was my suggestion,' Andee admitted, 'and I suppose I didn't really think it would be, but it was worth asking. Any news on the author with a second home in Norfolk?'

'He's sold it, apparently, so she can't be there. Maurice suggested I talk to Jeannie's niece, Mallory in New Zealand. Apparently she was at Howarth Hall from October until just before Christmas. I'm waiting to hear back from her to set up a time. Do you know if Guy Symonds is coming to Kesterly this weekend?'

'I believe that's the plan. I've arranged to call him in about twenty minutes. He should be in his car on his way out of London by then. I should have said, please don't mention to Guy what I told you about my sister and how long she was missing. At this stage it really won't help.'

'No problem,' Cara assured her. 'Maurice Bisset tells me that his bosses are talking about offering a reward for information.'

Andee was about to respond when Natalie Rundle came into the room. 'I thought you'd be out at the estate,' she commented, going to touch elbows with her old friend.

'I've just come back – three arrests and one fatality. What a world we live in, huh? So, how are things here?'

With a glance at Cara, Andee said, 'We still don't seem to be much further forward, I'm afraid. Jeannie's phone and bank card records would be a big help . . .'

'You've put in the requests?' Rundle barked at Cara.

'I did it straight away,' Cara assured her, 'but I haven't had anything back yet.'

'OK, I'll get onto it. Anything else?'

Cara said, 'I spoke to Guy Symonds's ex-wife, Kate Gorman, this morning. She says she hasn't seen either of them in she can't remember how long, but as far as she's concerned they deserve one another.'

Rundle grunted. 'No sour grapes there then. Any more on Neil Roberts?'

'We haven't spoken to him again yet,' Andee told her, 'but we will. Apparently Athene are talking about offering a reward for information.'

Rundle nodded slowly. 'I suppose we should have seen that coming,' she commented. Then, 'OK, keep me in the loop and I'll chase up those records.' She was almost at the door when she turned back. 'Do you want to know what I think?' she asked.

'I'm sure you're going to tell us,' Andee responded dryly.

'OK, here goes: this woman, as far as we can tell, had no good reason to want to walk out of her life. So we can explore the possibility that she has a secret lover, or someone's holding her, or covering for her, or her car's somewhere upside down in a ravine, but I reckon we're looking at something a whole lot more serious.'

'The potential of it has always been there,' Andee pointed out, 'but we still don't have a shred of evidence to say that it's true. So, that leaves us saying she could be anywhere and, no matter what we do, we'll never find her.'

Rundle's eyes narrowed slightly as she said, 'I accept that people can disappear without trace, and no one knows that better than your family, but there's always a reason why someone wants to go. Your sister was a fourteen-year-old rebel without a cause when she went. What's Jeannie, apart from a successful businesswoman who's in good health and happily married – as far as we know?'

Conceding the point, Andee checked her watch. 'We're about to speak to Guy Symonds. Do you want to stay for it?'

'I can't, Gould was expecting me half an hour ago. Come and find me when you're done.'

Ten minutes later Guy Symonds was on the speaker-phone with Cara listening as Andee spoke to him. 'No, I'm sorry, we don't have anything ground-breaking to report,' she said, 'but I've heard that Athene are considering offering a reward. Did you know about that?'

'Yes, I did. The CEO called me last night. What I said – apart from thank you, obviously – was: let's try anything that might get us some answers.'

'OK, in that case, how would you feel about doing a televised appeal for her to come back? Or for someone to get in touch if they know where she is?'

'To be honest,' he replied, after a pause, 'it makes me feel slightly sick, but I guess it's a good idea given where we are.'

'Great, I'll talk to DS Rundle about setting it up. Are you on your way to Kesterly now?'

'I should be there in a couple of hours. Neil and Zac have been keeping a check on the house so I already know she hasn't miraculously turned up.' After a moment he added, 'As the days go on, I'm starting to fear that I might never see her again and I don't mind admitting . . . Oh, hell! I don't believe this! Christ! *Sorry. Sorry.* I've just rear-ended someone,' he told them. 'I'm afraid I'll have to call you back.'

After they'd rung off, Cara and Andee sat wordlessly looking at one another.

In the end Andee said, 'I'm not sure if my own history is complicating this, so tell me, do you think Jeannie's still alive and off somewhere living an alternative best life?'

Cara didn't have to consider it for long. 'If she is, I

can't see her being on her own, can you? Which means someone has to know where she is at the very least.'

'Is that what your gut is telling you, that she has chosen to go?'

Cara slowly shook her head. 'Not really,' she admitted.

Andee sighed and got to her feet. 'Let's hope the phone or bank records tell us something when we get them. Meantime, I'd better go and square off this press conference with Madame Rundle. I have a feeling she won't be happy, because those things always bring society's worst out of the woodwork, and there can be so many of them.'

CHAPTER TWENTY-SIX

Yesterday, as I walked along the lane behind the café – it's out of lockdown now with Christmas approaching – I noticed a fire escape leading up to the second and third floors of the building. I didn't climb it, of course, but I couldn't help thinking how easy it might be to break into her flat.

Someone should warn her about that.

CHAPTER TWENTY-SEVEN

FLISS

December 2020
Three weeks before Jeannie's disappearance

'What the hell do you mean you've sold my car?' Fliss cried, hardly able to believe she'd heard right.

'Calm down,' Zac tried to soothe. 'I got a great price for it and, let's face it, how else were you going to afford to buy me a Christmas present?'

Still reeling, she looked at the table where he'd fanned a stack of twenty-pound notes in a casino-like display of winnings, money she desperately needed, but she still couldn't get past the loss of her *car*. 'You had no right to just take it,' she told him angrily. 'How the heck am I going to get around?'

'We still have the van,' he reminded her, 'and unless we're making deliveries, we can't really go anywhere anyway. So, I thought to myself, why not pop over and have a chat with Sam Blakeford – you know Sam, he's got the car showroom . . .'

'Yes, I know him, and I also know he wouldn't give you this much . . . How much is there?' How could she not be drawn to it when she was in such dire need?

Zac grinned. 'Eleven and a half gs. Which, I admit, is slightly over the going rate for a Golf as old as yours . . .'

'*Slightly!*' she echoed incredulously. 'You mean like double.'

'You're doing the old girl a disservice,' he scolded. 'She was in really good nick, low mileage, MOT up to date . . .'

'Your father's behind this,' she declared hotly. 'This is your way of getting money out of him . . .'

He laughed. 'No way is Dad going to buy that old banger for eleven and a half grand.'

'Oh, so it's an old banger now. What happened to the great condition?'

'All of it true, or Sam wouldn't have wanted it. I'm not going to deny he's paid over the odds . . .'

'So part of it is a loan?'

'No, not exactly. Not at all, in fact. I just promised him free breakfasts for a year if he gave me my asking price, so you've got to admit, I pulled off a great deal.'

Not at all sure how much of this was making any sense to her, Fliss ended up doing the only thing she could think of for the moment, burying her face in her hands and laughing.

'OK, I know it was bad of me,' he confessed, 'but it doesn't take a genius to work out you've gone into debt thanks to the pandemic. I don't know if this cash puts much of a dent in it, but it's got to be better than nothing.'

Oh it would help, if only in a small way. 'To be honest,' she said, 'I was thinking about selling the car myself.'

'I thought as much, and I didn't want you to have to bother with it when you've got enough going on.'

How could she not love him for being so sensitive and assertive, and just for being him? 'You managed to get a way better price than I would have.'

'Because, like I said, I want a decent Christmas present. So, a trip to Down Under to see Mallory when she goes back, might do it, or a new car . . . Maybe not that, as we've just got rid of one.'

She flung her arms around him. 'Oh, Zac, sometimes I love you so much I could explode with it.'

'OK, let's not do that,' he protested, still hugging her. 'Instead, how about I go down to the café and find something for our supper while you do your end-of-day office stuff? Then we can either talk about how we're going to spend our loot, apart from on me, or we can catch up on the next episode of *Outlander*.'

Fliss's eyes sparkled delightedly. 'An evening with Jamie Fraser, I think so,' she responded. 'But first, let's get this money in the safe, and then you can bring in the Christmas tree that I know you remembered to pick up for us.'

'Oh shit,' he groaned. 'I left it on Dad's truck. But we'll have it tomorrow, no probs. The one in the café looks fab though, right?'

'It does,' she agreed, reliving for a brief moment the joy of decorating it last week with the Corona Girls, almost as if everything was normal in their lives, when actually it was all going mad. One minute the café was able to open, the next it wasn't – but only after she'd committed to big food orders for the festive season. Tier two one day, tier four the next. Masks, double masks. Six people outside, then none. Five unrestricted days over Christmas, then only one, with limits and no overnights. And as if all that wasn't enough to make her head spin, there was Zac's growing attachment to Mallory and his dread of her leaving.

Looking up as he returned from the café with a large

231

bowl of lasagne, she clicked off her phone saying, 'I can't get hold of Dad. I might have a new client for him.'

'He was going to Howarth Hall on his way home,' Zac told her, setting the oven to heat up. 'Jeannie's thinking about extending the wall either side of the gates. Once he gets talking to her, he could be a while.'

Fliss turned round at the ironic note in his voice.

His eyes were full of laughter as he threw out his hands. 'Don't ask me what they find to chat about that takes so long,' he said, 'but there always seems to be something.'

'Do they still go for walks in the woods?' Fliss asked, her smile feeling stretched, the words seeming heavy on her tongue.

'Oh yeah, those are still happening,' he replied, taking out a couple of plates, 'though I guess less now the weather's not so great.'

'I don't suppose he's ever mentioned them to Estie?'

'I shouldn't think so, you know what she's like, best not to bring Jeannie's name into anything when she's around, especially not right now. Apparently she's really on edge and snapping everyone's heads off for no reason. Although I suppose we could call that situation normal for her.' He gave a laugh as he went back to the former subject. 'You know, Mallory and I can't work out whether Jeannie's got a thing about Dad, or if it's the other way round.'

Fliss's heartbeat slowed. Could it be true that while she'd never got over Neil, while she'd continued to long for him and had never tried to make him cheat on Estelle, he was doing it anyway, with somebody else? With Jeannie? 'What about Guy?' she asked hoarsely.

'What about him?'

'Doesn't he mind about all the time they spend together?'

'He's hardly ever there, is he, so he might not even know.'

Fliss couldn't think of anything else to say, so she went to set the table and tried to refocus her mind on the accounts. It wasn't easy, but at least it was good to know the eleven and a half thousand pounds was there; however, before working out which of her debts was the most immediate, she should talk to the accountant Andee had put her in touch with. With any luck he might agree to her keeping a little back for Christmas presents, if only for Zac and Chloe.

By ten o'clock, after some warmed-through lasagne and two episodes of their current favourite series, Fliss cried off the third, feeling certain that for once she was tired enough to sleep through till morning.

She was just settling into bed, eyes already half-closed and dimly able to hear Zac in his own room on the PlayStation with his mates, when suddenly she was wide awake again. For no reason at all, her tiredness had evaporated, her eyes were open and her mind was spinning around every anxiety it could conjure in less than sixty seconds. Guy; Jeannie and Neil; Zac and Mallory; her dependence on the Corona Girls; Estie's odd behaviour lately; the very real possibility she'd end up having to sell the café. But who would want to buy it while the country was in such a state? And even if a new owner could be found, they'd either want the flat for themselves, or rent from her which she couldn't pay.

She shouldn't have extended the café and apartment when she had, right before a pandemic. Obviously she hadn't known it was going to happen, but what kind of monstrous fate had set its sights on her then?

At least she had Zac, for now.

And her home and café, so she needed to calm down.

Whatever happened, no one was going to end up dead this time, the way they had before.

In the end she must have dozed for a while, perhaps even properly slept, for when she opened her eyes again she saw that it was just past three in the morning. A hellish time to be awake, absolutely the worst, but at least she'd managed to sleep for a few hours without the help of Zolpidem.

The question was, should she take one now to get her through the rest of the night, or was it too late?

She lay staring at the closed curtains, made festive by the glow of Christmas lights shining up from the Promenade. She listened for what might have woken her, but there was only the rhythmic sound of waves in the bay, no traffic, no voices drifting over from the beach. How grateful she was that her son wasn't amongst the druggies that congregated there; how deeply sorry she felt for the parents who were struggling to keep their youngsters away from gangs and other criminal activity during this impossible time.

Aware of how awake she was, she decided to get up and make herself some tea. It was foolish to think she'd get back to sleep now without some help, but rather than be groggy in the morning, maybe she could take a look at a couple of the business models that Angie, one of the Corona Girls, had sent her way. They wouldn't get the café properly open again – nothing could do that until the government gave the go-ahead – but apparently other hospitality venues had found some ingenious ways to keep going, so maybe one would work for her.

As she passed the main bathroom, she felt a draught wrap itself around her bare legs and, going inside to check, she found one of the tall casement windows was at least halfway open. For a heart-stopping moment, she wondered if someone had broken in, was maybe even now somewhere in the flat.

She stayed very still, listening for the sound of someone moving around, but there was nothing.

Maybe Zac had gone out this way.

Except why would he? He had keys to let himself in and out of the back door. Nevertheless, she tiptoed to his room, and was relieved to find him sprawled out on the bed and snoring. For a moment she stood staring along the hall towards the door that led up to the next floor. There was nothing up there – it was used only for storage these days, and she doubted she'd ever get round to converting it into another apartment, not at this rate anyway.

Going to the door, she gingerly turned the handle and found, to her relief, that it was locked. Next she checked the sitting room and kitchen, entry hall and cupboards, and finding everything as it should be, she returned to the bathroom and tugged down the window, wincing at a flash of back pain. Had she opened it herself? She was so horribly forgetful these days – or perhaps just distracted, with so much on her mind – that she could have. When chatting with the Corona Girls, she light-heartedly put her absent moments down to brain fog, as if it were nothing to worry about, when she knew that her reliance on painkillers and sleeping pills was really the cause. Still, she couldn't manage without either, and what did it matter who had opened the window? It was closed now and no harm was done, so why not just make a cup of tea and go back to bed with the business modules?

*　　*　　*

A few hours later, when Zac yawned his way into the kitchen for breakfast, still in boxers and an old T-shirt, she said, 'Did you open one of the bathroom windows for some reason?'

Giving his head a shake, he said, 'No, why?'

She shrugged. 'I found it that way last night and I don't remember it being open when I went to bed. I was worried that someone might have broken in.'

That woke him up. 'Have you checked?' he asked, looking around worriedly. 'Shit, you put the money in the safe, didn't you?'

'Don't worry, it's still there. Nothing's missing at all, so I guess there wasn't a burglar.'

'Did you hear anything?'

She shook her head and put some coffee in front of him. 'I don't suppose you did either. You wouldn't above your snoring.'

Shooting her a menacing look, he said, 'Well, my money's on you opening it up in your sleep.'

'What! I've never walked in my sleep.'

'How would you know if you're not awake?'

Conceding the point, she said, 'Let's just make sure it's properly locked from now on; after all the fire escape's right outside and we don't want any old riff-raff – or a burglar –coming in, do we?'

'But it's OK for a psychopath?'

Flipping him with a tea towel she said, 'You need to get a move on. The manager at Tesco is expecting you to pick up a crate-load of donations by seven.'

CHAPTER TWENTY-EIGHT

ESTELLE

December 2020
Three weeks before Jeannie's disappearance

Estelle was staring out at the marina, where only a few Christmas lights burned in the evening gloom and empty masts were rocking back and forth in the wind. She only had to think of her mother – the woman who'd given birth to her; that softly spoken, beautiful, ugly hypocrite – to feel disgust at herself and a fury that was almost impossible to control.

Why had Estie allowed her to walk away, as if all that mattered was how *she* felt and what *she* wanted? Why hadn't she shouted after her, knocked her to the floor, told her exactly what she thought of her and her self-preservation?

She had more information now about Serena's children, Aubyn and Talia, and her husband, Sir Jerome Fellowes. How were they going to feel when they found out there was another member of their family, someone who'd been so cruelly rejected by their mother and wife? Surely they'd only be able to see her as a monster after that.

'It doesn't end here,' she said silently, as if Serena could hear. 'I hope you know that. I will not let you get away with the way you treated me.'

The same words, the same raging sense of injustice, over and over and over. It was all she felt, all she could think about. There would never be anything between her and her mother – no love, no pride, no laughter, no relationship at all. Serena's only concern was to shield her legitimate family from the living, breathing shame that was Estelle Fields.

Carrying two glasses of wine from the apartment kitchen, Guy said gently, 'I'm sorry I haven't been able to see you sooner. It's been hectic at the hospital. I didn't even get back last weekend.'

'I know, you told me,' she said, still staring out at the night.

'But I rang,' he reminded her, 'and I worried about you.'

That comforted her and, as she turned around she said, 'You still haven't told me who this flat belongs to.'

Passing her a glass of wine, he said, 'A friend of Jeannie's, Val Clayburne. We've been keeping an eye on it until she can get here herself.'

'It's a nice place. Do you bring all your girlfriends here?'

A flash of disapproval passed across his eyes.

'Sorry, I shouldn't have said that. Apart from anything else, I'm not a girlfriend.'

'No, you're someone who's not in a good place right now, which is perfectly understandable considering what you've been through, but I don't think you need to see it quite as bleakly as you do. It was just a first meeting.'

'But she said—'

'I know what she said, and maybe she meant it at the time, but going by the other things you've told me about

238

her, she doesn't sound as though she can just cut you off as if you'd never met at all. I'm sure she'll be in touch again. Maybe not right away, but sometime in the New Year.'

Sinking into one of the sofas, Estelle took a sip of her wine and watched him sit into an armchair. She wondered, fleetingly, what he'd do if she took off her clothes to show him the lingerie she'd had delivered today especially for tonight. Then she pushed the thought away, knowing she'd never do it. It wasn't what he wanted from her; he didn't give the impression of wanting anything at all.

'Why do you bother with me?' she asked, suddenly needing to know.

He smiled in what looked like surprise. 'I don't see it as a bother,' he told her. 'Far from it, in fact. I've enjoyed our walks on the moor, and our chats.'

'I don't understand why, when I'm always talking about myself and there's always something wrong.'

Amused, he said, 'You're far more interesting than you seem to think, and anyway, it's not true that you only talk about yourself.'

'I have lately.'

'Because you've had a lot going on, and I know you're still hurting over what happened with Jeannie. That bothers me.'

She swallowed and looked away. She didn't like him talking about Jeannie, or maybe she would if he'd criticize or denigrate her once in a while. She never allowed herself to think about the two of them together at Howarth Hall, living a happily married life. She almost couldn't bear that he belonged to that woman in so many more ways than he'd ever belong to her.

'I'm not sure I can repair it,' he continued, 'but I'd like

to think that at some point I can get the two of you together again.'

Hating the idea almost as much as she longed for it, she said, 'Why would you care?'

'Maybe because of how much it would mean to you. She might not know it, but I think it would mean a lot to her too.'

Unable to believe that, Estelle sipped her wine and let several minutes pass before she spoke again. 'I hated my mother when she walked away,' she said, 'I mean in a horrible, almost violent way, but after you and I talked on the phone . . . I'm sorry for ringing you at work . . .'

'It doesn't matter. I'm glad you did.'

'It made all the difference to me, talking to you,' she said. 'I felt able to start breathing again, and functioning in a way that wasn't all about revenge.' She'd never tell him just how dark her thoughts had become, or that she feared they'd come back again when she was unable to see him; she didn't want him to know just how ugly she could be inside.

He put his glass down and, sitting forward, rested his elbows on his knees as he looked into her eyes. 'Do you know what really concerns me about you, Estelle?' he said. 'It's that you always seem so lonely and unsure of yourself when you have no reason to feel that way. You have a good – a *great* – husband and a beautiful daughter. You have a very loyal and caring friend in Primrose. You have a wonderful extended family in Zac and Fliss, and yet I know, when you're feeling the way you are, it probably doesn't feel as though it matters.'

'You're right, it doesn't,' she said, and got up to go and

refill her glass from the bottle he'd left in the kitchen. She kept her back to him as she said, 'But my life isn't the way you see it. Of course I love my daughter, and I'm grateful for Prim, but Neil . . . I know you think highly of him, everyone does, but he's no saint.'

Guy laughed. 'I'd be worried if he were.'

'I mean, he's done things . . . Awful things, and got away with them.' She turned around and found him regarding her curiously.

'Such as?' he prompted.

She shrugged, awkwardly, knowing she shouldn't go on, but she wanted to, felt utterly compelled to. 'There was this woman,' she said, 'a while back, a client who lives on the Heights. He . . . They were . . . She ended up accusing him of assault.'

'You mean he was violent towards her?'

Suddenly not wanting to discuss it any more, she took a large sip of wine and said, 'He regrets marrying me. He probably wouldn't admit it, certainly not to me, but I know he does. The trouble is that nothing could ever persuade him to leave Chloe. So he stays with us in spite of still being in love with Fliss.'

As she looked at him again, she saw confusion and what seemed to be doubt in his eyes.

'He never left Fliss, in his heart or in any other way,' she told him. 'She's the one who left him, not because she didn't still love him, but because she got drunk one night and ended up driving into a delivery van. Fliss herself was in a critical condition for over two months and, when she was finally released, she was charged with causing death by drink-driving.'

'Oh my God,' he murmured, clearly shocked. 'I didn't . . . I didn't know any of that.'

241

'Why would you? They don't talk about it. Mostly they carry on as if it didn't happen, but it did. She ended up serving time. When they let her out again, Neil was waiting for her. He was ready to forgive her, to try and rebuild their life together, but she wasn't able to forgive herself.'

Guy took a breath, seeming for the moment unable to find any words.

She was glad, because she was sure he felt sorry for Fliss and she didn't want to hear it. She also wasn't feeling very proud of bringing it up. Maybe she'd had too much to drink herself. 'I've always known that he only married me because of Chloe,' she ran on. She gave a short, painful laugh and downed the rest of her wine in one go. 'Do you know, I've never been able to talk to him the way I can to you, and how long have we known each other? A few months. But, just my luck, you're in love with someone else.'

Getting to his feet he came to the kitchen and put his hands on her shoulders. 'We're already breaking the rules by being in here,' he said, 'so how about we break them a bit more,' and pulling her into his arms he held her close, smoothing her hair and rocking her from side to side. He said, 'I know it must feel as though everything is piling on top of you right now, but something will change, I promise, because something always does.'

CHAPTER TWENTY-NINE

CARA

Thursday 21 January 2021
Fifteen days since Jeannie's disappearance

This day was going on and on, like it might have no end, which was possibly why Cara was finding it a bit difficult to get her head around what she was hearing. Sure she was tired, and her understanding of literary techniques was grounded in not very much, but Mallory Haines and her aunt definitely seemed to exist in their own kind of world. 'So do you think it's possible Jeannie is in Vienna?' she asked carefully, certain she'd got the wrong end of the stick, though not sure how, or if there even was a stick. 'If she said there were other ways of getting there . . .'

'Yes, through imagination,' Mallory Haines explained. 'It's our most powerful tool, especially for writers and editors. Sometimes my aunt calls it her "transport".'

Cara stared at her pretty young face on the screen thinking, *OK, different to a bus, but whatever works.* 'So do you think she's there?' she repeated.

'Not physically, no. I just think it's something she could be working on.'

'But you don't know where she could be doing this work?'

Mallory shook her tousled waves. 'I know Guy and Maurice have both spoken to the author, Dylan Frank, but apparently she hasn't been in touch with him. Mum and I are really worried about her, you know.'

'OK. When you were staying with her, did she mention anything about going away somewhere – or with someone – in January?'

Mallory's eyes grew round. 'No, she didn't.'

'Did she ever seem afraid of something, or someone?'

Mallory took a short breath, blinked and glanced away.

Startled by the reaction, Cara gave it a moment and decided to come at it another way. 'Did anything happen while you were staying with her to cause you some concern?' she asked.

Mallory shook her head, but she still wasn't looking at the screen.

'I'm getting the impression that something did,' Cara pressed, sensing that Andee and the DS, both out of shot, were listening more intently now.

'I'm really sorry,' Mallory said. 'I want to find her as much as you do, but when I left, just before Christmas, everything was . . .' She shrugged. 'Normal.'

Why the hesitation before normal? 'Was anyone joining them for Christmas?' Cara ventured.

'Uh, no . . . No.'

'You're not seeming too sure about that.'

'Until I left, we were the only ones at the house. Me, Jeannie and Guy.'

'Was that the case for the whole time you were there, just the three of you?'

'That's right.'

She wasn't being truthful, Cara felt sure of it, and half-expected (and hoped) that the DS would take over now.

She didn't.

'No visitors, no staff?' Cara prompted.

'The cleaner came in on her regular days. The gardener, landscaper, he came too.'

'You mean Neil Roberts?'

'Yes, and Zac, his son.'

Deciding to roll with this now the name had come up, Cara said, 'Did Neil Roberts spend much time at the Hall?'

Mallory frowned. 'I suppose as much as he needed to.'

'Was there anything in particular that struck you about him?' *Was that question as dumb as it sounded?*

'I don't know what you mean.'

'Did you ever think that there could be more to his relationship with your aunt than the client-gardener thing?'

Mallory's face became pinched. 'They always got along well when I saw them together,' she said. 'Guy is good friends with him too. He's a really nice bloke. We all went surfing together a few times.'

'I guess you know Neil Roberts is married to the writer, Estelle Fields?' Cara said, not quite sure of where she was going with this. 'Did your aunt see her at all while you were with her?'

'Not that I'm aware of, and I'd be surprised if she did. They don't exactly get along.'

Cara was about to ask her next question when Mallory said, 'Someone we did see, maybe back in November, was Estelle Fields's assistant.'

'Primrose Barnes?'

'That's her name. We didn't speak to her or anything. She was too far away, opposite the Seafront Café. I only remember it because I thought she was staring at us.'

'And was she?'

'I don't really know. The sun was quite dazzly that morning when it came out, and by the time it went in again she was walking away.'

Not sure what, if anything, to make of that, Cara said, 'OK, back to your stay at the Hall. We're trying to establish if something unusual happened while you were there that could have made your aunt end up taking off without telling anyone where she was going?' Long question, but at least it was to the point.

Looking both miserable and helpless, Mallory said, 'My uncle says she does go off sometimes, but she's never been gone this long before.'

Cara stared at her hard, wishing that Andee or the DS would come in right now, because something was definitely awry, and she couldn't be the only one sensing it. From the corner of her eye she saw the DS give her a nod, the signal to keep going.

'You didn't exactly answer my question. So did something happen?' Cara pressed.

Mallory shook her head. 'No. Nothing. Or not that I saw.'

'So something did, but you didn't see it?'

'I-I . . . Well, my dad turned up unexpectedly, but I didn't actually see him.'

Sensing how surprised Andee and the DS were to hear this, Cara said, 'When exactly was this?'

'Uh, four days before Christmas. He broke the Covid restrictions, which is why we haven't mentioned it before.

246

Anyway, I would have stayed another day, but my . . . My flight was booked so I left . . . when I did. Actually, if you don't mind, time is getting on and I need to be at a lecture in the next half an hour.'

Receiving no instruction to keep her talking, Cara thanked her for getting up so early and watched the screen turn dark. She turned to Andee and DS Rundle, having no idea just yet how this had gone. When no one else spoke, she rubbed her eyes and said, 'I don't know about you, but there was a minute there when I started thinking Jeannie might have time-tripped off back to nineteenth-century Vienna.'

Rundle chuckled and Andee said, 'It was an interesting interview on several levels. Let's start with Primrose Barnes at the Seafront. Any thoughts?'

Cara shrugged.

'Maybe you need to speak to Ms Barnes again,' Natalie suggested.

'OK,' Cara agreed, 'except it's going to seem a bit weird me asking her why she was staring at Jeannie Symonds on some random day back in November, isn't it?'

'Any weirder than doing the staring?' Rundle countered.

Moving them on, Andee said. 'I'm sure we all got the same impression that the girl deliberately avoided her father when he turned up unexpectedly. Has Guy ever mentioned anything to you about Jeannie's brother – Paul, isn't it? – visiting around Christmas?' she asked Cara.

Cara shook her head.

'I'll give him a call,' Andee said, 'and at the same time I'll tell him we're going to hold off on a press conference for now?'

'Just a couple of days,' Rundle confirmed.

As soon as she was through to Guy, Andee put the call on speaker and said, 'Hi, have you sorted out the rear-ending business?'

With a tired laugh he said, 'Yes, finally, and it was totally my fault. Sorry, I should have got back to you straight away, but I had another call come in, and then that led to another. You know how it goes.'

'Of course. Where are you now?'

'Just about to leave the M5 towards home. I should be there in about half an hour, but I'm happy to talk now if you are. I'm just trying to remember where we were before I drove into someone's car. Actually, before we go ahead with that, I want to ask you about the conversation I had with Cara yesterday. Unless I'm imagining things, it left me with the impression that Neil might know more than he's saying. Is that true? Have you spoken to him again?'

'Not yet,' Andee admitted, 'but we intend to.'

'I'd be shocked if it turned out he was keeping something back,' he said. 'I can't imagine that he would, he's been so keen to help find her.'

Not running with that, Andee said, 'We won't be asking you to go in front of the cameras just yet. There are still a couple of things we need to straighten out first.'

With a sigh he said, 'I can't say it's not a relief, although I'll do it as soon as you think the timing's right.'

'Good to know. Meantime, we've just spoken to your niece, Mallory, and she told us that her father, Jeannie's brother Paul, was with you at Christmas?'

There was a short pause before he said, 'He turned up a few days before, and only stayed for one night. I didn't mention it before because . . . Well, I thought he'd left

248

the country long before Jeannie disappeared, and I still don't have any reason to think he didn't. Listen, can I call you back when I get home? I don't want to bang into anyone else, and I do need to tell you about this.'

CHAPTER THIRTY

I haven't been to the café for a while, but I still think about her all the time; it lowers the breath in my lungs and stirs the blood in my veins. I imagine loosening her thick blonde hair and running my fingers through the cool, glossy texture of it; I see it spread out around her shoulders; I hear her murmuring my name.

She is sensuous beyond measure; her lambent blue eyes and exquisitely full mouth so entrancing to watch. I try not to stare when I'm there, but I can't help being aware of the effect she has on me.

Should I do something about it?

I long to, of course, but I have to be sure of doing it at the right time, in the right way.

CHAPTER THIRTY-ONE

JEANNIE

Monday 21 December 2020
Sixteen days before Jeannie's disappearance

'Darling, there you are,' Guy exclaimed, looking relieved as he came from the house to open Jeannie's car door. 'I was worried when I got home and you weren't here.'

'Didn't I leave a note?' she responded in surprise. 'I meant to. Sorry. I just popped to the supermarket to get a tart for dessert this evening and I forgot to take my phone.' She stepped out of the Lexus and stretched up to kiss him. 'Isn't Mallory here?' she asked.

'No sign of her when I got in.'

'She'll be in her room talking to her mother or mates in NZ. She usually is around this time of day.'

Settling into the circle of his arm as they walked to the Hall, she felt a swell of pleasure to see the Christmas lights Neil had wound through berry-laden garlands around the front porch. Beyond the forecourt, nothing could be seen of the garden, for sea fog was settling in a ghostly nimbus all over the Heights. It was wonderfully atmospheric, she thought, redolent of old black-and-white films where Gothic towers seemed to float in misted landscapes and restless souls walked past empty windows. 'I guess he hasn't arrived yet?' she asked quietly before they went inside.

'No, but he's on his way. He should arrive sometime in the next hour.'

'Provided he can still find the way. It's been so long and on a night like this . . . Let's hope he doesn't have an accident.' Did she mean that? Probably, but a non-injury collision would hold her brother up at least for a while, and she wouldn't mind that at all. Of course, by rights, he should be quarantining for the next ten days at least, but Paul Haines had only ever lived by his own rules.

Stepping into the entrance hall, she felt the warmth greet her like a smile. The sound of Oasis coming from Guy's study told her it was where he'd been until he'd heard her pull up outside. 'Will you have to work this evening?' she asked.

Taking her coat he said, 'Maybe, for a while, but don't worry, I've no intention of leaving you to deal with Paul alone.'

Grateful for that, she made a concerted effort to detach from her nerves and started for the kitchen. 'Mallory's saying she won't see him,' she said, over her shoulder. 'If she doesn't, he'll blame me for it, but how can I make her do something she's so set against?'

'Would you like me to talk to her?' he offered, going to pour them both a drink.

Sighing, she gave it some thought. 'I don't know that it'll do much good, and I expect you want to get back to your study while you can?' Her eyes twinkled the question, letting him know that tonight she didn't mind if he did. Sometimes his preoccupation with other people's issues was an irritant, other times not.

'I have a few calls to make,' he admitted, 'but I shouldn't be long – and if he arrives before I'm done . . . Well, I'll hear him, so I'll make sure I'm the one to open the door.'

'Thank you.' She looked up into his eyes and wished it could be just the two of them for dinner – three, she corrected; she wouldn't want to exclude Mallory.

Picking up his glass he left her to unpack the cartons Magda had collected from the seafood restaurant in Kesterly that morning. A full three-course meal for four, all Jeannie had to do was heat and serve. It was much easier entertaining this way when she was so busy – and so apprehensive about her brother's unwelcome visit.

She was in the middle of sharing a mackerel pâté between four plates – one for Mallory to have upstairs – when she spotted Guy's precious notebook on the centre island. Knowing he was likely to need it, she decided to save him the bother of coming to look for it. However, before taking it to him, she couldn't resist a little peek at the most recent entries.

As usual it was mostly medical jargon beyond her powers of comprehension, but there was a number and set of initials printed at the bottom of a page that seemed significant, although nothing to say why it should be. Taking a quick shot of it with her phone, she went through to his study.

'You forgot this,' she said, putting the book down on the desk in front of him.

Casting a glance at it, he said, 'So I did. Thank you.'

She smiled, and wondered if he'd actually left it behind on purpose as he sometimes did, wanting her to find an entry to excite or perplex her. She considered asking about the number, but decided against it until she'd tried it herself. 'If Paul's jet-lagged,' she said, 'and wants to go to bed early, I was thinking we could watch a movie after dinner. It might help to distract me from the fact he's in the house.'

'Sounds good to me. Did you have anything in mind?'

She shrugged as she suggested, '*Rear Window*?' and took a sip of the wine she'd brought with her.

He held her eyes for a long moment, but only said, 'You know I'm a Hitchcock fan.'

She touched a finger to his lips and was about to plant a kiss on his forehead when she froze. 'Is that a car pulling up?' she asked, turning to the heavily curtained window.

Using a remote to lower the music, he listened for a moment, but the night outside was still.

'Nerves,' she said with a self-conscious laugh. 'Sorry. I should leave you to it and carry on in the kitchen.'

Grasping her hand as she turned away, he said, 'You've had this out with your brother once before. Maybe he's coming to apologize.'

As much as she'd like to believe it, she said, 'If that were the case, he'd have made it clear when he rang.' Frowning she added, 'I guess we had to invite him to stay the night?'

Guy was sardonic. 'He's come all the way from New Zealand and the local hotels are shut, so I don't see we had a choice. I take it one of the guest rooms is made up ready?'

'I'm sure it will be. Magda's very good about that, but with Mallory in the east wing, I suppose we ought to put him at the other end of the house, closer to us.'

'Do you think she's afraid of her father?' he asked curiously.

Jeannie tilted her head as she thought. 'I'm not sure afraid is the right word. I think she just likes to avoid confrontations with him – and there's going to be one tonight, we can be sure of that.'

Shaking his head, he said, 'Personally, I'm not convinced, but we'll see. Now, let me finish up here and I'll come and lay the table.'

As she walked away, leaving the door ajar behind her, she heard him answering his phone and was tempted to stay and eavesdrop, but she was too uptight tonight to give in to the urge.

'I take it he's not here yet,' Mallory said from the stairs.

Looking up, Jeannie smiled. 'No, he isn't, but you know he'll want to see you so—'

'It's not going to happen,' Mallory interrupted. 'I know he's here to bully me, and if he'd just listened when I last spoke to him, he'd know already that I'm flying home the day after tomorrow.'

'Well, we can tell him that tonight.'

'What are you going to do if he starts on you again? I think he will, you know.'

'I'm afraid you're right, but what's done is done, Mallory. We can't change anything, and if it's going to take another showdown to convince him of that then I'm already bracing myself.'

Mallory stiffened at the sound of the gate buzzer. 'It'll be him,' she declared. 'I'm sorry if you feel I'm letting you down . . .'

'I don't, so put it out of your head.' She turned as Guy came out of his study. 'He's here,' she murmured.

Guy nodded and glanced at Mallory as he pressed a button to release the gates.

'I'm sorry,' Mallory said and, moving light as a feather, she disappeared back up the stairs.

Aware of how hard her heart was beating, Jeannie watched Guy go to the front door, heard a car crunching over the gravel and urged herself to take strength from the determination that whatever happened during her brother's visit was not going to be her fault.

'Paul,' she heard Guy say with just the right amount of warmth in his tone. 'You made it. I was half-expecting you to call to—'

'I almost did,' her brother cut in, his voice coming out of the fog as gruffly familiar as it was unwelcome.

Jeannie remained where she was, watching Guy disappear into the night, no doubt bumping elbows and uttering pleasantries before he returned to the Hall with a large holdall. A beat later the enormous, dreadfully familiar bulk of her brother filled the doorway; self-assured, arrogant, and as forbidding as ever. His hair was long, thinning at the temples and falling in dark, damp strands around his collar. His face was large and clean-shaven, with bulging veins on his forehead, narrow, flinty eyes and a thinly smiling mouth.

'Jeannie,' he stated, making no move towards her. 'You're looking well.' His eyes flicked around the spacious entrance hall with its ornate rosewood staircase, oak-panelled walls and vaulted ceiling. Then he looked at her again, his eyes frank and scornful, as Guy relieved him of his coat.

Jeannie forced herself to say, 'What brings you here, Paul?'

Ignoring her, he said to Guy, 'Is she still running you around in circles with that psychotic personality of hers?'

'We keep each other on our toes,' Guy retorted mildly.

'Can I get you a drink? Maybe you'd like to freshen up before we eat?'

'Yeah, maybe I would.' He rubbed his huge hands together as if meaning business. 'It's a hell of a journey from NZ. Easier, of course, if you can go first class, but that's a long way out of my reach.'

Guy said, 'You're lucky to be able to travel at all when most of the rest of us can't.'

'That's because most of the rest of you have shit governments, but hey, let's not get into politics before I'm even properly in the door. Now, where's my daughter?'

Jeannie watched him look around again, as if Mallory might be hiding in a shadow or behind the dazzle of a lamp. Eventually his eyes came to hers in a way she knew was meant to intimidate. It did, but she held firm, refusing to be the first to look away.

'Where's Mallory?' he repeated. 'I thought she'd be here to greet me.'

'She's in her room,' Jeannie replied, 'and I believe she's already told you that she's flying home the day after tomorrow, so exactly why are you here?'

'To make sure she leaves, of course. She should never have come, and wouldn't have if I'd had anything to do with it.'

'Then lucky you didn't.'

'Is this your only bag?' Guy asked, referring to the holdall he'd placed on the floor.

'It's all I need for now,' Paul replied. 'I've some duty-frees in the car for the girls, and some Scotch for you. I remember you have a good taste in liquor.' He looked Guy up and down with a wryness that was so false it made Jeannie's skin crawl. 'You know, it's good to see you my friend,' he declared, bumping Guy's elbow again. *I never thought you'd stay with her for this long*, he didn't add, but Jeannie heard it anyway.

'I'll take you to the room you stayed in before,' Guy said.

Paul said, 'Let's hope we don't get lost on the way, huh? This place is so big it could take days to find your way out again. Bit of a fire hazard that, I should think.'

With a warning glance at Jeannie not to rise to it, Guy picked up the bag and directed Paul to the stairs.

'I should have dinner ready in about half an hour,' Jeannie said, stiffly, 'but come down earlier if you'd like a drink first.' *Keep it civil; there was nothing to be gained from stooping to his level, or showing that he was getting to her.*

Paul was part-way up the stairs when he stopped and looked over the banister. 'By the way,' he said, 'I hope we're not going to get into anything . . . unpleasant tonight. First, I'm jet-lagged, and second, a lot of water has flowed. Hasn't it?'

Not enough to stop the comment about a fire, Jeannie wanted to say, or to prevent you from coming here, or to wash away the ugliness inside you. She said nothing, simply turned away and returned to the kitchen.

Moments later Mallory appeared at the foot of the back stairs. 'Are you all right?' she asked, coming to refresh Jeannie's wine. 'I heard what he said . . .'

'I'm fine and it doesn't matter,' Jeannie assured her. 'We can get through this, but I think it might be easier if you joined us for dinner. He'll hate knowing you're in the house and ignoring him.'

'I really don't care. He deserves it for coming all this way to force me into leaving, and we know that's why he's here.'

Jeannie nodded slowly, not wanting to contradict her niece, because on one level she was probably right, but there was more to it, she was in no doubt of that.

'Here's Guy,' Mallory said quietly as her uncle came into the kitchen.

Turning around, Jeannie met his eyes and, knowing he was probably regretting ever taking Paul's call, never mind agreeing to let him come here, she made a small attempt at irony as she said, 'So, my darling, how is this working out for you?'

'It's only for a night or two,' he reminded her. 'I think we can handle it. Are you going to join us for dinner?' he asked Mallory.

She shook her head. 'Sorry. I can't face it. If it's OK with you guys, I've arranged to leave early tomorrow so I'll be gone before he gets up. I can stay at a hotel near Heathrow before my flight.'

'Oh no,' Jeannie protested, 'I don't want you to leave like this.'

'It'll be easier if I do. I've already spoken to Zac. He's going to borrow one of his dad's vans to drive me to the airport. I know it means we'll be breaking the rules, being in the same car, but I won't be coming back here, so you don't need to worry.'

'I'm sure you'll be safe with him,' Jeannie said, thinking of how negligent of the rules she and Neil often were when they walked in the woods. It was as though the virus, masks, endless hand-washing and government warnings belonged to another world.

'I'd be happy to drive you myself,' Guy told her, 'but I'm not keen to leave Jeannie here alone with Paul.'

'I know, and you shouldn't,' Mallory replied. 'Zac's

going to meet me at the gates at six. I'm sorry,' she said, to Jeannie, 'it's not how I wanted to say goodbye. I've had such a wonderful, special time here, I wish I could stay for ever.'

'I wish you could too,' Jeannie murmured, stroking her hair. 'But the good thing is that you have some exciting times ahead, and let's not forget that being in New Zealand is a lot safer right now than being here.'

Unable to deny that, Mallory caught Jeannie's hands in hers. 'You've taught me so much,' she said softly. 'I shall always treasure this time we've had.'

'Me too, but we'll see one another again very soon on Zoom or FaceTime, and before we know it you'll be back here, or Guy and I will be Down Under. And I'm sure Zac will too,' she added with a tender smile.

Mallory's eyes were swimming in tears as she nodded. 'I really wanted to take you back to the Seafront Café before I left so I could say goodbye to Zac's mum.'

'I'll pass the message on,' Jeannie assured her, 'or Guy will. Now, if you're serious about leaving in the morning, you should probably go and pack.'

After hugging her hard, Mallory said, 'I'll deal with Dad when we're back in New Zealand. He'll know by then what an absolute idiot he's made of himself, chasing across the world to try and bend me – and you – to his insufferable will.'

As it turned out, Paul was overwhelmed by jet-lag so didn't make it down for supper, and nor did Jeannie and Guy watch a movie. They went to bed early, and though Jeannie woke around three to hear her brother padding about the landing, she didn't get up to ask if he needed anything. He knew where the kitchen was, and wouldn't be shy about helping himself if he was hungry. He would also find out soon enough, should he go in search of Mallory, that she'd locked the door leading into the east wing.

'You have no reason to be afraid of your brother,' Neil had told her yesterday morning as they'd left the garden behind and strolled into the woods. 'What happened to your parents was terrible, devastating, but more for you than for him. If he can't see that then he doesn't deserve to be let into your home.'

She couldn't be sure what had made her open up to Neil about her parents' death and the way her brother had responded with such horrible accusations. She never normally discussed it with anyone, apart from Guy, but they'd already been married when it happened so he knew about it anyway. Maybe it was because, during one of their rambles, Neil had told her why he and Fliss had broken up, and she'd wanted him to know that she understood what it was to be the victim of tragedy. It was as though digging into their pasts and sharing secrets had buried the roots of their relationship even deeper, and she was sure it felt the same for him. In fact, they'd become so close that she looked forward to seeing him and being with him almost as much as she did spending time with Guy.

It was just before six in the morning when she dressed and wrapped up warmly to go and help Mallory carry her bags to the gate. She didn't want her to go off without a final hug; she didn't want her to go at all.

'You mean so much to me,' Mallory whispered as they reached the roadside, her words tumbling into the cold, salty air in shapeless white puffs. 'You're my favourite person in the world next to Mum. OK, you're fierce,' she grinned, 'and unpredictable, and a very tough boss, but, guess what, you don't scare me.'

With a laugh, Jeannie pressed a kiss to her forehead. 'Scaring you is the last thing I want to do,' she said, blinking back tears. How long was it going to be before she saw this treasured girl again? When would the world open up to allow them to be in each other's time zone, never mind each other's embrace?

'I'm sorry about Dad,' Mallory whispered.

'You shouldn't be apologizing for him.'

'I don't know why he's so convinced you're some kind of monster, when he's the one who behaves that way.'

'What happened back then,' Jeannie said, 'he knows the truth of it, I'm sure, he just doesn't want to see it.'

They turned as the sound of a car engine came to them through the fog, and soon two headlights appeared, faint and hazy, gradually brightening as Zac pulled up alongside them. He jumped out of the van and grabbed Mallory's bags as she gave Jeannie one last hug.

Moments later her niece had gone, leaving only the lingering sense of their shared embrace against Jeannie's body, and the loss of her already deepening in her heart.

I wonder, she thought to herself, as she walked back through the gates, *if I too could disappear into the mist and go to a place where no one could reach me.*

What would you do then, Guy? How afraid would you be?

CHAPTER THIRTY-TWO

FLISS

Monday 21 December 2020
Sixteen days before Jeannie's disappearance

'Are you OK?' Neil asked, as Fliss returned to the counter after unlocking the café to let him in. It was only six thirty in the morning, still dark outside, but he presumably had a busy day ahead with Zac going off to the airport with Mallory.

'I'm fine,' she assured him coolly. 'Are you?'

Frowning, he said, 'I'm good, but am I sensing there's something going on—'

'You mean between you and Jeannie?' she cut in without even thinking. Where was the anger coming from? She hadn't even been aware of feeling it, and yet here it was, spilling out of her. 'So is it?' she demanded.

He blinked in astonishment. 'I don't know what you're talking about. Why are you saying that?'

'I've heard all about how you walk in the woods with her – even your own son thinks there's something—'

'Stop!' he cried, putting up a hand. 'She's a client. I happen to get along pretty well with her, and I like her. Whatever else you might be telling yourself is in your own head.'

'Is it? OK, if you say so. I don't want to fall out with you when Leanne and Claudia are likely to turn up at any second.'

He shook his head in confusion and watched as she turned on the coffee machine to begin filling it with beans.

'Do you want a hand with anything?' he offered, glancing around.

'No, it's fine, I can manage.'

'Fliss, for God's sake . . .'

Rounding on him, she said, 'I don't care who you sleep with, OK? I really don't. It's none of my business, apart from the fact that you're married, and so is she, but apparently that doesn't count. Does Estie know?'

His expression was dark with anger as he said, 'I can see there's no reasoning with you while you're in this mood. Let's hope you're in a better one for Christmas.'

After he'd gone, she began setting out the breakfast trays and trying not to think of how big a fool she'd just made of herself.

Or had she? After all, he hadn't actually denied it.

CHAPTER THIRTY-THREE

ESTELLE

Monday 21 December 2020
Sixteen days before Jeannie's disappearance

It was a little after seven in the morning as Estelle drove through the clouds of rolling sea mist towards Howarth Hall, hoping she might see Guy. Of course no one was around, why would they be at this hour, but she'd been unable to sleep and so here she was.

Somehow she had to get herself through Christmas, to do her best for Chloe, but she already knew that nothing she did was ever going to be enough when she felt so alone and worthless. Fliss would be the life and soul of the big day. Maybe she, Estelle, should feel thankful for that, and to Prim for deciding to stay instead of returning to her parents for the festivities. She didn't feel thankful though, she only felt sick and resentful and wholly undeserving of the way her life was turning out.

'I've never done anything to harm anyone,' she kept telling herself, 'so why is this happening to me? What is wrong with me? Why does no one want me?'

Why doesn't Guy call?

He was obviously too busy with Jeannie, too wrapped

up in the Christmas they were going to spend together to consider anyone else.

How could she not see that as yet another rejection? As Jeannie winning while she was losing?

Hearing her phone ping with a text, she picked it up from the seat beside her and felt her heart plummet with despair. It was Prim asking where she was.

Why didn't her mother call to say she was sorry, that she'd acted too hastily and that – now she'd discussed it with her family – she wanted to meet her again? It was all Estelle wanted, it would change everything for her, and even now, in the very depths of her despondency, hope wouldn't die. It burned and yearned and brought false light to the terrible darkness she was in.

What was she going to do? Who could she turn to now that Guy seemed to have given up on her too?

CHAPTER THIRTY-FOUR

JEANNIE

Monday 21 December 2020
Sixteen days before Jeannie's disappearance

'What do you mean she's gone?' Paul spat, unsightly in his tiredness and yet still strangely handsome in a ravaged, don't-fuck-with-me sort of way. Jeannie had always felt bewildered by his looks, which were on the one hand almost pleasing, on the other so sour and foreboding.

'I said, what do you mean she's gone?' he repeated harshly. 'Gone where?'

'Back to New Zealand,' Jeannie replied, putting a coffee in front of him. 'She left first thing this morning.'

Seeming momentarily at a loss, he said, 'Why would she leave without seeing me? She knew I was here.'

'Yes, she did, but she knows what you're like, Paul, and she didn't want to be marched out of the door by an overbearing father, or listen to you sounding off at me the way you always feel compelled to.'

His face darkened with resentment. 'Well, I guess she's away from you, so that's one good thing. You know I don't want her under your influence, I don't actually want her anywhere near you. You're poisonous, Jeannie. You do things to people that destroy them, and I'm not letting that happen to my daughter.'

Wishing Guy would come in now, Jeannie said, 'I don't care what you think of me, Paul, all the things you keep telling yourself, the lies, the twisting of facts, and your refusal to accept what you did to our parents . . .'

'What *I* did?' he roared. 'You're the one who burnt the fucking house down with them in it.'

Jeannie flinched and turned away. She felt sick, terrified, wanted this to stop, but knew it wouldn't.

'That wasn't me, Jeannie,' he raged on. 'I was on the other side of the world when you set fire to our family home and made sure they couldn't get out.'

'Stop!' she yelled, spinning back again. 'You know it isn't true, so why do you keep saying it?'

'Because I know it *is* true. They were putting me back in the will. Dad told me that himself, and when you found out you made sure it couldn't happen. You are evil, right to your core. You are the very worst kind of human being—'

'No! It's you, *you* who are evil,' she yelled. 'You come here accusing me of doing things only *you* could do . . .'

He ducked as she hurled a pan at him.

'Shut up!' she shrieked furiously. 'Stop saying those things. I would never have hurt our parents, much less do—'

'The house burned down and the candle that started it, that was left on a locker between their beds, had been put there by you.'

'And I've never denied it. I know I'm responsible for leaving it burning, and I have to live with that for the rest of my life, but it wasn't deliberate. I had no idea that the leaves in the wax were flammable. It was a design fault. Every investigation has concluded that . . .'

'But you knew about the leaves, didn't you? It's why you chose *that* candle. It had already been withdrawn from sale, but you happened to have one and you used it.'

'No!' she seethed, covering her ears. 'I loved them. I was always there for them and you never were.'

'Oh, play me another. It's the oldest story in the book, Jeannie. Someone in your position should know that. You did it to make sure everything they had went to you! Look around you. How long did it take for you to get this place, to start playing lady of the manor? You'd burned down the one we grew up in, so here's another—'

'That's enough,' Guy said darkly as he came into the kitchen. 'We can't keep going through this, Paul. There was an inquest, as you know, and no charges were ever brought . . .'

'Because she's fucking clever, that's why! So fucking clever that she's walked off with everything that should have been mine and never looked back. But you're not having my daughter, Jeannie. I'm telling you that now. I know you're trying to turn her against me—'

'You're doing that yourself,' Jeannie cried furiously. 'Look at you. Listen to yourself. I don't need to do anything. She can see you for what you are . . .'

'Which isn't a parricidal maniac, and that's what *you* are. I might not be able to prove it, but we both know it's true. You meant them to die in that fire. When you left the house, you made sure all the doors were locked—'

'Paul, I've already asked you to stop,' Guy cut in angrily. 'If this is all you've come for . . .'

'Of course it's all he's here for,' Jeannie shrieked. 'He pretends to care about Mallory, and our parents, but he's the one who was stealing from Dad's company. He's the one who left for New Zealand with fifty thousand pounds that Dad *gave* you to start again, even after you'd embezzled over a million out of the company. He did it to protect you from the scandal; he still tried to help you in spite of the humiliation he suffered, knowing that his own son was a dirty thief. All you've ever cared about is yourself and the money that was *never* going to be yours.'

'Yes, I care about the money, but at least I admit it, unlike you, and I repeat, I did not kill my own parents to get it.'

'Paul, it's time for you to leave,' Guy told him, coming to stand between them.

'Oh, I'm going, don't worry,' Paul snarled, 'but let me tell you this, sister dearest. It's not over. You won't get away with it. Even if the law won't hold you responsible for what you did, I do, and you're going to pay.'

She flinched as he smashed his coffee mug into the sink and stormed upstairs to collect his belongings.

Minutes later he was in his rental car, heading for the gates, while Jeannie stood in Guy's arms, still shaking and praying with all her heart that this would be the very last time she saw him.

PART TWO

CHAPTER THIRTY-FIVE

CARA

Saturday 23 January 2021
Seventeen days since Jeannie's disappearance

In spite of it being the weekend, Cara was at her desk by eight, reading a message from Mallory Haines. In it she explained that her father had returned to New Zealand on Christmas Eve, and on Boxing Day evening he'd fallen and broken his ankle.

Cara sent the information to Andee and DS Rundle, and was about to update the whiteboard when her mobile rang.

Seeing it was Richie from the *Kesterly Gazette*, she clicked on, hoping he might be inviting her out for a drink, while knowing he couldn't, thanks to the Covid rules.

'Hey, how are you?' she asked, going to pour herself a coffee. She'd long had a crush on him, but wasn't at all sure the feeling was mutual. Still, she could always hope.

'I'm good thanks,' he replied. 'How about you? Any news on Jeannie Symonds I could use?'

'Nothing you don't already have,' she countered. 'Maybe there's something you'd like to share with me?' They'd done this on a case she'd been attached to before, a little quid pro quo, and it had worked quite well.

'I've heard the Symondses have an apartment at the marina,' he confided.

'Right, yeah. Not actually theirs, but it has been checked, and she's not there.'

'OK. I saw Primrose Barnes down that way yesterday morning.'

Cara stopped pouring. She'd been there herself yesterday morning, but why did he think it was significant that Primrose Barnes had been too? What did he know that she didn't?

'Really?' she said. 'What time was that?'

'Around midday.'

An hour or so after she'd left.

'She was driving out of the gates,' he continued, 'so I have no idea where she'd been in the complex, just thought it was an interesting coincidence, what with you having been there earlier.'

Guessing Colin on security must have told him that, she said, 'There have got to be half-a-dozen restaurants doing takeout meals in the marina.'

'Except none of them open at lunchtime,' Richie pointed out.

The marina was a big place, so Primrose Barnes could have been going anywhere, and Cara couldn't see why she would be visiting the flat the Symondses took care of. She said, 'OK, thanks for the call, Richie. I'll get back to you as soon as there's anything I can share from my end.'

CHAPTER THIRTY-SIX

FLISS

Saturday 23 January 2021
Seventeen days since Jeannie's disappearance

It was just after three in the afternoon when Guy came into the café looking tired and hassled – in fact not at all like the cool and contained man Fliss had come to know. She wasn't surprised, given it was over two weeks now since he'd first come in to ask if she'd seen Jeannie; clearly the worry was taking a toll.

Nevertheless, he managed to inject a note of warmth into his tone as he said, 'Sorry if I'm overdoing the visits and phone calls. I know how unlikely it is that one of your regulars will have seen her after all this time, it's just that—'

'It's OK,' Fliss assured him. 'I understand how hard this is for you, especially with it being so long now. I just wish I had something positive to tell you. Have you spoken to Andee today?'

He nodded. 'Briefly, this morning. Nothing's changed I'm afraid.'

Wanting to make some sort of gesture to help him feel better, she said, 'I know we're not supposed to, but if you'd like to drink your tea over there, at the end of the bar . . . There's no one around at the moment, and if someone wants to come in, I can take their order out to them.'

Clearly moved by the kindness, he looked around, saying, 'God how I've missed sitting in a café. It's something we were all taking for granted not so long ago, yet now it feels like a luxury.'

'Glad to hear you think of the Seafront that way,' she commented teasingly. 'The bar stools should be there, just pull one out and I'll slide a tray along to make sure I keep my distance.'

Settling into place, he started to remove his mask and stopped.

'You won't be able to drink your tea with it on,' she pointed out.

He was smiling as he peeled it away, and she felt faintly surprised to realize that seeing him without it was like recognizing someone she hadn't seen in a while.

'Thank you,' he said as she slid a tray of tea his way and, with a self-conscious smile, added, 'can I offer you a cup?'

Why not? she thought and, pushing along another teacup, she watched him fill it and declined the milk and sugar.

'You realize you now have to take your face covering off too,' he said as he pushed the cup to his arm's length.

As she lifted her visor, she felt for an odd moment as if they were flirting, revealing parts of themselves that hadn't actually been accessible before. Then she realized he was no longer looking at her. His eyes were fixed on Jeannie's photograph, clipped to the bottom of the day's

Specials board on the wall behind her. It wasn't easy to read his expression, although she could tell he was struggling and, after all this time, she feared he had good reason to be thinking the worst.

'There's something I haven't told you,' he said, and because his gaze was still on Jeannie, she wondered if he was speaking to her. 'I was planning to leave her,' he said quietly. 'We hadn't talked about it. I hadn't told her, so she wouldn't have had any idea. Or I didn't think she did until she suddenly disappeared on me.'

Thrown by the unexpectedness of his confession, Fliss wasn't sure what to say. 'Do . . . do you think she found out?' she finally managed.

'If she did, I don't know how.' He looked up and smiled sadly.

'Have you told Andee?' she asked.

He shook his head. 'I saw no reason to when I hadn't even mentioned it to Jeannie. I thought it would just complicate things because it couldn't be why she left if she didn't know about it.'

Fliss wanted to ask why he'd decided to end his marriage, but didn't feel that she could.

'Ending a relationship is never easy, is it?' he sighed. 'Especially when the last thing you want is to hurt someone you care for.'

Thinking of the devastating break-up of her own marriage, and all the pain she'd caused, Fliss's heart flooded with feeling. She wished she could reach out for his hand; a proper gesture of comfort was what he needed now, an unspoken empathy, definitely not the story of her own failures. But touching wasn't allowed, so after a while she said, 'Is it because you've found someone else?'

He seemed surprised by the question, and said, 'No, no, there isn't anyone else. I just simply didn't want to be in the marriage anymore. I don't suppose that's changed, although it's hard to know how I'm feeling now, with the way things are.'

CHAPTER THIRTY-SEVEN

CARA

Monday 25 January 2021
Nineteen days since Jeannie's disappearance

Looking up as Andee came into the incident room, Cara grimaced as she said, 'I have some news. DS Rundle wanted me to tell you as soon as you came in.'

Andee unwound her scarf and put down her keys and phone as she said, 'Why do I get the feeling it's not going to be good?'

'It is, and it isn't,' Cara replied. 'Thanks to pressure from the DS, the phone company's finally coughed up their records. That's the good bit. Here's the bad: there's been no activity on Jeannie's mobile since January the sixth.'

Andee stilled as she took this in.

'The last call,' Cara continued, 'was the one she made to Maurice, her assistant. After that, no communications, and no way to track it because the finder wasn't activated. And as you know, we've never found any evidence of a second phone.'

Andee sank into a chair. 'This definitely isn't good,' she murmured. 'How about in the days or weeks leading up to the sixth? Any significant calls there?'

'Not that I've found so far, but I'm still going through it. Mostly they seem work-related, apart from calls or texts to Guy and her niece.'

'OK. What about the credit cards? Anything back on them?'

'Both, and no transactions on either since an online purchase on January the third from John Lewis for some La Prairie cosmetics.' Reading from her notes she added, 'The parcel was delivered on January the sixth at ten forty-four by DPD.'

'Only hours before she left.' Andee was clearly trying to work out what this might mean, and eventually said, 'I'll find out from Guy if these expensive cosmetics are still in the house, but if it was a purchase made in time for her departure, it's still not going to tell us where she is. Natalie!' she shouted as Rundle shot past the door.

'Not now,' Rundle shouted back.

'Yes now, or I'll take it to Gould myself.'

A moment later Rundle was in the room. 'What is it?' she asked tartly, clearly not thrilled to be summoned, or threatened, on her own territory.

'I take it you already know that Jeannie's mobile and credit cards haven't been used since January the sixth—'

'I didn't,' Rundle interrupted, looking at Cara. 'I just passed the records on when they came in.'

Andee said, 'And in case you need more to take to Gould, I learned something interesting from Fliss at the weekend. Apparently Guy Symonds was planning to end his marriage.'

Rundle's eyes widened.

'He's never mentioned that before,' Cara stated.

'Apparently not to Jeannie either,' Andee told her, 'which

is why he didn't tell us. He says she had no idea it was his intention, so he didn't want to complicate things by suggesting it could be why she left.'

Rundle couldn't have looked more sceptical if she'd tried. 'Are you buying this?' she asked, clearly ready to heap more scorn.

'I need to speak to him.'

'Do it now,' Rundle instructed, 'I'd like to hear what he has to say.'

Minutes later, Guy Symonds was on a video-link explaining to Andee why he hadn't mentioned wanting to end his marriage when he'd first spoken to her about Jeannie's disappearance.

'I really didn't think it was relevant,' he insisted, 'and I'm still not sure that it is. Jeannie didn't know it was my intention, and I had no plans to do anything about it until I'd worked out with a solicitor the best way to handle it. By the best way, I mean one that would cause her the least amount of distress.'

'Is there any way she could have found out if you didn't tell her?' Andee asked. 'And that's why she left?'

He took a moment to think. 'I keep a notebook,' he said, 'you may have seen me using one to jot down reminders or ideas for lectures, sometimes just idle thoughts. I haven't seen my last one for a while. I assumed I'd left it in London, but now that you're asking about it . . . Well, it's quite possible that I jotted down the divorce lawyer's name and number and Jeannie . . .' He gave a helpless sort of gesture. 'She wouldn't know who it was unless she googled the name, and I don't recall seeing it in her search history when I checked her computer.'

'But she might have called the number?'

'It's possible. The solicitor I'm dealing with hasn't mentioned it.'

'Can you let us have his or her details?'

'His. Of course. I don't have them to hand. Shall I put them in an email after we've finished here?'

'Thank you. So, do you think Jeannie might have taken the notebook with her, given you can't find it?'

He looked doubtful. 'I can't think why she would have.'

'Is there anything else in it that might have caused her some upset, or to be angry with you?'

'You mean angry enough to leave and not be in touch for almost three weeks? As I said, they're mostly medical notes.'

Andee glanced briefly at Rundle and Cara and, sensing they had no more for now, she began wrapping things up.

'Before you go,' he said, 'I should let you know that I've managed to rearrange my schedule for the next couple of weeks. It's hard to concentrate with all this going on, so I felt it would be in everyone's interests if I was at Howarth Hall for the time being.'

Moments after the call ended, Andee received the email he'd promised and Cara quickly checked the lawyer's number against Jeannie's phone records.

'OMG,' she muttered. 'She called it at eleven forty on January the fifth.'

Andee and Rundle exchanged glances. 'How long was the call?' Andee asked.

Cara checked. 'Twenty-three seconds.'

Andee said. 'Long enough to find out who the number belongs to, or maybe to leave a message of some sort?'

Rundle got to her feet. 'I'm escalating this as of now,'

she stated. 'I'll speak to Gould to make it official; mean-time I want you, Cara, to start briefing DCs Shari and Johnson. The main incident room has come free so you can set up there.' To Andee she said, 'Are we agreed that a husband's lies – or omissions of truths – make him suspect number one?'

Andee said, 'It would certainly be the conventional route to take.'

Rundle scowled at her. 'As soon as you've got a better one, be sure to let me know,' and a moment later she'd gone.

Cara looked at Andee. 'She won't have forgotten about Neil Roberts,' she said.

'No, I'm sure she hasn't,' Andee agreed, 'but she's right to be worried about Guy. I hope you are too. You might want to take that.'

Realizing her mobile was buzzing, Cara saw who it was and put the call straight on to speaker.

'Hello Ms Barnes,' she said, reaching for a pen, 'thanks for getting back to me. I wanted to ask you about a trip you made to the marina—'

Primrose cut in, 'Is it OK for me to ask if you've found Jeannie Symonds yet?'

Cara glanced up at Andee as she said, 'No, we haven't. Is there something you'd like to tell us?'

'Can I come there?' Primrose asked. 'I'm happy to fit in with a time that suits you, but there are things . . . Something's been happening that I think you need to know about.'

CHAPTER THIRTY-EIGHT

FLISS

Tuesday 26 January 2021
Twenty days since Jeannie's disappearance

'First I need to thank you for the tea on Saturday,' Guy said, raising his voice a little to make himself heard over the low, incessant roar of the waves, 'and now this.'

Fliss smiled. 'I'm glad to take a break,' she assured him, thinking what an understatement that was, given how stressed she'd been lately, and how thrilled she'd been when he'd made the suggestion. 'It doesn't happen often these days.' And it wouldn't have today, had Wilkie from the Corona Girls not insisted she could cope for an hour, longer if necessary.

With a laugh she added, 'I can't remember the last time I did this walk. Funny how you don't take advantage of what's on your doorstep when you live in a place. I'd almost forgotten how much I love the sea air.'

'It's certainly exhilarating,' he agreed, stepping sideways as a skateboarder whizzed past, narrowly missing him.

It was neither a sunny, nor warm day, but at least the wind wasn't hurling a gale as it had been lately, and so far today there was no sign of rain. It really was good to be outside.

'Didn't you want to be there while the police searched the Hall today?' she asked, hoping he wouldn't mind her mentioning it. It had been in the news, so everyone knew, and she couldn't help wondering if that was almost as bad as having his home ransacked.

He shook his head, and said, 'I did and I didn't. In the end I thought it wiser to let them have free rein. If I was there watching them sort through all our private belongings . . . Well, I was afraid it might not bring out the best in me, and getting in their way wouldn't help any of us.'

Admiring his ability to downplay the awful situation he was in, she said, 'What do you think they're actually looking for?'

Catching his scarf as it tailed into a sprightly breeze, he said, 'I guess they won't know until they find it, but I'm sure they'll take Jeannie's computer and files. Mine too, given my status as Suspect Number One.'

She looked at him worriedly. 'If they thought that, they'd surely have called you in for questioning by now?'

'It'll happen when they're ready. I'm the husband of a woman who's been missing for almost three weeks and unfortunately I don't have a proper alibi for when she disappeared.'

'But I thought you were in London.'

'I was working from home on the Wednesday. No one else was there, I didn't go out, or have any visitors. Luckily the car was on the drive the whole time, and my phone was with me, so maybe my suspect status will be downgraded once they've finished running their checks on that.'

They parted for a moment to pass either side of a couple with a pushchair and slow-walking toddler.

'What's concerning me a lot at the moment,' he said,

when they were close enough to communicate again, 'is them deciding to dig up the garden. That's what seems to happen in cases like this, isn't it?'

Knowing that each thrust of a spade and turn of soil, never mind destruction of gazebos, fountains, dry-stone walls and rugged pathways would feel like a body blow to Neil, she said, 'But it was all done long before Jeannie disappeared, so there would be no reason to do that, surely.'

He threw her a grateful smile. 'I'm letting my imagination run away with me,' he grimaced, 'of course you're right,' and he took out his phone as it rang. Seeing who was calling he said, 'This will only take a moment,' and turning from the wind, he said, 'Jason. Thanks for getting back to me.' He listened for a while then said, 'Actually, that's a good idea. I'll do it today, thanks,' and he rang off.

As they walked on he said, 'That was the lawyer I contacted about separating from Jeannie. He's advising me to engage someone who specializes in crime.'

Fliss's heart contracted. A criminal lawyer! She felt wretched for him. It seemed so wrong that he, of all people, who spent practically every day saving lives, should have to be going through this. 'Have you spoken to Andee since they made the search official?' she asked.

'Yes, she called last night to remind me that this was what we wanted and that if – when – it happened, the going would probably be tough. She's right about that, and this is just the beginning. Of course, I haven't helped myself by not admitting straight away that I wanted to end my marriage. I guess at that point I still believed we were going to find her, so there didn't seem any point to it.'

'And you don't believe that now?'

He shook his head despondently. 'I've no idea what to think now. The fact that she hasn't used her phone for all this time . . .' He trailed off, clearly not wanting to put any more of the thought into words.

Pulling her padded coat more tightly around her, Fliss walked on beside him, her long legs easily keeping up with his, her heart pounding with sympathy and trepidation. If something awful had happened to Jeannie, and it seemed foolish now not to think that it had, he really was in the worst imaginable position.

'I know you and Neil are still quite close,' he said, after a while, 'I just wondered . . .' He glanced at her briefly, then shook his head. 'Sorry, I don't . . .'

'Wondered what?' she asked, moving in a little closer so she could hear him better.

Keeping his eyes fixed straight ahead, he said, 'I probably shouldn't ask this, but has Neil ever talked to you about Jeannie in a way . . .' He looked at her again. 'Did he ever give you the impression they were . . . close?'

Fliss's heartbeat slowed as the understanding of what he was asking seemed to burn inside her. 'I think . . . They're friends,' she said, not wanting to give it any more status than that. 'He speaks highly of her.'

He smiled. 'Yes, she does of him too. Actually, she's had a bit of a crush on him for a while, I've even teased her about it . . . I just can't help wondering if it ever went . . . any further?'

Fliss could feel herself becoming light-headed at the thought of all the terrible implications it could have for Neil if there was any more to the relationship. 'Please tell me,' she said hoarsely, 'that you don't think Neil has done anything to hurt her.'

'Oh God, no,' he cried. 'Oh, Fliss, I'm sorry. Believe me, that's not what I'm saying. I know the police have spoken to him because he was the last one to see her, but I'm certain someone's seen her since. There has to have been someone else, unless she's . . . done something to herself.'

Flinching at that, she said, 'Do you think she would? If she thought you were going to leave her, maybe she . . .' She stopped; it was too awful for words.

'She's not someone who gives up that easily,' he said, 'so no, I don't believe she'd harm herself, and certainly not for that reason. I'm not sure why I said it. I mean, there's no note, we never had a discussion of any kind, much less a fight . . .' He paused. 'And yet, here we are.'

He slowed his steps and, breaking away from her, went to lean his elbows on the iron railings over the beach. As she joined him, a few feet away, he said, 'I'm sure you already know that the national press has started to take an interest in the case, so it won't be long before our entire lives are exposed for the edification and probable titillation of all.'

Sensing his dread of becoming a doctor at the centre of a scandal, the surgeon who was no longer recognized for what he did, but more for what he might have done, Fliss said, 'Maybe she'll see it and come to her senses before things go any further.'

'We can but hope,' he responded, not sounding convinced, in fact not seeming as if he was even really with her anymore.

She let the silence run, filled with the sough of waves and screech of gulls and a speedboat that roared out of nowhere to cross the bay. She was thinking of what he'd asked her about Neil, and how she hadn't seen much of him since they'd exchanged words. She wanted to call him now, and yet wouldn't know what to say if she did.

It was a moment before she realized Guy was speaking.

'. . . so please let's stop talking about me,' he was saying, 'I'd like to hear about you. I know you own the café, and you have a very handsome young son who Jeannie's niece is quite smitten with, but that's about it.'

Coming into the moment, she said, 'There isn't much else, apart from the struggle to keep going through these lockdowns and what kind of state we'll be in once we're out of them. Please let it be business as usual. Maybe it'll be even better than before if staycations really do take off.'

He was watching her and his expression had softened as he took in the hope and concern in her words. 'Have you ever thought about doing anything else?' he asked. 'Or maybe catering is in your blood?'

With a laugh, she said, 'No, it's not. My father was a biochemist, he died when I was seventeen; and my mother was a primary school teacher. She's gone now too. Eleven years and I still miss her. We were very close and she saw me through some pretty difficult times. What about your parents?'

Turning his back to the sea, he said, 'They've both gone too. Dad was a heart surgeon, the planter of footsteps, so to speak, and Mum was a midwife. They had me quite late in life. No brothers or sisters. You?'

'I'm an only child too. As is Neil. It's why we decided early on that we'd definitely have more than one . . .' She stopped, not wanting to go any further with that. 'Do you have any children?' she asked.

'No, I'm sad to say, because I always wanted them. I

just seem to have met women who don't. In Jeannie's case it was a little late anyway, and my first wife was very driven by her career. You and Neil must have been quite young when you got together.'

'We were both in our second year at uni. By the end of the third year I was pregnant with Zac and, because we were madly in love, we couldn't wait to get married. The folly of youth, huh?'

'Let's be thankful for it, life could be very dull otherwise. Have you ever met anyone since Neil? Sorry, that's none of my business . . .'

'It's OK. The answer is no, I haven't, or no one I could get serious about.'

He smiled, seemed about to say more, but then turned to walk on towards the marina.

As she caught up with him, he said, 'Do you like to sail?'

'I used to,' she replied, 'but I haven't been out in a while. How about you?'

'It's probably one of my favourite things to do, apart from surfing, but Jeannie's not so keen, unless it's a couple of weeks in the Caribbean or off a Greek island.'

'I think I'm on Jeannie's team,' she responded dryly.

He smiled. 'A friend of ours, Valerie, keeps a boat here during the summer – it's in the South of France now – she also has an apartment in the first block. Maybe you already know that, Cara and Andee have searched it. I'm thinking of asking if I can stay there for a few days while all this police activity is going on.'

Realizing how hard it must have been for him at the Hall, even before the search was made official, she said,

'That sounds like a good idea, and with the security here you'll probably be able to escape the press.'

He stopped and turned to look back along the Promenade. 'It's quite peaceful now the wind's dropped,' he commented, seeming to take it as a lull in his personal chaos. He took out his phone as it rang again and his face paled slightly as he said, 'It's the police.'

Wanting to give him some privacy, she began to walk back towards the café, hoping with all her heart that nothing terrible had been found.

It wasn't long before he was beside her again, and in a frustrated, yet ironic tone, he said, 'They're about to leave the Hall and don't have any keys to lock up, so time for me to head back there, I'm afraid. Wish me luck and thanks again for the walk.'

It wasn't until later when she was at home with the café closed and Zac in the bath, that Fliss allowed herself to reflect on all that she and Guy had talked about. Though she was undeniably worried for him – so much so that she'd already texted to tell him to call any time if he needed to talk – her greatest concern was for Neil. She wanted to ring and ask him about Jeannie, to get his reassurance that there hadn't been anything going on, that there was actually nothing to be concerned about, but how could she do that without it sounding as though she suspected him of something far more sinister than an affair?

CHAPTER THIRTY-NINE

ESTELLE

Tuesday 26 January 2021
Twenty days since Jeannie's disappearance

'Neil! Where are you going?' Estelle cried urgently.

As he turned around to find her standing on the stairs, dressed to go out, she felt her heartbeat quicken. If she hadn't spoken, he'd have left without even knowing she was there, so why had she called out to him?

'I could ask you the same,' he countered, taking in her coat, scarf and boots.

She stared at him, unsure of what to say, only wishing that she hadn't stopped him.

He came to the foot of the stairs, took her hand, and turned it over in his own. 'You're cold,' he told her. His eyes weren't warm, but he did seem concerned, as though he knew they were in separate places, on parallel tracks, but not sure whether he wanted to join them.

'I'm fine,' she insisted, taking her hand away.

He looked surprised and bewildered. 'I'm worried about you, Estie,' he said. 'Please tell me what's wrong.'

'It's OK,' she snapped, 'you can stop pretending that Prim hasn't told you about my *birth* mother. I know she has.'

He didn't even try to deny it, he simply regarded her with so much intensity that she was forced to look away. 'I'm sorry things turned out the way they did,' he said. 'It must have been terrible for you. I'm sure it still is, but we can help you get through . . .'

'Where are you going?' she repeated forcefully, in spite of the shake in her voice.

'To the police station. They want to talk to me about Jeannie.'

'Again? Why?' she cried shrilly. 'What have you done?'

Appearing shocked he said, 'I haven't *done* anything . . .'

'But you were the last one to see her. Everyone knows that, so they obviously think . . . Where is she? Do you know?'

Taking a step back he said, quietly, 'I've no idea where she is, Estie, but the fact that you seem to think I do . . .'

'That's not what I said . . .'

'It's exactly what you said, and now I'd like to know if it's what you're going to tell the police when they interview you, that you think I know where she is.'

'Why would they want to interview me?' she blurted. 'I've already told them I don't know anything.' She looked around, as if something somewhere could save her from this, but there was nothing, and no one, only the truth that she didn't want to speak.

'I know what you're thinking,' he said. 'You're remembering how I was accused of assault before . . .'

'She dropped the charge.'

'But now you're asking yourself if I was guilty and got away with it.'

'No! I . . . Neil, please,' she cried as he turned away in

anger. 'You're wrong. It's not what I was thinking,' but the door had already slammed behind him.

Sinking onto the stairs, she began to count her breaths, and to remind herself that everything was going to be all right. She just needed to stay calm, to let everything play out the way it had to. She had nothing to be afraid of, no reason to start panicking and accusing Neil of something he could never have done. That was what she'd told herself when he'd been arrested before, that he could never have done it. The woman was a liar, a fantasist, someone who'd lashed out after he'd rejected her advances.

The police had ended up believing him and so had let him go.

She couldn't imagine they'd do so again, and the mere thought of it made her feel sick to her soul.

CHAPTER FORTY

CARA

Tuesday 26 January 2021
Twenty days since Jeannie's disappearance

It had taken next to no time for everything to kick off once DS Rundle had spoken to the brass upstairs; in fact, Cara's head was spinning with how fast things were happening. A full-on SOCO team had been up at Howarth Hall for most of the day, another was at work on the Symonds's London house, and a PolSA unit – an official police search team – was already on standby. Right now DCI Gould was talking to the press outside the station, where Cara had made sure that Richie Franklyn from the *Gazette,* who'd also been commissioned by a national paper to cover events, had a front-row seat.

For her part, she'd been stuck in the incident room all day, living with the shame of having failed to uncover the fact that Neil Roberts had once been arrested for assault. True, it had never escalated into a charge, but a complaint had been made six years ago, by a female client, that he'd attacked her when she'd tried to break off their relationship, and it had taken Leo Johnson all of a few minutes to find it.

However, she might yet save face, for half an hour ago she'd finally received an email response to a request she'd made on day one of being assigned to the case. She wasn't sure what she'd expected from it, it had been more of a 'covering all bases' exercise really, but it seemed she'd done the right thing, and now she was extremely keen to hear what the DS had to say about it.

An hour later there was a gathering of at least six detectives, plus Andee, behind Cara's chair as she talked them through what was happening on her screen. 'This is a video that Jeannie posted on her Facebook page of a party at the Hall last summer,' she began. 'I sent it to the techies to see if they could zoom in on this particular section, where you can see a man walking across a field next to the house. I know you can't tell from this, but I'll show you in a minute who it is. He's heading towards the woods and, as the drone overtakes him, you'll see . . . Yes, there she is, there's a woman standing by a gate who looks as if she might be waiting for him.' She clicked open a file containing two separate close-ups, of both the man and the woman, and sat back so everyone could see.

'Well, well,' Rundle muttered, glancing at Andee.

'It's Guy Symonds,' Andee stated, 'apparently on his way to meet Estelle Fields.'

'Are there any shots of the two of them together?' Rundle asked Cara.

'No, the drone's already moved on before he gets to her, but he's close enough to the gate that he can't have *not* known she was there.'

Rundle turned back to Andee. 'Did he ever mention anything about Estelle Fields to you?'

Andee shook her head.

'So Jeannie's husband and sworn enemy are . . . what? What are they doing here?'

'We won't know until we ask him,' Andee replied.

To Cara, Rundle said, 'Get him up on screen. I want to hear what he has to say about this.'

As Cara made the connection, Noah Shields, one of the detectives, took an incoming call on one of the landlines.

'Neil Roberts has arrived,' he told Rundle.

She nodded, and after moving the other detectives out of shot, she took over Cara's chair and focused her attention on Guy Symonds as his tired, almost gaunt-looking face appeared on the screen.

'Good evening, detective,' he said. 'I was just about to leave to go to the marina apartment.'

'Actually,' Leo Johnson said quietly to Rundle, 'I think a forensic team is still there, so maybe he can hold off until tomorrow?'

'I heard that,' Guy said, 'and it's no problem. So is there something I can help you with?'

Coming straight to the point, Rundle said, 'We have some video here of you meeting with Estelle Fields on the day of a party held at the Hall last summer. Would you care to tell me about that?'

Seeming too tired for surprise, he said, 'I'm guessing this is the footage Jeannie posted on her Facebook page. I'm not sure if she even noticed the part where I left and went over to the woods; I wasn't even aware it was there myself until I checked her social media accounts after she disappeared.'

So he hadn't tried to remove it, Cara noted, which had to be a point in his favour.

'I went over to talk to Estelle,' he explained, 'because

I saw her watching the party and I couldn't help feeling sorry for her. I knew how upset she'd been by the breakdown of her relationship with Jeannie, and I realized when she sent a house-warming card after we moved in that she probably wanted to repair the situation. I must admit, when we got talking that day, I was surprised to find that the whole thing still bothered her so much. I ended up trying to persuade her to come and join us, but she wouldn't hear of it.'

'Is that the only time you've met with Estelle Fields?' Rundle asked tonelessly.

'No, actually,' he replied. 'I've had a few chats with her since, mainly because of how lonely she always seems. I think it's been her hope, since the day of that party, that I might provide some sort of bridge back to Jeannie, and I'm guilty of allowing her to think that, because I thought it might be good for Jeannie too if there was some sort of resolution and closure around what had happened between them.'

Rundle glanced up at Andee, who gave a small shrug as if to say, *It sounds plausible, but whether it's the truth I've no idea.*

Turning back to the screen Rundle said, 'Did you talk about anything else when you met with her, besides the situation with Jeannie?'

'Yes. We talked about her birth mother and whether she should be in touch with her. She was, just before Christmas, and it turned out to be a difficult meeting that she found hard to cope with.'

Puzzled, Rundle said, 'So why come to you with it?'

He shrugged, as if not quite certain himself. 'I'm going to say that strangers – or near strangers – are sometimes easier to talk to than family members. They don't have the same emotional investment in whatever the issue might be, so I guess that's why Estelle chose to talk to me. She might have told those closest to her by now, I don't know.'

'When was the last time you saw her?' Rundle asked.

He frowned as he thought. 'I can't recall the date,' he said, 'but it was probably about three or four weeks ago.'

'Before or after Jeannie disappeared?'

'It would have been before. No disrespect to Estelle, but I had other things on my mind after Jeannie left.'

'Have you ever discussed Jeannie's disappearance with her?'

'No. As I said, I haven't seen her since it happened.'

'Is it possible Jeannie was going to meet her when she left the Hall on January the sixth?'

He seemed both surprised and troubled by that. 'I've no reason to think it,' he replied, 'because as far as I was aware they were never in touch. But you have Jeannie's phone records, and her computer now. I didn't find any communication between them myself when I went through the emails and messages.'

'How many times did you meet up with Estelle?'

He shrugged. 'Four? Five at the most.'

'Did she ever say anything that led you to think she might want to cause Jeannie some harm?'

He shook his head doubtfully. 'There was still a certain amount of animosity on her part, but it was more defensive than intentional, I'd have said.'

Rundle looked back to Andee, and receiving no prompt to go further she said, 'OK, Mr Symonds, we'll leave it there for now. Thank you for your time, we'll be in touch again soon.' As the screen darkened she rotated in her chair to address Andee. 'Do you believe him?' she asked bluntly.

'On the face of it, I've no reason not to,' Andee replied, 'but I know what you're thinking. Here's something else he didn't tell us about until we found it out for ourselves.'

'Until Cara found it out,' Leo Johnson put in.

Cara shot him a grateful smile.

'It's good that you followed it up,' Rundle told her. 'I don't know where it gets us, yet, but there's clearly some sort of peculiar dynamic between those two households. Guy Symonds and Estelle Fields; Jeannie Symonds and Neil Roberts . . .' To Andee she said, 'Care to comment?'

'Not at this stage,' Andee replied.

'Someone else we should talk to,' Rundle continued decisively, 'is Fliss Roberts.'

'Really? Why?' Andee queried.

'From what I've heard, she and Symonds have struck up a bit of a friendship in recent days, and she was once married to Neil Roberts? Presumably she still talks to him?'

'Yes, but I don't see—'

'I'm not accusing her of anything,' Rundle interrupted, 'but she could know more than she realizes.' Turning to Cara she said, 'What's happening with Primrose Barnes?'

Cara grimaced. 'She was supposed to come here at two this afternoon, but she didn't show up and I haven't been able to get hold of her.'

Rundle turned back to Andee.

Andee said, 'I'd like to be in the gallery for your interview with Neil Roberts, if that's OK,' and, apparently having no problem with it, Rundle led the way downstairs.

CHAPTER FORTY-ONE

FLISS

Tuesday 26 January 2021
Twenty days since Jeannie's disappearance

Fliss scanned the text from Guy, thanking her for taking time for a walk and letting her know he was moving to the marina now the police had cleared the scene. She'd offered to be there for him any time he needed to talk, and he promised to take her up on the offer if needs be. She put away her phone and looked up as Zac came into the kitchen, wrapped in a towelling robe and smelling of her bubble bath.

'Everything OK?' he asked, taking a beer from the fridge.

'Yes, I think so,' she replied. She wanted to ask him about his father and Jeannie, what he'd actually seen, if anything, but she bit it back, knowing it would upset him to think she had any doubts about Neil while all this was going on. She wasn't entirely sure that she did, except – given how worried she was – she accepted that she must have some concerns.

'Have you seen Estelle recently?' she asked.

Fixed on his phone, he shook his head. 'Not for a couple of weeks.'

Fliss hadn't seen her either, at least she hadn't been into the café while Fliss was there. 'I think I'll give her a call,' she said and, scrolling to Estelle's number, she clicked to connect.

Estelle answered on the first ring. 'Fliss, is everything OK?' she asked. 'Are you calling about Neil?'

Fliss's heart turned over. 'Why do you ask that?' she said.

'The police have called him in again,' Estelle ran on, 'and he's been gone for quite a while. I thought you might have some news. Will you ring me if he gets in touch with you first?'

'Of course,' Fliss promised. 'And you'll ring me?' but Estie had already gone.

CHAPTER FORTY-TWO

CARA

Tuesday 26 January 2021
Twenty days since Jeannie's disappearance

Cara was with Andee in the viewing gallery, watching and listening as DS Rundle and Leo Johnson questioned Neil Roberts. He was looking smarter today than the first time he'd come in, when he'd worn his work clothes. Maybe he was trying to make a good impression.

Leo had begun by asking about the nature of his relationship with Jeannie; if they ever socialized, or spent time together away from the Hall. All things Cara had been through before, but now the questioning was official and necessarily more detailed.

'The furthest we've ever been from the Hall is into the nearby woods,' Roberts replied, his eyes seeming calm and remarkably blue above his mask, Cara noticed.

'And that would be for work purposes, or something else?' Leo prompted.

Roberts's eyebrows met in a frown. 'She doesn't pay me to go for walks with her, if that's what you're driving at,' he countered.

'So they're for pleasure?'

'I'd be more inclined to say recreation and education. She's interested in learning more about nature, and so I share what I know.'

DS Rundle glanced towards Andee, although there was no way she could see her through the one-way glass.

'Did you go to the woods often?' Leo asked.

'I wouldn't say often, no. More in the summer, less at this time of year.'

'Did you walk with her on Wednesday the sixth of January?'

'No. I've already told you, I saw her through the window that day . . .'

'Did she invite you into the house?'

'No.'

'Have you ever been inside?'

'Yes.'

'For what reason?'

'Before the pandemic, I often went in to discuss designs or ideas for the garden with her and her husband. It's against the rules for me to go inside now.'

'Which doesn't mean you don't go.'

'Well I don't.'

'Were you having an affair with Jeannie, Mr Roberts?' Rundle asked.

His eyes went to her; he stared at her hard and for so long that Cara couldn't even guess at what he was going to say.

Rundle held the gaze.

In the end he said, 'I'm here for a second time to tell you what I remember about that day. I want to be helpful, but *this* . . .'

'It was a simple question, Mr Roberts, and I have to wonder why you're finding it so difficult to answer.'

'I was not having an affair with her,' he said tightly.

Without missing a beat, Rundle said, 'Tell me about Sarah Hansell.'

His face paled, and Cara felt Andee tense beside her.

'I have nothing to say about Sarah Hansell,' he retorted. 'It's in the past and has nothing to do with this.'

'I believe she was a client you attacked when she tried to end your affair,' Rundle stated.

Roberts's jaw tightened. 'It was not an affair, and I absolutely did not attack her.'

'Is it your usual MO to become violent with a woman who wants to end—'

'Sarah Hansell was a client who *wanted* an affair,' he cut in furiously. 'When I refused . . . It was investigated at the time and I was never . . .' He got to his feet. 'This is all bullshit and you know it,' he growled. 'If you want to speak to me again, I'll make sure I have a lawyer with me.'

After he'd left the room, Leo announced the departure and stopped the recording.

Andee said to Cara, 'I need to make a call. Tell Natalie I'll see her in the morning.'

CHAPTER FORTY-THREE

ESTELLE

Tuesday 26 January 2021
Twenty days since Jeannie's disappearance

Estelle flinched as Neil came through the door. He tossed his keys and phone on the kitchen countertop and tugged open the fridge for a beer. 'Where's Chloe?' he asked, flipping the top.

'Next door with Prim, watching a movie,' she replied. 'How did it go with the police?'

'They asked about Sarah Hansell.'

Her heart skipped a beat. 'But they know she ended up admitting she was lying,' she pointed out.

He took a long draught of his beer. 'Yes, they know that, but I'm pretty sure they're doubting it now.'

Afraid they might be, she said, 'So how did you leave it with them?'

'I said I was going to get a lawyer.'

'Yes, you should do that. They can't get away with accusing you of something you didn't do.' Were they talking about Sarah Hansell now, or Jeannie Symonds?

They both looked at his phone as it rang. Estelle saw

it was Fliss, and felt annoyed that the woman hadn't even bothered to wait for her to call.

'Hi,' he said shortly as he answered.

Estelle heard Fliss say, 'Andee just rang, she says you need a lawyer . . .'

'Is she recommending someone?'

'Of course, she's already called Helen Hall. I'm worried, Neil. What did they say?'

'Not now,' he said. 'Just send me Helen's details if you have them and I'll speak to you tomorrow.' He was already heading for the stairs as he rang off.

Unsure whether or not to go after him, Estelle remained where she was, her breathing shallow, her heart racing in a way that made her feel sick and shaky. The police would call her in next, she knew it, and she still had no idea what she was going to say to them.

She started as the back door opened and Prim came in.

'I need to talk to you,' Prim said, closing the door behind her. 'I should have gone to the police today, but I didn't—'

'I can't deal with this now,' Estelle broke in and, before Prim could get any further, she ran upstairs and locked herself in her writer's room.

CHAPTER FORTY-FOUR

FLISS

Wednesday 27 January 2021
Twenty-one days since Jeannie's disappearance

The intention today had been to walk on the beach for an hour, provided Guy wasn't called in for questioning, and so far he hadn't been; however the weather was too rough and the tide too full to stay with the plan. So Fliss had driven to the marina, where he'd been waiting outside the apartment block to show her where to park. He'd then led the way into a splendid Victorian pavilion adjacent to the boats, where they could shelter from the wind and enjoy the coffee and cider-apple doughnuts she'd brought with her.

As they ate and drank, seated either end of the slatted bench, the waves beyond the harbour crashed up over the headland in a frenzy of foaming surf, while masts clanked and rattled like wildly chattering birds, and feisty gusts howled around the ornate roof.

For a while he talked about the phone calls he'd received last night, including one from the hospital trust, and others from the colleagues who were covering for him, or who wanted to express some moral support. She could see how much it bothered him to be cut off from his world like this, and wished there was something she could say to help ease the stress of it all.

'So you're in the flat now?' she said, putting her coffee mug down on the bench beside her as he bunched up the empty doughnut bag and used the napkins she'd brought to wipe his fingers.

'I am,' he replied, 'although I didn't bring much with me. I can always go back if I need more.'

'Are the press still hanging around the Hall?' There had been quite a bit on TV about him and Jeannie last night and again this morning, but Fliss hadn't watched much of it. For some reason it felt disloyal to both him and Neil to try and get information that way, especially when there was so much random and even spiteful speculation.

'They weren't there when I left first thing,' he said, 'but it was before six. They could have turned up again by now. I think the police are intending to carry on searching at some point; they'll let me know if they do.'

Imagining how intrusive and disruptive it must be to have strangers crawling all over his home and his life, she felt her heart go out to him. 'Did you know that Neil was questioned again last night?' she asked.

He looked at her quickly, worriedly. 'No, I didn't,' he said.

'He sounded pretty stressed when I called him, so I don't think it went well. He's speaking to a lawyer today.'

Guy nodded, as though agreeing with the decision. 'With the way things are, I think we're all going to need one,' he commented distractedly. Then, 'I had a chat with one last night. She sounds pretty good, although I don't have anything to measure it against.' Seeming suddenly restless, he got up and walked to the front opening of the pavilion, where he stood with his back to her, staring past the boats out to sea. His hair blew about in the wind, his face was pale, and she wondered how in touch he still felt with the life he'd known before any of this had happened, the ordinary day-to-day living of coming and going from London, of focusing on other people's diseases and conditions, of knowing his wife would be there when he got home. Did it all feel as remote as he seemed right now; she couldn't imagine how it wouldn't.

After a while he turned to look at her and his expression caused a surge of unease to go through her. 'There's something I need to tell you,' he said, 'or ask you, really.'

Certain it was going to be about Neil, she braced herself, but then noticed that a wryness had crept into his smile and a spark of humour was in his eyes.

'It's actually rather embarrassing,' he confessed, 'or certainly it is for me, but anyway, here goes: has Jeannie ever talked to you about me?'

Confused and taken aback, she said, 'We've never had an actual conversation about you, if that's what you mean.'

'It is,' he confirmed. He pushed a hand through his hair and came to sit down again as he said, 'I need to explain, and this, I'm afraid, is where it gets embarrassing. You see, she knows that I . . . Well, that I'm attracted to you, and there have been times in the past, when she's suspected something similar, that she's made it her business to go and speak to the woman concerned.'

Fliss blinked, not quite past the bit about him being attracted to her.

'If you're wondering how she knows,' he continued, 'it's partly because she picks up on these sorts of things,

310

I think a lot of women do. I mentioned once or twice that I was worried about how difficult the lockdown might be proving for you.'

She felt an unsteady rhythm start in her chest. 'I had no idea,' she said, 'that you were even thinking about me, much less about the disastrous state of my business.'

Regarding her with concern, he said, 'Is it really that bad?'

She quickly shook her head. 'No, I mean yes, but I'll work it out.'

He seemed about to say more, but was interrupted by his phone.

'Yes, speaking,' he said in answer to the caller. He listened for a moment then said, 'No, as I'm sure I've said before, she had no other computers, tablets or phones that I'm aware of, but you could try speaking to someone at Athene. It's possible they issued . . . OK, then I have no other suggestions I'm afraid.'

As he rang off, Fliss watched him bunch the mobile in his hands as he struggled between this reality and the other that was out there closing in on the rest of his life.

His phone rang again.

'Not a number I recognize,' he said, 'but I guess I should take it. Hello, Guy Symonds speaking.' He listened, then said, 'Four-five, four-six,' and ended the call. 'Apparently a search team has turned up at the Hall without the gate code. They want to take a look around the garden and surrounding area.'

Feeling almost as dismayed by that as he must, she said, 'Did they mention digging anything up?'

'No, but I think they have to have a special warrant for that.'

Of course, she should have realized, and destroying the garden was hardly what mattered, was it? 'She left in her car,' she pointed out, 'so why are they searching . . . ?' She didn't finish the question; they both knew the answer and it didn't need to be spelled out as a result of her eagerness to defend him.

He looked up as the first fat drops of rain began to splash onto the roof.

Though she really didn't want to leave, she said, 'I guess I should be going before it gets any heavier.'

He didn't respond, and she realized he probably hadn't even heard her.

She started to stand but had to stop as a spasm of pain shot through her lower back.

'What is it?' he asked, turning to her worriedly.

'It's OK,' she assured him. 'It'll pass.'

'Sit back down. If you can.'

'I probably ought to try and stand.'

'Then hold onto me.'

His arm was strong and firm as she gripped it and, as the pain slowly subsided, she finally got herself to an upright position. 'Fine now,' she assured him, knowing she probably looked far from it. 'It comes and goes. I'll be turning cartwheels within the hour.'

Smiling, he said, 'Now that I have to see.'

Realizing she was still holding his arm, she looked down at her hands and said, 'So there went our attempt at social distancing.'

'Sorry,' he said, and took a step back. 'I didn't think.'

'Please, don't apologize. You were just coming to my rescue.'

He laughed. 'Are you having it treated?'

'I have in the past. It's an old injury from a car accident I had many years ago.'

'Well, it shouldn't still be playing you up like this. Maybe I could recommend someone for you to see?'

Touched and surprised that he hadn't suggested himself, she said, 'That would be good. Thank you.'

The rain was starting to come down quite heavily now, yet neither of them attempted to leave.

'I know we shouldn't,' he said, 'but would you like to come inside for a drink? The side entrance is right there, and we can always keep a distance inside . . .'

'I'd love to,' she replied and, gathering up the remains of their small picnic, she ran with him to the double-doors between two closed boutiques. In next to no time they were out of the rain.

CHAPTER FORTY-FIVE

ESTELLE

Wednesday 27 January 2021
Twenty-one days since Jeannie's disappearance

'Tell us about your relationship with Guy Symonds, Mrs Roberts.'

Estelle didn't make the correction; after all, technically it was her name, even if Fliss still used it. 'I don't have a relationship with him,' she replied, keeping her hands under the table, tightly bunched between her knees to stop them from shaking. She was glad of the mask too, so no one could see how utterly wretched and afraid she was feeling, although it probably showed in her eyes.

Both detectives stared at her, as if they had all the time in the world for her to come up with an answer that was better than the one she'd given. The male was called Leo Johnson; he had thick red hair and pale blue eyes that seemed quite friendly; the female was Natalie Rundle, biracial, striking, but not someone who seemed very interested in being friendly.

'I don't have a relationship with him,' she said again.

'According to him you do,' Rundle told her.

Estelle flinched and tightened the grip on her hands.

'What I mean,' she said, 'is we're not . . . It's not *that* kind of relationship.'

'I see. Shall we call it a friendship then?' And without waiting for an answer, 'Tell us about that.'

Estelle swallowed dryly, her words seeming too far away to reach. These detectives were already making her feel as though they wouldn't believe her no matter what she said. 'He's . . . He's been really kind to me over the last few months,' she told them. 'I've been going through a difficult time and . . . Well, I find him easy to talk to.'

Rundle's eyebrows arched. 'You chose the husband of a woman you have a long-standing grievance with to be your confidant?'

'I didn't *choose* him, it just happened.'

'How?'

'I spoke to him one day, back in the summer and . . . I guess he was kind to me. He's like that.'

Rundle sat back in her chair and folded her arms. 'How often do the two of you get together?' she asked.

Estelle shrugged. 'Not very. He's in London a lot of the time.'

'When did you last see him?'

'Um, earlier this month. Actually, it was New Year's Eve, during the day. We met on the moor in his car.' Were they going to bring up something about Covid restrictions now? If they did, Estelle had no defence for that.

'What did you talk about?' Rundle asked.

'Mostly my birth mother. I met her for the first time before Christmas and I was quite upset about it after. Guy knew that and he wanted to check how I was doing.'

Rundle looked puzzled. 'Why would he care?'

'I told you, he's like that.'

'Does your husband know about this friendship?'

'No. It was . . . It's something for me. I want to keep it to myself.'

'Why?'

She shrugged awkwardly. 'I just do. Neil has his secrets, I have mine.' Why had she said that? It wasn't something she should have mentioned, not here, not now.

'What secrets does your husband have?'

'I don't know, he – he doesn't share them with me, apart from the fact that he still cares for his first wife. He finds that too hard to hide.' What were they going to think of that? What did it matter? She was only telling the truth.

'His first wife was Fliss Roberts?'

'That's right.'

'What do you know about his relationship with Jeannie Symonds?'

'I-I know that he works for her at Howarth Hall.'

'Do you have any reason to think it might be more than an employer/client relationship?'

Estelle could feel her blood running hot as she forced herself to look straight into the detective's eyes. 'All I can tell you is that a lot of women find Neil attractive, so I wouldn't be surprised if Jeannie does.'

Rundle nodded slowly, taking this in. 'Did you ever suspect an affair between them?'

'I . . . I'm not sure. I mean, I suppose there could have been. I wouldn't have any way of knowing for certain.'

'How has he been reacting to her disappearance?'

'I . . . Uh, he's been worried, the way everyone has, but he hasn't really spoken about it much.'

Rundle stared at her hard; it was a strange sort of look,

316

unsettling and disorientating, making Estelle want to squirm, although she managed not to.

'Do you know if he's seen Guy Symonds since Jeannie vanished?' Rundle asked.

'Yes, I'm sure he has. Guy called the weekend after he got back from London to ask if Neil had seen her, so Neil went over there. I think he knocked on doors with Guy initially, and they searched the woods together. It might have been Neil's idea to talk to Andee Lawrence when the police weren't interested, but I'm not certain about that.'

'Did you help Guy Symonds with the search?'

Feeling suddenly ashamed of her inaction, she said, 'I didn't take it very seriously at first, and anyway, everyone knows that I can't stand her, so it would have looked odd if I suddenly made out like I cared where she was.'

'Do you care now?'

Her shrug was jerky. 'I don't know. I suppose so, but I have my own issues going on, so I don't think about it very much.'

'Your own issues being those with your birth mother?'

'That's right.'

Rundle gave her another of those peculiar looks, as if she was seeing right through to something that even Estelle didn't know was there. She felt like a specimen trapped under a magnifying lens.

'Where were you on January the sixth?' Rundle suddenly asked.

Estelle almost stopped breathing; her head started to spin. 'I-I was at home, under lockdown, the same as everyone else.'

'Can anyone verify that?'

'I'm sure my PA can, Primrose Barnes. She might not have been with me all day, but she'd only have been next door.'

'Do you recall what time your husband arrived home that day?'

She tried to think, but everything was starting to feel disjointed, as though it had happened a very long time ago. 'I expect it was around five,' she said. 'Probably no later, as it would have been dark by then.'

'Were you surprised when he was called in for questioning again last night?'

'I-I'm not sure, but I don't think he knows where she is.'

'Why?'

'I just don't think that he does.'

'What about Primrose Barnes? Might she know?'

Estelle frowned in confusion. 'I don't see how. She never has anything to do with Jeannie. Neither of us do.'

'Why isn't she returning our calls?'

'I don't know. I hadn't realized she wasn't, but she's already talked to someone here, I'm sure of it. I don't expect she's got anything to add.'

'Have you?'

Estelle shook her head.

'Apart from the fact that you have a secret friendship with Guy Symonds?'

Her throat tightened. She wanted desperately to get out of here now but couldn't think how to bring it to an end. Then she remembered what Neil had done and said she thought it would be a good idea if she spoke to a lawyer.

Finally she was back out on the street, walking away from the police station, trying to remember where she'd left her car, where she needed to go next, what she must do.

How was she going to find a lawyer? Could she use the same one as Neil? Should she call Fliss to ask if she knew of anyone else? Or Andee . . . She thought of her mother; she was a solicitor specializing in crime, but the mere thought of calling her made her feel sick to her core. Serena Fellowes hadn't wanted anything to do with her firstborn daughter before, and she definitely wouldn't now.

CHAPTER FORTY-SIX
CARA AND ANDEE

Thursday 28 January 2021
Twenty-two days since Jeannie's disappearance

Cara was in the front passenger seat of Andee's Mercedes, using her mobile to try to get hold of Primrose Barnes as they sped along the coast road on their way to Westleigh Heights. DS Rundle and the rest of the team were already at the Hall, as were forensics and photographers. Apparently a search helicopter and canine unit had also been put on alert.

All the increased activity around the house had come about because a note had been found in the pocket of one of Jeannie's coats yesterday saying, *Woods? Half an hour?* There was no name, no date, nothing to suggest when she'd received the note, although, as Leo had pointed out, if she'd received it on January the sixth, wasn't it more likely to have been in the coat she was wearing when she'd left the house?

Regardless, it was now in their possession and in the process of being fingerprinted, before going on to forensics for further analysis if necessary.

To Cara's surprise, Primrose Barnes suddenly answered, just as she'd expected to be bumped to messages again.

'Primrose?' she said eagerly. 'Ms Barnes?'

'Yes, who's this?'

'It's Cara Jakes from Kesterly CID. When we spoke a few days ago you told me you were coming in . . .'

'I know what I told you but I was . . . It was a misunderstanding. I'm sorry to have wasted your time.'

'Would you like to fill me in on what it was anyway, just in case?'

'No, really, it wasn't important. I'm afraid I need to go,' and that was that, line dead, Primrose gone, Cara high and dry, and Andee was now on the phone.

Cara could see it was Richie Franklyn from the *Gazette*, and she felt a little lift in her heart. Anything to do with Richie interested her, including the fact that his dad had apparently once been a spy for MI5.

'. . . no luck so far,' he was telling Andee, 'but don't worry, I'm on it.'

'Great. We'll need police help to get access to the CCTV of local stations, but if you could make a list of the possibles . . .'

'Have you checked Kesterly already?' he asked.

'Yes, we have, but we were looking for Jeannie then, so we need to go through it again. I'm sure you can sweet-talk Henry, at the station, into giving you what you need.'

'No sooner said. I'll get back to you as soon as I have anything on the car rentals,' and he was gone.

Cara turned to Andee, 'Car rentals?' she blurted. Then, 'Is Richie working with you on this?'

'Since yesterday,' Andee replied, indicating to overtake

a tractor. 'He and I sometimes join forces when we think it'll be in both our interests. In this instance, I've asked him to try and find out if Guy Symonds rented a car on or around January the sixth.'

Cara's eyes widened. They'd learned yesterday, from his Range Rover's tracker system, that it hadn't moved from outside the London house that day. His phone had located him there too, but apparently these alibis weren't enough for Andee.

'He could have hired, or borrowed a car,' Andee explained, 'and just left his phone at home.'

'So you think . . . Actually, what do you think?'

'I'll have a clearer idea of that once Richie's done his stuff, but it's not only about doubting Guy's word, a thorough check like this could also help him.'

Cara had to think about that.

Andee smiled. 'If there's no sign of him coming or going from this area, and by that I mean stations as far afield as Bristol, Bath, Castle Cary, Taunton, Exeter, and no record of him hiring a car, I think we can all feel satisfied that he really was at home in London that day. I also think that he – and his lawyer if it gets that far, and I'm sure it will – will thank us for putting it beyond doubt.'

Cara turned to look straight ahead, taking this in while trying to remember what else she wanted to ask. 'Does DS Rundle know you're doing this?' she finally said.

Andee laughed. 'Of course. With resources being what they are, she's happy to take all the help she can get, and trust.' She glanced in the mirror as the sound of sirens reached them, and as she pulled over Cara saw Leo Johnson and Noah Shields whizz by in an unmarked car.

Andee was straight on the phone to Leo. 'Anything you'd like to share?' she asked.

He laughed. 'I thought that was you in the Merc. No, nothing, just wanted to get there a bit quicker. Have you got anything for me?'

'I'm not sure yet. Cara and I are on our way to see Ambrose Austin.'

'Who?'

'He's an eighty-five-year-old curmudgeon who'd rather cut out his own tongue than speak to the police.'

'Sounds fun at parties. And he's of interest because?'

'He lives in the last house on Westleigh Heights before the moor, which is about fifty yards from Howarth Hall's gates on the opposite side of the road. You could be forgiven for missing it, it's so overgrown, but it's there all right. Guy and I knocked when we were asking the neighbours if they'd seen anything and got no reply. I understand the same happened during the door-to-door yesterday. Whether we're going to be any luckier today remains to be seen; however, we have a secret weapon this time.'

Intrigued, Cara turned to look at her.

'I've got to hear this,' Leo chuckled.

'My mother,' Andee smiled. 'She knew him many years ago, and I found out last night that throughout the lockdowns she's been organizing his shopping. She could be the only person on the planet he actually likes or lets through the door – she could also be the only person hereabouts who remembers he's alive.'

'OK, good luck with that,' Leo said. 'I'll catch up with you later.'

By the time they approached Howarth Hall, taking a while to get through the press blockade fifty yards or so

323

before the gates, there was no sign of Leo or Noah, only the car they'd left with a dozen other vehicles and white vans parked alongside the woods.

As Andee brought the Mercedes to a stop only metres before they reached the moor, Cara saw right away how easy it would be to overlook the house they were next to, for it was barely visible through the jungle of overgrown trees and tangled hedges surrounding it. Just the odd glimpse here and there of a windowpane, a few red bricks, and a sooty chimney pot. From where they were sitting, it didn't come over as unoccupied so much as totally derelict.

Andee led the way in through a rusted front gate and along a cracked, death-trap of a footpath to the side of the house. There was a porch that might have had a fresh coat of paint some time a century ago, and a glass conservatory that appeared to be choc-full of cannabis plants. There was also the sorry ruin of a small barn with trees growing out of the roof, some rusted machinery lying about the yard, and a large wooden shed with a padlock on the door and sawn-off planks nailed randomly over the single window.

'You bring me to all the best places,' Cara commented under her breath.

Andee laughed and said, 'Don't bother with your mask yet, it'll only put him off if he is in there. He might think we're bandits.'

Suspecting they might need the gas variety if they did manage to get in, Cara kept her dainty little lilac covering in her pocket and watched Andee step into the open porch and knock on the door.

'Mr Austin! Ambrose?' she shouted. 'Are you in there? It's Andee Lawrence, Maureen Lawrence's daughter. Can I have a word with you?'

Silent as a grave, if the shufflings of birds and drips of rain were ignored.

Andee moved around to the front of the house, pushing aside thickly gnarled foliage and a decayed bird-feeder and banged on the bay window. 'Mr Austin! It's *Maureen* Lawrence's daughter. She said you were here. Can we have a quick chat please?'

As the door next to her creaked open, Cara started so violently that she almost fell over.

A tall, rangy man with ragged grey hair, sagging cheeks and a thick, silvery beard stared at her through smeary half-specs. His clothes looked as old as he did, brown, shiny, flecked with dirt, and about ready to walk off on their own.

'Mr Austin,' she said, loudly enough for Andee to hear.

'You don't have to shout,' he told her sharply.

'Ah, you're there,' Andee declared, clambering back to the porch. 'I'm so glad. Are you all right?'

'Yes,' he said gruffly, 'why wouldn't I be? Who's she?' He nodded at Cara.

'She's a friend of mine. Cara Jakes. And I'm Andee—'

'Yeah, I gathered, Maureen's daughter. How's your mother?'

'She's fine. Asked me to send her regards. Is it possible we could come in for a minute?'

Oh no, please let's not, Cara managed not to beg.

'We've brought masks in accordance with the regulations,' Andee told him, holding hers up for him to see.

'Bollocks to that,' he snarled and, turning around, he disappeared back inside, leaving the door open for them to follow.

Deciding to put her mask on, never mind the bollocks, Cara followed Andee into a large, dimly lit hall with a wide wooden staircase climbing one wall, an enormous stone fireplace dominating another and a number of closed doors that looked as though they could lead straight to Shelob's Lair. Above was a huge skylight all covered in muck and leaves.

'Through here,' Ambrose Austin shouted.

Andee went first, glancing down as a tabby cat twirled itself around her ankles, and came to a sudden stop at the threshold of the kitchen. Only a step behind her, Cara realized right away why she'd stopped; the smell was so rank it could knock a person out.

Doing her best not to retch, she moved forward with Andee, and nearly lost it at the sight of a skinned rabbit on the draining board. Clasping a hand over her mask, she sat down heavily at a rickety table next to Andee and swallowed hard. The old boy was filling a kettle, and the sink full of filthy dishes was making Cara queasier than ever.

'You don't need to go to any trouble for us,' Andee assured him, and Cara could have kissed her. No way would she be able to drink out of a cup from this kitchen. Even the cat bowl looked more inviting.

'So what do you want to talk to me about?' he asked, reaching for a pipe but not lighting it. 'I suppose it's to do with all that business down the road. Bloody police swarming about all over the place. I don't want the buggers anywhere near me, I'm telling you that now.'

'It's OK, they're not coming,' Andee assured him, 'but I am hoping you might be willing to help me find Jeannie Symonds.'

'She's the woman what lives there, yeah?'

Andee nodded.

'The one they're saying disappeared?'

'That's right.'

'Yeah, well, I don't know nothing about that. I've never even spoke to her, nor her husband.' He sucked noisily on the empty pipe and briefly bared his brown teeth in a grin so ghastly Cara could already feel the nightmares coming on.

'What we're really interested in finding out,' Andee told him, 'is whether you might have seen anything.'

'January the sixth, that's when they reckons she went, isn't it?' he said, proving he followed the news. 'Yeah, as a matter of fact I did see something that day that might or might not be of interest. In fact, I saw a few things and, before you ask, I know it was January the sixth because I had a log delivery and the bastards left them piled up outside my store so I had to stack 'em up inside myself. That's how come I was out in the yard for so long and how come I saw the van parked up at the edge of the woods, right across from here in the layby. It was there for ages. I kept thinking it would go any minute, but no, every time I looked up it was still there.'

'What sort of van?' Andee asked. 'Do you remember the colour, or make, or anything else about it?'

'I can tell you exactly whose van it was. Her from the Seafront Café, Fliss. She's who was parked up there that day; or her van was. I could see it plain as day. Ages it was there, then the next thing I looked up and she was gone.'

Cara looked at Andee, knowing she had to be as thrown by this as she was.

'What time would it have been?' Andee asked, betraying nothing.

He shrugged. 'About midday, I suppose, maybe a bit

after. Then next thing the gardener's truck turns up. You know, that Neil bloke. I saw him unloading something or other before he drove on and let himself in through the gates. That was about one o'clock, give or take.'

Quietly stunned by all the information that this one man who'd refused to talk to the police was providing, Cara could only feel glad Andee was in charge, for she had no idea where she'd go next.

'Did you see him leave?' Andee asked.

'No, can't say I did, but I saw her go. That was later, around half three. It was starting to get dark, anyway, and I was only out then because I couldn't find the cat.'

'When you say her, do you mean Jeannie?'

'She's got a white Lexus, right?'

Andee nodded. 'Did you notice which direction she turned in?'

'Down towards town.'

'And was anyone in the car with her?'

'No idea. Too far away for me to see. I told you, it was getting dark.'

Andee took a breath and sat back in her chair.

He watched her, beady-eyed, chewing on his pipe and flashing his terrible grin on and off, as if it were some awful beacon for the undead.

'You've been extremely helpful, Mr Austin, thank you,' Andee said, 'but I'm going to have to ask you to give a statement to the police telling them—'

'Oh no, you can forget about that. I'm not having any of them in here. Can't stand the bastards ever since they stitched up my poor brother for something he never did. He ended up killing himself over it, so no way are *the boys in blue* getting anything from me.'

Cara touched her foot against Andee's as she said, 'I can understand how you feel, Mr Austin, so don't worry, we'll find another way to track down Jeannie.'

He stared at Cara hard, a malevolent gleam in his eyes. 'Do you think I'm stupid,' he growled. 'You've recorded everything I said on one of them phones, haven't you? Well, that's all right, I got no problem with that, as long as you're not a cop in my house. You can give it to them if you like, makes no difference to me. Just warn them not to come knocking on my door again, because I'm an old man with a shotgun and not much longer to live.'

DS Rundle's expression was one of utter disbelief as she listened to what Andee was telling her. 'Was there some kind of circus going on up there that day that no one else knows about?' she exclaimed. 'Or is this bloke winding us up?'

Neither Andee nor Cara attempted an answer.

'So he tells you that Fliss from the café was parked next to the woods around midday on the sixth?' Rundle looked from Andee to Cara and back again, as if expecting one of them to tell her she was misunderstanding this. 'Is he to be trusted?' she pressed. 'Is he sure he has the right day?'

'I've checked with the log supplier,' Cara said, 'and that was when they delivered.'

Rundle sat back in her chair, clearly not sure for the moment where to go with this. 'Have you spoken to Fliss?' she asked Andee.

'No, not yet,' Andee replied, 'and we don't actually know that she was in the van. It could have been one of the staff; one of the Corona Girls even.'

Seeming to accept that, Rundle said, 'What about Neil Roberts, turning up and dumping something in the same spot before going into the house? Did this Austin bloke know what it was?'

Cara shook her head.

'Did you take a look at the layby before you left?'

'Of course,' Andee replied, 'and there's nothing there that shouldn't be. Or not that we could find.'

'I have photographs,' Cara assured her.

'So what are we supposed to conclude from this?' Rundle demanded in frustration. Without waiting for an answer, she said, 'Could your bloke be certain it was Jeannie he saw driving out of the place at three thirty?'

'It was a white Lexus,' Andee replied, 'but too dark to see who was in it.'

Rundle shook her head in bemusement. 'Neil Roberts is downstairs, consulting with a lawyer prior to further questioning,' she told them. 'We brought him in because of the note, which could have been sent this time last year for all we know.'

'Who's the lawyer?' Andee asked.

'Does it matter?'

'Only that – in the interests of disclosure – you might want to inform whoever it is of what you now know.'

Natalie nodded agreement, but said, 'I'm going to need some time to think this through. Cara, find out if Gould's in his office.'

As Cara reached for the phone it rang. 'DS Rundle's office,' she announced.

Rundle was about to speak to Andee when she caught the shock on Cara's face. 'What is it?' she demanded, shooting a hand out to take the receiver.

'They've found a body,' Cara told her, starting to shake.

'Where?' Rundle barked down the line as Andee hit speaker. 'Is it her?'

'It's trapped in the rocks below the woods on the far side of the peninsula,' Leo Johnson replied. 'We can only just see it from where we are, it's so far down, but we reckon it's a woman. DI Townsend's here. I'll put him on.'

'Natalie,' the inspector running the search shouted above the wind, 'it's possible a lifeboat can get in; otherwise we're going to need mountain rescue plus helicopter.'

'Have you contacted anyone?'

'Being done as we speak.'

'Any idea if it's her?'

There was a pause before he said, 'We've got binoculars on it now and . . . Hang on . . . She's face-down, but going by the burgundy-coloured coat, black trousers and length of floating hair, I have to say it's looking likely. Poor thing, how the hell did she end up down there?'

CHAPTER FORTY-SEVEN

JEANNIE

Wednesday 6 January 2021
The day of Jeannie's disappearance

Jeannie hadn't got far from the house when she decided to return for a warmer coat. It wasn't raining, or windy, but the temperature wasn't far above freezing and her navy Barbour just wouldn't do it.

Once ready, she checked again that she had everything she needed, and pulled the back door closed behind her to start across the field towards the woods. She felt so glad to get out, she could dance. All morning she'd barely had time to think, never mind eat, drink, scratch her nose, or pee, with so many calls coming in, video meetings to attend, decisions to make. By the time she'd finished speaking to Maurice, twenty minutes ago, she'd been on the point of screaming, especially when she'd spotted Neil outside. She'd really wanted to talk to him, had felt the urgency of it playing havoc with her concentration, but the call had been too important to cut Maurice short. In the end, Neil had gone before she could get to him, and though she could have rung to ask him to come back again, she had reminded herself that he had other clients, other commitments.

Then she'd gone through to the kitchen to make herself a coffee and had found the note on the table.

Woods? Half an hour?

It was as if he'd read her mind, had actually sensed her need to see him, so to hell with everything else, she was going to go and find him.

On reaching the kissing gate she pushed through, letting it clang behind her, and strode on into the woods. No rain, thank God, but nothing in the way of sun either, just a drab January day with the barest bud of a flower in the field and not a single sprig of leaves on the deciduous trees. It was as if the world had ground to a halt; no signs of life, no breath of wind, nothing at all apart from a deadly virus that no one could see, hear, smell or touch, and yet it was holding more prisoners than anything or anyone ever had.

Neil was nowhere in sight yet, but she knew more or less where she'd find him, so she pressed on, feeling her heart starting to twist with the thought of what she wanted to talk to him about.

Bessington, Hicks and Rayford. It was the name of the law firm she'd found in Guy's notebook a few days ago, and a quick call to the number had told her that they specialized in divorce.

Why would he be in touch with someone whose role in life was to tear apart marriages? Surely he wasn't intending to do that with theirs.

At first she'd told herself that someone at the firm must be a patient, or the relative of one, or maybe they were reaching out because Guy had some information they needed. There could be a hundred different reasons why the name of this firm was written in his book but, whatever they might be, she couldn't stop herself thinking the worst.

That he might be planning to leave panicked her almost beyond reason. The game of leaving was one she played, although never completely carried through. It wasn't one that he played too.

The humiliation of him abandoning her would be impossible to bear. People would crow and snigger behind her back, pity her, congratulate him for getting away intact. Oh, she knew how unpopular she was with some, how they'd do almost anything to bring her down either professionally, or personally, it didn't matter which.

What they didn't know, and certainly wouldn't care about, was that she actually loved him, and wanted with all her heart to stay married to him. She'd thought it was what he wanted too. It was true she could be difficult, unpredictable, bossy, moody, demanding – she had so many faults – but she'd always believed her idiosyncrasies, her penchant for spicing things up in unusual ways, were what he loved most about her. It was what he said, or what he used to say, anyway; but she realized he hadn't told her in a while.

Had he written the lawyer's name in his notebook intending her to find it? He knew she sometimes read it, so was this his way of starting the conversation?

She knew very well that at times she'd upset him a lot, repelled him even, especially when she'd actually believed he was seeing other women. Her way of dealing with it had been 'unusual' he'd said, 'undignified and frankly bizarre.' For her part she'd considered it highly effective, since the women she'd spoken to had backed off right away. She'd never told him the terrible things his ex-wife had said about him; the shockingly scathing attack on his character had been so hysterical and undeserved that Jeannie had slapped the woman's face before walking away.

'Don't go there again,' he'd told her sharply when he'd found out she'd been. 'And you can keep away from me too until I'm ready to put this behind us.'

She'd been so infuriated by his reaction that she'd taken off to Paris with an author and hadn't bothered to tell him where she was going or when she'd be back. Let him worry, let him think she'd had enough and gone for good. He'd soon realize what a mistake he'd made and come looking for her.

He hadn't. She'd waited an entire week for him to call, and in the end had returned to their London house not sure what to expect, only knowing how afraid she was that he might have left. He'd arrived home an hour later and their reunion, immediate and passionate, had launched them into a second honeymoon. Yes, he still loved her, of course he did, he'd never stopped, he'd just been angry and upset by her behaviour, but now it was over, and they wouldn't talk about it again.

After that she'd never found reason to suspect anyone else, apart from Fliss, of course, but as appealing as Fliss undeniably was, Jeannie couldn't make herself believe he was *seriously* attracted to her. True, he'd written a few things about her in his notebook, but Jeannie had known she was meant to see them. They were his way of getting back at her for her attraction to Neil. So no, not Fliss. She just wasn't his type. Sensual yes, and a sweet personality, but it was all a test to find out if she, Jeannie, would have a similar chat with Fliss as she'd had with the others.

Actually, she had tried a couple of times, but it was hard to get Fliss on her own, and as she hadn't really been worried, she'd let it go.

Glancing up now as a rowdy flock of gulls wheeled overhead, she pressed on into the woods, hoping that Neil hadn't already given up on her and left. She'd feel quite bereft if he had. Funny how he had that effect on people, on her anyway; that when he went she was left feeling as though he'd taken a small part of her with him. Or perhaps it was that something of him lingered that she didn't know how to deal with unless he was there.

One touch of nature makes the whole world kin.

The words were Shakespeare's, but it was Neil quoting them that resonated with her. The sharing of these woods had certainly brought them closer together. She loved talking to him, listening to him, and testing him on what he did and didn't know about literature, poetry, nature and life in general. She knew already that when she told him about the lawyer's number she'd found in Guy's notebook, he'd let her rant until she started to see for herself how ridiculous she was being.

She was some way into the woods by now, and starting to slow her strides, slightly breathless and warming through. She came to a stop and leaned against an old beech tree, letting her head fall against it with eyes closed. She took several long moments to centre and listen to the rustlings and birdsong, and to the distant rush of waves. She found these moments as soothing as any amount of yoga or relaxing massages. It was a special form of meditation that didn't necessarily require a still mind or mood music, it simply invited in everything around her – all the scents, sounds, the feel of the air, the taste of the wind.

She wasn't sure how much time had passed when she opened her eyes again. It didn't matter. She was in no hurry; her phone was in her bag so if anyone needed her they could call. She fished around in her pocket for Neil's note, just in case he'd put a time on it, but then remembered it was in her other coat, so she just walked on.

Eventually she reached the mossy stump where he sometimes stood, making her laugh as he shouted poetry, or made up ditties, or maybe talked prosaically about what help they could give to the woodland wildlife without upsetting the National Parks. She sat down on it and delved into her bag for Guy's notebook. He'd probably realized by now that he'd mislaid it again, and would ask later when he rang if it was somewhere at the Hall. She'd tell him it was, so perfectly safe. She wouldn't mention anything about the lawyer.

Now she was calmer she could see how she'd make herself look foolish if she did.

She'd never really talked to him about Fliss either, although she had teased him a little, but they'd never discussed the reason Fliss's marriage to Neil had ended.

Such a sad story that Neil himself had told her. A tragedy that should never have happened, much like the one her own parents had suffered, for that shouldn't have happened either. Paul, her brother, could tell himself as often as he liked that she'd deliberately set fire to the house, but he was wrong, would always be wrong – she was just thankful that no one had believed his monstrous accusations at the time. Yes, she'd known that her father was intending to put Paul back into the will, but she'd had no problem with it. There was plenty for them both, and what had mattered far more to her than the money was seeing how much it had meant to her parents to be ending the rift with their only son.

The timing of it all couldn't have been worse. When the fire happened, her father hadn't yet spoken to a lawyer about his change of plans, but he had already told Paul. So was it any wonder that Paul believed she'd set the blaze deliberately?

She'd have told him right then that she was ready to share the inheritance, but his horrible, cruel accusations had stopped her, made her want to punish him for thinking so ill of her.

It was time, though, for this hatred and sense of injustice to be brought to an end. After the awful scene at Christmas, she'd talked it over with Guy and had decided to settle a large sum on Paul now, and to change her will so that, when the time came, Mallory would inherit everything. Guy had agreed it was the right thing to do, in spite of his vague plans for them to retire early and live the high life somewhere exotic and warm. She knew he wasn't really serious about that; in fact he'd said himself that they already had plenty of money, and he was sure doing the right thing by Paul and Mallory was what her parents would have wanted.

Hearing a noise behind her, she felt her heart lift. So Neil was still here. She stood up and started to turn around, but then stopped as she spotted someone ahead through the trees. Presumably it was some random hiker, although it was rare to see anyone out here at this time of year. Frowning, she tried to make out if they were coming towards her, or walking away. It was hard to tell through the tangle of branches, until they stepped into a clearing and – realizing who it was – she felt a jolt of shock go through her.

'What are *you* doing here?' she asked, annoyed and confused and suspicious now that this was not a chance meeting, but it was all happening too fast for her to be sure of anything. She was trying to take a step back but something, someone was behind her, blocking the way. It must be Neil.

She started to turn, expecting to see him, but suddenly her face was being smothered with something soft and sweet-smelling. She started to struggle, trying to wrench herself free, but her limbs grew quickly heavy, were too hard to move and, as her knees buckled, she could feel herself sinking down and down, slumping awkwardly and unstoppably into darkness.

CHAPTER FORTY-EIGHT

FLISS

Thursday 28 January 2021

'I don't understand why you're asking me this,' Fliss said, starting to become anxious. Andee seemed so serious, worried even.

Going to close the door to the café's office, Andee said, 'A body has just been found on the far side of Howarth Woods . . .'

Fliss clapped a hand to her mouth in horror. 'Is it Jeannie?' she asked, barely a whisper.

'They don't know for certain. It seems to be female, and she's in the water at the bottom of the cliffs, but what's concerning me right now is that your van was seen parked on the edge of the woods on Wednesday January the sixth at around midday.'

Fliss stared at her, taking a moment to catch up.

'January the sixth,' Andee repeated for emphasis. 'At some point you're going to be asked what it was doing there on the very day Jeannie disappeared. *I'm* asking what it was doing there. Maybe you weren't driving it?' she prompted, sounding hopeful, although if it wasn't Fliss it was going to be someone else they knew, so there were no good answers here.

'I can check,' Fliss said, terrified it had been Zac, though not entirely sure yet what to be terrified of.

Quickly she opened up her computer's calendar, feeling thankful she was being asked this by Andee first, and not the police. She needed to gather her thoughts, to calm down and remind herself that she had nothing to hide, nor did Zac, but her fingers were shaky as she clicked on the first week of January. When she saw the entry for the sixth she unravelled with relief. Zac hadn't been making deliveries that day; she had.

'I remember now I'm looking at this,' she said, seeing where she'd been that morning. 'I pulled over . . .' She broke off, afraid it might not be wise to go any further.

'Why did you stop?' Andee persisted. 'This is really important, Fliss. The police are going to be in touch with you any time now. I shouldn't even be here, telling you this. So why were you parked on the edge of the woods on *that* day? And why have you never mentioned it?'

Turning hot as all the implications of it crowded in on her, Fliss said, 'I was up that way because I'd dropped some hot soup and rolls at the Shooting School. You know Annie and David are taking meals—'

'Yes, yes. So you left the school and . . .'

'Then I stopped at the woods on the way back because I was falling asleep at the wheel. I really shouldn't have driven anywhere that day. I try not to if I've taken a sedative the night before, but I'd promised Annie someone would deliver what she needed and no one else was free.'

'Oh God,' Andee murmured, pressing a hand to her

341

head, her reaction alone telling Fliss that this was a lousy alibi. 'As soon as you found out Jeannie was missing, you should have told me . . .'

'I would have, if I hadn't forgotten it was that day. It didn't feel like a big deal, no one was around . . .'

'But you were seen, and right now I'm not sure what that's going to mean. However, given your friendship with Guy . . .'

Fliss's temper flared. 'What has that got to do with anything?' she cried. 'It only started a few days ago. He was just a customer before . . .'

'And what is he now?'

Fliss's cheeks burned. 'You can't ask me that,' she replied, looking away.

Andee sighed, and allowed a moment for them both to cool down.

'Fliss, I'm not judging you, I swear it,' she said, in the end, 'I'm simply trying to prepare you for when the police get in touch, because they will, you can be certain of that.'

Fliss regarded her in fear and disbelief. 'You surely don't think I had anything to do with Jeannie's disappearance,' she demanded, wondering where their trust and friendship had suddenly gone.

'No, of course not, but it's not me you have to convince. It'll probably be a detective you've never met before, because you know Kesterly CID too well. They won't be interviewing you.'

Fliss threw out her hands in fury. 'I don't believe this!' she cried, turning away and back again. 'I pulled over to take a nap thinking it was the right thing to do, and now I'm being accused of . . . What am I being accused of? Tell me, because you're really starting to scare me.'

'I'm sorry, I don't mean to, but you need to talk to Helen Hall. I've already put in a call—'

'You think I need a *lawyer*?'

'This is a potential murder case now, so yes, I do. One of Helen's associates, Oscar Radcliffe, is with Neil at the station even as we speak.'

Fliss reeled. 'They're talking to Neil again? This is the third time . . .'

'A note's been found that he might have written.'

'What sort of note?'

'I'm sorry, I can't say, but I will tell you that he was seen dropping something off in the layby at the edge of the woods not long after you left it. Do you know anything about that?'

Fliss was dumbfounded, and so thrown by the way this was going that she couldn't think what to say.

As Andee waited, it was clear that she was hating every minute of this too.

In the end Fliss said, 'No, I don't know anything about it, but Andee, this is Neil we're talking about. You know he'd never hurt anyone, so whatever they're saying, and whatever they've found, you and I both know that he is *not* involved in this.'

Andee didn't argue, simply held Fliss's eyes in a steely gaze as she said, 'Promise me you'll speak to Helen before you speak to the police.'

They both turned as the door opened and Zac came in, holding out Fliss's mobile.

'It's Guy Symonds,' he told her. 'He says it's urgent.'

Taking the phone, Fliss waited for Zac to close the door and said, 'Guy? Are you OK?'

'No, I'm afraid not,' he said, hoarsely. 'A body's been

found on the rocks below the woods. They seem pretty certain it's her.'

'Oh God, I'm so sorry,' she murmured, looking helplessly at Andee. 'When will they know for sure?'

'I think they probably already do, because they've asked me to go and identify her. Someone's on their way to pick me up. It's why I'm calling, to let you know that we won't be able to meet today.'

'That's all right. I understand. Would you like me to come with you?'

'No, it's fine, but thanks. I'm not even sure if it would be allowed. I'll call again as soon as I have some news.'

As she rang off, Fliss stared at Andee, the shock and confusion of it all silencing her again.

Andee put a hand on her arm. 'I'm sorry,' she said softly. 'I know you've become close to him, but for your own sake, I think it would be a good idea if you don't see him again until all this is over.'

CHAPTER FORTY-NINE

ESTELLE

Thursday 28 January 2021

Estelle was at home again now, sitting on the edge of the indoor pool that none of them used often enough. She was staring at the swaying water she'd just climbed from, barely hearing someone come in, or even registering her own name as it was spoken.

'Estie, please look at me.'

She stayed as she was, swimsuit clinging to her skinny frame, hair plastered to her head and face.

'They've found a body,' Prim told her.

Estelle tensed. Everyone had been expecting it, even if they hadn't wanted to admit it. 'Is it hers?' she asked hoarsely.

'It hasn't been confirmed yet, but given where it was . . .'

Estelle's eyes still didn't focus; her mind seemed to be stuck with the motion of the water, back and forth, up and down, so many thoughts swelling in horrible, tumultuous silence and dropping away again.

Reaching for a towel, Prim draped it around her shoulders.

Estelle blinked back tears as she said, 'I'm not going to pretend I'm sorry. I detested her.'

Prim turned to look out at the garden, as though not wanting to stay here, but not wanting to leave either.

'Have you heard from Neil?' Estelle asked, suddenly remembering he was at the police station.

'He hasn't called me. Shall I fetch your mobile to see if he's tried to contact you?'

Estelle shook her head. She'd find it herself.

Tightening the towel around her, she rose to her feet.

For several moments they stood where they were, Prim watching Estelle, Estelle staring at the floor.

In the end Prim said softly, 'I know what's been happening, Estie.'

Estelle looked up at her, eyes suddenly wide, searching, temper rising. 'What are you talking about?' she demanded. 'Nothing's been happening . . .'

'I'm not judging you, Estie, I'm just saying that—'

'Leave me alone,' Estelle snapped, cutting her off.

'I saw you with Guy Symonds, Estie. At the marina. He let you in through a side door of an apartment building . . .'

'You don't know anything,' Estelle growled. 'You might think you do, but you've got it wrong. OK? You've *got it wrong*,' and shoving Prim out of the way, she stormed for the door, ignoring the splash as Prim fell into the deep end, and the fact that Prim couldn't swim.

CHAPTER FIFTY

CARA

Thursday 28 January 2021

Neil Roberts's lawyer, Oscar Radcliffe, had come in person to the station to support his client. So many were doing it by video-link these days, but Radcliffe was seated right next to Roberts, wearing a visor. He was about forty, with bushy brown hair, sharp dark eyes and a couple of days' worth of stubble around his jaw. He was apparently part of Helen Hall's A team, which made him one of the South-West's leading criminal solicitors.

They'd only been in the interview a few minutes before DS Rundle, also in a visor, produced the note that had been found in Jeannie's coat pocket. 'Do you recognize this?' she asked, pushing the plastic bag across the table to Roberts so the words on the torn-out page could be easily read.

Woods? Half an hour?

'Yes,' he replied. Once again Cara was struck by the blueness of his eyes above his mask; his hands, resting on the table, were dirt-ingrained and strong; the kind of hands that worked hard for a living – that could be seen as gentle or cruel.

'So you wrote this?' Rundle pressed.

'I did.'

'When?'

He shrugged. 'A few weeks ago. I can't tell you the exact date.'

His answers were no surprise, for he'd already admitted ownership of the note in his prepared statement; he'd also said that he'd left it under a stone on an outdoor table for Jeannie to pick up and that it had been some time before Christmas. However, the DS had wanted to gauge his reaction when she put the note in front of him, just in case it unsettled him in some way.

'Did Jeannie meet you that day, whenever it was?' she asked.

'No, it turned out she was too busy, she couldn't take a break.'

Rundle eyed him for a long moment and Cara expected her next question to be about the Devil's Scoop, but instead she changed direction. 'You were seen offloading something from your truck into a layby close to Howarth Hall at around one o'clock on the day Jeannie disappeared,' she declared. 'What was it?'

Seeming surprised and slightly rattled by the question he said, 'It was a pile of stones I'd been given by Ron Frobisher, a farmer up on the moor. Jeannie wants her front wall extended, and these stones match what's already there.'

'So where are they now?'

'Where I dropped them, as far as I'm aware.'

'In the layby?'

'No. I unloaded about ten feet from the gates, so whoever said it was in the layby got it wrong.'

After checking to make sure Cara had made a note of the moor farmer's name, Rundle switched back to the woods and said, 'Did you and Mrs Symonds ever go as far as the Devil's Scoop on your woodland walks?'

He frowned in puzzlement, but sounded wary as he said, 'No, we didn't.' He didn't know yet that a body had been found, but he'd clearly sussed that he was being asked about this notorious spot for a reason.

'Is it a part of the woods that you're familiar with?'

'Not especially. It's a good mile and half from Howarth Hall, and the terrain over that way isn't safe, it's eroding. If you're not careful you can end up going over the edge.'

Cara could feel herself tensing as she wondered if he had any idea what he was saying. Could he be so matter of fact if he actually knew what had happened?

'When were you last over there?' Rundle asked.

He took a moment to think. 'A couple of years ago, maybe three? I can't give you an exact date. Jeannie and Guy wanted to tour the woods after they moved in, so I went with them to point out various routes. We only went as far as the Scoop because Jeannie was keen to see it after I'd mentioned how dangerous it could be.'

'Did she ever go there again?'

'Not that I'm aware of. As I said, it's a good distance, and not that easy to get to. The views, on the other hand, are pretty spectacular.'

'Did Guy Symonds ever go there again?'

'I have no idea, but I'd be surprised if he did. He doesn't walk in the woods as often as she does. But I'm not at their place every day and, even when I am there, I don't actually know what their movements are.'

'But you do go surfing with Guy Symonds?'

'We've been a few times, yes, with my son, Zac, and Mallory – that's Jeannie's niece. They were sort of seeing each other when she was here.'

Rundle nodded slowly and looked down at the notes in front of her. After a good few moments of silence that no one attempted to fill, she said, 'Did Jeannie ever confide any suicidal thoughts to you?'

His eyes widened in clear alarm as he said, 'No, never. Why are you . . . ?' He broke off as Oscar Radcliffe put a hand on his arm to stop him.

'I'm calling this interview to a halt, detective,' the lawyer said, looking up from his phone. 'I don't know if you were aware, before we came in here, of what I've just been told by text, but I hope you weren't.'

Rundle's expression was stony as she stared back at him.

'I need to take further instructions from my client,' he told her and, getting to his feet, he gestured for Neil to leave with him.

Before they closed the door, Rundle ended the recording and said, 'We won't delay you any further today, but please bring your work notebooks in for analysis, Mr Roberts, and we'll let your lawyer know when we're ready to speak to you again.'

After they'd gone, Rundle gathered up the note and other paperwork on the table, looking as grim as Cara had ever seen her. 'There's sure to be someone up at the scene who can check on these stones,' she said.

'If need be, I don't mind driving up there,' Cara offered.

Rundle nodded. 'Of course, he could have moved them since January the sixth,' she said, 'but if he did you'd have to wonder why, when he didn't know until today that anyone had seen him drop them.'

'You didn't mention anything about Fliss having been there,' Cara pointed out.

'There wasn't a chance. We were lucky to get what we did before someone notified Radcliffe that a body had been found. If they'd known in advance, he might have advised the "no comment" route, at least until we had the cause of death.' She checked her watch. 'She should be with the pathologist by now, God help her, although it's a bit late for that, I suppose.' She sighed sadly and pressed her fingers to her eyes. 'They had to remove her arm to free her shoulder from the rocks, did you know that? I guess I'm just glad I wasn't there to see it.'

Feeling the same, and as dispirited by it all as the DS clearly was, Cara said, 'Have you heard if Guy Symonds has ID'd her yet?'

Rundle nodded and held up her phone. 'Leo texted about twenty minutes ago. It's definitely her; or the clothes are hers. I don't think she's in much of a state to be looked at.'

Upstairs, in the incident room, they found everyone glued to aerial news footage of the woods, cliff-face, and huge, brutal rocks where giant waves slammed in from the sea, covering the spot where Jeannie's body had been trapped, quite possibly for the last three weeks. It looked so bleak and godforsaken and such a cold, sinister place to end up that Cara found herself wanting to cry. No one deserved to die like that, to be so alone and undiscovered for so long, and what made it even worse was that someone must have known she was there.

Unless she'd gone too close to the edge and the ground had given way beneath her.

351

Checking who was calling her mobile, Cara saw it was Andee and showed the DS before clicking on.

'Ask her if Richie's come up with anything regarding Guy Symonds and a hire car,' Rundle said, before Cara could speak.

'I heard that,' Andee said, 'and the answer is, he's still working on it.'

Cara relayed the message and said, 'Neil Roberts has admitted the note is his, but claims he left it before Christmas. And apparently he dropped a pile of stones about ten metres from the gates to the Hall. Not in the layby.'

'OK, that's interesting,' Andee responded. 'Has it been checked out yet?'

'I'm just about to get on to it.'

'And where are things standing as far as Fliss is concerned?'

Cara glanced at Rundle as she said, 'A couple of special interrogators should be here by tomorrow to interview her.' Rundle nodded confirmation. 'They're taking over all the interviews from here on,' Cara added.

'I thought that would happen,' Andee responded. 'It's common practice in a case like this. I'll tell Fliss's lawyer. Helen Hall's representing her.'

'Of course it could have been an accident,' Cara said lamely.

With a sigh Andee said, 'I know you don't believe that, Cara, and I don't either,' and with an assurance she'd be in touch again soon, she ended the call.

Turning to address the room at large, Rundle said, 'If anyone wants me for the next half an hour, I'll be with Gould prepping for the new interrogators.' She'd been gone only a moment before reappearing in the doorway. 'Does anyone know if Guy Symonds has got himself a lawyer yet?' she asked.

'Yes,' Shari Avery replied, rapidly digging around on her desk, 'it's a woman, I know that . . .'

'OK, call and tell her that we want to interview her client tomorrow. We'll give her a time once I've spoken to the pathologist.'

'Here it is,' Shari said, waving a piece of paper. 'She's London-based and her name is Serena Fellowes.'

CHAPTER FIFTY-ONE

ESTELLE

Thursday 28 January 2021

'What the hell were you thinking?' Neil demanded furiously. 'You know very well she can't swim. It's lucky for you she managed to get herself out . . .'

'I didn't do it on purpose,' Estelle shouted back. As if she would. Why would he even think that?

'She says you did.'

Stunned, she cried, 'Has she lost her mind? Why would I do that?'

'It's a good question.'

Realizing he was waiting for an answer, she gaped at him in disbelief, while inside she was silently screaming. 'I'm not having this conversation,' she suddenly snapped. 'But if it'll make everyone happy, I'll go over there now and apologize.'

'She doesn't want to see you.'

Her eyes widened in shock. Prim never refused to see her, ever. 'I'm going anyway,' she declared, starting for the door.

'Before you do, maybe you'd like to tell me where Chloe is.'

'She was in her room . . . Isn't she there now?'

'I don't know, I haven't looked, but you clearly haven't been keeping a very close eye on her. You're supposed to be home-schooling, for Christ's sake.'

Enraged, she cried, 'Don't you dare lay that on me when it's *you* who's been at the police station for half the day. And it's *you* the police suspect—'

'Stop it!' Chloe yelled, appearing in the doorway, hands clasped to her ears. 'I hate it when you two argue.'

'It's OK,' Neil soothed, quickly going to her. 'It's just a misunderstanding.'

'Why have you been with the police?' she asked him as he sat her up on the counter.

'One of my clients has died,' he replied, 'it's nothing for you to worry about.'

'Why don't you go and see Prim?' Estelle suggested to Chloe. 'She had a nasty shock earlier. I expect she'd like you to go and cheer her up.'

'What sort of shock?' Chloe asked.

Glaring at Neil, Estelle said, 'She *fell* into the pool. She's OK now, but it wasn't very nice for her.'

'Because she can't swim. How did she fall in?'

'It doesn't matter. Just go and make sure she's all right and ask if she's coming over for supper.'

As soon as Chloe had gone, Estelle rounded on Neil again. 'So what did the police say to you? Why have they called you in *three times* now? Do you have to go again?'

'I don't know yet. Possibly.'

She watched him scrolling for a number on his phone, and cried, 'Who are you calling?'

'Guy Symonds. In case you've forgotten, his wife's body has been found . . .'

'You can't be serious. You must be the last person he'd want to talk to right now.'

'Then why don't you speak to him?' he challenged, holding out the phone.

She drew back as if it might scorch her. 'I-I wouldn't know what to say,' she stumbled.

He was still staring at her as his phone rang and he put it to his ear. 'Fliss,' he said. 'Yes, I'm at home now. Everything's fine. You don't need to worry. Is Zac with you?'

As he listened to the answer, Estelle stayed where she was, not knowing what else to do. She was in such a state of agitation and anxiety she'd almost lost track of what was happening, of how everything seemed to be spiralling out of control.

'. . . and Helen Hall is the best,' Neil was saying. 'You just have to tell her . . . Be straight with her. You have no reason not to be. What time are you going? OK, you'll be allowed as much time with her beforehand as you need and just because you were in the layby next to the woods . . . Yes, someone saw me too. I've no idea who . . . Fliss, honey, please don't be scared. Is Andee with you? Good. I'll come if you want me to. OK. Shall I talk to Zac? All right, get him to call me when he's finished.' As he rang off, he sighed heavily and pushed a hand through his hair.

Estelle's eyes were bright, almost manic, as she cried, 'What layby? What's going on?'

He shook his head. 'It doesn't matter. It'll all be sorted.'

'Don't brush me off like I'm a child.'

'Then maybe stop behaving like one,' he growled. He went to the cupboard and poured himself a very large Scotch.

She watched him drink and felt as if she was with a stranger. He wasn't her husband, never had been really,

not in his heart, and now . . . What – who was he now?
'I don't know what to do,' she said wretchedly. 'I'm starting
to feel very isolated here. First Prim's not talking to me,
now you—'

'Maybe if you stopped making it all about you,' he
cut in irritably, 'you'd see that other people also have
issues . . .'

'Well, we all know you'll worry about Fliss long before
you'd ever worry about me.'

His eyes closed as he raised a hand and clenched it into
a fist. 'Pull yourself together, Estie,' he said, 'think about
what's really going on here . . .'

'Oh, don't worry, I am. I can see it for what it really
is, and I've always been able to.'

Before he could answer, his phone rang again and he
clicked on. 'Zac. Mum said you were talking to Mallory.
Is she OK? She's coming over? Yes, of course she would.
What about her dad? When are they due to arrive? I don't
think they have to quarantine at a hotel if they come
straight . . . Yes, I suppose that makes sense. All right,
son. Stay with Mum for now and call if you need me.'

As he rang off he said to Estelle, 'Apparently Guy's
moving back to the Hall, so Jeannie's brother and niece
can use the marina apartment.'

Estelle was staring at nothing, feeling the words sliding
off her like water over stones. 'Did Zac tell his girlfriend
that you've been talking to the police?' she ventured.

'I don't know, I didn't ask. Estelle, why are you behaving
as though you think I'm guilty of something?'

Before she could answer, Chloe came in, looking worried
and confused.

'Prim's gone,' she said.

Estelle's heart twisted. 'What do you mean, *gone?*' she cried.

'She's not there. Go and see for yourself.'

Running out of the door, Estelle raced over to the annexe and into Prim's little kitchen. The place had been stripped of her knick-knacks, no coats were hanging on the hooks, and only an old pair of ripped Wellies was in the rack.

She clasped her hands to her cheeks, starting to shake. Prim surely must have known that the pool thing was an accident, so what had made her go off like this without even saying goodbye?

Feeling nauseous with dread and despair, she raced all over the house, looking for a note, or something to say that she hadn't actually gone, but she clearly had.

She ran back to the house and grabbed her mobile. No text, IM or email.

She could hear Neil and Chloe in the sitting room as she tried to compose a text, shaking so badly that it took three attempts to get it right.

Where are you? We need to talk. Can't bear that you'd leave like this. Estie x

She began to pace. What should she do? She needed to talk to someone, to speak out loud what was spinning around madly in her head, to try to get everything straight. But there was no one. She had no other friends, no parents, no family to call on, and she'd almost rather die than try to speak to Guy now.

In the end she sent another text saying, *Please, Prim, I have to see you.*

There was no reply to that one either.

'Oh Prim, *Prim,*' she sobbed. 'Please come back. You can't abandon me too. Not now. I won't be able to bear it.'

CHAPTER FIFTY-TWO

CARA

Thursday 28 January 2021

OK, that was something Cara really wasn't going to do again – ever. Viewing dead bodies clearly wasn't her thing, especially ones that had been in sea water for over three weeks, and had the backs of their heads caved in. If only the pathologist hadn't turned her over, Cara might never have had to bolt for the door, only just making it outside in time to bring up her boots.

DS Rundle had been quite sympathetic when she'd finally joined her, had even admitted to a similar response when she'd had first sight of a dead body herself as a young beat officer – a psycho knife job, apparently, that had left the victim with no breasts or internal organs . . . Cara had begged her to stop there or she'd be heading for a ditch again.

Now they were back at the incident room where everyone was gathered for a briefing, and DS Rundle was ready with her precis of the pathologist's findings so far. 'We've got Dai Jones on the case,' she began, 'who's probably known to most of you, so I'm sure you'll all agree we're in good hands. He says we're lucky to have found Jeannie when we did, a couple more days and her trapped arm and shoulder would have decomposed enough for the tide to have carried her out to sea. I'd say it was what was intended, that she'd never be found, presuming we're looking at foul play. Unfortunately, Dai can't be certain that it was. The blow to her head could have been dealt before she went over the cliff, or it could have happened when she hit the rocks. And heaven only knows what's been feeding on her since she fell, or was thrown, into the abyss.'

After a moment's grim silence, Leo said, 'Was the blow to the head the actual cause of death?'

'Dai believes it was.'

'Can he give us any idea how long she was actually there before she was found?'

'He thinks our date of January the sixth is probably about right for time and date of death, and for duration in the water, but it's not possible to be any more precise than that.'

'If the head injury didn't happen when she hit the rocks, does he have any idea what might have been used?'

'All he'll commit to is a blunt instrument, so we could be looking at a heavy stone, a hammer, some sort of iron bar . . . There's a team up at the woods now, checking for anything that might have potential, also for footprints, something snagged on a tree, signs of a scuffle around the cliff edge. It's pretty dangerous terrain, as we know, so they don't have an easy job.'

'Is it possible it was an accident?' Shari Avery asked. 'Maybe she walked too close to the edge and the ground gave way?'

Rundle regarded her bleakly. 'Yes, it's possible,' she agreed, 'and so is suicide, although I don't think either is the reality of what happened. Does anyone else?'

Everyone shook their heads.

'It's highly probable,' Rundle continued, 'that the weapon, if there is one, has already been disposed of, or was cleaned and returned to its usual place in a toolbox, or a garden shed.' She watched the room as a murmuring broke out and Neil Roberts rushed to everyone's minds, just as she'd intended.

Leo Johnson said, 'I'll organize the search warrant.'

Rundle nodded. 'I'm not sure how many premises he has, so someone needs to find that out to make sure they're all given a thorough going-over.'

'Are you going to arrest him?' Noah Shields asked.

'Not yet. I want to talk to Guy Symonds first. Cara, can you call his lawyer to set it up asap, and we need to search the Hall again with this new knowledge in mind. It's possible Neil Roberts has some sort of storage facility there – a shed, a greenhouse – and if so it will be of particular interest.'

Cara said, 'Now that Jeannie's body has been found where it was, are we assuming that someone else was driving her car when Austin Ambrose saw her leaving on January the sixth?'

'We are,' Rundle confirmed, 'and if we could find that car it would probably give us most of the information we need. In fact, right now, it's all we have to say that this was a murder. If it turns up in some car mechanic's place and we're told she was given a lift back to the Hall after dropping it off, we might not have a case at all.'

Leo said, 'There's been enough publicity for a mechanic to have come forward by now, and even if that did happen, she surely wouldn't have gone over to the Scoop in the dark.'

'Maybe she went the following morning. Without an actual date and time of death we're having to make it up as we go along.' She looked across the room to where

DCI Gould was standing with his shoulders propped against the wall and arms folded. Though no words were spoken, it was clear that they shared a mutual concern over the way this was looking.

As the others began setting up for the new searches, Cara called Guy Symonds's lawyer and arranged for him to be interviewed at midday. After that she rang Ron Frobisher, the moor farmer who'd supplied a truckload of stones to Neil Roberts, and received confirmation that it had happened late morning on 6 January. Next she called Andee to ask if Richie had anything interesting to report on the car-hire enquiries.

'He's spoken to over two dozen firms in London,' Andee replied, 'and Guy Symonds isn't on anyone's records for any dates, never mind the ones we're asking about.'

'So you're thinking that he really was at home on Wednesday the sixth?'

'It's looking that way, but Richie's about to start trawling through CCTV around the West Country stations. He'll be in touch right away if there's anything. Now I have a question for you. Have the special interrogators from HQ arrived yet to interview Fliss?'

'Yes, they have. I haven't seen them, they're in one of the conference rooms familiarizing themselves with the case.'

'OK, if you can find out their names it could be useful. What else is happening over there? Any news from the pathologist yet?'

After relating what was known so far, Cara said, 'I think the DS is seriously worried that whoever did this is going to end up getting away with it.'

'Yes, I'm sure she is. Has she shared with you yet who she actually thinks did it?'

'No, but as it stands it's definitely between Neil Roberts and Guy Symonds. What do you think?'

'Frankly, I don't want to believe it of Neil, I really don't, but we've all been wrong about people in the past . . .'

'So you think it was him?'

'That's not what I said. Let's see how the interview with Guy Symonds goes. I'll check with Natalie first, and if she OKs it, I'll join you in the gallery in just under an hour. One last thing which could be significant: Fliss tells me that Primrose Barnes has disappeared.'

Cara started. 'As in, like Jeannie disappeared?' she asked worriedly.

'All I know is that there's been no sign of her since yesterday. Her car and most of her belongings have gone, she hasn't been contactable by phone, and there was no note to say she was leaving or why. I'm trying to get hold of Estelle to see if she has a number for Prim's parents in Cornwall. If she's not there . . . Well, if she's not, it'll be anyone's guess where we try next, but I can tell you this, there was some sort of showdown between her and Estelle yesterday that didn't end well.'

'Do you know what it was about?'

'Apparently Estelle is saying it's no one else's business, and when Neil spoke to Prim, before she left, she wouldn't say anything either, only that she couldn't take much more.'

Cara had no idea what to make of this. 'So she told him she was going to leave?' she asked.

'Not in so many words, but she did mention something about going to talk to Guy Symonds. Whether she did or not I can't say, but you might want to pass this on to Natalie so she can decide what to do with it.'

CHAPTER FIFTY-THREE

FLISS

Thursday 28 January 2021

Seeing Guy's number come up on her phone, Fliss asked Andee to give her a moment and left the café to go through to the office. 'Hi, how are you?' she asked softly as she closed the door behind her and clicked on.

'I was wondering the same about you,' he replied, his voice low and slightly gravelly. 'I'm sorry I couldn't take your call earlier, I was talking to my lawyer. I'm on my way to the station now for the interview.'

'Is your lawyer going to be there?'

'No, she's attending by video-link. She seems pretty much all over it, though. I have confidence in her.'

'How did you find her?'

'She was recommended by a friend. Anyway, I wanted to let you know that I'm definitely moving back to the Hall tonight. I wasn't sure when Mallory and her father would arrive, but it'll be some time tomorrow, so I thought the place should be cleaned before they get there.'

Fliss's eyes went down as she said, 'That's a good idea.'

She hadn't meant to go over to the apartment last night; she'd promised Andee she wouldn't see him again until all this was over, but the pull of him, the desire she felt when it had been so long, had been too hard to resist.

'I can't stop thinking about you,' he told her softly. 'I know I shouldn't be saying that, given where we are, but it's true. You're so beautiful, even more than I imagined. I can hardly wait to undress you and make love to you again.'

His words were reigniting the intensity of her desire and sending an electric heat through her pulses. 'I want that too,' she whispered.

'We'll make it happen,' he promised, 'I just wish it could be right now, this minute.'

She started to imagine how that would be, and jumped as the door suddenly opened. Seeing it was Neil, she felt a terrible guilt surge through her. It made no sense, she wasn't married to him, owed him no loyalty of this sort at all, and yet she couldn't deny that she felt she'd been caught cheating. 'I need to ring off now,' she said to Guy. 'Thanks for the call.'

For several moments she and Neil simply stared at one another, neither of them seeming able to find words to break them out of this tense and awkward standoff. She didn't even know where it had come from; it was as if the chemistry between them had a language, a communication and understanding all of its own.

'Who was that?' he asked in the end.

'Guy Symonds,' she replied, seeing no point in lying.

'What did he want?'

'Nothing really. Just to tell me that he's on his way to the police station.'

'And why would you want to know that?'

She shrugged. 'I-I guess he doesn't have any friends around here, apart from me, and you . . .'

'And Andee, but he chose to call you.'

She didn't know how to handle his anger, what to say to make him understand that she'd never look at another man if she could have him, that she was still confused about his relationship with Jeannie. If she hadn't done what she had all those years ago, they'd still be together, and she wouldn't even be tempted to satisfy her pent-up needs with somebody else. It was all her fault, she knew that, but he couldn't expect her to live like a nun when he was suffering no such existence. It had already gone on for far too long.

'Why are you here?' she asked, getting to her feet. 'Is there any news on Prim?'

'No. We've spoken to her parents but it doesn't seem she's there.'

'So where can she be?'

'I've no idea. Maybe we should ask Guy. She said she wanted to talk to him . . .'

'He hasn't seen her.'

'And you know that because?'

Her eyes flashed. 'Don't speak to me like that,' she cried. 'You have no right to make me feel guilty about anything when you're *married* to somebody else.'

'And his wife's body has just been found at the bottom of a cliff, so is this really a good time to be starting an affair? Or has it been going on for a while?'

She made to slap him, but he caught her hand, twisted it behind her and stared harshly into her eyes.

In spite of hating him in that moment, she could feel herself weakening, as if her body had a will of its own, had found where it really wanted to be, pressed against his. Her heart was right there too, but she wasn't going to let him get away with this.

'Let go!' she seethed, pushing him back. 'You can't come barging in here acting as if you own me. I have a right to my own life, and I don't have to answer to you.'

'I never said you did, but you can't be ignorant of the fact that I am suspect number one right now . . .'

'If that was true, they'd have arrested you.'

'And they still might. As we speak, they're out there, searching my nurseries, garages, storage facilities. The house will be next.'

Shocked by that, she cried, 'But they won't find anything.'

'They'll find plenty if they want to, like the note they think I left for Jeannie on the day she disappeared, asking her to meet me in the woods. Never mind that it was written weeks before, I can't prove that, and as far as they're concerned it's more evidence to say that I'm in this up to my eyes. Now tell me this, do you think I would have done anything to hurt her?'

She didn't even hesitate. 'No, of course not. I know you wouldn't.'

'Then who else do you think it could be?'

She felt the blood rush to her head as she understood what he was saying. 'I don't think it was him,' she said quietly.

'Well, it had to be someone,' he growled. Turning away from her, he walked out of the office, leaving the door open behind him. She stood still, feeling more confusion than she could cope with right now, given her own impending interview with the police.

CHAPTER FIFTY-FOUR
CARA AND ANDEE

Thursday 28 January 2021

There were nine of them in the incident room, including DCI Gould, DS Rundle, Andee and Cara. They were all watching the interview taking place downstairs between the special interrogators and Guy Symonds. Thanks to some sort of technical hitch, they couldn't see his lawyer, Serena Fellowes, but they could hear her clearly enough when she spoke, which so far had simply been to introduce herself for the recording.

They'd been going for almost an hour by now, and it was hard to say exactly what was special about the two detectives from Avon and Somerset, when they were simply going over everything Guy Symonds had already told Andee and Cara in his initial interviews with them. Cara guessed this was a forensic style of questioning, delving into cracks that were already filled just in case something gave, while double-checking facts to ensure they remained the same and the right conclusions had been drawn.

'Your man's coming across as pretty relaxed,' Gould commented, when they finally got to the point where Symonds admitted he'd been seeking to end his marriage.

'Too relaxed for someone who's just lost his wife the way he has?'

'He looks quite drawn to me,' Andee responded, 'and tired, but remember he's someone who's used to holding it together in difficult situations. It goes with his job.'

No one argued, they were too intent on the progress of questioning as it moved on to Guy's movements on January the sixth.

'So what exactly did your work at home involve that day?' DS Kerry Greenfield asked. She was a large woman in her early fifties with a pronounced Scots accent and a headmistressy sort of air.

'Haven't you established that yet?' Gould asked incredulously.

'Of course,' Rundle assured him, 'they're just double-checking.'

'To be honest,' Symonds said a little sheepishly, 'I was asleep for some of it. I'd had a surgery the day before – a tumour under the brain of a fifteen-year-old boy – that turned out to be even more complicated than we expected, and it ran much later. I was pretty exhausted by the time I got home, but wired, so I couldn't quite switch off.'

'Didn't you have any hospital commitments on the sixth?' Greenfield asked, her eyes on the statements in front of her that backed up the story about the surgery. 'I thought you neurosurgeons were run off your feet? Or has Covid changed all that?'

'It's better now than it was,' he told her, 'we're catching up on our backlog, but we also schedule in lighter days to follow those that we know are going to be strenuous. A tired surgeon isn't much use to anyone, but I did go into ICU at around seven thirty that morning to check on the patient. After that I returned home and caught up on some sleep.'

'My client also had several phone consultations with patients during the afternoon,' Serena Fellowes put in. 'These can be checked.'

Kerry Greenfield nodded acceptance and, after consulting her notes, she said, 'We know that your wife was at a place called the Devil's Scoop before she met her death. Is this somewhere you've visited together?'

'Only once, as I recall, with Neil Roberts, our landscaper. It was just after we moved in. Jeannie was keen to see it, so he showed us the way. I'm not sure either of us could have found it again, the path was quite disjointed, disappearing altogether at times, and it was very overgrown. Also, we knew it was dangerous over there, so it was kind of out of bounds.'

'Did Neil Roberts have any trouble finding the path?'

'Not that I recall.'

Andee's hand tightened on the desk in front of her and Cara understood why. Symonds had just wittingly, or unwittingly, added more weight to the case against his landscaper.

'You were aware of a friendship developing between Neil Roberts and your wife?' Greenfield made the statement a question.

'We've always got along well with him. He's very personable.'

'But your wife had a closer friendship with him?'

'Yes, I think so. Actually, she had a bit of a crush on him, if the truth be told, and I think the feeling was mutual, although I shouldn't speak for him, obviously.'

'Did you ever suspect they might be having an affair?'

'The thought did cross my mind.'

'Would it have bothered you to find out you were right?'

'Yes and no. No one likes to be cheated on but, as I've already stated, our marriage had come to an end, for me anyway.'

'But she didn't know that?'

'We never discussed it, although obviously we would have if . . . Well, if things hadn't turned out the way they have.'

Rundle said to Gould, 'Would you be sobbing by now if you were talking about your dead wife?'

'I don't expect so,' he replied mildly, making Cara smile, for everyone knew there wasn't much love lost between Gould and his ex.

'Did you want to leave your marriage because you'd met someone else?' Greenfield asked.

If the question took him by surprise, he showed little sign of it, simply said, 'That was part of the reason, yes, although I had not entered into a relationship with the other woman. I don't think she was even aware of my feelings until recently.'

Cara tensed. This was new.

'And who is this person?'

'Felicity – Fliss – Roberts. She owns the café in town.'

Cara turned to Andee and could see that this was not a surprise to her.

Making a note, Greenfield said, 'If she's aware of your feelings now, does that mean you're in a relationship with her?'

'It's still early days.'

'Can you be more specific?'

'We've seen one another on a couple of occasions.'

371

'Since your wife disappeared?'

'That's right.'

'Are your feelings reciprocated?'

'I think you'd have to ask Fliss that.'

'I'm asking you.'

'Then yes, I believe she feels the same.'

Andee sat back in her chair, clearly not liking how this was going, but she said nothing as Greenfield continued.

'Did you arrange to meet Fliss Roberts in the layby near your home on January the sixth at around one o'clock?'

He seemed puzzled by that. 'No. As I've already told you, I was in London that day.'

'So you can't explain why she was there?'

'I'm afraid not. No.'

'Have you ever asked her about it?'

'This is the first I've heard of it.'

'Does it concern you to know that she was there?'

'I'm not sure . . . I . . . Maybe it does somewhat, yes.'

'Could she have been meeting your wife?'

Clearly taken aback he said, 'I'd've thought she'd go to the Hall if she wanted to see her.'

Greenfield leaned in to her partner, DC Alan Bryant, who'd been jotting down notes all the while, and listened as he spoke quietly in her ear. He was a wiry, po-faced man in his thirties, with thinning fair hair and large-framed glasses. As he finished speaking, Greenfield took a sheet of paper from him and put it on the table in front of her.

'Do you know someone by the name of Primrose Barnes?' she asked.

Seeming thrown again, Symonds said, 'I wouldn't say I know her, but I know who she is.'

'Did she come to talk to you last night?'

'No.' He sounded confused. 'I don't know why she would.'

'She hasn't been seen since yesterday, and the last she said to anyone was that she was going to talk to you.'

He still seemed baffled. 'I've no idea why she'd say that, but maybe she went to the Hall looking for me. I was at the apartment, and she certainly didn't come there.'

'What would she want to talk to you about?'

'I have no idea. As I said, I don't even know her.'

'Can anyone verify your presence at the apartment last night?'

'Actually, yes, Fliss was with me.'

Andee put a hand to her head.

'In spite of the Covid restrictions,' Rundle muttered.

'All night?' Greenfield prompted.

'Until the early hours. She felt she had to get back then, for her son. She wanted to be there when he got up this morning.'

'Jesus,' Andee murmured.

'Makes a change for you not to know everything,' Gould commented dryly.

Rundle said, 'Tell me why I've stopped liking this bloke. I'm not sure I ever really did, but here he is, an eminent surgeon, well-spoken, good-looking, and I find myself believing every word that comes out of his mouth . . . Yet something's not right here, I can feel it in my gut.'

'Everyone speaks highly of him,' Cara reminded her. 'His colleagues, friends, patients, all those we've spoken to, and you'll have seen them on the news saying the same.'

Rundle nodded and turned to Andee. 'Do you think he's genuine?' she asked.

'Insofar as it goes,' Andee replied. 'He can't fake who he is, it's too easy to check.'

'But you've got to see that he's trying to stitch up Fliss and Neil? Isn't he? Or am I imagining—?'

'And right there,' Gould interrupted, 'is why we need these special interrogators, because you're too close to Fliss and her ex to be objective.'

Rundle regarded him darkly. 'You've known Fliss a lot longer than I have,' she reminded him. 'Are you saying you think she's played some sort of role in this?'

'I know she was in the layby on that day,' he pointed out, 'apparently asleep.' He shook his head. 'It's not much of an alibi . . .'

'She was in the café during the afternoon,' Andee informed him. 'I personally can vouch for that.'

'But there's still a period of time unaccounted for, when we know she was in the vicinity of the house. We also know that her ex, Neil, doesn't have an alibi for any time after lunch that day, whereas Guy Symonds does.'

Andee's eyes flashed. 'Are you seriously suggesting that Neil and Fliss did this together? Come on, Gould, you can do better than that?'

He simply shrugged. 'I'm just pointing out a couple of things that I don't think you guys want to see,' and getting up from his chair he left the room, just as Greenfield and her sidekick brought the interview to an end.

CHAPTER FIFTY-FIVE

FLISS

Thursday 28 January 2021

Fliss had known Helen Hall for almost as long as she'd been in Kesterly, but only ever as a customer at the café, so it felt bewildering to be here now in this spacious, high-ceilinged law office, with its ornate fireplace and elegant furniture, explaining why she'd been parked in a layby on the edge of Howarth Woods on January the sixth.

'So you weren't there to meet someone?' Helen prompted, her quiet voice as calming as her sky-blue eyes were direct and concerned. Her hair was an unruly mass of auburn curls, and the freckles across her nose made her seem far younger than her fifty or so years.

'No, absolutely not,' Fliss assured her. 'As I said, I was afraid of falling asleep at the wheel, so that's why I pulled over. I didn't even pay much attention to where I was.'

'They're going to cast some doubt on your reason . . .'

'But who would they think I was meeting?' Fliss cried in frustration.

'I'm not sure yet, but we do know that Neil was seen after you'd left. Apparently he dropped off a pile of old stones for a wall he's intending to build. Although,' she went on reading from her notes, 'he told Oscar, his lawyer, that he offloaded them next to the gates, not in the layby. I believe subsequent enquiries have proved that to be the case. Nevertheless, you were both in the vicinity at around the same time.' She looked up as Andee came in, already half out of her scarf and coat.

'Sorry to be late,' she said breathlessly, 'how are things going here?'

'I don't think there's much to worry about,' Helen replied. 'They'll just be covering all bases, talking to everyone, until they have more to go on.' She raised a hand for a pause as she took a call on her mobile. 'Oscar,' she said. 'You have some news?'

As she listened, Andee said quietly to Fliss, 'You were with Guy last night?'

Fliss's eyes widened as her heart skipped a beat. 'How do you know?'

'Guy just told the interrogators during his interview.'

Feeling herself burn with embarrassment, Fliss said, 'Why did he . . . ?' The 'why' didn't feel as important right now as the fact that she'd hidden it from Andee. 'Please don't judge me . . .'

'I'm not, but I'm worried. Is that why you and Neil argued this morning?'

'You heard that?'

'I saw him leave and clearly something had upset him.'

'It had nothing to do with what happened to Jeannie—'

'At the moment, *everything* is to do with that,' Andee interrupted, 'which is why I advised you not to see Guy until it's all been resolved. Have you told Helen you're sleeping with him?'

Fliss shook her head, starting to feel ashamed now of how easily she'd given in to the power of her physical desires, while knowing that if he asked her to see him again later, she'd probably find it almost impossible to say no.

'She really won't want to find out from the police,' Andee said, 'so you need to tell her. I didn't see your van outside. Did you walk here?'

Fliss nodded. 'Zac took it this morning. He's helping Guy move back to Howarth Hall. Mallory and her father are going straight to the flat to quarantine when they arrive.'

'OK,' Helen said, ending her call. 'Apparently the police are still searching Neil's workplaces and vehicles.'

'What do they expect to find?' Fliss demanded angrily.

Helen's eyes flicked briefly to Andee as she said, 'I'm sorry to be blunt, Fliss, but top of their list right now will be a potential murder weapon, or something that ties—'

'But that's absurd,' Fliss broke in, turning to Andee.

'It's OK,' Andee soothed, 'Oscar will take care of it. It's you we need to concern ourselves with now.'

Fliss checked her phone as it rang. 'It's Leanne,' she said. 'She's running the café today,' and clicking on she said, 'Hey, is everything—'

'The police are here,' Leanne told her, sounding rattled. 'They've got a search warrant so I've had to let them in.'

Stunned, Fliss looked at the others. 'They're searching the café,' she informed them. She clicked off and reached for her bag. 'I need to go.'

'No,' Helen cautioned. 'Let them do their job.'

Fliss stared at her, having no idea what to say or do. This was getting so out of hand she was starting to feel genuinely afraid.

377

'I need you to tell me,' Helen said, 'if they're likely to find anything that could incriminate you in some way.'

Fliss was dumbfounded. 'I've already told you, I had nothing to do with it . . .'

'In that case, let them search.'

In the end she nodded agreement. 'Yes, they can turn the whole bloody place inside out if they have to,' she said tightly, 'they'll soon discover they're wasting their time.'

Andee said, 'Fliss, I know it's hard, but you need to put this out of your mind now and focus on the upcoming interview. The police are expecting you in under an hour.' To Helen she said, 'Fliss has something to tell you about her relationship with Guy that might or might not be significant, but it's best you know.'

CHAPTER FIFTY-SIX

ESTELLE

Thursday 28 January 2021

'Estelle! Where are you?' Neil called out from the bottom of the stairs.

Realizing it was him, Estelle quickly rushed from her study onto the landing. 'Why did you knock on the door?' she cried angrily. 'I didn't know who it was—'

'I can't find my keys,' he cut in. 'What's wrong? Where's Chloe?'

'I'm here Dad!' Chloe called from her room. 'I'm doing an English exam online, can't come now.'

As Neil went through to the kitchen, Estelle hurried down the stairs to go after him. 'Have you heard from Prim?' she demanded. Then, registering the way he was tearing open drawers and cupboards and rifling through them, she started to panic. 'What are you looking for?' she cried.

'My spare keys. Do you know where they are?'

She tried to think, but everything was out of kilter, things just weren't adding up . . . 'How did you get in if you don't have them?' she asked, unable to make sense of this.

'I turned the handle and the door was unlocked.'

Unlocked! Why hadn't she realized that? She was trying to be so careful while she and Chloe were here alone.

'Are you sure you don't know where they are?' he demanded, going through to the utility room.

'Why do you need them?' she asked, baffled and shaken by his urgency as she followed after him.

'The police are going through everything at the nurseries, and the fact that I can't unlock file cabinets, or cupboards, or desks, is not going down well. They'll probably be here soon so you need to prepare Chloe.'

'What! Why?'

'Because I live here,' he said as if she were stupid. 'Ah, thank God,' he sighed, pulling a bunch of keys from the pocket of an old Barbour and snatching them into his fist.

'Don't go!' Estelle implored as he started back to the kitchen.

'I need to take these to the nurseries,' he explained. 'The police are waiting . . .'

'Neil, please!'

He frowned, clearly annoyed, but also concerned. 'Estie, what's wrong with you?'

Knowing how crazed she probably looked, and sounded, she tried to force herself to calm down. 'Nothing, I just . . . I don't know how to explain this to Chloe. What am I supposed to tell her?'

He glanced out to the hall, then back to her. 'I'll go and talk to her,' he said, 'and then I'll have to go.'

As he ran up the stairs, Estelle stayed where she was, staring after him, seeing nothing, and feeling so afraid she didn't know what to do anymore. Then, worried about what he was going to say to Chloe, she ran up to the landing and stood outside the bedroom door, watching and listening as if she didn't quite have the right to go in.

He was sitting on the end of Chloe's bed; she was turned around in her chair, looking at him earnestly as he said, '. . . mistakes are made all time, you know that, and I'm afraid this is a pretty big one that I have to help sort out. I don't want you to worry about anything . . . You're not, are you?'

'I think so, a little bit,' she admitted.

Patting his knee, he held out his arms for her to go and sit with him. In spite of being almost ten now, and rarely willing to be babied by any of them, she went to him and rested her head on his shoulder as he lifted her onto his lap.

'I'm not going to be gone for very long,' he assured her softly, 'and when I come back we'll have a nice long chat about everything, OK?'

She nodded, made to put a thumb in her mouth, then remembered she didn't do that anymore. 'Can I come with you?' she asked, placing a hand on his face and tugging it round so he was looking at her.

'I'd love to take you, sweetheart, but I can't this afternoon. And you've got schoolwork to be getting on with, remember?'

She snuggled in tighter and put her arms around his neck. 'I don't want you to go,' she murmured into his neck.

'I know, and I wish I didn't have to, but it won't be for long.'

'Do you promise?'

'You have my word, I'll be home as soon as I can. While I'm gone, will you look after Mum? She's feeling quite sad about Prim leaving . . .'

'I'm sad about that too. I love Prim.'

'And she loves you, which is how we know she'll be back soon, because she wouldn't want you to be worried.'

'Why did she go?'

'I'm not sure really. Maybe she just needed some space. People do sometimes.' He tightened his hold on her and, as he pressed a kiss to her hair, his eyes met Estelle's.

'I need to go now,' he said and, standing with Chloe in his arms, her skinny legs wrapped around his waist, he carried her to her desk and sat her back on the chair.

Minutes later, Estelle was closing and locking the front door behind him, listening as he drove away with her forehead pressed to the frosted glass. He'd always been so much better with Chloe than she had; seemed to know the right things to say and how to give love in a way that she, Estelle, found so hard. It wasn't that she didn't feel it, because she did, especially for Chloe, but nothing she said or did ever resonated with her daughter the way she wished it would. Prim never had a problem reaching her, and nor did Fliss. It was just her, the wretched, foolish, motherless woman who was always an outsider; the one who didn't fit, no matter what she did. She was a failed writer, an unwanted daughter, an unloved wife, a terrified friend who had no real place in the world, nor even in her family. She was, as her adopted mother had once put it, a sad little crow amongst blackbirds.

CHAPTER FIFTY-SEVEN

CARA

Thursday 28 January 2021

Cara looked up in surprise as Andee came into the incident room. 'I thought you'd be with the DS watching Fliss's interview,' she said, turning from her computer.

'I was expecting to find her here,' Andee replied. 'I guess she's in the gallery?'

Cara nodded. 'She went down a few minutes ago. I can take you if you like, swipe you through all the doors.'

'Thanks. Tell me first how the search is going.'

'Are you interested in Neil Roberts's premises, or the woods, or Guy Symonds's place?'

'All three.'

Cara grimaced. 'Nothing much from any of them, actually. The SOCOs in the woods are having a really difficult time of it. There was so much rain the week after Jeannie disappeared that they've more or less ruled out finding any footprints, partial or otherwise, that will be of any use. Even if they do, we know that both Neil Roberts and Guy Symonds have been there looking, so they wouldn't be much help. Unless they're off the usual beaten tracks, of course, but apparently there's no sign of anything yet.

They're also saying that parts of the cliff edge have fallen away in the past few days, so there's no way of telling if anything sank or broke off before that.'

Andee nodded thoughtfully as she took this in. 'So, as things stand, we still can't say for certain that a crime has been committed?' she stated.

Cara regarded her regretfully. 'Except there has to have been, unless we're prepared to believe that Jeannie walked over to the Scoop on her own that day and the ground went out from under her. No sign of her bag yet, by the way, but it's reckoned that was swept off by the tide.'

Andee inhaled deeply, letting it go in a sigh of quiet frustration. 'OK let's go and join Natalie,' she said. 'Is Gould down there too?'

As it turned out, Rundle was on her own in the viewing gallery and barely looked round as Cara and Andee came to join her.

'How's it going?' Andee whispered as she took one of several empty chairs in the darkness.

Rundle shook her head and kept her eyes on the interview taking place on the other side of the one-way glass. Everyone in the room beyond was wearing a mask – Fliss didn't have a smile on hers today; it was a plain peppermint green that contrasted prettily with her sky-blue eyes, and her thick blonde hair was tied in its usual ponytail at the nape of her neck.

For the moment everything seemed calm and civilized.

'More and more old ground,' Rundle murmured, 'nothing we haven't heard before.'

'Did you really expect anything else from Fliss?' Andee asked.

Rundle shrugged. 'I've got to admit the thing with Guy Symonds took me by surprise this morning.'

Andee didn't respond, simply switched off her phone before it could ring and turned her attention to the interview.

'So you're saying that your relationship with Guy Symonds didn't start until *after* Jeannie disappeared?' Kerry Greenfield was asking, as if needing to clarify what Fliss had just told her.

'That's right,' Fliss replied.

'Is it serious? I mean for you?'

'I-I'm not sure.' Fliss's long fingers knitted and unknitted themselves on the table. 'I guess it could be, if circumstances were different.'

'You mean if his wife hadn't just died in suspicious circumstances?'

Fliss swallowed. 'Yes, I suppose that's what I meant.'

'Tell us what you know about those circumstances.'

'Only what I've read or heard in the media.'

'Which is?'

Fliss took a breath. 'That Jeannie was found trapped in the rocks below Howarth Woods, and that she could have fallen while out walking.'

'Do you believe that?'

'I-I try not to make judgements until I know all the facts.'

Greenfield nodded. 'So you're not sure it was an accident?' she prompted.

'I don't think anyone is sure.'

'Unless someone was with her when she fell. Were you?'

Fliss's eyes shot open in shock. 'No!' she cried. 'I have no idea how she came to fall. I swear it.'

Greenfield's expression was unreadable. 'You said, a moment ago, that you could be serious about Guy Symonds. I guess it's going to be much easier now that he no longer has a wife.'

Fliss stared at her incredulously.

Helen Hall leaned in to speak quietly to Fliss, and whatever Fliss had been about to say didn't materialize.

Not letting go, the detective said, 'Do you want to pursue your relationship with Mr Symonds?'

'I just want all this to be resolved,' Fliss retorted, 'so that we . . . *he* can get on with his life.'

Cara was aware of Andee wincing, but no one spoke, only continued to listen as Greenfield said, 'You were parked in a layby next to Howarth Woods on January the sixth at around midday to one o'clock?'

Fliss nodded. 'Yes, I was.'

Greenfield took a moment to check the statement she was holding. 'Because you "needed to take a nap"?' The way she quoted the words made them sound utterly implausible.

'That's right,' Fliss replied, defiantly.

'Why have you never mentioned anything about this nap before? I believe it's only come up in the last couple of days.'

'Because I-I didn't take a note of the date when I was there. It didn't seem important at the time.'

Still looking as though she didn't believe a word of it, Greenfield said, 'Do you often need to sleep in the middle of the day?'

'No, not really. Not unless I've taken something the night before?'

'By something you mean some sort of drug?'

Fliss's hands tightened together on the table as she said, 'That's right. It would have been Zolpidem.'

'Do you think it's wise to drive when you're under the influence of a narcotic?'

'No, probably not.' Fliss made to say more but Helen Hall put out a hand to stop her.

'Are you sure you weren't in that layby to meet someone?' Greenfield pressed.

'Yes, I'm sure.'

'Did you get out of the car at all?'

'No.'

'Maybe you were waiting for your ex-husband?'

Fliss's tone was sharp as she said, 'I *wasn't* waiting for anyone.'

'So not Guy Symonds, or your ex-husband?'

'No, neither of them.'

Greenfield opened a file on the desk in front of her and took some time to look through it. In the end, only half-looking up from the page in her hand, she said, 'You have a history of driving under the influence, don't you, Mrs Roberts?'

Fliss didn't answer the question, but a flush of colour was rising up from inside her mask. Cara wasn't sure what was happening, but from the way the atmosphere had suddenly changed in the gallery and in the interview room, she could tell something was afoot.

'In fact,' Greenfield continued, 'you've killed someone before, while under the influence . . .'

'It was an accident,' Fliss cried angrily.

'But you went to prison for it, so you were held responsible for *two* people's deaths. One was a young woman by the name of Penny Reeves. The other your own son,

387

Adam Roberts. You killed them when you lost control of the car while you were driving with more than the legal limit of alcohol in your blood.'

Fliss's head was in her hands as Helen Hall began arguing heatedly with Greenfield, but Cara couldn't hear what was being said, because Andee was shouting at the DS.

'Did you know they were going to do this?' she seethed, already on her feet.

'No, of course not,' Rundle replied, looking genuinely shocked.

'Then make it stop.'

Rundle nodded for her to look back at Fliss. Helen Hall had clearly called for a break, and was leading Fliss out of the room.

'Why did that happen?' Andee demanded furiously of Rundle.

'I don't know *why*,' Rundle replied, 'but they obviously looked into Fliss's past and saw she had a record . . . You know how it goes.'

'But it has nothing to do with Jeannie Symonds. The two cases aren't even similar.'

'Listen, you know as well as I do that those guys aren't going to leave here until every last stone has been turned and someone is held accountable for Jeannie's death. Andee!' she cried as Andee started for the door. 'I'm sorry, OK. You're right, Fliss's past shouldn't have been thrown at her like that, but you know what Gould would say if he was here: he'd ask if we'd be reacting this way if Fliss was someone we didn't know?'

'Yes, we would,' Andee retorted. 'Or I would. That woman has been through hell since she lost her baby son *fifteen years ago.* And allowing this . . . *this* . . . *pantomime* to go any further will not help anyone to find out what happened to Jeannie. Now, if you'll excuse me, I need to go and see how much unnecessary damage has been done.'

As the door shut behind her, Cara sat quietly in the darkness, remembering how her old nan had once said that Fliss had something dark to hide. She guessed this was probably it, that Fliss had been at the wheel of a car and over the limit when a woman and her own little boy had died.

Several more minutes ticked by before Rundle said, 'I had no idea it was going to go that way, Cara, and I want you to know that I agree with Andee: it had no damned good reason to.'

CHAPTER FIFTY-EIGHT

FLISS

Thursday 28 January 2021

While thankful that her police interview was not going to be continued this evening, Fliss was still in turmoil as Andee drove them away from the station. Greenfield's disbelief about why she'd been parked in the layby, the suspicion that she'd been waiting for someone, that she'd been somehow involved in Jeannie's death in order to further her relationship with Guy . . . It was unthinkable, unbearable . . .

But worse – far, far worse than anything else – was the way they'd tried to use the accident of fifteen years ago against her. She'd never imagined for a minute that it would be brought up today, and neither had Helen Hall, which was why she'd ended the interview so abruptly. She was now, apparently, in a meeting with DS Rundle and DCI Gould, voicing strong objections.

It felt as though the world was going rapidly crazy, throwing up suspicions and doubts, questions, fears, old nightmares, new ones . . .

'I managed to get hold of Neil before we left the station,' Andee said. 'He's going to meet you at the flat.'

Neil. Oh God, *Neil.* 'Did you tell him?' she asked over

the wrenching in her heart. 'I mean that they talked about Adam?'

'Yes,' Andee said softly. 'I think he's the only one who can help you with this tonight.'

Knowing how true that was, and grateful to Andee for realizing it, she turned to look out at the darkness shrouding the bay and tumbleweed skimming along the Promenade. She hadn't talked about Adam in so long, only ever whispered his name to herself in quiet, lonely moments when she allowed herself to believe that they might still be connected in some way. Having his loss thrown at her so brutally was making her feel sick inside, as all the self-loathing, guilt and shame crowded in to remind her of what she'd done.

She should never have got into her car that night; she should have left Adam where he was, at her mother's, safe and fast asleep. She could have driven home alone, or stayed the night too. There had been no need to leave. Zac had been with Neil on a dads and lads camping trip in Devon; they hadn't even been expecting to see her. So why in God's name had she decided to pack Adam up and strap him into his car seat when she'd had a large glass of wine and no dinner and he was already settled in his grandma's spare room?

Her mother had tried to persuade her not to go, but one glass wasn't anything to worry about, she'd insisted, she'd be fine, and it was always easier to start the day at home. She'd have everything she needed to hand, and Adam usually slept through until eight in his own bed. Plus she could have everything ready for Neil and Zac when they got back around midday. There were so many good reasons to go home.

'Goodnight, Mum, love you,' she'd said, kissing her mother's silky cheek. 'Thanks for having him today. I'll call to let you know when we're home.'

She'd spent the next five days fighting for her life in ICU. Both legs were broken, her spine and ribs fractured, one lung had collapsed and her head had suffered such a traumatic blow on impact that the damage to her brain, at that time, had been the cause of greatest concern.

When she'd finally been brought out of the induced coma, she'd remembered nothing of the accident, and she still couldn't in any detail after all these years. There was only a blurred, spinning sensation, a sense of jarring and crunching and flashing of lights; no memory of pain or fear, or of being cut from the car. What she did remember, however, and knew she would never forget, was Neil's grief-stricken face when he'd told her that Adam hadn't made it. He'd barely been able to get the words out, and had sobbed so hard when he finally did that a nurse had hurried to comfort him. Then had come the other horrifying news, that a young woman of twenty-three had also lost her life, because she, Fliss Roberts, had driven a car when she'd known she shouldn't have.

She couldn't be certain now exactly when she'd realized she could never be trusted as a mother again, that she must stand aside and allow Neil to take full custody of Zac. Maybe she'd already been in prison by then, sentenced to five years for causing death by driving while over the legal limit. Not far over, apparently, but even the small amount had been enough to end the lives of her baby son and an innocent woman.

Neil deserved so much better than her, and so did Zac. She had failed them in the worst imaginable way; she couldn't even look at them without being reminded of what she'd taken from them, a brother and a son. Neil had fought her, begged her, even threatened to kill himself if she tried to divorce him, but she'd known he wouldn't do that. He'd never have done it to Zac, or to himself, no matter how devastated he was.

In the end, though they'd lived apart following her release from prison, they hadn't divorced until after Estelle had fallen pregnant with Chloe and had decided she wanted to be married. Neil had agreed, but had always remained adamant that Fliss must be a part of their son's life. Even if they didn't live under the same roof, or share the same lives, Zac would always know who his mother was, and Fliss would never miss out on any stage of her son's development.

As the café came into view and they saw a single marked police vehicle parked outside, Fliss's heart contracted with the sheer awfulness of where they were now, today. 'They surely can't still be searching the place,' she said. There were no flashing lights, thank God, or actually any signs of life at all from where they were. The café was in darkness and so was the flat upstairs, but the car must be there for a reason.

'Zac's not back yet,' she remarked, looking for the van as Andee drove into the service lane so they could use the back door. Two uniformed officers had to move out of the way so she could pull into an empty parking bay. The lights were on back here, showing them other ghostly figures in white protective suits going through the garage and storerooms. 'Where's Zac?' Fliss said, trying to recall where he'd said he was going today. 'He was helping Guy to move,' she remembered. 'Maybe Mallory's here by now. I should give him a call.'

'Let's go inside first,' Andee suggested.

As they got out of the car, one of the men in white suits approached them. He was holding something in his right hand, a long, narrow plastic bag with an object inside that wasn't immediately definable in the shadows.

'Leo?' Andee said, recognizing him.

'We're just about done here,' Leo Johnson answered.

Fliss was staring at the bag. 'What's that?' she asked.

He held it up and glanced at her regretfully as he said, 'It's a spade we found in your garage.'

Puzzled, she said, 'There are always spades there. What's special about this one?'

With an uncomfortable glance Andee's way he said, 'It needs to go to the lab.'

'But why?' Fliss protested, refusing to connect with the obvious. 'It'll just be Zac's or Neil's. They're always leaving things here.'

Leo looked over his shoulder as someone called for him, and raised a hand for them to wait. Turning back to Fliss he said, 'Where's Zac?'

'Uh, I'm not sure,' she replied, feeling her heart rate quicken as the potential of this began to gather its own momentum. 'I was about to call him.'

They all turned as headlights flooded the lane. As the Seafront van came to a stop, Zac got out.

'What the heck's going on?' he demanded, coming towards them. 'Mum? Are you OK?'

'Yes, I think so,' she replied, leaning into him as he put an arm around her.

Leo Johnson said, solemnly, 'I'm really sorry to tell you this, Fliss, but Neil was arrested about twenty minutes ago.'

CHAPTER FIFTY-NINE

CARA

Thursday 28 January 2021

Neil Roberts hadn't actually been charged yet, but DS Rundle, DCI Gould and the special interrogators were closeted with the CPS lawyer, and everyone was expecting him to sign off on it soon.

Cara was in a state of high anticipation, as was the rest of the team as they waited for news. Richie had been in touch to ask if it was true that Neil Roberts was under arrest, but Cara hadn't dared to answer. She could only guess at who might have dropped the rumour; she only knew that she wasn't going to risk her job by sharing information with the press that might not even be accurate by the time it went public.

She'd been told she could go home, that there was nothing more she could do tonight, but there was no way she could leave the station until she knew for certain what was happening.

Her head was spinning with this new reality: Neil Roberts had killed Jeannie!

She couldn't work out whether she was more shocked

or confused. She had no idea yet how he'd done it, apart from that he'd obviously pushed her off the cliff.

But why?

She wished Andee would call or come in; she must surely have heard about the arrest by now, but she was probably still with Fliss, which was why Cara hadn't contacted her herself.

What a terrible day this was for Fliss: that insane interrogation she'd been put through, the arrest of her ex-husband for murder, and now Cara could only wonder if she knew yet that it was actually going to get worse.

CHAPTER SIXTY

FLISS

Thursday 28 January 2021

Fliss's face was ghostly white as she stared at Leo Johnson in disbelief. 'This can't be happening,' she murmured, starting to feel light-headed. *Neil, arrested?* 'Please tell me I'll wake up in a minute.'

'What's the charge?' Zac demanded, as if they didn't already know.

'No charge yet, as far as I know,' Leo replied.

Zac looked down at the spade Leo was holding. 'Why have you got that?' he demanded.

Speaking quietly, Leo said, 'Zac, I'm afraid you're going to have to come with me.'

Fliss turned cold to her core. 'Leo, you have to stop this,' she cried in panic.

Zac was backing away, arms in the air. 'I haven't done anything wrong,' he protested.

'No one's saying you have,' Leo assured him, 'but we need to clear some things up.'

Andee said, 'Leo will explain everything once you're at the station, Zac. Dad's lawyer will be there. His name's Oscar Radcliffe. Find him and introduce yourself.'

Looking more afraid by the minute, Zac turned to his mother. 'Are you coming too?' he asked.

She attempted a nod, but Andee said to Zac, 'There won't be anything she can do, so I'm going to take her inside. We'll wait up for you. If you need a lift, call and I'll come to get you.'

Pulling him into her arms, Fliss held him so tight that neither of them could breathe. 'I love you,' she whispered. 'If you see Dad, tell him I love him too.'

He drew back to look at her. 'It's going to be all right,' he assured her with an earnestness all fractured through with fear.

She managed a smile. 'Of course it is,' she said, wanting to believe it so badly that in the moment she did – but then she saw Leo passing the spade to another officer as he stripped off his protective gear and felt herself starting to collapse inside.

'Call as soon as you can,' she told Zac, and somehow she made herself let him go, never taking her eyes from him as Leo led him to a car and allowed him to get into the passenger seat before driving away.

As soon as she and Andee were in the flat, Andee put the kettle on and pressed Fliss into a chair in the sitting room. 'It's been a stressful day and you're tired,' she said. 'Let's try to wind things down for a moment and we'll go back over everything when you're ready.'

Fliss nodded, and let her head fall against the cushions. A moment later she was panicking again. 'I can't believe they've arrested Neil,' she cried helplessly. 'Oh God, Andee, I feel as though I'm losing my mind. And now they've taken Zac.' She sat forward, burying her head in her hands.

Andee came to sit beside her and gently rubbed her

back. 'Let's try to stay calm,' she said, 'we need to have our wits about us as things unfold, and try not to worry about the spade. I'm sure they've taken others, and all sorts of tools, but they won't find anything on them . . .'

'How do you know?' Fliss cried, turning to look at her. 'I don't want to believe it, but what if they do? Oh God,' she cried, suddenly struck with guilt. 'I should have called Estie. She'll be beside herself by now.'

As she went to get her phone, Andee said, 'Check to see if she's called you. She might have left a message.'

Fliss shook her head. 'No, no calls from her,' she said, and scrolling to Estelle's number she waited for the connection. 'Estie, it's me,' she said to the voicemail, 'are you OK? I'm sure you know that they've arrested Neil. Maybe you were with him? You could even be at the station waiting for him now. Please call me when you can, don't worry about the time.'

As she rang off, she said, 'I hope to God Chloe didn't see anything. She'll be terrified if she did. I'll try Prim to see if she's with her . . . Except Prim's not there, is she? So where's Chloe?' she cried, more fear building inside her.

Taking the phone from her Andee said, 'I'm sure Estelle's at home with Chloe and she'll call back at any minute.'

Fliss took several breaths in an effort to calm down. She felt so wretched, drained and panicked; her head was thumping, she needed to take something to ease it. She started to get up and jumped as her phone rang. *Neil? Zac? Estie?*

'Guy,' she told Andee, and clicked on. 'Hi, how are you?' she asked, trying to collect her thoughts, to focus on him now instead of herself.

'I'm fine,' he answered, 'back at the Hall. Zac was a great help today. He must be home by now?'

'Yes, he's . . .' She couldn't tell him what had happened, not yet anyway, so she said, 'Have Mallory and Paul arrived?'

'They should be at the apartment sometime in the next hour. How did your interview go with the police today?'

'It was . . . Not really what I was expecting. I'm going back again tomorrow.'

'Really? Why?'

'I-I'm not sure. I think there are still some questions they need to ask.'

'You sound upset. Would you like to come here? Or I can come over?'

'No, no, it's OK, Andee's here, but thank you.'

She could hear a TV in the background and a moment later he said, 'Oh God, it's just come up on the news about Neil . . . I'm sorry, I . . .'

'Zac's at the station too,' she blurted.

Sounding shocked, he said, 'Surely they don't suspect him of anything.'

'I don't know. I'm waiting for some news. It's a nightmare and I'm not sure where or how it's going to end.'

'It'll be all right,' he assured her gently. 'It's only an arrest, not a charge. I'm sure they'll let them both go again by the morning.'

Trying desperately to cling to the words she said, 'But what if they don't? What if they've found something?'

'Sssh, I'm sure that's not the case. It'll all be sorted out, and once this is behind us I'll take you away from here. We can start a new life together where you won't have to worry about the café, or debts, or anything else, and there'll be no reminders of things we'd rather forget.'

Fliss sat holding the phone, unsure what to say, or even to think. To go away with him, a new life, far from here . . . ? It wasn't what she wanted at all. Had she ever given him that impression? Surely not.

'Would you like that?' he asked softly. 'Just the two of us?'

She remained silent as her eyes moved to Andee.

'It's OK, you don't have to give me an answer now,' he said. 'It was the wrong time to bring it up. I just want you to know that I'm here for you and that you mean a great deal to me. Will you call if you want to talk? I'm probably not going to sleep much tonight.'

Dimly wondering what it must be like for him to be back at the Hall and on his own, she said, 'Yes, of course. Thanks.'

After clicking off the line she put her mobile on the table and looked at Andee again.

'What is it?' Andee prompted.

'I don't know,' she replied. 'I just . . . He sounded . . .'
Andee waited.

Fliss shook her head and decided to change the subject. 'Won't Graeme be expecting you?' she asked, referring to Andee's partner. 'I've already taken up so much of your day.'

'I spoke to him just after I called Neil,' Andee assured her, 'and he's fine about me staying here. I'll pop back in a while to pick up some things, but I want to be around in case you get a call in the night.'

Sighing, Fliss reached for the tea Andee had put on the table. 'What do you think's going to happen when I go back to the police station tomorrow?' she asked, not sure she wanted an answer, but she had to face it whether she liked it or not.

'I don't see any reason why they'd want to talk about the accident again,' Andee replied, 'that was just a tactic to shake you up, get you off balance so you'd end up saying something to incriminate yourself, or someone else. I hate that method of interviewing myself, I thought it was extinct by now, but apparently not.'

'I don't have anyone else to incriminate,' Fliss said, 'because I don't know anything.'

'And that's all you need to remember.'

'I had no reason to want to harm Jeannie, and I had no way of getting her into the woods, never mind to the cliff edge.'

'Exactly.'

'But they think I helped someone do it, and Neil doesn't have an alibi, does he?'

Andee shook her head.

Fliss's mind spun. 'But it's crazy to think that he and I would . . . We had nothing against her . . .'

Very carefully, Andee said, 'Do you know for certain that Neil wasn't sleeping with her?'

Fliss wanted to shout, 'Of course he wasn't!' but how could she when she didn't know. 'Even if he was, it doesn't mean he'd want to kill her, for God's sake.'

'Maybe it wasn't intentional . . .'

Fliss could hardly believe it. 'What are you saying? You surely don't . . . Andee . . .'

'If there was some kind of argument,' Andee persisted, 'maybe one of them tried to break off the affair . . . These are the sorts of questions the detectives are asking themselves, and they know what happened with Neil and Sarah Hansell . . .'

'She withdrew the complaint.'

'Yes, but it's still on record, so in their eyes he has a history of violence against women who reject him.'

Fliss shot to her feet. 'That is such nonsense,' she cried, 'and even if it wasn't, why the heck would *I* help him do something so monstrous?'

'They only see what's in front of them, some of it unexplained, or not adding up in the way it needs to.'

'And now they're collecting things that could have been used to break Jeannie's skull, like the spade from my garage, so they're going to think I took it from Neil and brought it here. Or Zac did? Dear God, they can't seriously think Zac . . . It's why they've taken him in, isn't it? Is that why he's at the station now? Of course it is. Christ, what's the matter with me? Why am I taking so long to catch up? We have to do something, Andee. I have to make them understand that Zac had nothing to do with this – none of us did.'

'Don't worry, Helen and Oscar will take care of it, and I'll lay money that Zac will be home before midnight.'

As it turned out, it was just after eleven when Zac came in, tired, dishevelled and ravenously hungry in a way only a lad his age could be after the ordeal he'd just experienced. 'I only saw Dad for a minute,' he told Fliss as she embraced him, and Andee got up to make him a sandwich. 'I gave him your message and he said to tell you not to worry, it'll all be sorted out.'

'Did they ask you about the spade?' Andee wanted to know.

'Only if it was mine. I said it belongs to the company.'

'Which it does,' Fliss confirmed, as if that explained everything, when actually it explained nothing at all. 'What else did they ask you?'

'Where I was on January the sixth. Like anyone knows what day of the week it is, never mind the date during these lockdowns.'

'So what did you tell them?'

'That I was either helping out here, at the café, or doing deliveries, or maybe I was working for Dad. I said I'd check the diaries and let them know tomorrow. Why have they arrested Dad, for God's sake? They must know he didn't do anything.'

'Of course he didn't,' Fliss assured him, 'but things are taking a while to straighten out. He'll probably call any minute to say he's on his way home. Was Estie there, at the station?'

He shook his head. 'I don't think so, but she could have been in a different part.'

Fliss looked at Andee. 'Do you think I should try her again? Yes, I should.'

There was still no reply from Estelle, so Fliss left another message and put down her phone.

Zac said, 'Mallory's at the flat now. I should call her; I just don't know what to say about the way everything is. You remember how close she was to Jeannie, and here's me and Dad being questioned—'

'Has she called you?' Andee asked.

He nodded. 'About half a dozen times, which means she's probably seen it on the news so I owe her an explanation.'

Andee said, 'Why don't you text to say you'll call in half an hour? That way you can have something to eat first and take some time to clear your head.'

He closed his eyes, still seeming undecided about what to do; however, he put his phone on the table and caught his mother in another embrace. 'We'll get through this,' he told her, as if sensing she needed the reassurance, or perhaps hearing himself say it brought its own sort of comfort.

'Of course we will,' she said, holding onto him tightly.

'Maybe you don't need me to stay now that Zac is back,' Andee said, wiping her hands on a kitchen towel. 'But I'm not far away if anything comes up. Just call, don't worry about the time, especially if you hear anything from Neil or Estie.'

CHAPTER SIXTY-ONE
ESTELLE

Friday 29 January 2021

It wasn't quite seven the next morning when Estelle pulled up outside the café and rang Fliss's mobile number. She could see no signs of life inside, but Fliss and at least one of her trusty Corona Girls were probably in the kitchen preparing breakfasts by now, and the lights would go on in the shopfront at any moment.

'Estie!' Fliss cried when she answered. 'Where are you?'

'I'm outside,' Estelle told her, forcing her voice to stay calm. 'Chloe's with me. Can she come in?'

'What? Yes, of course. Aren't you coming too?'

'I can't. I have to be somewhere. She's got her laptop and an overnight bag, if that's all right. I'm not sure when I'll be back.'

'Estie, what's going on? Where do you have to be? Have you spoken to Neil?'

Estelle rang off and pulled Chloe into a tender embrace. 'I'm sorry about this, sweetie,' she said, swallowing her tears, 'but you know how much you love being with Fliss and Zac, and I'll be back as soon as I can.'

'Why won't you tell me where you're going?' Chloe complained. 'And where's Dad? He promised he'd come home last night, but he didn't.'

'Fliss will explain,' Estelle said and, leaning across her daughter, she pushed the passenger door open. 'Look, there she is, just opening up. Off you go now, and tell her I'll call her later.'

Moments later she was driving away, not even glancing in the mirror to check that Chloe had made it into the café – Fliss would make sure of it, so she didn't need to worry. She wondered fleetingly how Fliss could carry on as normal, serving coffees and bacon rolls, rising to all the chitchat with her customers, who dripped through one at a time when the world was falling apart around them.

She didn't care. Fliss could take care of her own problems – and Chloe – while she, Estelle, worked out what needed to be done about her own. She couldn't do it with Chloe around, she was too afraid of something happening to her; she wasn't strong enough, or clever enough, to keep her safe.

Of course she knew she was being paranoid, that she'd lost all sense of where she was and what she should be doing, but at least she'd had enough sense to get Chloe out of the house before Neil came home again. *If* he came home, and there was no guarantee of that, but if he did and he found his precious girl still there, and his wife seeming to hide behind her . . .

No! Estelle wasn't going to think about that. She just needed to put her foot down now, because at any minute she was going to drive past the gates of Howarth Hall. If there had been another way to get home, she'd have taken it, but there wasn't.

Her speed was nearing seventy as she left Westleigh Heights behind. She hadn't noticed the stones Neil had dumped there on January the sixth, or the layby, or the woods, but she hadn't been looking, and anyway, she didn't care.

She just wanted to get home, to close and lock the doors again and decide what had to be done.

Finally she was pulling up outside the house, the one she'd designed that she knew Neil had never really liked. He'd only ever been here for Chloe, never for her.

As soon as she got inside, she slid the bolts on the front door, pulled a curtain across the frosted glass panel and went to check that all the downstairs windows were locked.

She was so busy running around, breathless and muttering to herself, that she didn't hear any other movements in the house. She thought, truly believed, that she was there alone, that she was safe, and so was Chloe, until she went through to the kitchen and realized with a stuttering stop to her heart that someone else was there.

'Prim,' she said hoarsely. 'Where . . . where have you been? How did you get in?'

CHAPTER SIXTY-TWO

FLISS

Friday 29 January 2021

'She's upstairs with Zac now,' Fliss told Andee over the phone. 'I didn't get the chance to speak to Estie before she drove off, but Chloe says she's been acting really strangely lately and it's clearly scaring the girl. I didn't feel I could question her any further than that without making matters worse, but something's obviously going on.'

'Have you tried calling Estie since she left?' Andee asked.

'She's not picking up or returning my texts. Oh God, if only I could speak to Neil. Will they let him go today, do you think?' She knew she was probably being foolish to hope, but it was impossible not to.

'I don't know,' Andee replied, 'but I'm on my way to the station as we speak, so I'll be in touch as soon as I have some news. Meantime, hold on to that dear little girl. She needs you right now.'

As she rang off, Fliss went to join Leanne and Wilkie in the kitchen. She'd decided not to do front of house today; too many customers would have questions, or knowing comments, or the kind of sympathy she really didn't want to engage with. Much better that Angie dealt with the public, while she helped out behind the scenes and was free to take calls the instant they came in.

Where the heck would she be without the Corona Girls?

Guy rang next, but she let the call go to messages and didn't even check to find out what he'd said. She didn't have the heart even to think about leaving with him, much less to plan for it – she wondered when she'd given him the impression it was what she wanted to do. Her café was here. Her family was here. Right now, all she wanted was to see Neil walk through the door, and to hear him say that everything had been sorted. 'The arrest was a stupid mistake,' he'd tell her. 'They've found out it really was an accident, so our lives can go back to normal.'

Her phone rang again and, seeing it was Zac, she clicked on.

'I'm supposed to be ferrying the old folk to the town hall for their vaccines today,' he reminded her, 'so I'm going to take Chloe with me.'

'Good idea,' she said, and closed her eyes as the craziness of the world made her head start to spin. 'Does that mean you're using the van?'

'No, you need it for deliveries, so Leanne said I can take her car. We'll be back about four then we'll walk over to the marina to see Mallory.'

Knowing he'd spent over an hour talking to Mallory last night, Fliss let it go there. She didn't need to get involved in his relationship at this time; it was enough to know that Mallory wasn't holding him responsible for something that was absolutely not his fault. 'I'll call if I hear anything from Dad,' she told him.

Minutes later, Helen Hall rang to let her know that her next interview with the police had been put off until the following day. 'I'm afraid I don't know why,' Helen replied when Fliss asked, 'but I've already made it clear to DS Rundle and DCI Gould that we will not be discussing the accident of fifteen years ago, unless someone can explain why it is in any way relevant to what's happened to Jeannie.'

CHAPTER SIXTY-THREE
CARA AND ANDEE

Friday 29 January 2021

'Are you crying?' Andee asked as she entered the incident room to find one of the young DCs dabbing her eyes.

Looking up from the paperwork in front of her, Shari Avery gave a self-conscious laugh as she said, 'I'm just reading through the letters Guy Symonds's patients have sent to him. There are so many, and some of them are really getting to me.'

With a sympathetic smile, Andee glanced at Cara, who didn't seem to have heard any of what had been said, or even to have registered that someone else had come into the room. Her computer screen was displaying row upon row of numbers and, as she went through them, she was making notes on a pad next to her.

For an incident room, it was quiet, though that didn't mean nothing was happening, only that everyone was busy elsewhere. 'Is Natalie around?' she asked.

'I'm here,' DS Rundle replied, coming into the room behind her. 'I was just coming down to get you, but apparently they let you through.'

'Barry Britten's on the front desk,' Andee explained.

'You know he gives me a free pass, once you've OK'd it, of course. So what's happening here?'

Rundle threw out her hands as if to say everything and nothing. 'The search continues of Neil Roberts's premises, Howarth Hall, and the woods; still nothing of concrete consequence from the pathologist, and forensics won't be back to us for a while on the potential blunt instruments that were collected yesterday. The Avon and Somerset guys are busy interrogating already.'

'Who's with them now?' Andee asked.

'Neil Roberts. I was there at the start, but there are only so many times you can listen to the same thing over and over, and I can't see him changing anything until new evidence comes in to change it for him.'

'What prompted the arrest last night?'

'Apparently, they wanted to keep him in, so they decided they had enough to justify it. Frankly, they do, so I didn't even try to argue. That sort of scare can change a person's story quite dramatically, as we know.'

'But it hasn't happened yet?'

'No. He's shaken up, you can see that, and his lawyer kicked up a bit of a fuss. However, right now, whichever way you look at it, things are not looking good for him. How was Fliss after her ordeal?'

Taking off her coat as she sat down, Andee said, 'Upset, obviously, and things weren't helped by Zac being pulled in . . . Did anything actually come of that?'

'Not that I've heard, but you've got to understand why he's of interest. He works at Howarth Hall; he's Neil Roberts's son, and as far as I understand it, he hasn't yet come up with an alibi for January the sixth himself.'

413

Andee closed her eyes in exasperation. 'You can't be serious.'

Rundle turned to Cara. 'Morning you over there,' she called out, 'what's so fascinating? Should we call a conference?'

'Soon,' Cara replied, not even looking around, just keeping her checklist going between page and screen.

'She's been on that since she arrived this morning,' Shari piped up.

Rundle said to Andee, 'I suppose you'd have told me if Richie had come up with anything regarding a hire car, or station sighting?'

Andee was checking her phone as she nodded. 'Of course,' she said, and looking up added, 'I think we're going to have to accept that Guy Symonds really was in London on January the sixth and seventh and returned to Kesterly on the eighth.'

Rundle's frown showed her dissatisfaction with that.

Andee said, 'You must have asked yourself why he would kill Jeannie when he'd already contacted a divorce lawyer? It doesn't make any sense.'

'OK, it doesn't, but I can't help feeling we're missing something somewhere. Tell me your gut isn't saying the same. Maybe he paid someone to do it?'

'OK, this is important,' Cara declared, turning to face them, her youthful eyes bright with excitement. 'I've been through all of Guy Symonds's phone records, and I can't find a single call or text to or from Estelle Fields.'

Andee felt a frisson of understanding as Rundle said, carefully, 'Go on.'

'If they were friends,' Cara explained, 'the way they both say they are, they surely had to have communicated

414

with one another somehow, so I'm guessing that he must have another phone.'

Rundle turned to look at Andee. 'It makes sense to me,' she declared.

'Me too,' Andee agreed.

'OK, Cara, see if you can get him up on a video-link.'

Rundle was seated at the computer herself by the time Guy Symonds appeared on the screen.

'Good morning, detective,' he said, looking unusually unkempt for him. 'How can I help you?'

Coming straight to the point, Rundle said, 'We can find no record of communication between you and Estelle Fields, so I'm wondering how you arranged the friendly meetings you told us about?'

He seemed surprised. 'I have a personal phone as well as my work phone,' he told her. 'I thought you knew that.'

It was Rundle's turn to be thrown. 'I don't recall it ever being mentioned,' she said, sounding annoyed. 'Where is it now?'

He appeared at a loss. 'I assumed it was taken when the house was searched. Unless I left it in London but, even if I did, surely the officers who carried out the search there would have found it. It's not a secret.'

Picking up a pen, Rundle said, 'Can you give me the number, please? And service provider?'

After doing so, he said, 'I'm sorry if it's caused some confusion, but I'm sure you'll find that you already have it.'

As soon as the call was over, Rundle said to Cara, 'See if you can find out where this phone is, and I'll contact O2 with an urgent request for information.

415

Where are you going?' she called out as Andee made for the door.

'To see Estelle Fields,' Andee replied, and a moment later she'd gone.

CHAPTER SIXTY-FOUR

ESTELLE

Friday 29 January 2021

Estelle was sitting at the kitchen table with a mug of coffee between her hands. The exhaustion etched on her face seemed a reflection of the exhaustion inside her. Everything was feeling surreal, almost otherworldly, even though she was now over the shock of having found Prim in the house. Of course Prim had been able to get in – she had keys.

'So where have you been for the last two days?' Estelle asked, as Prim sat down with her own coffee and regarded her with those familiar toffee-brown eyes.

'With my parents, but I asked them to say I wasn't there.'

Estelle shook her head. 'I couldn't believe it when you just took off like that.'

Sounding both sorry and defensive, Prim said, 'I had to go. Staying was no longer an option – surely you realized that?'

Tensing around a truth she didn't want to face, Estelle said, 'I didn't mean to push you in the pool, you have—'

'It wasn't about that, and you know it,' Prim cut in impatiently. 'The police keep trying to get in touch with me, and one of their first questions is going to be whether or not I can give you an alibi for January the sixth. We both know that I can't.'

Estelle's heart contracted as she clutched her mug more tightly in her hands. The burn was easier to cope with than the fear.

Changing the subject for a moment, Prim said, 'Where's Chloe?'

Stammering slightly, Estelle said, 'With Fliss. I was too afraid to keep her here.'

'Why?'

She wondered if Prim had gone mad to ask such a question, but then realized she might genuinely not know the answer. 'Have you seen the news?' she asked brokenly. 'Have you seen what he's done?'

Prim nodded her understanding. 'It's why I came back,' she said. 'I could hardly believe it . . . Estie, have you spoken to him?'

Shrinking from the question, Estelle said, 'I can't. He said I shouldn't call and I'm afraid of what he'll do if I try.' She looked at Prim with haunted, terrified eyes. 'He's hired my *mother* as his lawyer,' she cried wretchedly. 'He knows who she is, and he's *using* her to help clear his name.'

Calmly, Prim said, 'It's why I came back. When I saw that, I realized I had to. So let's talk about it, Estie. Tell me what really happened and I'll do whatever I can to help you. But I can't lie to the police. I need you to understand that, OK?'

Estelle sobbed as she inhaled. 'I don't want you to,' she said wretchedly. 'I just want this to be over, but before I tell you, can you call Fliss? Please? Ask her if she can come. I need her to understand why I can't tell anyone anything until she knows what it's going to mean for her.' She started at the sound of someone ringing the doorbell. 'Oh God, it might be him,' she panicked, leaping from her chair. 'Don't let him in, Prim. Please. Let's just not answer.'

Getting up from the table, Prim put a comforting hand on her shoulder as she passed. 'We need to find out who it is,' she said. 'Just stay where you are.'

Moments later, Estelle heard voices at the door, and almost unravelled when she realized the caller wasn't male. She listened, trying to make out who it was, but could only recognize Prim's voice and footsteps as she returned.

'It's Andee Lawrence,' Prim said evenly. 'I think you should speak to her.'

Estelle's head jerked as she nodded. 'OK,' she said, 'but I still need Fliss to be here. Please. I'll wait upstairs until she comes.'

CHAPTER SIXTY-FIVE

FLISS

Friday 29 January 2021

'Of course I'll come,' Fliss assured Andee down the phone.
'And you say Prim is there?'

'Yes.'

'Is she all right?'

'She seems to be.'

'So where did she go?'

'I'm not sure of anything yet, but I think we'll have a
much clearer idea in the next hour or two. I'll tell Estelle
you're on your way.'

After ringing off, Fliss quickly made sure it was OK
with the Corona Girls if she left for a while and, grabbing
the keys to the van, she ran outside. She could have kissed
her son when she found it had a full tank of petrol.

Zac rang as she reached Hope Cove. 'Mum, Mallory's
dad wants to talk to the officer in charge of the case. I
said it was DCI Gould, is that right?'

'Yes, or DS Rundle. She's much more hands-on. How's
their jet-lag?'

'Working through, and they've just tested negative, so
they're coming out of quarantine today. Apparently Paul's

pretty steamed up about something, although from what I can tell that's kind of his normal state. Anyway, I should call Mallory back now. Chloe sends love, see you later,' and he was gone.

Fifteen minutes later, Fliss was driving past the gates of Howarth Hall when Guy rang, almost as if he'd sensed she was nearby. It unnerved her slightly, although she couldn't think why when it was clearly no more than a coincidence.

Instead of answering, she let the call go to voicemail. She didn't want to have to find an excuse not to see him today. Or any other day. She'd realized during the night that she'd made a mistake in thinking she was falling for him; she'd been blinded by his good looks and charm and her pathetically desperate longing for the kind of male attention she really only wanted from one man.

On arriving at Neil and Estie's place, she pulled up next to Andee's car and quickly checked her messages.

'Hi, it's me,' Guy said softly. 'I think I might have misspoken last night, trying to go too fast, too soon. I'm sorry if I alarmed you. I hope we might get together today, but I understand how difficult things are for you right now with Neil being where he is. I still can't believe he did anything to hurt Jeannie; it has to have been some bizarre sort of accident – that's what I keep telling myself anyway. I guess we still don't know one another well enough for me to admit to all the things that keep going around in my mind about you, but please know I'm finding it hard to think of anything else. I only have to picture you in my mind's eye to feel the need to see you, to hold you in my arms and to make love to you again and again. Please call when you can.'

Unsettled by the way her body reacted to his words, in spite of her resolve not to see him again, she was about to put the phone in her bag when it rang again.

Seeing it was Helen Hall she clicked on.

'Fliss, good morning,' the lawyer said. 'I'm afraid I have some bad news that I thought I should share with you right away.'

CHAPTER SIXTY-SIX

CARA

Friday 29 January 2021

Cara found DS Rundle in the custody area, talking to a Crown Prosecution lawyer who she knew was back again about Neil Roberts. 'Sorry to interrupt, ma'am,' she said, when Rundle spotted her hovering. 'Jeannie's brother, Paul Haines, is in the front office demanding to see you.'

Rundle's eyebrows arched with interest. 'Is he now? I thought he was supposed to be in quarantine.'

'He says he and his daughter have both passed their tests and this can't wait.'

Turning back to the lawyer, Rundle excused herself and left him with the Avon and Somerset detectives while she followed Cara out of the suite. 'I'm keen to speak to Mr Haines anyway,' she said as they started along the corridor, 'so let's go find out what he thinks is so urgent.'

A few minutes later they were in a soft interview room with Paul Haines and his daughter seated on large leather sofas around a scratched coffee table.

'First of all,' Rundle began, 'I'd like to express our sympathies for the loss of your sister, Mr Haines.'

'Yes, thank you,' he said, gruffly, tugging his mask back

up over his nose, 'and now I'd like you to go and arrest the bastard that did this to her. I know it was him – I'm talking about her husband, Guy bloody Symonds, just in case you haven't already worked it out.'

Hiding her shock, Cara glanced at Rundle who, entirely composed, said: 'Can you tell me why you think that?'

Haines sat forward, resting his large arms on his thighs. 'It doesn't take much figuring out,' he retorted, 'especially if you're me. My sister spoke to me on New Year's Eve, it was probably still the thirtieth here, whatever. Check her records if you like, you'll see I'm right. It was Mallory she called on WhatsApp and Mal was with me on account of this.' He tapped the medical boot supporting his injured ankle. 'Jeannie said she was tired of all the hostility between us, that it had to end, and so she was going to make Mallory her main beneficiary when the time came, and meanwhile she'd be transferring the equivalent of three million quid to me in various stocks and shares. It was about what I'd have got if my father had been able to change his will before the fire put a stop to it.

'Now the same bloody thing has happened again. Just as I'm about to get what's rightfully mine, my sister goes over a cliff edge before she's had chance to speak to a lawyer. Now that's a funny coincidence, don't you think? First my parents, now Jeannie. So you tell me Guy Symonds isn't behind it. I'll even go so far as to say he burned my parents' house down to make sure Jeannie got the lot before any of it came my way. I know I'll never be able to prove it, I'm just saying it wouldn't surprise me if he swapped those candles and gave Jeannie the one he knew was a fire risk. Maybe not a fail-safe way of doing it, but it worked, didn't it? And it's damned well worked again.

He made sure she didn't get to speak to a lawyer after she rang us,' he reached for his daughter's hand, 'because the last thing he wanted was any changes to her will or transfers of wealth taking place and putting it all out of his reach.'

Cara was watching Mallory, trying to gauge what she was thinking, but it didn't appear she was going to say a word to contradict her father.

Rundle said, 'How do you think he did it, Mr Haines?'

'I don't know. I wish I did, but I'm telling you he did, and it's your job to make sure he doesn't get away with it.'

Rundle didn't argue, simply said, 'Thank you very much for coming in, Mr Haines. Cara here will bring you refreshments while you wait, and then perhaps you'll be willing to go through it again for the record.'

CHAPTER SIXTY-SEVEN

FLISS

Friday 29 January 2021

'What is it? What's happened?' Andee asked, clearly alarmed to see how pale Fliss was as she opened the front door to Neil and Estie's house.

'I've just had a call from Helen Hall,' Fliss answered shakily. 'The CPS is at the station, and they're about to charge Neil, so I won't be able to come in. I have to speak to Zac before he hears it on the news and I don't want to break it to him by phone.' She looked past Andee as Estie, white-faced and clearly frightened, came down the stairs with Prim behind her. She was about to apologize and ask if they could talk later when Estie said, 'It won't matter if they charge him, because they'll soon let him go.'

Fliss regarded her in confusion, looked to Prim, then to Andee and back to Estie. 'What do you mean?' she asked.

Estie didn't answer, just turned and walked, almost trance-like, into the kitchen.

'Come in,' Andee said quietly. 'I understand your concern for Zac, but we need to hear what she has to say.'

'Let me just send him a text,' Fliss insisted, and after firing off a few words that she wasn't entirely sure made much sense, she followed the others into the kitchen.

Estie was already seated at the large table with Prim and gestured for Fliss and Andee to sit at the other end.

How ingrained social distancing had become now, skewed though this arrangement was, and no windows were open as far as Fliss could tell.

To her surprise, Andee held up her phone as she sat down and said, 'Do you mind if I record this, Estie?'

Alarm flashed in Estie's eyes, and it seemed for a moment that she was going to panic, or run, or at least shout at Andee to put it away, but then the stark reaction was gone and she said, 'Maybe you should. It might save me from having to go through it all again at the police station.'

Unable to imagine where this was going, just praying that Estie was right about them letting Neil go, Fliss braced herself as she watched Andee set the phone on the table.

In halting and quiet tones, and with her small hands bunched together on the table, Estie said, 'I didn't know what he was going to do, I swear it. I'd never have gone along with it if I did. You probably won't believe that . . .' She took a breath that was more like a gulp and her eyes remained lowered as she said, 'You're going to say I was stupid, ignorant, delusional even, not to have guessed long before I did, and you'll be right, because I was. My only excuse, I suppose, is that I kept hoping it was going to work out the way he told me it would; that somehow Jeannie and I would be on good terms again, and . . .' Her voice fell into a dry, wrenching sob and she put a hand to her mouth to block it.

'He said it would bring my mother – my birth mother

– back into my life,' she said, 'and that this time everything would work out, because he and Jeannie would make sure it did.'

Fliss glanced at Andee and, seeming to read her mind, Andee said to Estie, 'We're talking about Guy Symonds, is that right?'

Estie nodded dully, and Fliss felt as though she was unravelling and tensing all at the same time, but at least it wasn't about Neil.

Andee said, 'How did you become involved with Guy Symonds, Estie?'

In a low and halting monotone, she told them about the summer party and how he'd come to talk to her by the kissing gate. 'I met up with him a few times after,' she continued. 'We walked and talked, but what really matters is the time I saw him during the day on New Year's Eve . . . She inhaled a shuddering breath. 'That was when he asked me to help him with a surprise he had for Jeannie that would probably work out well for me too.' She glanced up, looked at each of them almost as though they were strangers, then turned her head stiffly to one side.

'I know you'll find this hard to believe,' she said, staring out at the garden, 'or maybe you won't, but I was – I became – besotted with him. I only had to look at him, or think about him . . . I don't mean in a sexual way, but if he'd wanted that, I know I would have gone along with it. I was even expecting it, hoping for it, I suppose, but we never . . . It didn't happen. We just met and talked, mostly about me, and now, when I look back on it, it feels like he was hypnotizing me, luring me into a sense of security that was . . .' She seemed unable to describe it, 'Blinding, I suppose,' she said in the end. 'I know that probably sounds crazy, or as if I'm trying to excuse myself, but he made me feel like I mattered and I . . . I was taken in by it. I was taken over by him. It was like I wasn't able to do anything unless I talked to him first. He was so kind and patient, understanding in a way that I needed far more than I realized, and I couldn't get enough of it. I felt I could tell him anything and he'd never think badly of me.' She took a breath, and then another, and Prim put a steadying hand on her arm.

'He told me that all I had to do,' Estelle continued, staring at Prim's hand, 'was drive to London on the morning of the sixth, pick him up at his home and bring him back to Kesterly. "It's not a big thing to ask, is it," he said, and the way he said it, it didn't seem big at all, probably because I'd have done anything for him, whatever he asked, just to keep him as my friend, and maybe more when he was ready – or not if everything worked out between me and Jeannie. I don't know really, I didn't rationalize any of it then, I was just ready to do whatever he wanted. He said at one point, "This is going to help a lot with your birth mother, you just wait and see. It will all come good for you, Estie, I promise." Her voice seemed stuck inside her for a moment, as though it couldn't find any breath to release it until the words suddenly came in a gulp. 'And now he's . . . he's hired her as his lawyer,' she sobbed, 'and when I saw that, I felt as though I was losing my mind.'

Fliss was mesmerized, horrified as she watched Prim use a tissue to dab Estie's tears. It was clear what this was leading up to now, and she almost didn't want Estie to have to go through the torment of reliving it.

Taking a sip of water from a glass Prim had put in front of her, Estie forced herself to go on. 'Before I left him on New Year's Eve, he told me not to call or message him again, just to come on the following Wednesday morning at nine and he would be waiting. So that's what I did. Before anyone was up at home, I got into my car and drove all the way to London where I picked him up a little after nine and brought him back here. On the way he was talking to people on the phone, patients, other doctors, his secretary, I don't really know who they were. He just seemed busy and grateful that I was helping him with this surprise for Jeannie.

'I suppose it was about half past twelve or one o'clock when we got to Howarth Hall – I wasn't checking the time, but I'm sure it was around then. He told me not to drive in or it might spoil things, that I should park at the edge of The Enclave, you know the executive new-builds across the road and down a way?'

Andee nodded.

'We waited for a while, then he told me to stay where I was, he wouldn't be long, but as he started to get out of the car, Neil pulled up outside the Hall in his truck. We watched as he unloaded some stones, then he let himself in through the gates. Guy said something about not having expected this. We stayed where we were for maybe half an hour, then Neil drove out again and went right past us. He didn't even look in our direction. After that, Guy told me again to stay where I was and he'd be right back. He ran over to the gates, let himself in and, just as he said, he was back in a matter of minutes.'

'Did he tell you why he'd gone over there?' Andee asked.

Estie shook her head. 'I presumed he'd spoken to Jeannie, but that's only what I thought. It's not what he said.'

'Did he mention anything about a note? Or did you see one?' Andee prompted.

Again Estie shook her head. 'All I can tell you is that I was starting to get worried by now, or confused – maybe afraid, even – but then he told me to follow him, so I did. He seemed quite excited, so I thought everything must be going to plan and, like Jeannie, I'd find out soon what it was all about. We crossed the road and went into the woods not far from where Neil had piled the stones. Guy was holding my hand, telling me to take care not to fall because I wasn't wearing the right kind of shoes. Nor was he, but it didn't seem to bother him. He just led me on through the trees, holding back brambles and pointing out roots I might stumble on. He was so attentive and kind . . . I had no idea, not for a single minute . . .' She pressed a hand to her mouth, as if stopping the words might in some way stop the horror of it all.

Prim lifted the water glass and Estie took it again, fingers trembling so hard that Prim's hand stayed with hers as she drank.

Fliss and Andee looked at one another; Fliss could only wonder if Andee was thinking about how she, Fliss, had also been drawn in by Guy Symonds . . . and so had Andee, in her way.

Estie's eyes were tightly shut as she continued. 'When we got to where we were going . . . I didn't know where that was until I saw Jeannie sitting on a tree stump in a kind of clearing. She was holding her bag in her lap. She didn't seem to know we were there . . .' She broke off, took a breath and started again. 'Guy indicated for me to stay where I was, but as he circled round behind her, she must have heard him because she got up.

431

'I didn't move, at least I don't think I did, but I must have, because she spotted me through the trees and asked me what I was doing there. I didn't answer, there wasn't time to because Guy was suddenly putting a cloth over her face, like it was a blindfold, a game . . . She started to struggle, but he was stronger than her and didn't let go. Then she dropped down to her knees. He went down with her, keeping the cloth over her mouth and nose, holding it there, pressing it hard into her face . . . She couldn't fight any more, I could see that . . . I told myself she wasn't supposed to, that it was all a part of the surprise. It was easier to think that even though I knew . . . In my heart . . . I . . .' Her head dropped forward and Prim held her as she sobbed.

'Take your time,' Andee said gently, and went to refill the water glass.

Eventually, Estie spoke again, her voice thick with tears. 'He lifted her on to his shoulder,' she said, 'and began carrying her through the woods. He told me to follow and, because I didn't know what else to do, I did. When she got too heavy to carry, he dragged her for a while and I . . . Oh God, oh God,' she choked wretchedly, 'I helped . . .' Her hand shot to her mouth as she dry-retched on the horror of it all.

Prim looked at Andee. 'Maybe you have enough now?' she asked quietly.

Estie shook her head. 'No, I need to tell . . .' She drank more water and forced herself on. 'Eventually we were near the Scoop,' she said, 'and he picked her up again, not over his shoulder this time, but like she was a child . . . Like she was an offering, or a bride he was carrying over a threshold, except her head and arms were hanging down and he wasn't looking at her at all. He just walked forward with her in his arms and when he reached the edge he . . . he let her roll away . . .' She clasped her hands to her face as she cried, 'He threw her away like she meant nothing, and I just stood there watching. I-I couldn't believe what he'd done. I couldn't speak, or move. I hadn't even tried to stop him. I don't know if I could have . . . Then he came to put his arms around me. He said . . . he said, "Let's try not to pretend you're upset about this, OK? We know how you felt about her and, now she's gone, you don't ever have to think about her again."

'I don't think I answered. If I did I can't remember what I said. I just let him walk me away, glad he was taking me in the other direction and not pushing me over the cliff too.

'On the way back to the car, he told me that everything would be all right as long as I didn't contact him again, or tell anyone what I'd seen. "If you do," he said, "remember, you will be an accomplice."' She broke off, sobbing so hard now that Prim wrapped her in her arms and held her until she was ready to go on.

'When we got back to the car, he didn't get in,' Estelle said, finally straightening up. 'He said he was going to get Jeannie's Lexus and that I should follow him when he drove out of the Hall. "When we get to the marina," he said, "I want you to wait outside on the Promenade while I take the car in. I'm counting on you not to let me down, but I know you won't because we don't want anything bad happening to you, do we? Or to that lovely . . . lovely little girl of yours."' Her breath caught and caught again as she apparently recalled the threat to both herself and Chloe.

By now rain was slamming into the skylights, and ferocious gusts of wind were rushing at the bifold doors, as if all the wickedness Estie had experienced that day was trying to find its way in. Fliss could only feel relieved that no one was expected to speak, for she had no idea what she'd say; she didn't even know what was the right thing to feel in these tense and terrible moments.

'So when he drove out of the gates in Jeannie's car,' Estie finally continued, 'I did as he said and followed him in mine. He wasn't in the marina for long, and I didn't see where he went while he was in there, but when he came to get into my car he told me he'd left the Lexus in the car park under the apartment building, next to the one where his and Jeannie's friend has a place.'

'Why did he take the car?' Andee asked quietly.

Estelle blinked, as if she'd forgotten, but apparently it came back to her because she said, 'He said if it wasn't at the Hall then everyone would think she'd gone of her own accord and it would take them longer to find her, or they might end up not finding her at all.'

Thinking of the raging tides and storms that had ravaged the area over the first days of Jeannie's disappearance, destroying all traces of what had happened in the woods and on the cliff edge, Fliss could only feel sickened by how calculated it all was. Indeed, it was a miracle that the body had been discovered, for the tide really should have swept it away.

'Do you know if the car is still at the marina?' Andee asked.

Estelle shook her head. 'Maybe he's moved it by now. He said he'd covered it with a tarpaulin, the same as lots of other cars parked there, so it wouldn't stand out, and when the time was right he was going to change the plates and take it somewhere it would never be found.'

Several minutes ticked by, as if she'd finally been struck dumb by the horror of reliving it all.

In the end Andee said, 'Did you drive him back to London then?'

Estie shook her head. 'No. I thought I was supposed to, but he said that I'd been away from home for too long already when we weren't supposed to be travelling anywhere. So he got me to take him as far as Chippenham Station. Before he got out of the car, I asked him why he'd done it and he said, "I have my reasons." Then he squeezed my hand, and said, "All you have to do now is get yourself an alibi for today and then forget it ever happened. You weren't there, you didn't see anything and, whatever you do, don't contact me." I thought he'd get out of the car then, but he carried on sitting there, and then he said, "Funny Neil turning up when he did today. I hadn't bargained on that, but really it couldn't have worked out better." I asked him what he meant but he didn't answer. He got out of the car and I haven't seen or spoken to him since.'

Her eyes were tormented and swollen as she looked across the table straight at Fliss, and Fliss felt her heart twist with a mix of pity and apprehension. Surely there wasn't more. She wasn't even close to processing all she'd heard so far, could hardly believe how she'd been taken in by him too.

'I know I should have come forward and said all this sooner,' Estie said, as if Fliss was the only one there now, 'but I was afraid that he might get to Chloe before I could make anyone believe what I was saying. So when I talked to the police earlier in the week, I told the truth, as far as I could, that it didn't matter to me that Jeannie was dead. I suppose it shouldn't matter, except it does, because no one deserves to die like that. I'll never stop seeing him spilling her out of his arms, like she meant nothing to him at all. She was helpless, had no idea what was happening, no way of defending herself . . .' She stopped and seemed to hunch inside herself, as if trying not to feel any more emotions.

Fliss waited to see if anyone else wanted to speak first. When no one did she said, 'What changed, Estie? Why have you decided to tell us this now, today?'

Estie lifted her head, and looked at Fliss as she said, 'It's because of Chloe. I can't carry on keeping his secret, knowing he's out there and able to do her some harm just to make sure I never speak up. I don't know if he ever would, but I never imagined he'd be capable of doing what he did to Jeannie.' She paused a moment and said, 'I might be a bad mother in many ways, I know I am, but I love my little girl and I want to be sure, when I go to prison, that you will take care of her.'

Fliss hardly knew what to say, although of course she would.

Attempting a smile, Estie said, 'You survived it once, so maybe I can too.'

No one looked at anyone else as the words misfired in the way Estelle's often did. Fliss knew she might be the only one wishing that Estie had said something about wanting to save Neil from going through any more than he already had for a crime she knew he hadn't committed. Maybe it had been part of her reason for telling the truth today, and she just hadn't yet thought to say it.

Turning to Prim, Estie said, 'Thank you for being my friend, and I'm sorry for not always showing how much I appreciate you. I guess I'm not very good at getting relationships right . . . Well, I've proved it now with all that I've just told you. I don't know what happens next, except I realize this probably leaves you out of a job.'

Prim regarded her sadly. 'It's all right, I've already decided to move back to Cornwall, so you don't have to worry about me.'

Estelle nodded and Fliss realized that she probably wouldn't worry about Prim for a moment longer.

Looking at Fliss again, Estelle said, 'I've always been jealous of you, for lots of reasons, but mostly because no one ever finds it hard to love you. I know Neil's still in love with you, but it's the way Chloe is with you that has been the hardest for me to take. I wanted to be number one for her, the centre of her universe, the way a mother should be, but you were always there too.'

Fliss wasn't sure what to say, how to defend herself, or even if she should. Fortunately Estie hadn't finished.

'And now Chloe is going to need you while I'm gone,' she said with a teary smile that might, previously, have been accompanied by a little jump. 'I know you'll take really good care of her, and I hope you'll tell her some good things about me, and even bring her to see me when you can.'

Before Fliss could think how to respond to that, Estelle turned to Andee.

'I hope I've given you enough to prove that he did this,' she said, 'and now, if you're ready to leave for the police station, I am too.'

'No!' Fliss said sharply. As everyone looked at her in

surprise, she said, 'Estie, you can't just hand yourself in without speaking to Chloe. She needs to see you before you go.'

Estie was already shaking her head. 'Neil will explain everything to her,' she said. 'He's always been good at that—'

'I don't care,' Fliss cut in angrily. 'You're her mother, goddammit, and I will not let you run away from this. I'll drive you to the café now – Andee can follow us – but you are going to speak to Chloe before we take you in.'

Estelle looked very much as though she was going to resist, but in the end the fight seemed to go out of her as she nodded, and said, 'I will if you'll agree to be there too.'

CHAPTER SIXTY-EIGHT

CARA

Friday 29 January 2021

'Andee Lawrence wants you to call her the instant you get this message,' Shari Avery declared as Cara and DS Rundle returned to the incident room after seeing Paul and Mallory Haines out of the station.

'OK, get her on the line now,' Rundle instructed, 'and put it on speaker. You all need to hear what I'm about to tell her.'

As soon as she'd reached Andee, Shari said, 'The DS is here, Andee, she—'

'Great,' Andee interrupted. 'Can she hear me?'

'I can,' Rundle confirmed and, before she could get any further, Andee said, 'I'm on my way back into town, but you need to know now that Estelle Fields has just confessed to being an accessory to Jeannie's murder. It was Guy Symonds who actually carried it out. I've recorded it all, with Estelle's permission. I'll send the audio file as soon as I stop.'

'Where are you headed now?' Rundle barked.

'To the café. Fliss is taking Estelle there so she can say goodbye to Chloe. It would be a good idea to send someone over ready to bring Estelle in when she's done. I'd do it myself, but obviously I don't have the power of arrest, if it comes to that. Please tell whoever goes not to make a big deal of it in front of the child if they can help it.'

'No problem,' Rundle responded. 'Shari, that's yours. Leo and Noah, get yourselves a warrant for Symonds, but no call to him or his lawyer first, we don't want him taking off before anyone can get there.'

'His lawyer,' Andee said, 'is Estelle's birth mother.'

Cara blinked as Rundle exclaimed, 'What?'

'I'll fill you in when I get there,' Andee replied, 'insofar as I understand it, and I'm not entirely sure that I do. Nor am I at all clear on why he did it.'

'Maybe I can help there,' Rundle responded, pulling up a chair to sit nearer to the phone. 'I've just had a very interesting chat with Jeannie's brother. He is not a happy man, and I can't say I blame him, if what he's saying is true.'

She filled Andee in on the interview with Paul Haines, and Cara watched everyone's expressions as they listened intently.

When the DS finished, there was a pause before Andee said, 'Do we know that Guy Symonds is the main beneficiary of Jeannie's will as it stands?'

'Haines is certain he is, but we need to contact Jeannie's lawyer to be sure.'

Andee said, 'If he is, this could change things considerably for him. By the way, you need to check apartment blocks three, four and five at the marina. They're the only ones with underground parking. It's possible you'll find Jeannie's Lexus in one of them, unless he's already moved it.'

'Are you serious?' Rundle cried. 'It's been sitting right under our noses all this time?'

'Hate when that happens, don't you?' Andee said, wryly. 'I'll call Richie now to find out if he's checked Chippenham Station CCTV. Apparently that's where Estelle dropped Symonds for his return journey to London on January the sixth. Anyway, you'll have everything I've got when I get there, and obviously you'll be able to speak to Estelle when she comes in. Please tell me now that you didn't get as far as charging Neil Roberts.'

'We didn't,' Rundle confirmed, 'but nor can we let him go until all this has been verified.'

'Of course, but try at least to make sure he doesn't spend another night in a cell for something he didn't do.'

After Andee had rung off, Cara gave herself no time to pluck up the courage, simply said straight out to the DS, 'Can I tip Richie off about Guy Symonds's arrest?'

Rundle's eyebrows shot up in amazement until, suspecting why Cara was asking – who wouldn't have a thing for Richie at Cara's age? – she said, 'Wait until the lads are on their way up there. Then do it, by text, and show me first.'

Having no problem with that, Cara hurriedly tapped out a message ready to send as soon as the DS gave the word. *Drop everything and go to Howarth Hall now. Breaking news, your exclusive.*

Then she sat back in her chair and felt the exhilaration drain away as she looked around at the whiteboards and was reminded of what this was really about – a woman who had lost her life in an appalling way, and another who was about to lose hers too, albeit in a different sense.

And then there was the man behind it all.

Cara had to admit that never in a million years had Guy Symonds struck her as someone who'd kill his own wife to make sure he kept her money. She felt sure he had to be pretty well off himself, doing the job that he did, so maybe there was still more to this that had yet to come to light.

CHAPTER SIXTY-NINE

FLISS

Friday 29 January 2021

'Chloe's on her way,' Fliss said, looking up from the text on her phone. 'I've asked Zac to wait in the café.'

Estelle's head jerked nervously as she nodded and, wringing her hands, she paced to the window and back. 'What did you say to Zac when you knew you were going to prison?' she asked suddenly. With an awkward little laugh, she added, 'I never thought I'd be asking you for this sort of advice, but you're the only person I know who's had the experience.'

Trying to be more gracious than the reminder made her feel, Fliss said, 'Zac was a lot younger; he wouldn't have understood if I'd said too much, whereas Chloe will know if you're not being straight with her. So I can only suggest that you be as honest as you can, without going into the details of what actually happened to Jeannie.'

Estelle nodded, seeming to take it in, but then she said, 'Should I mention Jeannie?'

'Maybe not, as Chloe didn't know her,' Fliss said. 'Or did she? Did Neil ever take her there?'

'No, I don't think so.' Estelle threw out her hands in

despair. 'This is so awful,' she cried, eyes flooding with tears. 'What is she going to think of me? She'll hate me and I won't be able to bear it. But she'll be all right. She'll have you and Neil. That'll be good, won't it, you two together again? It's what he's always wanted, never me. I'll divorce him. You can tell him that, if you like, or I will.'

Fliss wanted to point out these moments were meant to be all about Chloe, nothing else, but it was too late, Chloe was coming through the door and all Fliss wanted to do was scoop her up and do whatever she could to protect her from the next few minutes. She shouldn't have insisted on this happening, had lost sight – in all the craziness – of the way Estie was unable to see things through someone else's eyes, even her own daughter's.

'Mummy! I didn't know you were here,' Chloe cried, dropping the heavy bag she was carrying and kicking off her shoes. 'We've had a really busy day, me and Zac, taking people for their vaccines, and some of them are so funny. There was one lady who knows Daddy and she said if you ever leave him, she'll be first in the queue to take your place and she's *ninety-one*. Zac said—'

'Chloe, sweetheart,' Fliss gently interrupted, 'come and sit down for a minute, Mummy's got something to tell you.'

Startled, Chloe looked at her mother and, finally clocking how anguished she looked, she quickly went to her. 'It'll be all right, Mum,' she soothed, taking hold of her hand. 'You don't need to worry. I promise, it'll be all right.'

It took Fliss a moment to realize that Chloe had no idea what she was talking about, only that this was what she always said when her mother was upset. How had she, Fliss, not noticed this before?

'Oh, I'm not worried,' Estie tried to smile. 'I'm just having one of those days, you know me. But Fliss is helping out and I'll be fine before we know it.'

Chloe turned to Fliss for reassurance.

Before Fliss could summon the right words, if they even existed, Estie sat down on the sofa and pulled Chloe to her. 'Something awful has happened,' she said, lacing her fingers through Chloe's, 'but you don't need to worry about it. I've got everything sorted out, I promise, but it's going to mean that I have to go away for a while. I'm not sure how long yet, and I wish I could take you with me – well, you wouldn't want to come where I'm going, but I shall miss you a lot while I'm there. What really matters is that you'll be all right, because you'll be with Fliss and Zac, and I know how much you love them and they love you too.'

Frowning, Chloe glanced at Fliss again, then put her arms around her mother's neck and whispered, 'I'll come too so you won't be on your own.'

Fliss swallowed hard, and could hardly bear to look as Estelle's face crumpled into a mask of misery.

Drawing Chloe into an embrace, Estelle said, 'I really wish I could take you, my darling, but honestly it's not a place for children. You see, it's a prison, because I've done something bad.' As Chloe made to break away, she clutched her harder and closer. 'I didn't mean to do it,' she vowed, 'and I really wish I hadn't got involved in it, but I was very silly because I didn't think about anything except myself. I know that's not a very good excuse, but there it is . . .'

'What did you do?' Chloe demanded, struggling free.

'Oh, it was horrible. I didn't do it. Someone else did,

but I was there and I'm going to be blamed too, but like I said, Fliss will take care of you while I'm gone and she'll bring you to see me.' She looked up at Fliss and, after receiving a nod, continued, 'You'll be able to come whenever you like, and we'll speak on the phone every day.' Again she looked to Fliss for confirmation. She went on: 'We'll write lots of letters, and I'll want to hear everything about what you're doing and you must send me lots of photographs. Will you do that for me?'

Although Chloe tried to nod, her chin was starting to wobble and Estie said, too sharply, 'Now you mustn't cry. It won't solve anything . . .'

'But you are.'

'I know, but that's different.'

Chloe said to Fliss, 'Where's Prim? Has she come back yet? She always knows how to help Mum when she's feeling upset.'

Aching inside, Fliss said, 'She's gone to be with her parents in Cornwall, but we can call her if you like. I'm sure she'd love to hear from you.'

'Yes, I think we should,' Chloe decided. 'Can we do it now?'

'Maybe a little later,' Fliss replied. 'She'll be driving now.'

Chloe turned back to her mother and put her arms around her again. 'I wish you didn't have to go,' she said, 'but I promise I'll write and come and see you.'

Fliss wasn't sure what was breaking her heart more: the fact that this dear little girl didn't have a proper connection with her mother, or indeed a clear understanding of what was going on, or that Estelle had singularly failed to mention Chloe's father, who Fliss knew couldn't love his daughter more.

They all looked up as someone knocked on the door. Fliss stepped out into the hall with Andee.

'Is she ready to go?' Andee asked quietly.

'I'm not sure she'll ever be that. Are you taking her in?'

'If she wants me to, but Shari Avery is downstairs, she can go with her if she prefers.'

'We'll let her decide. Before we go back in there, do you know if they've released Neil yet?'

'I don't think so, but it'll be imminent.'

'And what about Guy Symonds? Have they arrested him?'

'It should be happening as we speak.' Andee regarded her searchingly, but Fliss turned her head away.

'I made a terrible mistake,' Fliss murmured, hating even to think of it.

Putting a reassuring hand on her arm, Andee said, 'You weren't the only one to be taken in by him. We all were.'

Fliss nodded. 'And in comparison to poor Jeannie and Estie, we've got off lightly,' she said. She started to turn back to the door and stopped. 'What are we going to do if she kicks up a fuss in front of Chloe?'

Andee shook her head. 'There's only one thing we can do,' she replied, 'and that's deal with it.'

Bracing herself for a harrowing few minutes, Fliss pushed open the door and found Estie and Chloe playing a handclapping game as if nothing in the world was wrong.

'. . . *girl having fun,*

Here comes Prim with a pickle up her bum . . .'

Chloe squealed with laughter and said to Fliss, 'We used to sing that to Prim when I was little, and she'd chase me round the room saying she'd show me what a pickle was.'

Smiling, Fliss looked at Estie, but her eyes were already on Andee.

'You're not going to use handcuffs are you?' Estie asked, turning paler still.

'I'm not a police officer,' Andee reminded her.

Chloe's eyes widened with apprehension. 'Where's Daddy?' she asked shakily. 'I want Daddy.'

Going to her, Fliss lifted her up onto her hip and kissed her head. 'He'll be here soon,' she whispered.

Estie stood up and, with a strangled sob, leaned in to kiss Chloe's cheek. 'I should eat you all up,' she tried to joke, 'and then I could take you with me.'

Chloe stared at her, eyes full of tears as she dug her fingers hard into Fliss's back.

Putting on a playful smile, Estie attempted one of her silly little jumps, as if trying to make light of it all, then she walked out to the hall ahead of Andee. 'Don't forget to write now, will you?' she called over her shoulder. 'And I shall ring as soon as I can.'

Fliss rested her head on Chloe's as she stared after her mother, seeming not to know what to do or say. For a few moments they could still hear footsteps on the stairs and voices getting quieter until they were no longer there.

'How about some chocolate cake?' Fliss whispered.

Chloe nodded, but her eyes were still on the open door, then she tensed at the sound of someone charging up the stairs.

Oh God, no, no, no, Fliss cried silently, certain it was Estie coming back.

'Zac!' Chloe cried shakily as he appeared in the doorway. 'Mummy's gone to prison.'

Zac's bewildered eyes went to his mother.

'She has,' Chloe insisted, as if he might not believe her.

'What the heck's going on?' he demanded. 'I just saw the news. They've arrested Guy Symonds?'

Fliss nodded and went to cup a hand round his face. 'And Estie?'

She nodded again. 'Although it's not quite what you're probably thinking.'

He turned away and back again. 'Shit, this is crazy,' he muttered. 'Where . . . where does it leave Dad?'

'Can we call him?' Chloe asked. 'I want to speak to him.'

'I think he might be here soon,' Fliss answered. 'Let's text him to make sure he knows where we are.'

Sliding down from Fliss's arms she went to fetch her phone.

Zac was already sending a message; so was Fliss.

'Do you think I should go over there, in case he needs a lift?' Zac asked, looking worriedly at Fliss.

'Let's wait until we hear from him,' she replied. 'Andee's just gone with Estie, so there's a good chance she'll bring him back with her.'

'I've sent it,' Chloe declared, 'and now I'll send one to Mum. I just have to try and think what to say.'

'Why not tell her that you love her and you hope she calls soon?' Fliss suggested.

Seeming happy with that, Chloe set to work while Fliss turned back to Zac. 'Is everything OK downstairs?' she asked. 'Is it all locked up?'

'Leanne and Angie are seeing to it,' he assured her. Then clutching his hands to his head, exposing his midriff, 'Jesus! I feel like I'm totally spacing out here. Just tell me everything's going to be all right with Dad.'

'It will be,' Fliss promised, 'I just don't know how long

it's all going to take.' She glanced down at Chloe, and said, 'How about that cake? I expect Zac would like some too. We know it's his favourite.'

He started to protest but, catching his mother's eye, realized he needed to agree. 'I should call Mallory,' he said. 'I'm supposed to be seeing her tonight, but I want to be here when Dad gets back.'

Going to the kitchen, Fliss said, 'Do you think they had any idea about Guy?'

He shrugged. 'All she said to me was that her dad wanted to speak to the police and she'd tell me after what it was about. She must know by now that he's been arrested.'

'Hello Daddy,' Chloe suddenly said into her phone, 'I just wanted to let you know that we're at the café, like I said in my text, and it would be good if you could come home soon. We have a lot of things to tell you and you'll never guess what they are. Well, you might, because you always know everything, or you like to think you do, but you're not as clever as me.' She giggled awkwardly and added, 'Love you,' before ringing off and looking up in surprise as Fliss laughed and Zac came to swing her up in his arms. 'I just thought he might like to hear my voice,' she explained. 'He says it always cheers him up, but I don't know if that's true.'

'Oh it is,' Zac assured her, 'it very definitely is.'

It was almost seven by the time they finally received a text from Neil to let them know that Andee would be dropping him off in the next ten minutes.

CHAPTER SEVENTY

CARA

Friday 29 January 2021

'Are you serious?' Rundle cried furiously. 'Guy Symonds isn't being brought here, to this station?'

DCI Gould was unapologetic. 'We have six cells in our custody area, and five are already taken, thanks to the anti-lockdown protest earlier. Estelle Fields is headed for the sixth. Symonds's arresting officers have already been rerouted to Dean Valley HQ.'

Rundle's eyes flashed with outrage. 'So I will have to go there to interrogate him?' she protested. 'While Estelle Fields is here? Please tell me how I am supposed to be in two places at once?'

'Estelle Fields has already given a full confession; any detective here can make it official without any help from you. I'm sorry that you'll have to go to HQ to question Symonds, but you won't be alone – the guys from Avon and Somerset will be with you.'

Rundle looked about to explode.

'Unless he confesses too, of course,' the DCI pressed on, 'in which case it could save you a journey and they'll both be in front of a magistrate by Monday.'

451

'And if he doesn't confess?' she bit back.

'Then it'll take a little longer. Either way you need to get in touch with the CPS again. I don't see them having a problem signing off on a charge for either of them, do you?'

Rundle's expression was still taut as she turned and looked at Cara. 'Has Richie found any footage of Symonds at Chippenham Station yet?' she asked.

'I'll get onto him,' Cara replied, deciding now wasn't the best time to remind the DS that Richie had been at Howarth Hall for the past hour covering the arrest. She was just glad of an excuse to call him again, and was already excited about meeting up with him when all this was over and restrictions were lifted. Amazing that he'd suggested it when she'd rung to tip him off about the arrest. She'd almost given up hope.

CHAPTER SEVENTY-ONE

FLISS

Friday 29 January 2021

'He's here! Fliss! Daddy's here,' Chloe cried from her vigil by the window. Tearing out of the room, she raced downstairs and into the café to throw open the front door. Fortunately Zac was close behind with the keys, so there was only a short delay before they were embracing their father, and Chloe was urgently telling him that her mother had gone to prison, but she didn't know why, and she was going to write to her and take photographs to send and could they go to see her, because she'd said they could.

He was still carrying her in his arms as he came into the flat and, seeing how tired and dishevelled he was, Fliss wished she could walk him straight into a shower and soothe away all the stress and angst he'd been through. Instead she went to take Chloe from him while Zac passed him a beer and they all slumped down on the sofas with drinks and a plate of tasty samosas with a spicy chutney dip that Fliss had rescued from the café a few minutes ago.

As both children chattered on and Neil did his best to answer, his eyes kept coming to Fliss and she found herself remembering the young man she'd met at uni all those years ago; the one she'd married far too young and yet had already loved with all her heart. The anxious husband coaxing her through childbirth, twice, and the excessively proud father holding his perfect baby sons in his arms. She recalled how she'd smashed their lives apart with a single glass of wine; the unbearable, irreparable agony of losing Adam; the wrenching guilt and self-loathing that had followed; how she'd pushed him away, unable to forgive herself and never really thinking of how much more pain she was causing him. Throughout it all he'd still loved her and had done everything in his power to make sure she remained a mother to Zac. And now here they were at this strange and disorienting time in their lives, still very much together in almost every way that counted.

'Can I tell my friends about Mummy,' Chloe suddenly asked, 'and where she is?'

'Uh – I don't think you should do that yet, sweetheart,' Neil replied, running a large hand over her delicate curls. 'We're going to need to decide on the best way of saying things, and let's find out exactly what's going to happen first, eh?'

Seeming satisfied with that, she said, 'At least it's not as bad for me as it is for Leila Callaghan. Her mummy died, so she can't ever see her again. That's really sad, isn't it?'

'Yes, very,' he agreed, searching her innocent young eyes with his. Fliss knew he was trying to fathom what was really going on in her tender, nearly ten-year-old mind.

Giving him an impish smile, as though knowing she'd mystified him somehow, Chloe said, 'Are we going to be sleeping here tonight, because if we are I don't have my pyjamas or a toothbrush or any clean clothes for the morning?'

Fliss and Neil looked at one another.

'Tell you what,' Zac said, apparently making the decision, 'I'll drive you over to the house to get something now, and I'll pick up some stuff for you too, Dad, while we're there?'

Neil was still looking at Fliss, as if needing her to OK it.

'Yes, do that,' she answered, 'and I'll make us some supper while you're gone.'

A few minutes later she and Neil were alone in the flat. After going to fetch another beer from the fridge, she passed it to him and curled up at the other end of the sofa he was on.

'So how are you?' he asked softly as they looked into one another's eyes. 'Andee told me what happened when you were questioned—'

'It wasn't good,' she interrupted, 'but I'm more concerned about you right now and what you know about Estie and Guy.'

He sighed a mirthless sort of laugh. 'I had no idea there *was* an "Estie and Guy" until today. Did you?'

She shook her head. 'She says it wasn't an affair and I think I believe her. I still don't really understand what the relationship was, but to quote her she was "besotted" with him. And he was kind to her and understanding—'

'In a way I never was.'

'Oh, come on, you've always been good to her. She couldn't have wanted for a better husband or father for her child . . .'

He was shaking his head. 'But I didn't ever get close to her in a way I should have; or even try to find out what mattered to her. I mean, I asked, sure I did, but . . . Well, you only have to look at the business with her birth mother. Why couldn't she tell me about that? I still don't understand it, but perhaps we were already too far apart for her even to want me to share it.'

'Did you know,' Fliss said, 'that Guy Symonds has hired her birth mother as his lawyer?'

He turned to her, stunned. 'I didn't even know the woman was a lawyer,' he said. 'Why the hell has he done that? What is he trying to prove, for God's sake?'

'I have no idea, but I'm getting the distinct impression it's all a game to him, that nothing or no one really matters, which seems an odd thing to say about someone who's supposed to be all about saving lives.'

Clearly bewildered, he said, 'The name Shipman comes to mind, but it was patients he killed . . .' Then realizing where that could lead, 'Oh God, don't let's go there. This is bad enough.'

Agreeing, Fliss said, 'Did you see Estie before you left the station?'

He shook his head. 'They were already interviewing her, but I'm not sure they'd have let me anyway.' Clearly still taking it all in, he said, 'I knew she hated Jeannie, but to have allowed herself to get caught up in this—'

'I don't think she knew what was going to happen until it did,' Fliss interrupted. 'You'll understand what I mean once I've told you what she told us this afternoon.'

He listened quietly as she spoke, hardly moving, keeping his head back against the sofa, staring at the ceiling and saying nothing at all until she'd finally finished.

He surprised her then when he said, 'I remember her going out early that day, tiptoeing around the bedroom trying not to wake me . . . I actually wondered, not for the first time, if she was having an affair. I even hoped she was. Not because it would give me an excuse to leave her, although I wanted to, but so she'd have one to leave me. I never dreamt for a minute she was going off to meet Guy Symonds . . .' Turning to Fliss, he said, 'Does she have any idea why he did that to Jeannie?'

Fliss shook her head. 'I don't think so. He just told her that he had his reasons.'

'So she doesn't know about the money?'

Confused, Fliss said, 'What money?'

Sitting forward to put his bottle on the table, Neil said, 'Andee told me while she was driving me here. Apparently Jeannie was about to give at least half of what she has to her brother, and make her niece the main beneficiary of her will. It seems he didn't give her a chance to get round to talking to a lawyer. So I think we can presume that was why he did it, to make sure nothing got signed away from him.' After a moment he added, 'If they'd divorced he'd have probably ended up with half. Jeannie's plan left him with nothing.'

Fliss's eyes closed against the images that Estie had created for her today, of Guy simply letting his wife drop to the rocks below the cliff. How could that be the same man that she'd befriended here in the café, and had got so close to in recent days? She shuddered even to think of him touching her, and of how willingly she'd gone to him.

Finding Neil watching her, she decided that now wasn't the time to tell him what she'd done. There was too much else to think about tonight, too many other priorities.

'Does Estie have a lawyer, do you know?' she asked.

He nodded. 'Apparently one of Helen Hall's team is on it. I heard before I left that Guy Symonds was being taken to another police station, but I don't know which one.'

'I wonder if Estie will get bail? Do you think that's possible?'

Shaking his head, he said, 'I don't know, but to be honest, I hope for Chloe's sake that she doesn't. It would be very disruptive for her if her mother suddenly showed up again now, only to disappear again in however long. And you know how unpredictable Estie can be . . .'

He didn't have to finish the sentence, Fliss understood his meaning only too well. Moving away from the unsettling thought, she said, 'She's not a bad person, not even close, she's just . . . different, I suppose.'

With a dry and sad laugh he said, 'Yes, she is different, mainly, I think, because of how desperately she craves love. I can see that now in a way I couldn't before, maybe because I didn't try. Which isn't to say I didn't care for her. I did, and still do. She's my wife, but she's also like a child in some ways; maybe that's why I never knew how to be with her. I tried so many times to get through to her, to create some kind of bond between us apart from Chloe. I'd watch Prim to see how it was done, but I just couldn't get it right. If it hadn't been for Chloe . . . Well, we wouldn't have got married in the first place if it weren't for her, and obviously I'd never want to be without my girl, so what am I really trying to say here?'

Smiling, Fliss reached for his hand and held it between both of hers. 'You're too tired and wrung out to think very clearly about anything right now, but believe me when I tell you that Chloe knows how much you love her, and it's being so secure in that love that makes her the confident and resilient little girl that she is.'

Bringing her hand to his mouth he kissed it gently as he said, 'I must keep reminding her of how important she is to me.'

'That's good,' Fliss said softly. 'I don't think we ever get tired of hearing how much someone loves us.'

His eyes came to hers, just as blue and full of feeling as he said, 'It's been too long since we said it to one another, and I don't know about you, but I really want to say it right now.'

Moving closer to him she continued gazing into his eyes as she whispered against his lips, 'No one's stopping you.'

TWO MONTHS LATER

CHAPTER SEVENTY-TWO

ANDEE

Monday 29 March 2021

'I wasn't sure you'd come,' he said.

Andee pulled out a chair and sat down opposite him at the small metal table.

She'd been to this place before, more times than she cared to recall, so little about the ambient stench of stale male sweat and disinfectant was a surprise to her. All that was, was being here to see him, in spite of having grown used to the idea of him being in prison by now.

'You knew I would,' she responded, folding one leg over the other and sitting back, away from him.

Guy Symonds's alert grey eyes didn't convey much beyond sadness as he looked back at her, although his face covering made it hard to read him. Certainly there still seemed to be a magnetism to him, a sense of him wanting to connect on a deeper level; she could even feel herself responding to it. However, there was less lustre about him now than there used to be. In a place like this, no one could shine.

'So how are you?' he asked, sounding genuinely interested to know.

Determined not to be drawn in by him, she said, 'This isn't a social visit.'

His eyebrows rose in surprise.

'I mean,' she clarified, 'I'm not your friend.'

'Ah, I see.' He seemed hurt, and said, 'I'm sorry to hear that, but I guess it's not unexpected.'

'What is this about?' she asked. Today was the first day of prison visits since the latest lockdown had begun, so there had to be a reason why he'd chosen to honour her with the dubious privilege of being his first visitor. (She was sure he'd have preferred it to be Fliss, but that was never going to happen; Fliss had torn up all his letters and blocked his calls. He must have got that message by now.)

He was watching her, as if assessing whether or not this meeting was a good idea after all, or if he should just let it go and walk away. Whatever conclusions he came to, he said, 'I know you have a lot of questions for me, and I thought I'd give you the opportunity to ask them.'

She almost laughed. 'How very gracious of you,' she said.

He blinked, as though surprised by the sarcasm. Before she could speak, he said, 'I hear that Estelle's birth mother is representing her now.'

Since this wasn't quite true, she said, 'Serena's *firm* is acting for Estelle. It would be unethical for Serena herself to take the case.'

He nodded his understanding. 'But that must mean she's in touch with Estelle? And they're building a relationship?' he prompted.

'Insofar as it's possible, given where Estelle is.'

'Thanks to me?'

'Thanks to you.'

His eyes went down, and she looked at his hands, held loosely together on the table in front of him, thumbs circling one another, as if undecided where to be or when to stop.

'I know she entered a guilty plea at her recent hearing,' he said. 'I warned her she could receive a lengthy sentence for admitting to being an accessory, but apparently she did so anyway.'

Andee tensed. *He'd warned Estelle? Were they in touch? Or had it been part of a conversation they'd had before?* 'She's in good hands,' she said, not rising to it, 'and no one expects her to end up serving more than five years, maybe less with good behaviour.'

He nodded agreeably. 'You're probably right; it won't be for too long. Let's hope not anyway.'

She regarded him uncomprehendingly. In just about every way he was still the man she'd met at the café almost three months ago, who'd seemed so concerned for his wife's whereabouts, and grateful for any assistance he could get in finding her. Being here didn't seem to have changed him.

'Are you interested to know about Jeannie's funeral?' she asked, wondering if he'd even mention it if she didn't.

He swallowed as he said, 'Do you want to tell me?'

As she thought about it, she wasn't sure that she did. It might feel as though she was opening Jeannie up to him again, allowing him to share in something else of her, something that was perhaps even more personal and sacred than her life, and Jeannie didn't deserve that. So no, she wouldn't tell him that it was one of the saddest cremations she'd ever attended, not only because so few friends had been allowed to come, thanks to the times they were in, but mostly because it shouldn't have been happening at all.

In the end, she said, 'I'm told that you're going to plead not guilty at your hearing next week.'

He nodded; his eyes were still on his hands, as though he was only half-listening.

'On the advice of your new legal team?' she ventured.

'They think,' he said, eventually, 'that I should have my day in court.' With a certain wryness he added, 'They even think the jury might like me.'

She was finding it next to impossible to read him, to get any sense at all of what might be going on his mind. 'There's quite a lot of evidence against you,' she pointed out.

He frowned, and his eyes came up. 'I'm not sure I'd describe it as quite a lot,' he responded. 'To begin with, no one has ever come forward to say that they saw me in the vicinity of Howarth Hall that day, apart from Estelle, of course, but how do you know that she's telling the truth?'

Andee felt a jarring inside. It was true, she couldn't prove that Estelle's confession was real; however, she did know that Estelle's car had been picked up by police cameras going to and from London that morning.

Seeming to read her mind, he said, 'I know her car's whereabouts on January the sixth can be corroborated in various ways, but you must know by now that I wasn't in the car.'

Andee didn't know that; however, she had to admit that no one had been able to identify who was driving, or if there was a passenger, only that the timings and positions met with what Estelle had told them.

'I know,' he continued, 'that the CCTV at Chippenham Station – somewhere I've never been, by the way – has proved inconclusive, in that – out of all the people coming and going that day – they've only been able to isolate one man wearing a baseball cap and white sneakers who apparently could have been me.'

She didn't try to correct him, for it was true that CCTV at Chippenham Station hadn't actually identified him.

'And the note, asking Jeannie to go into the woods?' he said. 'My fingerprints were never found on it. They wouldn't be, because I never touched it, but I'm glad it was checked.'

Hating the way this was going, she said, 'Are you trying to suggest that Estelle left it on the kitchen table for Jeannie to find?'

He shook his head. 'I don't know who left it there. All I know is who wrote it, but you know that too.'

For one horrible moment Andee almost took the bait to argue, but she stilled herself and said, 'Who drove Jeannie's car to the marina?'

'I'm afraid I have no answer for that,' he replied. 'I can only tell you that it wasn't me.'

He obviously knew that his DNA had been all over the driver's seat of the vehicle, but there was no point in mentioning it; he'd simply remind her that the Lexus belonged to his wife. She said, 'There's no evidence of either Estelle or Neil having been in the car.'

He nodded. 'Yes, I'm aware of that.'

When he appeared to have no more to say about that, she said, 'Exactly why do you think Neil would have wanted Jeannie dead? I'm presuming that is what you want me to think?'

He shook his head, appearing completely baffled. 'I really don't know,' he said, sounding sincere and curious.

'Whatever went on between them . . . I have to say she never confided in me; I was only allowed to suspect that something might be happening, that was the way she liked things to be.'

Starting to feel an unpleasant heat spreading through her, Andee realized that she must, at all costs, resist getting caught up in this insidious web of doubt he was trying to spin.

'So you see,' he went on, 'the evidence against me isn't as solid or irrefutable as you seem to think, and it wouldn't be, because I didn't do it.'

Knowing that Estelle's confession wasn't as easily dismissed as *he* seemed to think, Andee pulled back from helping him to further his defence.

'We'll find out how consequential it is,' he continued, 'once the legal teams get to work on it.'

Having had enough of this now, she said, 'I thought I was here to ask questions, not to hear your theories on why the case against you can't be proved.'

'But you have to admit, it can't,' he countered. 'At least, not beyond a reasonable doubt.'

'We'll let the jury decide, shall we? Meantime, here is my first question: why did *you* want Jeannie dead? I can't believe it was all about money, not for someone in your position. So what was it really about?'

'Oh, I see,' he responded, 'we're going to run with the assumption now that I'm guilty. OK, if that's what you want. Why would I want to kill Jeannie, if not for money? Well, I have to admit I didn't like her very much. She wasn't a nice person, deep down. You only have to look at the way she treated Estelle to know that, and Estelle wasn't the only one.'

'Are you seriously asking me to believe that you inca-
pacitated Jeannie with chloroform, carried and dragged
her to the cliff edge before throwing her over, because
you didn't *like* her?'

He shook his head quite quickly. 'I'm not asking you
to believe anything. I'm just telling you why I might have
killed her, if I had, and one of the reasons could have
been that I'd stopped liking her.'

Realizing he was playing with her, she gave an impatient
sigh and reached for her bag.

'And as for the money,' he said, before she could get
up. 'You're actually right to think that someone in my
position has a good income, so why would I need to kill
my wife to get more, when all I had to do was divorce
her?'

Letting her bag go, she waited for the answer.

'It could be,' he mooted, 'that I have no real dedication
to what I do, and that I'd like to pursue a different sort
of life, one that might take some substantial wealth to
accomplish. A divorce settlement, in that case, probably
wouldn't do it. I'd need the entire fortune, including invest-
ments and properties, if I were to achieve this . . . what
shall we call it? Rarefied lifestyle?'

Remembering a passing reference to something like this,
way back when they'd first met – hadn't he said that he
and Jeannie had had words about retiring early the
weekend before she'd disappeared? – Andee said, 'Call it
what you like, but it would seem to me that when you
found out Jeannie had other plans for her fortune, you
acted swiftly to abort them.'

His eyebrows rose. 'We're talking hypothetically,' he
reminded her.

Feeling certain they weren't, while knowing she'd never get him to admit it, she said, 'I always imagined neuro-surgery to be a vocation, something a person would care about deeply, would make his or her life's work.'

He didn't deny it.

'So at what point did it stop being that for you?'

He inhaled deeply as he thought, glancing around the room at his fellow inmates and their visitors, almost as if surprised to see them there. Finally he said, 'My career is at an end now, whatever the outcome of this unfortunate business.'

It wasn't an answer, and to describe his wife's death as an unfortunate business was an abomination to her, if not to him. She pressed on. 'Your work, for many years, has been all about saving lives, or making them better, so what happened to change that?'

He appeared taken aback by the question. 'Nothing happened,' he assured her. 'I'm still a consultant, I retain the ability to perform specialized surgeries, to improve incurable conditions . . . Let me tell you this,' he said, suddenly changing tack. 'When you've seen as many people die as I have, some right there on the operating table in front of me, it can, over time, drastically alter your view on the whole business of life – its worth, its meaning, whether there is any point to it all. We are all going to die, we know that, but for some unfathomable reason we seem to think it's our duty, our mission even, to avoid it for as long as we possibly can, no matter what sort of quality it might be offering. Today, tomorrow, next month, next year, we are all headed in the same direction, whether we like it or not, and yet people in my position do whatever we can to try to prolong a life that might actually have been better relinquished to nature when it first came calling in the shape of a disease, or an accident, or maybe some sort of abuse. If everything happens for a reason, it could be wrong to stand in the way of whatever is controlling it, good or bad.'

Knowing this was a philosophical debate she might have got into at another time, and with someone else, she said, 'If you no longer care about human life, I'd say that would make it quite easy for you to take one.'

His eyebrows rose, although it was impossible to say whether in surprise or acknowledgement.

'Have you taken others, besides Jeannie's?' she prompted, thinking of Jeannie's parents.

Apparently bemused he said, 'Why on earth would you say that?'

Not prepared to voice her suspicions when she had no way of backing them up, she let the question go unanswered.

'How's Fliss?' he asked, changing the subject.

This didn't throw her as much as he probably hoped it would, and since she'd decided before coming that she'd tell him nothing about Fliss, she simply ignored the question. 'How many—?'

'Is she with Neil now?' he interrupted.

Ignoring that too, she saw his eyes narrow and felt she might finally be getting under his skin.

'Does he know that she slept with me?' he asked.

She simply stared at him, thinking the answer in strong, clear words in her head, and gaining no small pleasure from the fact that he had absolutely no way of getting to them. Yes, Neil did know about the very brief fling, or 'huge mistake', as Fliss preferred to call it, but they had moved on from it now. They had more important issues

471

to consider: a relationship to rebuild, two children with differing needs to put front and centre of their world. He might like to know, although Andee wouldn't tell him, that Neil and Chloe had moved into the flat above the café, and Estelle's house was soon to be rented to a family from London looking to escape the pandemic. Estelle herself had suggested it during one of her many phone calls. She wanted to keep the place, she'd said, at least for the time being. She might want to live there again one day, but meanwhile, she was excited about the book she'd already started to write, and her really big news last week was that she was soon to meet her half-brother and -sister.

'Fancy all this happening to me while I'm in prison,' she'd said to Andee during an unexpected call one evening a fortnight ago, 'and it's wonderful that my new family – my *real* family – want to come in person, which will be allowed from March the twenty-ninth. Of course, Chloe must be the first to come. I think Fliss and Neil are bringing her as soon as things properly open up, we're just getting it sorted.'

It had been at once sobering and perplexing to hear her in such good spirits, and not for the first time Andee had wondered about Estelle's conscience and the way it seemed to react on a different spectrum to other people's. She didn't actually seem to care very much that Jeannie was dead; she'd moved on from it, was in a new world now.

Apparently wanting an answer to his question, Guy said, 'So does Neil know that Fliss and I—?'

Andee said, 'Are you in touch with Estelle?'

He was still for a moment, then put a finger to his mask to push it further over his nose. 'Does it matter?' he countered.

Feeling that it did, she said, 'We all know how manipulative you can be, but why would you want to carry on proving it when she can't be of any use to you now? She's already entered a guilty plea.'

He merely looked at her, and it took her a moment longer than it should have to realize that, of course, Estelle would be called to give evidence at his trial. And if that happened, his lawyers would take her apart.

Annoyed with herself for feeling rattled, and determined to unsettle him at least once before she left, she said, 'Has anyone told you that Jeannie's brother is contesting the will?'

His eyes betrayed that no one had.

'The lawyers are saying that he has a good chance of winning his case; of course it will all be his if you're found guilty.'

His voice was steady, so were his hands, as he said, 'That's a big if.'

Though she didn't believe it was as big as he seemed to think, she didn't argue. Much better to leave him mulling it over, trying to come to a decision on how hard he should fight to hang onto his ill-gotten fortune. It could help his plea of not guilty if he agreed to let it go, though probably not enough to earn him his freedom.

As the buzzer for the end of visiting sounded, she reached for her bag and stood up.

Standing too, he said, 'Will you give Fliss a message?'

'No,' she replied and, leaving him with his next move unplayed, she walked away, never having felt more ready to leave this prison in her life.

CHAPTER SEVENTY-THREE
ANDEE AND CARA

Tuesday 30 March 2021

'So you think Estelle's still in touch with him?' Cara said, aghast, as Andee finished telling her about the visit to Guy Symonds the day before. 'She can't be. Surely she wouldn't . . . What the heck is wrong with her?'

Catching her hair from a sprightly breeze, Andee said, 'If she is, I'm leaving it to her mother to try and talk sense into her. I want no more of it.'

'But he's not going to get away with it!' Cara protested. 'I mean, he can't. We know he did it.'

'Knowing isn't proving,' Andee reminded her, 'but no, I don't think he will, no matter what he's telling himself, or his lawyers.'

They were either side of a picnic table across the road from the Seafront Café, taking advantage of finally being able to sit outside with a friend to drink coffee while soaking up the bittersweet salt air. Below them, a querulous tide was throwing itself up over the beach in foamy waves, while grey clouds scowled down from a low and thunderous sky. For the moment at least, the wind wasn't trying to wrench the takeout mugs from their hands.

Having been reminded of Estelle's parentage, Cara said, 'Did I tell you that I finally got to speak to her adoptive parents in Canada? No, I'm sure I didn't, because I haven't seen you since. Well, it was interesting, and quite sad really. Interesting because the mother said – I can't do the accent, but it was British-posh not Canadian – "Estelle only kills people in fiction, as she did with us. I'm sure she wouldn't hurt anyone in reality, at least not intentionally."'

Andee said, 'And that's not the sad part?'

Cara grimaced. 'She also said, "Estelle always was her own person; there was never any reaching her".' Allowing a moment for the coldness of that to resonate, she said, 'Do you know what I reckon?'

Andee shook her head.

'I reckon that woman never really tried. I mean, what sort of person says that about their own daughter, adoptive or not? "She always was her *own* person"? Talk about shirking any sense of responsibility. So that poor little girl went to a presumed good home as a baby, and from then on she probably didn't even come close to understanding what it was like to have someone to love her. Which doesn't stop the need, does it? It might even make it stronger. I can tell you it turns me inside out, it really does. And it makes my blood boil. People who don't take proper care of kids ought to be named and shamed and never allowed near them again. If it was left up to me, I'd make sure they suffered some of their own treatment, and it would be really bad . . .' She broke off, tugging a tissue out from her sleeve to dab her teary eyes. 'Sorry, getting too emotional here.'

'It's all right,' Andee said gently, 'I know you're working on a particularly difficult case of child abuse right now.'

'Oh God, tell me about it,' Cara wailed, letting her head fall back in despair. 'Honestly, I don't know if I'm really cut out for this job. It's killing me, knowing what happened to that dear little boy. You should see him, he's only six and he's terrified . . .' Realizing she was starting to get worked up all over again, she tried to centre herself and said, 'At least we've got the bastards who did it, and I'm pretty sure he's with a good foster family now, but you still can't help wondering what will become of him in the future, can you, after the experiences he's had. I just wish I could have taken him home with me – my mum would take really good care of him.' Her eyes finally alighted on Andee's and, feeling a comforting sense of anchoring, she pulled a face of anguished embarrassment. 'Sorry, rant over,' she said. 'I didn't mean to change the subject.'

'It's OK,' Andee assured her. 'If it makes a difference, being unable to take what happens to kids, to people, is the main reason I left the Force. I couldn't allow it to become my everyday existence anymore. It eats right through to your soul in the end, so that you stop seeing what's good in the world; you even stop trusting it.'

Blowing her nose and tucking the tissue away, Cara said, 'Am I allowed to say I miss working with you?'

Andee smiled. 'I miss you too. I think we made a good team, and if you ever decide you'd like to become a detective . . .'

'No, please don't go there,' Cara protested, holding up a hand. 'Or not if you're going to say the same as the DS. She wants me to get all the qualifications and go through two years—'

'I know what it takes to make the grade,' Andee interrupted. 'I'm just glad you know how highly Natalie regards you. And for what it's worth, if I were ever going to set up as a private investigator, you're the first person I'd want on my team.'

Cara's eyes widened with hope. 'Are you going to do that?' she asked, excitedly. 'I know everyone says you should, and I'd work for you in a heartbeat—'

'Hang on, let's not get ahead of ourselves,' Andee laughed. 'You being with the police was what really helped our investigation to go forward the way it did, remember that. So you're actually extremely valuable where you are. On the other hand,' she continued ponderously, 'we always have Leo and Shari – and Natalie when it suits her.'

'We do, we really do,' Cara responded, glancing over her shoulder as Andee waved to someone. Seeing who it was, Cara felt a lovely gladness swell up inside her. Fliss was on her way to join them.

'She doesn't know I went to see Guy Symonds yesterday,' Andee said quickly, 'so let's not mention it now?'

'Of course not,' Cara agreed, and as Fliss reached them she gave a gasp of exaggerated admiration. 'Wow! Check you out!' she declared. 'You look amazing.'

Simmering with delight, Fliss set down a tray of coffees and shook out her shoulder-length beach waves. 'All courtesy of Chloe,' she informed them proudly. 'She's quite good, isn't she? Needless to say, she's going through a phase of wanting to be a hairdresser when she grows up, but so far neither Zac nor her father will allow her loose with the clippers. No sense of adventure, is what I say. Anyway, I thought you might be ready for refills and, provided I'm not interrupting, I've brought one for myself.'

'Great that you did,' Andee said, scooting along the bench a little way to create the requisite distance for them to sit at the same table. 'Who have you left in charge of the café?'

'Zac, for the next half an hour, and as payment he wants a ticket to Thailand at the end of May. My response was something along the lines of "dream on".'

'Thailand?' Andee asked in surprise. 'I thought he wanted to go to New Zealand.'

'Oh yes, he wants to go there too. The plan, as I understand it, is for him and his mates to work their way around the Far East and Australia for a couple of months and then to head to the North Island sometime in late July/early August to meet up with Mallory and her friends for some skiing and, I quote, "anything else that comes up." This is all provided we're allowed to travel again by then, of course, and obviously they'll have to follow all the quarantine and test requirements of the countries they visit. It's not going to be straightforward, that's for sure, or inexpensive.' She raised her coffee. 'He deserves it, as far as I'm concerned, if only for being my rock this past year, but also for all sorts of other reasons. Luckily for him, his Dad has already said he'll foot the bill.'

With a smile, Andee said, 'You'll miss him, having had him at home for so long.'

'I will,' Fliss conceded wistfully, 'but it's time for him to start living his life again, and to be honest, it's not going to be half so bad when he goes now that Neil and Chloe are around all the time. I can't begin to tell you how wonderful that is, but I expect I already have, so I'll stop now.' She leaned in as she pulled an anxious face. 'We've got our first visit to Estie lined up for this Saturday,' she confided, 'and at the moment Chloe's saying she doesn't want to go.'

'Oh God, that's awkward,' Cara commented, glancing at Andee.

'I thought she was looking forward to it,' Andee said.

'So did we but, as of a couple of days ago, she's had a change of heart. Obviously we haven't told Estie yet, and I'm sure things will change by the weekend, we're doing our best to make them, but right now Chloe's keener to see Prim. That will also happen, as soon as Prim is allowed to stay over, which won't be until May the way things are going. Anyway, to be honest, all Estie ever talks about when she rings is her birth mother, her book, the letters she's had from her new half-siblings . . . She doesn't ask Chloe much about herself at all and Chloe's definitely started to notice.'

'Does she say anything?' Andee asked.

'She hasn't yet, but we can tell it upsets her, and it just breaks my heart to see how hard she's trying for it not to matter. She's such a sweet little thing, and so loving and brave . . . Things haven't been easy for her at school either, as you can probably imagine. Now everyone knows where her mother is, and what she did, she's lost a lot of friends and I think there's been a fair amount of . . . bullying? I don't know if it's as serious at that, but it's not good. Honestly, kids can be so cruel, and as for their narrow-minded, despicable parents . . . She's just a child, for God's sake. She can hardly be held responsible for what's happened, but apparently some of them think she can, so their precious little darlings should be kept at a distance. I can tell you, knowing who half of them are, I've a good mind to ban them from the café. I mean why would we want them coming through the door when they've got such a horrible prejudice against a ten-year-old girl? *Our* ten-year-old girl. The front of them, thinking I still want to serve them.'

'Have you spoken to any of her teachers?' Andee asked.

'Not yet. We will if it gets any worse, but in the end what can they do? I'm afraid it's only time that's going to get her through this, and maybe Zac. He's started picking her up from school lately and it actually seems to be helping. A lot of the baby-teens have a crush on him, and being a favourite with the older girls is turning out to be no bad thing for Chloe.' She broke into a laugh. 'Now, tell me, Cara, how are things going with you and Richie? Didn't I see you two together at this very bench a couple of Sundays ago?'

Cara felt herself glow with everything wonderful as she said, 'You did, and it was one of the rare times we haven't been virtual. Honest to God, this virus has taken online dating to whole new extremes. *But* the good news is that he's booked us a table for breakfast at the Seafront on the twelfth of April – the first day you can serve outside – and he's got us another reservation for drinks and dinner at The Mermaid that night.'

With wicked eyes, Fliss said, 'So what will you be doing in between?'

Cara choked on her coffee as she said. 'Working, I'm sorry to say. It's a Monday, remember, but I can't see us being able to socially distance for very much longer – it's peak agony, take it from me.'

As Andee and Fliss laughed, the sun broke out from behind a cloud and Fliss, unravelling her scarf, lifted her face to the warmth.

'Mm, heaven,' she murmured, soaking up the unex-pected rays.

'Pretty necklace,' Cara commented.

Still dazzled by the sudden burst of light, Andee turned to look and had to blink once or twice to bring it into focus. As she did, she felt strangely disoriented and then started to turn horribly cold inside. Wasn't that the necklace Jeannie had been wearing in the photograph they'd displayed on the whiteboard at the station? A diamond-encrusted heart.

Fliss's fingers were on the small pendant now as she said, 'I'm glad you like it. Neil gave it to me for my birthday last week.'

Andee's heartbeat was like an echo in her ears, the whole world seemed to be shifting.

Neil gave Fliss Jeannie's necklace?

Still smiling her beautiful, infectious smile, Fliss said proudly, 'He made it and had the diamond added after. It's gorgeous, isn't it? So delicate, and the detail is amazing.' She turned it over to show an inscription on the back, *With all my love, N*, and in that moment, as the sun disappeared again and Andee's eyes finally cleared, she realized that it wasn't Jeannie's pendant. They were similar, but this was a silver shell, not a heart.

Guy Symonds and his subtle insinuations had got to her more than she'd realized, because for one terrible moment . . .

'Are you OK, Andee?' Fliss asked. 'You look like you've seen a ghost.'

Andee broke into a smile. 'Sorry, I got distracted for a moment. It's lovely. I didn't know Neil was a silversmith.'

With a playful eye-roll, Fliss said, 'Believe me, there's no end to his talents, but that's for another time.' She glanced over her shoulder to follow the direction of Cara's eyes.

'No, don't turn back,' Cara quickly cautioned. 'He's coming this way and he'll see you looking.'

'Who?' Andee whispered as she and Fliss obediently kept their backs turned to whoever was approaching, both presuming it was Richie.

'It's this bloke who thinks the absolute world of himself,' Cara explained. 'I came close to a horrible run-in with him the other day when I was dropping my mum at work. Talk about arrogant. "You can't stop here, don't block that there . . ." My mum calls him a proper self-promoted God's gift, who's "really up himself". And the way he orders all the builders around . . . You should see it.'

'Who is this monster?' Fliss whispered, assuming outrage on Cara's behalf.

'He's the developer who's in charge of the extension to the health centre where my mum's a nurse,' Cara replied, 'and she never . . . she says . . .' She was starting to falter now, becoming aware that something wasn't quite right here. Fliss was tilting her head towards Andee, as if trying to tell her something. Finally catching on to what it was, Cara felt herself descend into a slow and horrible freeze. Oh dear God, she'd just dug herself into an enormous hole and she had absolutely no way of getting out of it.

Looking at Andee she said, 'Please tell me it's not . . . It is, isn't it?'

Andee was trying hard not to laugh as she nodded. 'I'm afraid so,' she confirmed, and turning as the monstrous God's gift reached them, she covered the hand he put on her shoulder with her own, saying, 'Darling, I wasn't expecting to see you here.'

'I was just going to get a coffee,' he said, blocking out everything else Cara could see, 'and I spotted you over here, so I thought I'd come and say hi. Fliss, looking good. Love the hair.'

She gave it a supermodel shake and said, 'I don't think you've met Cara, Graeme, have you?'

As his dark eyes came to hers – seeming way less threatening than she remembered, or her mother had described him – Cara stayed with her death wish as he said, 'So this is the famous Cara I've heard so much about. I'm glad to meet you at last.'

Thinking, *where was a mask when you needed one*, Cara said, to herself as much as to him, 'You're Andee's other half, aren't you?'

Andee said, 'Cara was just telling us how popular you are at the health centre.'

OK, Andee was going to pay for that.

Appearing both surprised and pleased, Graeme remained focused on Cara as he said, 'Really? Do you know someone there?'

'My mum's a nurse,' she explained. 'She doesn't really know anything . . . I mean, she does, but nothing important . . .'

Coming to the rescue, Fliss said, 'My guess is you're an absolute tyrant at work, Graeme, but we love you anyway. Are you going to join us?'

'I'd love to,' he said, checking his watch, 'but I'm afraid I don't have time. I don't suppose Neil's around, is he? I need to talk to him about the landscaping for the new-builds on Kesterly Mount.'

'He was in the office working on the computer the last time I saw him,' she replied. 'You might still find him there.'

'OK, great. Well, nice to meet you, Cara. Say hi to your mum for me,' and to Andee, 'I'll see you later, darling.'

As the county's hottest older bloke walked away, Cara kept her eyes on Andee as she mouthed, 'I'm sorry. Please shoot me now.'

Apparently enjoying every minute, Andee said, 'He's had far worse said about him, believe me.'

'I just didn't realize. I mean . . . Oh God . . . What am I like?'

'You're adorable,' Fliss assured her, 'and now tell me, what does everyone really say about Neil?'

ACKNOWLEDGEMENTS

Once again I am indebted to defence lawyer Nick Kelcey, for the guidance he so readily gave during the writing of this book. Thank you so much, Nick; I really couldn't have done it without you.

Also an enormous thank you to forensic scientist Claire Morse. It's always such a pleasure being in touch with you, Claire.

So many of us struggled through the lockdown of early 2021, including me. It was a pretty bleak time and keeping spirits up as well as creativity flowing was a challenge. I truly can't thank my editor, Kimberley Young, enough for the wonderful energy and insight she brought to this book at a time when I literally felt as though I was losing the plot!